Katie Fforde lives i nd
and some of her three chnuren. ... ...ing
and housework but, unfortunately, she has almost no
time for them as she feels it her duty to keep a close
eye on the afternoon chat shows. *Flora's Lot* is her
eleventh novel.

Praise for *Katie Fforde*

'Delicious – gorgeous humour and the lightest of
touches' *Sunday Times*

'A witty and generous romance . . . Katie Fforde is on
sparkling form . . . Jilly Cooper for the grown-ups'
Independent

'A heart-warming tale of female friendship, fizzing with
Fforde's distinctive brand of humour' *Sunday Express*

'Fforde's light touch succeeds in making this a sweet
and breezy read – the ideal accompaniment to a long
summer's evening' *Daily Mail*

'Old-fashioned romance of the best sort . . . funny,
comforting' *Elle*

Further praise for *Katie Fforde*

'A fairytale-like, gently witty read . . . Heart-warming – made for sunny days in the park' *Cosmopolitan*

'The romance fizzes along with good humour and is a good, fat, summery read' *Sunday Mirror*

'Joanna Trollope crossed with Tom Sharpe' *Mail on Sunday*

'A spirited summer read that's got to be Fforde's best yet' *Woman & Home*

'Acute and funny observations of the social scene' *The Times*

'Can be scoffed in one sitting . . . Tasty' *Cosmopolitan*

'Perfect holiday reading. Pack it with the swimsuit and suntan lotion' *Irish Independent*

'Fforde is blessed with a lightness of touch, careful observation and a sure sense of the funny side of life' *Ideal Home*

'Top drawer romantic escapism' *You Magazine*

'Warm, witty and entertaining . . . as satisfying as a cup of hot cocoa on a chilly night' *Woman & Home*

'Katie Fforde produces gentle cheering comedies that feature heroines whose waistlines are not what they were and who are gifted with humorous self-deprecation' *Sunday Times*

'Katie Fforde writes entertainingly about country life – and love' *Woman's Journal*

'Lively and engaging' *Woman's Weekly*

'Entertainingly written – a fine romance indeed' *The Lady*

'Bright and airy' *Closer*

'A winning tale of romance with a sense of humour' *The Good Book Guide*

Also by Katie Fforde

Katie Fforde
Flora's Lot

arrow books

First published in the United Kingdom in 2005 by Century

Arrow Books
The Random House Group Limited
20 Vauxhall Bridge Road, London, SW1V 2SA

www.rbooks.co.uk

Addresses for companies within The Random House Group Limited can be
found at: www.randomhouse.co.uk/offices.htm

The Random House Group Limited Reg. No. 954009

A CIP catalogue record for this book
is available from the British Library

ISBN 9780099502852

The Random House Group Limited supports The Forest Stewardship Council
(FSC), the leading international forest certification organisation. All our titles
that are printed on Greenpeace approved FSC certified paper carry the FSC
logo. Our paper procurement policy can be found at:
www.rbooks.co.uk/environment

Mixed Sources
Product group from well-managed
forests and other controlled sources
www.fsc.org Cert no. TT-COC-002139
© 1996 Forest Stewardship Council

Typeset in Palatino by Palimpsest Book Production Limited,
Polmont, Stirlingshire
Printed and bound in the United Kingdom by
CPI Bookmarque Ltd, Croydon, Surrey

To The Thameshead Singers,
especially the subversive second sopranos.
Thank you for letting me be a member.

Acknowledgments

None of this would have been possible without the following people. You know what you've done and I thank you.

Chris and Jean Arnison, Lindsey Braune, Elizabeth Poole, Paul Wakeman, Catriona Aspray, and all the staff at The Cotswold Auction Company. Elizabeth Lindsay and Cheryl Gibson for car boot sale help.

From Random House, in no particular order, Kate Elton, Georgina Hawtrey-Woore, Charlotte Bush, Justine Taylor, the wonderful sales team, Mike Morgan and everyone else who makes being published by Random House so much fun.

To Richenda Todd, as always a meticulous and sensitive copy editor and worth her weight in rubies.

To Sarah Molloy, Sara Fisher and the rest of the A. M. Heath team, who are kind, supportive and money grubbing in a good way!

And lastly, my family, who inspire me, support me and keep me on the straight and narrow (sometimes).

Chapter One

❧

A yowl from the plastic box at her feet made Flora look down anxiously. Was Imelda actually having kittens, or was she still just complaining about being shut up in a pet carrier on a hot summer day?

'Not now, sweetie, please!' Flora implored through gritted teeth. 'Just hang on until I've got this meeting over. Then I'll find you a nice bed and breakfast where they like cats.'

Aware that her pleadings were really a displacement activity, Flora picked up the yowling Imelda, hooked her handbag over her shoulder, hitched her overnight bag over her arm and went up the steps. She was slightly regretting her new shoes. They were divinely pretty with a heavenly fake peony between the toes, but not worn in and therefore killingly uncomfortable. Not one to sacrifice prettiness for comfort, Flora ignored the incipient blisters and pressed the bell. Seeing her own surname on the brass plate above it gave her a strange thrill. The family firm, and she was joining it.

The door was opened by a tall woman wearing a lot of navy blue. She was a little older than Flora, and had a no-nonsense look about her which inevitably made Flora think of Girl Guides. My shoes may be not quite suitable, thought Flora, to give herself confidence, but nor is that colour in this heat. In other circumstances, Flora realised, she would yearn to do a Trinny and Susannah on her.

'Hello,' said the woman, smiling professionally, 'you must be Flora. Do come in. We're so looking forward to meeting you. Especially Charles.'

Flora smiled too. 'I hope you won't mind, but I've got my cat with me. I can't leave her in the car in this heat. Apart from anything else, she's very pregnant.'

A little frown appeared between the woman's eyebrows as she looked down at the box. 'Oh, well, no, I'm sure it will be fine for a short time. Although I'm terribly allergic, I'm afraid.'

'Oh dear. I suppose I could leave her outside the door . . .' Flora bit her lip to indicate that in fact she couldn't leave Imelda anywhere except at her feet. 'But she might have her kittens at any moment.'

'You'd better come in,' said the woman, her professional manner beginning to fray. 'We're in here.' She opened the door of a room which was mostly filled with a table, around which were several empty chairs.

The room's sole occupant, a tall, conventionally handsome man wearing a dark suit and a very conservative tie, got up. Obviously Charles, her cousin fifteen million times removed.

Not promising. Flora depended on her charm to ease her way through life and had learnt to spot the few with whom this wouldn't work. He was a classic example, she could tell; he didn't like girls with pretty shoes, strappy dresses and amusing jewellery. He liked sensible girls who wore driving shoes, or plain leather courts with medium heels. His idea of good taste was a single row of real pearls with matching earrings, and possibly a bangle on special occasions.

When the woman who had brought her in (displaying all these signs of proper dress sense) touched his arm and said, 'Darling, this is Flora,' Flora wasn't at all surprised to see the sapphire and diamond engagement ring on her left hand. They made the perfect County couple.

'Flora,' said Charles, holding out his hand. 'How nice to meet you after all these years.' He didn't sound all that pleased.

'Mm.' Flora shook the hand, smiled and nodded; she wasn't that pleased, either. She had totally reorganised her life to take a part in the family business with, she realised now, desperately inadequate research. Charles and his worthy, conventionally dressed fiancée didn't want her, wouldn't make her welcome, and her spell in the country could turn out to be horribly dull. Still, she'd made her bed, and she'd have to lie in it – at least until the sub-let on her London flat expired. 'It's very nice to meet you, too. I can't think why we haven't met before.'

'You spent quite a lot of your early life out of the country,' he said soberly, as if she might have forgotten.

'I suppose that explains it. We did miss out on quite a lot of family weddings.' She smiled. 'Though perhaps I won't miss out on the next one?'

'Oh yes, haven't you two introduced yourselves? This is Annabelle, Annabelle Stapleton. My fiancée and possible future partner in the business.' His smile, though conventional, did at least prove he brushed his teeth, which was something.

3

'How nice,' said Flora, wishing she'd made more enquiries about the business before telling that nice man of course he could have her flat for at least six months, she wouldn't be needing it.

'Yes,' agreed Charles. 'Now, let's sit down and discuss your part in Stanza and Stanza.'

'Would anyone like a glass of water first?' suggested Annabelle.

'Oh, yes please,' said Flora. 'And could I post a little to Imelda? In the box? I need to check on her anyway.' Flora delivered one of her most appealing smiles to her distant cousin, a last-ditch attempt to get him on her side. 'I wouldn't have brought her if there'd been any alternative, I assure you.'

'That's fine,' said Charles smoothly, almost, but not quite, concealing his impatience. Then, when the water had been dispensed and the cat seen to, he said, 'Tell me, Flora, I hope this isn't a rude question, but how much do you actually know about antiques and the auction business?'

Flora took another sip of water. 'Ah well, you pick up things like that as you go along, don't you?'

'Do you?' asked Charles, who had, she now noticed, rather strange grey-blue eyes which, beneath his sceptical eyebrows, had the look of the North Sea in winter.

'Well, yes.' Flora tried to think of a suitable phrase, to indicate she knew more than what she had gleaned from a lot of recent, frantic watching of various afternoon television programmes on the subject. 'Cheap as chips' didn't seem to apply. 'Of course,' she said airily, 'having spent so much of my youth in Europe, I'm not so up on English furniture.'

'But you must be au fait with all those glorious ceramics,' said Annabelle. 'I adore ceramics.'

Just for a moment, Flora felt unsure what ceramics were. 'Oh, you mean china and stuff? Yes, I love it too. I collect teapots, funny ones, you know?'

Charles winced visibly. 'I think we'd better get on.'

'Well, yes, we'd better,' said Flora rashly. 'But I do wonder if we will.'

'What on earth are you talking about?' said Charles. 'Now . . .' He opened a file and drew out a sheaf of papers. He was not a man who would get behind with his paperwork. He had that look about him. He was a filer and a putter-into-alphabetical-order-er. It was painfully clear.

'Now,' he began, 'our mutual great-uncle left things slightly awkwardly.'

'Did he?' asked Flora. 'I thought it was all quite straightforward. You'd already inherited forty-nine per cent from your father, and I got fifty-one per cent when Uncle Clodio died. Clear as sixteenth-century window glass, or something. Although I realise I wouldn't normally have been expected to inherit,' she added as consolation.

'Yes,' explained Charles, openly irritable now. 'But it is awkward. You own more than me. And you know nothing about the business and I've been running this auction house all my life, more or less.'

'Well, obviously I'm not going to sweep in here and make huge changes!' Flora made an extravagant gesture with her arms, observing at the same time that a good sweep, on the floor at least, would be a good idea. 'I want to learn about the business I'm going to be part of.'

5

Charles and Annabelle exchanged questioning glances. 'That's encouraging,' said Charles warily, 'but it still doesn't quite settle the matter. I can't have you having more shares than I have. It doesn't make sense, on any level.'

The cat yowled, possibly showing solidarity with Charles.

'Sorry, I must have a peek. In case this is it.'

'It?'

'The moment when she really is going to give birth. It's her first litter, you see, and the kittens can come in about thirty minutes from when she starts. I've read all about it.'

While Flora fussed with the cat she thought about her own situation. She was obviously totally unwelcome and Charles was horrible. Which was a shame – she hardly ever disliked people. She'd probably better make an alternative plan. Staying in the depths of the country with a couple who deeply resented her presence was not going to be a lot of fun. 'If it wasn't for you, Imelda,' she breathed inaudibly, 'I'd hightail it out of town right now.'

'Tell me,' said Charles, when Flora was again upright, sitting back in her uncomfortable chair. 'What exactly do you hope to get out of your trip down here?' The grey-blue eyes were penetrating and cold – they really were just like the North Sea. Flora felt she was being interviewed for a job for which she had no qualifications – which, in a way, she was. She struggled to remind herself that, technically at least, she was more powerful than Charles.

She took a breath and didn't let herself be distracted

by Imelda's yowl. 'I haven't been brought up in the business like you have, but I have known about it. I didn't expect to inherit, as I said. It was such a shock to everyone when Niccolò was killed in that car accident and even then, I never thought Uncle Clodio – did you know him, by the way? He was lovely – would leave it to me.'

'No. I didn't know him.'

'It broke his heart when Nicki died, obviously.'

'It must have been terrible,' murmured Annabelle.

'But really, we – my parents and I – were totally surprised when we heard about how he'd left things.'

'Then I absolve you of forcing him to change his will on his death-bed,' said Charles dryly. 'But it still leaves us in a difficult position. In theory you could come in here and upset everything.'

Flora smiled. 'Yes I could, couldn't I?'

'Of course you won't,' Charles informed her firmly. 'But it would be much better if we could arrange things differently.'

'And how would you do that?' asked Flora, sensing they had the perfect plan all worked out.

'Annabelle could buy three per cent of your shares, so I would have one per cent more than you. Which, considering I am the senior partner, is only right and proper.'

'And Annabelle would have three per cent?'

'Yes.'

'And you're going to get married, so between you, you could do what you liked?'

'Yes, but you'd still have forty-eight per cent which

7

would bring you in a nice amount of money, when we make a profit.'

'Which you're not doing now?' Actually, Flora knew they weren't doing that well. She and her father had discussed it at length, but Charles was so prim and bossy that she wanted to make him say it.

'Not at the moment, no,' Charles admitted, 'but we do have plans to improve things.'

'Oh good. And now you've got me! I don't know all that much about the business, obviously, but I can learn. And two heads are better than one – or should that be three heads are better than two?' She glanced at Annabelle, who did not seem to be enjoying herself.

Charles frowned. '*Have* we got you, Flora? I was under the impression' – he glanced questioningly at Annabelle again – 'that you were only down here for a visit.'

'Well, yes, but I was planning to stay for quite a long time. Six months, at least. To see if I can stand – like – country life.'

'Six months!' said Annabelle. 'But where are you going to stay?'

Flora had been faintly hoping for an offer of someone's spare room, for at least a couple of days. As this was obviously not going to be forthcoming, she said, 'I thought a nice little bed and breakfast? Where they like cats?'

'Flora, before we get into the ins and outs of where you can stay, and I'm sure we can put you up for a short time—'

'No, Charles!' interrupted Annabelle. 'I'm terribly allergic to cats. You must have forgotten.'

'Sorry, yes I had.' He looked pained for a moment.

'But anyway, putting all that aside for one moment, I think I should make myself perfectly clear. There's really nothing for you to do in this business. It'll be better for us – I mean Stanza and Stanza – and ultimately you, if you just sell three per cent of your shares—' Imelda yowled again. 'Have a short holiday if you must, and then take yourself and your cat back to London.'

'Ah – well,' began Flora, not willing to admit to being temporarily homeless.

'Your parents still own that nice little flat in Lancaster Gate?'

'Yes.'

'And you live there?'

'When I'm in London, yes.' And I'm not in London now, you prig, and I've sub-let it for slightly more than I pay in rent to my parents so I can pay off my credit cards, she added silently, knowing not even thumb-screws would make her admit any of that to Charles.

'So you could go back?' asked Annabelle.

'I thought I was coming down here to live. For the time being, anyway. Downsizing!' she added glibly, not feeling remotely glib. 'It's terribly fashionable!'

'But if you sold me the shares, you'd have quite a lot of money. You could rent another flat, pay off your over-draft,' said Annabelle, who also had grey-blue eyes and an irritatingly patient tone of voice.

Bitch! thought Flora, she knows I'm short of money. She and Charles deserve each other. 'Well, put like that, your offer does sound quite tempting. Of course I will have to consult my father. Although I'm over twenty-one – obviously—'

'Not that obviously, actually,' murmured Charles, and

earned himself a flicker of a frown from Annabelle.

'I do usually discuss things like this with him. My parents aren't in the country right now, but we talk on the phone and email all the time.'

'Good,' said Charles. 'I'm sure he'd advise you to accept Annabelle's offer.'

'He might if he knew how much that was,' said Flora and smiled. 'Have you got a figure in mind?'

'Ten thousand pounds,' said Charles. 'Quite a lot more than three per cent is worth, of course, but we want to be generous.'

'That does sound generous,' said Flora, who had no idea if it was or wasn't. 'Do you mind if I think about it?'

'How long do you need? To get in touch with your father, discuss it, etc.?' asked Charles.

'A trip to the loo would be a good start.' Flora not only needed the loo, but to rinse her wrists in cold water, to clear her head a little. It was hot and she was tired. She didn't want to find herself bullied into something against her wishes by this *Country Life* couple with colour-coordinated eyes.

'Of course,' said Annabelle. 'Sorry, I should have offered when you first arrived. Stupid of me.'

'No, that's fine,' Flora replied graciously.

'Follow me,' said Annabelle.

'If you could just keep an eye on the cat?' Flora smiled endearingly at Charles, knowing it would annoy him.

Flora dried her hands on the roller towel in the dingy lavatory. Horrid soap, bad light and cheap loo paper, all things she would have changed if she'd been allowed.

But although she was very disappointed at the thought that all her plans for country living had been thwarted, ten thousand pounds would sort out her remaining credit-card bills, put a deposit down, and pay quite a few weeks' rent on a new flat. Or she could pay off the tenant in her parents' flat.

She should have felt excited about these new options, but somehow, as she emerged from the converted corridor that was now the Ladies', she felt flat and deflated. Her skills might not have been directly relevant to an auction house, but she did have them.

An elderly man in a brown warehouse coat stopped her before she'd turned into the main passage. 'Excuse me, are you Miss Stanza?'

'Yes.' He was silver-haired and well spoken and yet the shirt and tie, visible beneath the long coat, looked rather worn.

'I'm Geoffrey Whiteread. I knew your great-uncle, years ago. I'm the head porter.'

Flora struggled for a moment. 'The man who holds things up at the sales?'

The man smiled. 'Well, yes, but there is a bit more to it than that.' He looked about him, strangely furtive. 'Things are a bit difficult. I wanted to speak to you.'

Never one to refuse to share a trouble, Flora smiled, even if it did all seem a bit Gothic. 'Speak away.' The man looked kindly and a little troubled.

Just then they heard the office door open and both jumped. The Gothicness was obviously getting to them.

'This will improve the air circulation, at least,' they heard Charles say.

The old man frowned. 'We obviously can't talk here,'

11

he whispered. 'But perhaps we could arrange to meet later? It's very important you don't let that Annabelle woman get her hands on this business.'

'Why not?' Flora whispered back.

He made a gesture to indicate he couldn't go into it just then. 'Because she's a . . .' He paused, clearly on the verge of saying something very rude about Annabelle and then changed his mind. 'We can't talk here,' he repeated.

With the door open, Imelda's next protest was clearly audible. 'I'd better go back.' Flora nodded. 'Isn't there anything you can tell me now?'

The man shook his head. 'Not now. Just don't let her take control of the business. She's a holy terror.'

Scared lest her words be heard, Flora nodded again and set off slowly towards the door. She had obviously strayed into some sort of mystery novel, and she, Flora, would have to rescue this poor old man from the exploitative fiancée.

'She's a complete airhead,' she heard the exploitative fiancée say. 'But I expect she'll take the money. A fashion victim like her will jump at it.'

Fashion victim? Flora exchanged outraged glances with Geoffrey, who was listening with equal horror. She liked clothes, but fashion victim? Huh!

A chuckle, presumably from Charles, greeted this. 'Yes, she's obviously a natural blonde.'

Flora narrowed her eyes. 'Not as natural as all that,' she mouthed to Geoffrey.

'I never dreamt she'd want to stay,' said Annabelle.

Flora was confused. She knew she'd sent an email stating firmly she was going to take some time to learn what was what. She thought she'd been perfectly clear about it.

'I must say I would have thought even someone like her would have mentioned it. It's rude, not to mention inconvenient.'

'Actually' – it was Annabelle speaking – 'I think she may have said something about it in an email. I just assumed she'd take one look and run back to London.'

There was a small silence while Flora held her breath, terrified in case she made a noise and they discovered she was eavesdropping. 'Oh.' This was Charles. 'We'll just have to hope you're right.'

'No need to go on about it, Charles,' said his fiancée.

Even Flora, who wasn't exactly warming to Charles, thought this was a little unfair. He'd only said 'oh'.

'We'll have to try and convince her that staying is a bad idea and hope she takes the hint,' he said.

And before Annabelle could say anything more about her, Flora pulled back her shoulders and marched back into the room. Up until the 'natural blonde' comment she'd been in two minds, but that did it. No way was she going to let herself be chased back to London with a cheque for ten thousand pounds! Even without that sweet old man's Ancient Mariner-type mutterings, she was going to give this a go.

'Well,' she said, having made sure both Charles and Annabelle were looking at her. 'I've had a little think, and at the moment, I don't feel I want to take up your generous offer, Annabelle.'

'What? Why not?' said Charles, indignant and surprised.

'Because I really want to find out about my family

business, to work here, to learn about furniture and things.' She was aware that the 'and things' rather detracted from her grand statement, but she hadn't had long to prepare and hoped they wouldn't notice.

'My dear Flora,' said Charles, unwittingly using a phrase calculated to turn his cousin into a bra-burning shrew, 'you know nothing about the business. You have absolutely nothing to offer us. There's no room for you. There would be nothing for you to do.'

'Is that so?' Flora replied tartly. 'Then why are you advertising for a "general assistant" in the local paper?'

'When did you see the local paper?' demanded Charles, as if her buying it had been somehow illegal.

'Before I arrived. I was looking for bed and break-fast accommodation.' She was actually looking for somewhere she might rent, for when the kittens were born.

'The local paper is not the best place to look for that,' said Annabelle. 'And I'm afraid there's absolutely none available at the moment.'

'What do you mean? There must be. This is a very pretty little town. Someone must do bed and breakfast.'

'Lots of people do,' said Charles. 'But there's the music festival on at the moment. The town is seething with violinists.'

'Oh. I wonder what the collective noun for those is,' said Flora. A sound emerged from Imelda's box. 'Perhaps that about covers it.'

A tiny crinkle at the corner of his eyes told Flora that Charles found this quite funny but was not going to allow himself to laugh. Well, at least he had a sense of humour, even if he didn't ever use it.

'I had thought of renting, eventually.' In spite of her brave resolutions she was aware that her voice betrayed her misgivings.

Charles sighed impatiently, as if dealing with a toddler he wanted to smack but had to placate. 'We seem to have got off on the wrong foot somehow. We're not trying to stop you being part of the business, it just never occurred to us you'd *want* to.'

This was sufficiently annoying to give Flora another shot of courage. 'No?' Her brown eyes were limpid with disbelief as they met his cold, blue ones. 'But I sent an email. I thought I was quite clear about my intentions. Or didn't you get it?'

Annabelle cleared her throat. 'It, er, it only half down-loaded, so we didn't, quite. But I'm sure you can understand that Charles doesn't want you coming in here and messing about with things you don't understand,' she went on more briskly. 'Of course you will want to talk things over with your father, but I'm sure he'll advise you to be sensible and accept my offer.'

'Possibly,' said Flora. 'But I should point out that although he does advise me, I am old enough to make my own decisions.' Aware she was in a position of power, Flora's tones became low and gentle. Let them rant and rave if they felt like it.

'It will take a couple of days to get the legal stuff sorted,' said Charles. 'Perhaps if you had a few days' holiday down here, you might realise that a small market town really isn't the place for a metropolitan girl like you.'

'But where's she going to stay?' demanded Annabelle. 'I can't have her – she's got a cat!'

'And because I've got a cat, who might have kittens at any minute, I can't just go back to London. I might cause an accident. Imagine the News! "Ambulance called to help deliver kittens after pile-up on the M4. The RSPCA investigate".'

'Let's not get too worked up about this,' said Charles, not finding Flora's melodrama remotely amusing.

'No, let's not,' agreed Flora, disappointed that he couldn't crack a smile, even to be polite.

'Flora can stay in the holiday cottage,' he went on.

'Don't be ridiculous!' Annabelle dismissed this immediately. 'It's not fit for habitation. Otherwise we would have let it.'

'It's perfectly fit for habitation,' Charles contradicted. 'It's just not quite up to the standard required by the agency.'

'It's in the middle of nowhere!' protested Annabelle.

Charles didn't see this as a problem, in fact it was probably an advantage. 'Flora has a car.'

'Yes, I have.' Flora smiled, not wanting this lovers' tiff to continue in her presence. 'The holiday cottage sounds wonderful.'

'Honestly, you won't want to stay there,' said Annabelle. 'It's right out in the country, near some woods. You'll be terrified of the owls.'

'You think?'

'I don't want you ringing Charles at all hours of the night because you're frightened of the dark,' Annabelle explained.

'Of course not,' agreed Flora pleasantly. 'Just as well I'm not frightened of it. And owls don't bother me, either.'

'Sorry!' said Annabelle. 'It's just that most people

from London seem quite incapable of coping with country sounds: mating foxes, owls, cat fights, stuff like that.'

'When you've heard lions roar and elephants trumpet and there's only a thin bit of canvas between you and them, you don't worry about anything that can't eat you,' said Flora, believing this statement to be true, even if she had no experience of anything like that herself.

'Oh. Right,' said Annabelle, wrong-footed. 'I suppose not.'

'Does the holiday cottage have sheets? Saucepans, a corkscrew?' Flora enquired tentatively, not wanting to cause more annoyance than necessary.

'I'll pop home and fetch some things. I've got plenty of bed linen,' said Annabelle. She unhitched a service-able leather bag from a chair and extracted a large bunch of keys. 'All right if I take the Landy, sweetie?'

'Of course,' said Sweetie.

When she was alone with her cousin, Flora said, 'I think I should warn you, I do want to work here. I'll apply for the job as a general assistant, if you want.'

'I really don't think you'd like it.'

'You can't possibly know me well enough to say what I'd like and what I wouldn't! We've only just met.'

'I know but . . .'

'But what?'

'Did you used to go out with someone called Justin Mateland?'

Flora became wary. 'Yes. Do you know him?'

'We were at school together.'

'Oh, right.'

17

'Yes.' Charles's hard blue eyes drilled into Flora long enough to inform her that he considered she had behaved very badly to Justin. He didn't say it out loud, so Flora could defend herself, he just let her know that that was his opinion of the matter.

'Now we've discussed our mutual acquaintance perhaps we could go back to the matter in hand?' she said sharply.

'Which was?'

'The job? I was about to apply for it. If you could just give me a form I could fill it in.'

Charles sighed deeply. 'Oh, it's all right, you don't have to do that.'

'But if you've got other candidates to see . . .'

'No. There are no other candidates. We've been advertising for the post for weeks, and no one remotely suitable has applied.'

'Why not?' This was a bit worrying. Had Charles got a reputation locally for being mean-minded with no sense of humour and a horrible employer? It seemed perfectly possible.

'Because no one with anything about them wants to work here.'

'But why not?' She wasn't expecting him necessarily to admit to the reason, but she might get some clue.

'The wages, dear cousin, are crap.'

Flora bit her lip. Not good news, but not as bad as it could have been. 'I see.'

When he was quite sure that Flora was sufficiently subdued by the prospect of working for practically nothing, in a firm who didn't want her, while living in a remote cottage in the woods, Charles said, 'I must ring

18

the solicitor. Will you be all right here for a few moments? There are a few magazines . . .'

'I'll be fine. You go and do your thing.' She smiled again, from habit, but he didn't notice.

Chapter Two

While Flora was flicking through ancient copies of *Antiques Trade Gazette* and stroking Imelda's head through the box, wondering if she should just cave in and accept the ten grand, there was a knock on the door and someone's head appeared. It was the sweet old man. Geoffrey someone.

'Are you alone?'

Flora put down what felt like homework with relief. 'Yes. Charles is getting in touch with solicitors and Annabelle's gone to get things for the holiday cottage, where I'm going to stay.' Sensing a sympathetic ear, Flora took the opportunity to get her grievances off her chest. 'Do you know, she had the nerve to make out she didn't know I wanted to stay! I sent her an email making it quite clear. And apparently every b. and b. in the town is full of musicians for a festival.'

'That's right. Bishopsbridge has quite a reputation for music. Our choir opened the festival last week.'

Flora smiled admiringly while Geoffrey Whiteread came into the room. 'So you're not running off back to London then?'

'Not immediately, no.' Flora sighed. She was hot and tired and a bit despondent, and wasn't quite sure how long she'd be able to cope with being so unwanted.

'Good. You hang in there. This place needs someone to shake it up.'

'What makes you think I'm the one? I know nothing about the business.' All her early confidence had been dissipated by Charles's frigid attitude and the reality of her situation.

'You're young. And you're family. Not like that Annabelle.'

'When she marries Charles she'll be family.'

Geoffrey shuddered. 'Just because they've known each other for ever doesn't mean those two should marry! She doesn't even like the auctioneering business!'

'Then why marry into it? Buy into it?' she added, remembering the ten-thousand-pound offer.

'She likes control and if she marries Charles, she'll have control.' He perched on the edge of the table. 'She's already got some disastrous ideas for cost-cutting.'

'What do they involve?' asked Flora.

'Sacking me, number one,' said Geoffrey. 'She's right, I am old, but I've got more knowledge and experience of this business in my little finger than she'll have in a lifetime. She says we don't need a full-time porter, that we can depend on self-employed staff. But all their sorting has to be checked. Charles doesn't have time to do it.'

Flora sighed. 'The thing is, I know nothing about antiques and collectables, or whatever they're called. I can make them let me stay, but I could just make everything worse.'

'Or you could be the breath of fresh air this place needs.'

Flora shook her head. 'You make me sound like an

advertisement for a room fragrance, and I only know what I've picked up from afternoon telly programmes. A few editions of the *Antiques Roadshow* and that one where they have to buy things at an antiques fair and then sell them at auction. That isn't going to be enough.'

'I'll teach you,' said Geoffrey. 'I've forgotten more than you'll ever need to know. I was a dealer for years, before I came back here.'

Flora smiled at him. 'That's a wonderful offer, but it isn't only that. There's the whole living-in-the-country thing. Would I be able to cope with that? Charles and Annabelle obviously think I'm a waste of space already, and will fall apart if not exposed to a shoe shop and a wine bar at least twice a week. And that's before I've even made any awful blunders.' She regarded him seriously. 'I do like shoes, but I did want to give this thing a go.'

'If you really mean that, I might be able to help you fit into the way of life, too.' He smiled, his eyes crinkling at the corners in a friendly way. 'I can't point you to a wine bar within thirty miles, but there are other ways of keeping yourself amused.' He paused. 'Ever done any singing?'

'Apart from in the shower, you mean? I always sing in the shower. And I liked it at school. I was always asked to do the descants for the carols, and I sang a solo at the school concert once.' She frowned. 'It was a long time ago, though. Why do you ask? Are you offering to take me to a karaoke night?'

He chuckled. 'Not exactly. I was going to ask you if you'd like to join my choir.'

Flora almost laughed at the absurdity of the idea. 'What, the one that opened the festival?'

22

He nodded. 'It's a good way to get to know people, and although we've got high standards, we're a tolerant bunch. We need some higher voices. You'd be welcome.'

'But I couldn't possibly! I haven't sung for years and my sight-reading was never very good.' She couldn't imagine what her friends in London would say if she announced she'd joined a choir.

'Your sight-reading will really improve when you get back to doing it, and we'll all help you along.'

Flora considered. Geoffrey was the first person to make her feel remotely approved of since she'd arrived and she was touched. 'Are you sure? They won't think I'm an awful townie, and resent me?'

He chuckled. 'A pretty girl like you would cheer us all up. Not that we're all old, I don't want to imply that, but there's been no one young, single and female in the choir for years. You are single, aren't you?'

'Currently. A bit of a first for me, actually.'

He laughed again; he seemed to find her very amusing, but in a fond way, not because he found her ridiculous, unlike Charles and Annabelle.

'Then come along with me tonight, and see how you like it.'

It was tempting, particularly when the alternative was staying at home alone in a holiday cottage. And guessing at Charles and Annabelle's standards of what a holiday cottage required, she probably wouldn't even have a television to distract her from Imelda's yelling. Thinking of Imelda, she said, 'There's my cat. She might have kittens at any moment.'

'I'm sure she'll be fine – cats have been doing this for quite a while now. In fact, while there's no one here, why don't you let her out of her box for a bit? It may only be being shut up that's making her so vocal.'

Flora felt a rush of affection for this man; he'd said 'vocal' not 'noisy'.

'Then would you mind watching her while I go and fetch her litter tray from the car? I'm sure she would never do anything she shouldn't, but can you imagine how much Annabelle would hate me if my cat peed on the carpet?'

'About as much as she hates me, I should think.' He smiled. 'You go and get the litter tray and we'll let Imelda out for a bit.'

'You obviously like cats.'

'And so does my wife. I'm fairly sure that she'll be wanting one of the kittens when they're ready. This firm isn't the only thing which needs some young life.' He grinned broadly.

It was such a relief to be with someone who responded to her, who saw her as a person, not just a strappy dress, a pair of unsuitable shoes and expensive highlights, that Flora smiled fondly back. If this man wanted her to stay, she would stay, for his sake as much as her own. 'I'll go and get the litter tray.'

While Imelda was prowling round the office, after Geoffrey had gone back to work, Flora decided to give her best friend a call and got out her mobile.

'Hi! It's me! Good time?'

'Yes,' said Emma. 'I'm at home. How is it?'

'Well, not all that promising, to be honest, but I'm determined to stick it out. For a while, anyway.'

'What's the cousin like?'

'Absolutely dire.'

24

'Oh. That's a bit disappointing. I was hoping he would provide a bit of entertainment for you while you're out in the sticks. Is he married?'

'Engaged. And so stuffy he could do at-a-glance taxidermy.'

'And hideous? Or just spoken-for?'

'Well, I suppose his features are more or less in the right place, but he has minus amounts of charm and zero sense of humour. I think,' she added.

'So they're not exactly welcoming the new member of the family business?'

'You could say that,' Flora said grimly. 'They've already tried to buy me off. Annabelle lied to Charles about me wanting to stay, implying she had no idea I wanted to.'

'Oh no.'

'And I've got to live in a cottage out in the wilds. It might be a bit spooky.'

'But one of the advantages of being in the diplomatic service is surely that you've lived in all sorts of scary places with your parents, haven't you?'

'Yes, but the "with my parents" part is the thing. It's easy to be relaxed about cockroaches if you have staff.' She sighed. 'I am a bit of a poor little rich girl, Em.'

'Nonsense! You're a tough cookie. You'll be fine.' Emma knew what sort of reassurance Flora was seeking, and was quite happy to provide it.

Flora responded. 'I will, of course, and there's a sweet old man who's been really kind and asked me to join his choir.'

'Oh yes?' Emma sounded sceptical.

'No, really, he's terribly nice. Older than Dad, Ems. His wife might want one of the kittens.'

'She's had them already? My God! That must have been awful! Imelda having kittens on the boardroom floor with your cousin stuffing them with his evil gaze as they came out, one by one. You'll have to make some hideous installation with them, and enter it for the Turner Prize.'

'No!' screamed Flora, when she stopped laughing. 'She hasn't had them yet. You're right, it would have been awful. But Geoffrey's wife might have one when they are born. Annabelle's allergic to cats, of course.'

'Of course. Which is not remotely her fault.'

'No. Not at all. She's gone to get stuff for this holiday cottage. I hope she remembers a corkscrew. I might go and get some supplies. You'll have to come down for the weekend sometime. Quite soon, please!'

'I'm a bit tied up for the next couple of weekends, but I promise I'll come and see you as soon as I can.' Emma paused. 'And while I know you'll be absolutely fine, you and Imelda could always come and stay with me if you need to come back.'

Being given a get-out clause stiffened Flora's resolve to stick it out and give country life a proper try. 'That's really sweet of you, Ems, but how would Dave feel about that? Me, a cat and possibly six kittens?'

'I'm sure he'd be happy to have you.'

Something in her friend's voice alerted Flora. 'Everything all right between you two?'

'Oh yes, we're fine,' Emma sighed. 'In fact, I must call him.'

'I'll let you go. Oh my God! I can hear Annabelle and Imelda's loose!'

'Which no one would ever say about you, sweetie.'

'Oh shut up!' said Flora and disconnected.

Flora had just managed to scoop Imelda back into her box when Annabelle came in, her arms full of a plastic container.

'Right, I've got some basics. Sheets, pillow cases, a duvet, a couple of covers. How much do you cook?' she demanded briskly. 'Or are you a takeaway person?'

'Um – do I have much choice? Are there many take-aways in Bishopsbridge?'

'A couple of fish and chip shops, a Chinese and a Balti, which is very good, incidentally.'

'But no sushi bars?'

Annabelle raised her eyes to heaven just for a second, which told Flora her wind-up had worked.

'No.'

'Then I cook. Though not much,' she added, feeling sorry for Annabelle suddenly. It wasn't her fault she looked like a horse, and if she only dressed differently, she might be very handsome.

'But I don't think you'll need a Le Creuset casserole. It's unlikely you'll be making stews in this weather, even if you do cook.' Unaware she was the object of Flora's sympathy, Annabelle pressed on with the matter in hand. 'There are a couple of reasonable pans. Big enough to fit a boil-in-the-bag into, anyway.'

Flora decided to call a mental truce with Annabelle. She might be the nearest thing she had to female company, both literally and figuratively, and it would be much better if they were friends. Besides, Flora was itching to make a Trinny-and-Susannah-type raid on Annabelle's wardrobe, and Flora would have to be on quite good terms with her in order to get near it. She was willing to bet there were pie-crust collars, jumpers with sheep and trousers with stirrups in it.

'I'm sure whatever you've got is fine. Although a non-stick frying pan would be useful. You know how it is when you're tired, you just yearn for an omelette?'

'You've got one of those, but really, you'll need a proper pan for omelettes.'

Flora shook her head. 'A non-stick one is fine. I don't want to put you out more than I have to.'

Annabelle smiled back and Flora felt she should do it more often. It softened her considerably and she had very good teeth. A bit on the large side, possibly, but white and even. 'It's no trouble, really. We should have got the holiday cottage sorted out ages ago. You can tell me if there's anything hugely wrong with it, or missing.'

'I will.'

'There's a dear little garden. I don't suppose you like gardening? It would really help if you had time to clear a couple of the front beds.'

'I'm sure I could do that for you. If there's something to do it with, of course.'

'Oh yes, I was forgetting about tools. I'll see what I can organise. After all, you won't have much to do here, will you?'

Flora smiled. Charles probably hadn't had the opportunity to tell her that she'd applied for, and got, the job advertised in the paper. 'Not just yet, anyway,' she said. 'And it's such super weather at the moment. It would nice to be out in the fresh air.'

'Hmm.' Annabelle crossed the room and opened the

window Flora had closed so Imelda couldn't escape out of it. 'Talking of which – have you noticed? – there's a terrible smell of cat in here.'

'Ah. That might be Imelda's litter tray. I had to let her use it.'

'Oh.' She looked disconcerted. 'You know I can't have anything to do with it, I'm afraid.'

'Oh,' said Flora, forgetting her truce. 'Are you pregnant?'

'Certainly not! We're not married yet. I thought you knew that.'

'I did, but you know how it is in the country.' Flora couldn't resist. 'Very often men don't marry women until they've proved that they're fertile and can carry on the blood line.'

'You were joking, weren't you?' asked Annabelle after a few tortured moments.

'Yes,' Flora sighed. 'I was,' but I won't bother again, she added silently. 'Now, if you could point me in the direction of the nearest supermarket, I can go and get some supplies. Geoffrey will keep an eye on Imelda for me.'

'Geoffrey? Whiteread? You've met him?'

'Yes. We were chatting earlier.'

'Dreadful man,' Annabelle muttered. Louder she said, 'But he'll look after your cat?'

'I think so. If you could just show me where to find him, I'll ask.'

Thanks to Annabelle's remarkably precise directions, Flora found the supermarket easily. It was small, but seemed to have everything anyone could want. She was just hunting for some vegetable stock powder in among the gravy granules when a trolley wheel banged into her toe.

'Ow!'

'Oh my God, I'm so sorry!'

Flora looked up at the owner of a very nice voice. He had sun-streaked hair and a craggy, well-used face. His eyes were very blue against his tan. His shirt was open at the neck and had obviously once been expensive but was now faded and worn to the sort of dilapidation that was highly desirable. His trousers were similarly distressed. He was smiling down at her apologetically.

'I'm so sorry,' he said again. 'I've got a trolley that doesn't steer. Are you all right?'

Flora smiled back. 'I'm fine. It just gave me a bit of a shock, that's all.'

'And your toe isn't broken, or anything?'

They both looked down at her toe, the nail painted bright pink, matching the peony on her shoe. 'It seems fine,' she said.

'I would never have forgiven myself if anything had happened to such a pretty foot,' he said, a definite twinkle in his eye.

'I wouldn't have forgiven you, either,' Flora twinkled back.

He laughed. 'Are you new to the area? Or have I just missed you?'

'I'm new, but I'm glad to hear you don't hit everyone with your trolley, all the time.'

'I only hit people if my trolley's got a wonky wheel. I promise.'

'I'll take your word for it,' said Flora and began to move on. Much as she enjoyed flirting, Charles would be waiting to guide her to the cottage soon, and she didn't want to keep him waiting. He was bad-tempered enough already.

'Maybe we'll run into one another again?' said the man, grimacing at his inadvertent pun.

'Maybe,' Flora called over her shoulder with a grin.

Rather to her surprise, Charles wasn't bad-tempered when she turned up five minutes after the appointed time, he was apologetic.

'I'm most terribly sorry but something's happened to your car.'

'What do you mean?' Flora asked, confused. 'What can have happened to it? It hasn't been anywhere, has it?'

'No. It got run into.'

'But how could it? And who ran into it?'

He looked extremely embarrassed. 'It was Annabelle. She's terribly upset about it.'

'Too upset to tell me about it herself?' Flora snapped.

'Yes,' he said firmly. 'Although she's very sorry. Now let's put all this stuff into the Land-Rover and I'll take you to the cottage. Your car will be sorted out very soon. There's a very efficient garage that we use. Your cat's already in and making a hell of a noise.

'Annabelle's mortified about what happened to your car,' Charles repeated a few minutes later as they drove along in the Land-Rover, Imelda still yelling from her box.

'I know. She told me. It's all right.'

Once Annabelle had ascertained that Flora had not gone ballistic about the car, she had come out to apologise in person. Flora, trying vainly to ingratiate herself with these difficult people, had been very nice about it.

31

'Perhaps if you hadn't parked it quite so near the corner . . .' Charles said now.

Flora sighed. She was a little tired of people trying to make this small incident her fault. As she'd been in the supermarket when it happened, they were never going to convince her. 'She said that, too.'

'She's terribly upset. Nothing like that has ever happened to her before.'

'Oh well. I expect she's got PMS.'

'What?' Charles was horrified.

'Have you never heard of it? It affects women—'

'I know perfectly well what it is, thank you. Annabelle does not suffer from it!'

'Oh well, I expect she was distracted. By a cat or something. Perfectly understandable.'

'Anyway, the damage is very slight. You'll have your car back in days.'

'I know. We've been through all this.'

'You seem very calm about it, I must say.' He glanced at her, puzzled.

Privately, Flora felt she was only being calm in contrast to everyone else, but she said, 'Well, it's not my car. Why should I worry?'

'It's not your car!' Charles reverted to storm mode. 'Whose car is it?'

'My parents'. It's all right,' she said for the tenth time. 'They're not over-sensitive about cars, either.'

'Nor am I, but repairs cost money!'

'I do hope you didn't shout at Annabelle about it.'

'I never shout!' he said very loudly.

'No, of course you don't,' Flora replied, looking out of the window.

'Maybe, sometimes, when really pushed.'

'Rest assured, I will never push you, Charles,' she said, wondering how on earth they were going to get along. 'It is very kind of you to drive me,' she added meekly, to put things back on the level of boring politeness. 'And to lend me the holiday cottage in the first place.'

'It's Annabelle's cottage. I just see to the things that involve ladders and heavy lifting for her.'

Flora wondered which of these categories she came into. On balance, she preferred to be a ladder.

'She would have taken you now,' he went on, 'but she hates the Land-Rover. She's gone home for a cup of tea.'

'Good idea,' said Flora, suddenly desperate for a cup herself.

'It is quite basic in the cottage, but if you do stay, you'd probably be better off with something with four-wheel drive.'

'I'm sure I'll manage. I wouldn't want to buy another car.'

'The firm might have something it could lend you. In fact, that's what we'll do if your car takes too long to fix. You wouldn't want to drive this.'

'Wouldn't I?'

'It's very heavy.'

Flora sighed. Would she have to rescue someone from a burning building to convince Charles that she was not an airhead?

Possibly in solidarity, Imelda yowled.

'She's persistent,' said Charles, with a glance over his shoulder at the pet carrier. 'You have to give her that.'

'She's been cooped up for hours, poor little thing,' said Flora. 'If there'd been any alternative to bringing her with me, I would have taken it, I promise.'

'It would have been better if she hadn't been pregnant,' Charles observed.

'Yes. Unfortunately she was pregnant when I got her.'

'And couldn't whoever you got her from take her back? In the circumstances . . .'

'Not really. It was the Grand Union Canal. I found her floating in a carrier bag.'

'Ah.' He paused. 'I'm sorry. I didn't realise. You don't look like the sort of person . . .' He paused again, as if wary of causing offence.

'Who rescues cats in carrier bags?'

'Oh no.' He frowned. 'You look *exactly* like the sort of person who'd do that, sentimental and terribly soft-hearted. I meant you don't look like the sort of person who'd ever been near a canal.'

Amused, in spite of his insulting manner, she hurried to reassure him. 'Oh, it wasn't a real canal. It was in Little Venice. It's terribly smart just there. I was visiting a friend on a narrow boat.'

'That's all right then.'

Just for a moment she thought she spotted a glimmer of humour, but then it vanished.

'I do think you've possibly been a bit unfair to me,' she suggested mildly.

'Oh?'

'Mm. You're assuming things about me because of the way I look, instead of finding out what I'm like under my clothes.' A second too late she realised what she'd said. 'I mean, although I'm not wearing a lot, because

34

it's such a hot day, I am quite sensible and useful, really.'

'I realise you're a very attractive woman, Flora.' She had to be grateful he hadn't said 'girl'. 'But you'll find that you can't rely on your charm and your looks all the time.'

'No.' Flora felt almost as bad as if he'd slapped her.

'I'm sure you do have valuable skills,' he said, obviously not believing a word of it. 'It's just I doubt they're relevant to our business. You have absolutely no experience, after all.'

'I have worked in an art gallery,' she began. 'I was there for two years – up until last month. And I'm good with people,' she went on, knowing it was the sort of thing said about people who had absolutely no other talents whatsoever. 'And I worked at a management consultants' once.' She'd been a receptionist, and very good she'd been too.

'As I said' – his manner made Flora wonder if she could get through the journey without actually killing him – 'I'm sure you're a very accomplished girl—'

'Woman,' she snapped.

'Woman,' he corrected himself after a quick glance at her expression. 'But I don't think your particular – very valuable – skills are suited to an old-established family business.'

'And in what way are old-established family businesses different from new ones? Don't they need to get new business? Be efficient? Make a profit? Or don't they have bills to pay like every other business in the world?'

He sighed. 'Obviously we have expenses, although of course we own the building. We employ several people, have vehicles to maintain—'

'In other words,' she interrupted, 'you're the same as every other business: you need to operate at a profit. Do you operate at a profit? I do have the right to ask,' she added, when he didn't reply.

'No. But Annabelle has some ideas on how to change that.'

'Which are?'

'It's none of your—'

'It is my business, you know. Slightly more mine than yours, actually.'

Thunderclouds gathered in his dark, thick eyebrows. 'I don't think I can discuss these things without Annabelle being present.'

'Oh? I didn't realise she was a shareholder already,' Flora said innocently.

'She's not! But she's – she's been involved in the business for a little while now and it wouldn't be right for me to discuss things with you behind her back,' he said tightly.

'OK, seems fair enough. Tell me,' she went on, 'has Geoffrey . . . what is it?'

'Whiteread.'

'Oh yes. Has he worked for you long?'

'Not that long. But his father used to be a partner in my grandfather's time.'

'But he isn't now? I mean, Geoffrey didn't inherit from his father?'

'No. Geoffrey's father lost his share playing cards, but out of kindness, the family gave Geoffrey a job when he came back to the area.'

'And you'll keep him on until he retires?'

'If he ever does retire it would be a miracle. Here we

are,' he said, which didn't answer her question. He turned down a track. 'As you'll see, if the weather changes, you'd find the road almost impossible to negotiate. You'll regret ever coming here.'

If this was a barely veiled invitation to go back home, she wasn't going to accept it. 'If I'm not happy here, I'm sure I can find somewhere else to stay.'

'Not that easy with a pregnant cat.'

'But not impossible, either. Anyway, my little car is very solid, when it's not being banged into. And it was not that close to the corner,' she reiterated, to avoid a repeat of their earlier argument.

'Yes, but it's also quite low to the ground. It might bottom on some of the rocks in the road.'

'Is that one of the reasons you haven't let the cottage this year?' she asked, when they had bumped their way down a few yards.

'Yup. It needs money spending on it.'

'You might be better to sell it, perhaps?'

'It's not mine to sell.'

'I'd forgotten.' She hadn't, actually, but she was aware of an undercurrent that she didn't understand. Charles obviously disliked her, and not just because she was butting into his family business.

He sighed, possibly aware that his hostility was visible. 'There are a lot of things you will need to know if you stay around, but I don't want to explain everything if you're just a fly-by-night. It's complicated.'

'It always is. Oh, is that it? It's delightful!'

Isolated, the cottage was set against woodland and faced rolling hills. The late afternoon sun shone on to it, making the windows golden. It had a front door, a window on either side, and three windows on the storey above. A small shed leant against the side of the house, and a rambling rose scrambled up the porch and on to the roof.

'It is very charming to look at, yes,' said Charles, pulling on the handbrake. 'Not quite so easy to live in, as you'll no doubt discover. It was a gamekeeper's cottage. You'll find it very lonely.'

Determined not to rise to the bait, Flora took a deep breath, got out of the car, and walked towards her new home.

Chapter Three

When he had let them both in, and gone back to the Land-Rover to start unloading, Flora allowed herself a few moments to settle Imelda in the kitchen and have a look around before helping him.

The door opened straight into the only living room, which contained a fireplace, a staircase and a lingering smell of wood smoke. That could mean two things, she thought, either the fire smokes unbearably and the whole place is impregnated with it, or someone's had a fire quite recently.

She checked the kitchen, a lean-to at the back of the original cottage, was secure for Imelda, let her out of her box, and then went to get her litter tray.

'It's a dear little cottage,' she said to Charles, who was carrying a box of saucepans, a toaster, an electric kettle, and other things Annabelle thought necessary. 'Don't let Imelda out. She's in the kitchen.'

'I'm sure she'll be safe there. I hope you will be too.'

As Flora couldn't decide if this remark was meant kindly, sarcastically or threateningly, she ignored it, and dragged a suitcase out of the back of the vehicle. It was impossibly heavy, but she wasn't going to let Charles see it defeat her.

'Well, I'm here now,' she declared, perspiring freely

and hardly able to speak, dumping the suitcase in the sitting room. 'And you're just going to have to get used to me.'

He turned and stared down at her in a way calculated to make her aware of the sweat between her breasts, her wildly curling hair, the smear of mascara beneath her lashes. She stared back serenely. It would take more than being hot and smudged to put her out.

'I'm sure we'll find that a pleasure,' he said in a way that told her he felt there wasn't a cat in hell's chance he'd do anything of the kind.

Flora sighed. What was wrong with the man? Why couldn't he be more human and friendly? 'I'm not a brainless bimbo, whatever I look like,' she told him. 'Once you've accepted that, we'll get on much better.'

'My dear Flora . . .' His patronising tone affected her like nails down a blackboard. 'Flora,' he began again, possibly seeing her reaction to his first effort. 'I'm sure you're not brainless, and I don't know why you should assume I thought you were.' Lying so-and-so, she thought. 'But I do think it will be difficult for you to find a meaningful place as part of Stanza and Stanza.'

She regarded him, her head on one side. 'You know, if you hadn't said the name, my name, I might have been convinced. But you did. Stanza is my name as much as yours, and for that reason, even if it was the only reason, I feel I have to do what I can for the business.'

Charles sighed and Flora could see he was reining in his temper. 'The best you could do for the business is to go back to London and let Annabelle and me get on with running it. But as you're obviously not that keen on the company's welfare,' he continued sharply, 'we'd better get the rest of your gear unpacked.'

Flora made her way up the twisting staircase with handfuls of carrier bags. Charles seemed to have some other problem. It wasn't only his dippy cousin coming to mess with his favourite toy he was bothered about. But what on earth that problem could be, she couldn't think. She decided to ignore it, dumped her carrier bags on the bed and looked around at the bedroom. It was nearly filled by a large four-poster bed. It was an extremely pretty bed, but it meant that the chest of drawers had to go on the landing, as did the cupboard which did duty as a wardrobe.

The bathroom, when she went to inspect it, was a reasonable size, possibly because it had clearly once been a bedroom. It definitely needed brightening up: some plants, bright towels, or something, but it was fine. The second bedroom had two single beds in it, which meant that if Emma and Dave came to stay, Flora would have to give them her bed.

But it was very pretty, in a quaint, cottagey way. There was a fine layer of dust over everything, but basically it was clean and Flora felt she could be very comfortable there, once she'd got used to it being the only house for miles. And downstairs, there was a corkscrew. Flora checked this while Charles was lugging her case up the stairs. And later, when everything was unpacked, Charles said, 'Oh. There's something I've forgotten.'

He stalked back to the car stiff with irritation and came back with a bottle wearing a plastic sleeve, to chill it. 'Annabelle sent this. She feels guilty about your car, I suppose.'

41

'That's really kind of her!' And so unexpected, she added silently. 'Shall we open it?'

He shrugged. 'If you like. I can only have one glass, though.'

'I'll find some glasses,' said Flora, thinking that perhaps this was her last chance to get him to lighten up a little. She could have another glass on her own, later, and really relax.

The glasses were very dusty and didn't match. Hastily she washed them and dried them on one of Annabelle's clean tea towels.

'Shall I open it for you?'

'No, thank you,' said Flora, seeing him twitch with the desire to snatch the bottle of fizz out of her hand and open it himself.

'What will you do with the rest of the bottle?' Even watching her pour seemed to be agony for him, and she concentrated very hard on not over-filling the glasses.

'Put a spoon in the neck and drink it over the next few days.' She didn't think it would take her more than two days, actually, but didn't want him to get the impression she had a drink problem as well as everything else that was wrong with her. 'Here's to us, all like us, gae few and we're all dead,' she said.

Charles frowned and picked up his glass and sipped.

Casting desperately around for something for them to talk about, Flora said, 'So, you and Justin were at school together?'

'Yes.'

'And you've kept in touch all these years?'

'Well, no. He found out where I lived through Friends Reunited, and we met up.'

'Oh.' Flora nearly found herself asking, 'And what did you talk about?' just to keep the conversation going, but it really was none of her business. 'OK, here's another toast,' she said instead. 'To you and Annabelle getting the most out of my visit that you possibly can.'

Charles frowned at her. 'I think I've made it clear that we'd get on far better without you, Flora.'

'And I think I've made it clear that you're not chasing me back to London just yet.' She smiled brightly. 'You must come round for dinner as soon as I'm settled. Oh.' She lowered her glass. 'There's no table.'

They both regarded the four chairs, which sat, as if placed, round a table-sized space.

'Damn,' said Charles. 'I'd forgotten. We sold it.'

Flora laughed, and Charles looked at her, confused. Not having a dining table was not something to be taken lightly, obviously.

'It'll have to be a barbecue then, when you come for dinner with Annabelle,' said Flora, hating the idea. Barbecues were very informal things, not suited to the likes of Charles and Annabelle. Paraffin-flavoured sausages and burnt lamb chops were only fun with people you could relax with.

Charles possibly hated the idea of a barbecue too. 'It's all right, I'll bring you another table. Now, is there anything else you're likely to need?'

Flora was tempted to ask for champagne flutes, an ice bucket and a silver salver, but knew he'd just frown and not realise she was joking. 'I don't suppose there's a telephone?' she said instead.

'It's a holiday cottage,' he said, for what seemed the fifteenth time. 'And you've got a mobile.'

'I'll just see if I've got reception.' Flora's insouciance about living in a cottage miles from anywhere all on her own faded suddenly. If you can't ring the police, or your mate, in the middle of the night when you hear something go bump, things are all a lot more scary.

'On the other hand, it would be a good idea to have one,' Charles conceded, as Flora burrowed about in her bag. 'I'll see to it.'

'That would be kind.' Flora's words were more heart-felt than they sounded, so she smiled, to emphasise that she meant them. She found her phone, switched it on and peered at it. 'Not much of a signal. It'll probably be better outside.' She moved out of the front door, still studying her phone.

'No good if it's raining, or you're in bed,' said Charles.

The signal was a little better out of the house but it was still hardly functional. 'Annabelle won't want you to put a phone in here. It's a lot of hassle for a short-term thing.'

'I thought you were determined to stay.'

Flora frowned. 'I am. I was just thinking about it from Annabelle's point of view.'

'I'm sure Annabelle would like you to be as comfortable as possible for the duration of your stay,' he said evenly.

Flora grinned. 'Gosh. I didn't know people really used expressions like the "the duration of your stay" in real life.'

He raised his eyebrows. 'And I didn't know people still said "gosh".'

Flora bit her lip to moderate her smile. 'I bet Annabelle does.'

44

'She doesn't come from London.'

Flora wanted to say that she didn't either, but as she didn't really know where she did come from, she decided not to.

'I'd better go,' said Charles. 'Let me know what's missing – you'll probably find out as you go along.'

'Will you collect me tomorrow?'

'Why?'

'To take me to work?'

'Oh, don't worry about that. You don't have to start until Monday, and your car should be fixed by then.'

Flora opened her mouth to say, 'But you can't just abandon me here in the middle of nowhere with nothing to do,' but didn't, in case Charles suggested she take up gardening, like Annabelle had. 'Fine. I'll amuse myself until Monday then.'

Charles frowned, and Flora realised just what a nuisance her presence was for him. His sense of cousinly duty, a powerful force, was fighting with his extreme irritation at her presence. 'I could come and see how you're getting on, tomorrow,' he said reluctantly. 'And give you an update on your car.'

'It's all right. There's no need. I'll be fine.'

'Annabelle was devastated about the car, you know.'

'Yes, I know. I could see that she was. Even if you hadn't told me about fifteen times.'

'But you had parked it in quite a stupid place.'

Flora sighed. 'You can't make it my fault that Annabelle ran into me, however hard you try. But I admire you for trying. It's very loyal of you.'

He seemed to be confused. 'What do you mean?'

'You know what I mean. It wasn't my fault, it was

45

Annabelle's, but it's nice of you to stick up for your fiancée like that.'

'Oh.'

Flora suppressed another sigh. 'Could you please ring Geoffrey and explain I won't be able to come to choir tonight. I don't want to let him down.'

'Choir? You? Do you sing?'

'Of course. Doesn't everyone?'

'Yes, but Geoffrey's choir is very good. It has a repu-tation – oh, sorry, that must have sounded very rude.'

'Don't apologise. I'm quite used to it by now.'

'I'm sure I don't know what you mean.'

'I don't see why. I do speak English, most of the time.'

He shook his head. 'I must go. But you think you'll be all right?'

'Yes. I'll be fine.' She opened the door. 'Thank you very much for driving me here.'

'It really was the least I could do.' He regarded her for a few moments and then said, 'Goodbye,' and stalked out of the door.

Flora watched through the window as he drove away. Emma had once declared there wasn't a man in the world Flora couldn't charm if she really set her mind to it. Emma hadn't met Charles. Her mind went to the man who had run over her foot in the supermarket. If only Charles was a bit more like him, even a tiny bit, it would make life so much easier.

As she closed the front door and went to the kitchen to let Imelda out, Flora felt suddenly daunted. If she and Charles, and presumably Annabelle, were going to get on as business partners, it would be easier if they liked her. Charles would obviously turn into granite before he did any such thing, so she'd have to try and get Annabelle on her side. Otherwise she'd die of loneliness and despair.

If only Charles was remotely normal, she could have won him over with a little judicious flirting. Flirting worked with almost everyone and Flora did it almost as she breathed. Once, when faced with a particularly tedious job application form, she put it down as one of her hobbies. She got the job.

When Imelda was settled, Flora unearthed her radio from her overnight bag and switched it on. When her breathing and mutterings to Imelda were no longer the only sounds, she felt better. She would make this little house her home. And ask Charles for a television. A television was a perfectly normal thing to have in a holiday cottage, after all.

She had just begun to get bored with unpacking and sorting out her things and was wondering if putting butter on cats' paws to stop them roaming was really a good idea, or just an old wives' tale which would end up getting greasy marks everywhere, when she heard a car.

It was Geoffrey, and Flora met him at the front door. He was carrying something covered with a cloth.

'Edie's sent a cottage pie over for your supper, and when you've eaten it, I'm taking you to choir.'

'This is so kind!' said Flora, opening the door wider, forgetting about Imelda for a moment. Imelda, seeing the countryside in all its summer glory, shot out.

'Oh no!' Flora shrieked. 'What if she doesn't come back?'

'She will.' Geoffrey came into the house and set the dish down on a small table. 'Where is she going to go?

She won't spend the night outside, not if she's not used to it.' Geoffrey was very soothing. Flora found herself believing what he was saying, as if for Geoffrey to say something automatically made it true. 'You eat your supper, let her have a run around, and then we'll call her.'

They left the door open while Flora ate the still warm combination of tasty mince and mashed potato straight out of the Pyrex dish. Imelda could be seen, picking her way through the grasses, sniffing occasionally. When Flora was full, she put her plate down on the floor and called her cat.

Imelda, possibly hearing the sound of the dish landing on the floor, looked up and ambled back towards the house, her pregnant body almost triangular.

'That must seem awfully rude, but she always comes if she thinks I've put something down for her.'

He chuckled. 'That's all right. She might as well have what's left now. She's expecting, after all.'

'Are you sure it's all right to leave her?'

'I'm sure she'll be fine. Cats mostly like to get on and have their kittens on their own, anyway. Have you made a nice bed for her? They like cupboards, dark places. What about under the stairs?'

Together they made a space for Imelda, having first moved aside a pair of wellington boots. Then Flora fetched a pillow from the spare bed, checking first that it wasn't full of goose-down and therefore expensive to replace. A cardigan, that until that moment Flora hadn't considered old, went on top to make it smell familiar. And when Flora considered it comfortable enough for her cat she called her.

Obligingly, Imelda came to inspect her maternity suite, sniffing and then stepping on to it, her paws still dainty and discriminating in spite of her swollen body. After she'd circled, kneaded, settled and resettled for a while, Flora closed the door a little, to see if Imelda wanted it dark. She looked up at Flora and Geoffrey as if to say, 'That's fine, now run away and play.'

Feeling dismissed, Flora said, 'I expect the boots made her feel at home. She loved my shoe cupboard when I first brought her home, which was why I called her Imelda.'

Geoffrey chuckled in a fatherly way, and Flora realised that it was a while since she'd seen her own father, whom she loved dearly. Perhaps that was why she was drawn to Geoffrey.

'Now you go and get something warm to put on,' he said. 'It's quite chilly in the church, winter or summer.'

Flora bit her lip. It had been so hot in London everyone flopped about, sweating. It seemed even the weather was different in the country. 'The choir seems to start awfully early,' said Flora. Was going a huge mistake? Perhaps she should light a fire to keep the wolves away.

'Well, by the time we've got back to town, and you've popped in and said hello to Edie, it'll be time. We start at seven-thirty.'

'Right,' said Flora, wondering what on earth she'd let herself in for.

Edie, Geoffrey's wife, insisted on lending Flora a fleece, not considering her divinely pretty cardigan sufficient protection against the cold of St Stephen's.

'You could freeze to death in that church, even in high

summer. Don't worry about what you look like. It won't matter in there.' Edie smiled and patted Flora in a way that made Flora wonder if they had grandchildren. They'd be perfect grandparents: indulgent, wise, caring. 'Is your little cat all right?'

Flora nodded. 'We made her a place under the stairs. She probably won't have her kittens for days, but she's so enormous, and you can feel the babies moving about.'

'Well, you let me know as soon as they're born and I'll get Geoffrey to bring me along to see them. And now you two had better get along to choir. It would be nice if Flora could meet one or two of the others before you start.'

Fending off her ministrations and injunctions with fond good humour, Geoffrey ushered Flora back into the car.

'Why doesn't Edie come to choir?' Flora asked.

'Tone deaf. Besides, she usually goes to the pub with her friend on choir nights. Now belt up.' He glanced at his watch. 'We've got time to have a little tour round the town before we go. I can show you what's what.'

The town was a mixture of the stately old and the garish new. There was a row of town houses, one of which was occupied by Stanza and Stanza. Opposite was an ancient stone building which consisted of pillars that supported a small building above.

'That's the old butter market. Been in use since the thirteenth century. There's a very good fish stall here on Fridays.'

On the other side of the butter market was another row of shops, which were made up of two charity shops, an off licence, an Indian take-away – which must have been the Balti house Annabelle had referred to – and an ironmonger's.

'Fred, he's one of the basses, owns that shop. He's very helpful if you need anything for the house. He sells everything but he won't let you go home with the wrong thing, if you know what I mean. Down there's the abbey.'

Flora squinted down the road and caught sight of a pale stone building and a couple of flying buttresses. 'I'd love to see it properly.'

'We'll take you. We're all very proud of our abbey. It has a very nice tea shop, too.'

There was a much smaller church at the end of the street. 'Is that where we practise?'

'No. We sing there sometimes, and several of the choir worship there. There's a cleaning rota several of them are on, but I think it's just an excuse to go to the pub afterwards.

'That's the pretty bit over, but there are some useful shops down there.' He indicated a side street. 'A chemist, newsagent, optician, things like that. There's everything you need here,' he finished proudly.

Flora hadn't spotted anywhere you might possibly buy clothes apart from the charity shops, of which there seemed to be several more dotted about, but she didn't say anything. She didn't actually need clothes, after all, she just liked buying them. It was a pretty town if very quiet-seeming to city-bred Flora.

'Now, if you've seen enough we'll get on. St Stephen's isn't far but I like to be there early to get a parking space.'

Flora couldn't help feeling extremely nervous as Geoffrey ushered her up the aisle to the group of people standing by the piano. She was perfectly happy to go to parties by herself, to meet people in wine bars or pubs, but this little country church was daunting.

Geoffrey led her to a tall man with a commanding presence and a surprisingly shy smile. 'This is Flora, James. I hope you don't mind me bringing her along. She's new to the area, and likes singing.'

A thought gripped Flora like a pall of ice: she might have to do an audition. She could barely smile back at James. Why hadn't she asked Geoffrey about auditions? It was perfectly normal, after all, to check that someone could sing before allowing them into your choir, which had a very good reputation. Charles's words about the standard of the choir, which she suddenly remembered, added tenfold to her anxiety.

'Nice to see you, Flora.' James shook her hand. 'Soprano?'

Flora nodded. 'You probably don't need any more sopranos. I don't have to join the choir . . .'

James, possibly seeing how nervous she was, ignored this. 'You go and sit down over there. Moira will look after you.'

Moira, a tall woman wearing several layers of cardigans and sweaters, smiled and patted the seat beside her. 'Come and sit here, by me. This is Freda, and Jenny. We're the top sopranos. The seconds are the naughty ones, in the back.' She turned round and indicated three women who seemed to Flora to be models of respectability.

One of them said, 'We cherish our subversive natures,' so dryly that Flora couldn't decide if she was joking or not.

But even a joke that might not have been was something, and Flora began to relax a little. Other people drifted in and took their seats, which were arranged in two semi-circles near the piano. They all smiled at her in a friendly way which gave Flora courage to ask Moira, 'Will I have to audition?'

'Oh no,' she said. 'James will soon sniff you out if you can't sing.'

'And then what happens?'

'You get sent a letter with a black spot on it,' said Moira. Then she nudged Flora firmly in the ribs. 'I don't know! It's never happened! Just don't sing too loudly to begin with.'

Certain that no noise would be audible from her lips, however hard she tried, Flora nodded.

'Right.' James called the choir to order, and after a bit more chatting and catching up, he gained their attention. 'Welcome to Flora, who's come to give us a try. Let's do a few scales to warm up. On Ah!'

Flora found, after a few minutes, that she was really enjoying herself. At first, she had wondered why on earth she had elected to be in a freezing cold church, wearing someone else's fleece, on a beautiful summer evening, but as her voice remembered what it had done so easily when she was at school, the joy of singing in a group came back to her.

She was glad of the fleece. She would have appreciated fleecy track-suit bottoms to go with it. Her bare legs and peony sandals were soaking up the cold like water. But she still loved it. Looking over Moira's shoulder trying to sight-read, with Moira's strong, confident voice in her ear, she was sure she made no sound at all, but that was fine, she wanted to be quiet, not to make any mistakes. She badly wanted to be allowed to stay in the choir.

Flora was surprisingly tired when James finally finished with them. She mentioned it to Moira who said, 'It's probably because you haven't breathed deeply for years. You'll get used to it.'

'How was that?' asked James, when Flora went to say goodbye and thank you.

'Fine. I loved it. I'm a bit worried about the sight-reading though. I'm very rusty.'

'That will improve very quickly. I'm glad you enjoyed it. See you next week?'

'Definitely.' Flora felt a sense of achievement. It wasn't really anything to be proud of, stumbling her way through a choir rehearsal, but she felt she'd dipped a successful toe in the water of country life.

As Geoffrey drove her back through the countryside, some of Flora's optimism left her. Would she be able to cope without the comforts she was used to? Out here there would only be the sounds of wild creatures to disturb the night. Even the motorway was too far to hear unless you really listened. There wouldn't be the reassuring tick of taxis delivering people home from parties, the knowledge that a few streets away there was an all-night shop, willing to sell her anything her heart desired. There wasn't a cinema locally, and even the station was a half-hour's drive away. (Charles had informed her of the lack of facilities with dry relish.)

Then the thought of Annabelle, her undisclosed plans for cost-cutting, sacking Geoffrey, taking over the family firm, *her* family firm, stiffened her sinews. She could cope, would cope, admirably, and when she went back to London (which just now seemed something to be longed for, like Christmas was for small children), she would be a stronger, better-qualified woman.

It was a beautiful area, she admitted, observing the trees, the hedgerows, the hills beyond. Perhaps nature would sustain her in the way taxis and shoe shops had in the past.

Geoffrey offered to come in with her, to check everything was all right. She accepted gratefully.

Together they walked up the path. 'Well, the lights still work,' said Flora. 'I can see that.'

'Everything will still work. It's a good little house. I used to come and see to things when they let it last year. I know it's in good order.'

Flora opened the front door. 'I wonder how Imelda is.'

They went to the nest they had made for her so carefully. She wasn't there.

'Oh my God!' Flora's hands flew to her face. 'Where can she be?' Instantly she imagined Imelda escaping through an undiscovered hole and being set upon by foxes.

'Don't panic. She can't have got out of the house. Let's have a look around.'

It was somehow no surprise to Flora when they discovered Imelda, and four little multi-coloured shapes, in among the shoes she'd dumped out of their carrier bag into the bottom of her wardrobe. 'Oh Imelda! How could you? It must have been so uncomfortable!'

'I'll run down and get the bedding,' said Geoffrey,

'while you rescue your shoes. She might not like being interfered with but they need something more than just a heap of spikes to sleep on.'

Forgiving Geoffrey's dismissal of some of her favourite possessions, Flora stroked Imelda's head. 'You're very clever and I'm very proud of you, but do you have any idea how much those shoes cost?' Flora had lived on soup for weeks to buy some of them.

Imelda, who was very proud of herself and her kittens, didn't greatly care, but to Flora and Geoffrey's relief, she seemed to take quite kindly to being gently transferred from the jumble of Manolo Blahniks and Jimmy Choos to the bed Geoffrey brought up from downstairs.

Flora brought up a dish of cat food, which Imelda fell on as if starving, and another of water.

'Should I get some milk for her, do you think?'

'I wouldn't have thought so. Adult animals don't usually drink milk, you know.'

'No, and it does upset her, rather. Oh, I'll fetch the litter tray.'

When at last Imelda and her family were settled, Geoffrey said, 'I'd better be going.'

'Wouldn't you like a cup of tea or something?' Flora's social responsibilities came flooding back to her. 'You've been so kind.'

'I think I'll be getting back, but you have some hot chocolate or something before you go to bed. Help you sleep.'

Flora resisted the temptation to hug Geoffrey. He might not be used to being embraced by young women who were missing their dads.

Tired, but not sleepy, Flora ran a bath. At least the

cottage seemed to have an efficient immersion heater, which was something. She found some scented candles in one of her carrier bags and arranged them in the bathroom. Then she poured herself a glass of wine from the bottle that Charles had brought, switched on her radio, and got undressed. Country life was going to be all right.

Chapter Four

The following morning, Flora slept late. She'd been woken up three times by animals she hoped were foxes but sounded like the ghouls made of latex that were extras in the film *The Lord of the Rings*. The little suckings and breathings from Imelda and her brood had been soothing. Imelda was an extremely competent mother, even if in human terms she should be wearing a gym-slip.

After she'd fed Imelda and let her out for a few moments she went into the bathroom. Once she'd wrestled with the shower and the shower curtain and emerged more or less victorious, she went downstairs for breakfast.

That all done, she felt at a loose end. Of course, Imelda needed quite a lot of stroking, feeding and letting out, but apart from that, not all of which was truly welcome, there was nothing much for Flora to do. So she decided to clean the cottage and make it more homely. Then if Annabelle came to do a spot check, she would be ready for her.

Once she'd got into it, she quite enjoyed it; even if the hoover was heavy, inefficient and heaved out asthmatic sighs of dust with every pass, she felt pleasantly domestic, nudging the furniture out of the way and cleaning underneath it. She found polish and a duster and did quite a lot of spraying and wiping, but the smell of wood smoke still persisted. She didn't really object to it, she just wondered why the smell lingered so. Once everywhere shone as much as it could shine, given its nature, she rearranged the furniture. When she'd had a sandwich for her lunch and gone for a short walk, she moved it again, until she realised she'd put it back exactly as it had been when she'd arrived.

Rather than slump into a huge depression, which, she was aware, would have been only too easy to do, she went into the garden and hacked off some quite large branches of rambling roses, which she put in a chipped but attractive stone storage jar she found in the back of a cupboard. This she set in the fireplace.

'So I can make some sort of impression, a few changes,' she explained to Imelda later. 'Even if they are just cosmetic, they do have impact.'

She went to bed wondering if she would ever convince Charles and Annabelle that she could be remotely useful. Now that the kittens were born, it would be even harder to move back to London. She'd have to stay until they were a bit older, at least. As she lay awake in the moonlight, she came to the uncomfortable realisation that she was trapped.

The following morning, Geoffrey and Edie were on her doorstep before she'd cleared away her toast and Marmite.

'I couldn't keep her away, I'm sorry,' said Geoffrey, as Edie came in and went up the stairs, hardly pausing to say hello or ask the way.

Flora was delighted to have company, especially when the cottage was looking pretty.

'I won't disturb her,' said Edie, tweaking open the door to Imelda's cupboard.

Imelda, purring mightily, allowed Edie to inspect her brood, who were all well attached, pumping their little paws into their mother's body.

'I reckon they've grown already,' said Geoffrey.

'They definitely have,' Flora agreed. 'They were quite tubular yesterday. Today they're rounder, more like balloons.'

'We wondered if you needed to go shopping or anything,' said Edie. 'It's hard for you, stuck out here without a car. That Annabelle should be ashamed of herself.'

'Oh she is, very,' Flora assured her. 'And although I don't need much in the way of shopping – I stocked up the other day – I'd love to go out. Imelda's getting quite fed up with me asking how she is all the time.'

'We'll give you a little tour of the town, and you can see the abbey,' said Geoffrey.

'That would be lovely! I love old churches.'

'We're very proud of our abbey in Bishopsbridge,' said Edie, pleased with Flora's enthusiasm.

'Oh, and is there somewhere I could buy a book? I've nearly finished my current one, and there's nothing much to read in the cottage.'

'We have everything you need in Bishopsbridge,' said Edie proudly. 'Even a bookshop.'

The abbey was beautiful, and sited as it was, nearly in the middle of town, it seemed part of Bishopsbridge, rather than separate. Edie and Geoffrey showed her the tombs, the massive pillars, and the carved woodwork. Then she agreed to meet them in the shop and wandered round on her own, soaking up the mystery of being in a place where people had come to worship for nearly two thousand years.

She had just found the shop and had spotted Edie over by the cards when someone knocked into her. She moved out of the way with a murmured, 'Sorry,' when she saw it was the man who had run over her foot in the supermarket.

'Oh my goodness,' he said. 'I seem to be making a habit of this. Are you all right?'

'Of course.' Flora smiled back at him, pleased to see a familiar, handsome face. 'Unlike most of the contents of this shop, I'm not breakable.'

'"Lovely to look at, delightful to hold, but if you break me, consider me sold"?' he quoted, his head on one side.

Flora found herself blushing. 'I'm not like that,' she reiterated.

'Oh, I'm sure you're some of those things, but before we get that far, perhaps I should introduce myself. Henry Burnet.' He took her hand.

'Flora Stanza.'

'Oh – are you anything to do with . . .?'

'Yes. I'm a partner in the auction house. Although I'm very junior. An apprentice, really.'

'Ah. I know Charles Stanza a little bit.'

'I should think that's about the amount most people know him,' said Flora, wondering if she was being disloyal.

Henry Burnet laughed. 'He is rather reserved. So how long are you down here? Would you like a coffee? They do marvellous cakes in the café, all home-made.'

'Actually I'm with those people over there.' She indicated Geoffrey and Edie, who were now looking at her rather anxiously. It was a shame, it would have been pleasant to be with a man who wasn't a surrogate grandfather, or her stuffy cousin. She could do with some attractive male company.

'They might like coffee too,' suggested Henry, greatly to his credit, she thought.

'It would have been fun, but I don't think now is quite the time.'

Edie and Geoffrey had taken on the closed, solid appearance of parents in the presence of an unsuitable boyfriend met in the street, and moved round Flora protectively.

'Another time, perhaps?' said Henry.

'Perhaps,' said Flora. 'If you bump into me again.'

He laughed. 'I'm almost sure to. I'm terribly clumsy. I only came in to buy a birthday card for my sister.'

'And I'm being a tourist. The abbey is beautiful.'

'We are all very proud of it.'

'Are you ready to go now, Flora?' asked Geoffrey, pointedly.

She smiled at Henry, silently explaining why they had to part. He smiled his reply and Flora couldn't help thinking what fun it was to be able to communicate so easily with someone. Every single word was hard work with Charles.

'That's Henry Burnet,' said Geoffrey. 'He's got a bit of a reputation.'

'Oh. What for?'

'Womanising,' Geoffrey went on darkly. 'He's a philanderer.'

Flora sighed. 'Philanderer' was a very appealing sounding word.

'He's got a very nice house, though,' said Edie. 'But he's probably a bad lot. His wife left him.'

Well, at least he was single, she thought as she followed Geoffrey and Edie out of the abbey and they made their way to the pub to have lunch.

After she had been delivered home, and Edie had had another long goo over the kittens, Flora collapsed on the sofa with her new book. It would have been nice if she and Henry had been able to exchange numbers, but Bishopsbridge was quite a small place. They were bound to run into each other sometime. He did know her name, after all, and could contact her via the office, if all else failed.

She was going to have Sunday lunch with Geoffrey and Edie and felt quite content, but she was very glad when Monday morning came.

'We're going directly to the salerooms,' said Charles as he and Flora travelled down the track. 'We're having a sale the day after tomorrow and we're still getting stuff in.'

'Right. Good.' It was hard to know what she was expected to say.

'I'm sorry I didn't come and see you over the weekend. I know you were all right because Geoffrey told me.'

'I was fine.' Flora decided to be silent on the subject of whether it was right that Geoffrey, not after all a blood relation, should have been left with the responsibility of her welfare.

'We had to go to Annabelle's parents.'

'For the entire weekend?'

'Yes.' Charles's jaw took on the stubborn aspect of one who knows he is in the wrong. 'It was unavoidable. They're not as young as they used to be and they were very good to me when my own parents died.'

She refrained from comment and just said, 'Well, I was fine. Geoffrey and Edie were very kind.'

'I knew they would be.'

'Did you ask Geoffrey to look after me?'

'No, but he mentioned he was going to.'

'So that absolved your conscience?'

'No! I mean, I didn't have a conscience – why should I have? You're an adult, you're not helpless.'

'I would have been slightly less helpless if I'd had a car.'

Charles exhaled deeply. 'I know. I'm really sorry about that.'

'It wasn't you who smashed it.'

'No, but—'

'The cottage is a long way from the nearest shop.'

'Not if you're wearing the right shoes it isn't.'

Flora was not buying this one. 'When did you last walk from the cottage to the town?'

Charles gritted his teeth. 'I've never walked it.'

'It's a long way.' Thanks to Geoffrey and Edie she hadn't actually had to walk the distance herself, but she felt that Charles was being unacceptably blasé about abandoning her miles from anywhere.

'Well, don't tell me you had to buy cat food. You had mountains of the stuff the other day.'

'Imelda had her kittens.'

Charles frowned. 'Oh. I suppose that makes her eat more.'

'Yes. She had four,' she went on, furious with his blatant lack of interest. 'There's a ginger one, a tabby, a very pretty one with ginger and black patches on white, and a plain black one. Apparently cats can have kittens by different fathers in the same litter.'

'Oh.'

'Yes. I'm afraid Imelda must have been a bit of a slapper, although she's taking her responsibilities very seriously now.'

'Well, that's something,' he said absently.

'Can I have a cat flap in the cottage?'

'It's hardly worth installing one, is it?'

'What do you mean?'

'You might not stay long enough for the kittens to be able to use it.'

'Oh, I will. The kittens are far too small to move. I'll have to stay at least until they're bigger. Possibly for eight weeks, when they'll be ready to leave their mother. Anyway, Imelda will still need one.' She frowned, suffering a pang of sadness at the thought of the kittens living anywhere but with her.

'Well, if you insist and really think it's worthwhile.'

'I do. To both.'

'Very well.' He frowned again. 'How will Imelda manage until we get a cat flap organised?'

'She has a litter tray and—' She suddenly realised what she was about to confess.

'What?'

'I left the back door ajar. Only a tiny bit and I'm sure there are no opportunist thieves within miles.'

Charles sighed heavily – she was obviously living down to his expectations. 'Well, it's mostly your stuff they'd steal if they did break in, but don't for God's sake tell Annabelle you've left the door open. She'll have a fit! She's very hot on security. All her parents' cottages have burglar alarms and she was very cross with me when I didn't put one in there. I pointed out that there was no point in having something that shrieked like a banshee if no one would be able to hear it.'

'Thank you, dear cousin Charles. It's very nice to be reminded that if I'm attacked no one will be disturbed by my screams.'

He winced. 'I'll get on to the phone people straight-away. And you can certainly have an alarm if it would make you feel safer.'

'What would really make me feel safer is a car. Is there any news on mine?'

'I rang this morning. They're waiting for a part. They have to send away for it. I'd told them they'd better hurry, or there's no point in doing it.'

'I know what you're implying, but I'm not buying it. I'm staying, at least for the time being, and you might as well get used to the idea.'

'You realise you'll just be working as an office junior, the lowest of the low?'

'Yes. I don't mind learning from the bottom up. It's the best way.'

'And you'll stick it out for a while even though the cottage is very isolated?'

'Yes!' Too late she realised that she'd been tricked into revealing her feelings that the cottage was, indeed, very isolated. Still, she couldn't say anything now.

Charles didn't respond immediately. 'I'm sure Annabelle would offer to lend you her car if she knew how isolated you feel.'

'I don't want to borrow Annabelle's car . . . Though it's kind of you to offer,' she added, moments too late.

Charles's firm mouth twitched. 'Well, that's a good thing because I'm not sure she would have offered, actually. I really need an estate car or I'd offer you mine.'

'What about this Land-Rover? Is this needed for anything special?'

He laughed. 'I can't see you driving this behemoth.' It shuddered noisily to confirm its reputation. 'Even Annabelle finds it quite difficult to handle.'

Flora suppressed a sigh and tried very hard to keep all the sarcasm out of her voice. 'I think you might find I'm a better driver than Annabelle.'

'You think?' Charles pulled up at the side of the road. 'Then put your money where your mouth is and prove it.'

Biting her lip to conceal her grin of pleasure, Flora slid down from the vehicle and ran round to the driver's side. This was something she knew she could do. He'd have to lend it to her now.

Charles made the swap with slightly less alacrity. 'It'll probably be all right on the country roads but you might find driving through town a bit more difficult.'

The engine shuddered as Flora turned the key. She turned to him and said seriously, 'I think now is the time to confess that I haven't been a natural blonde since I was about ten years old. I think I'll be all right.'

Flora had to give Charles huge credit for letting a smile force its way from the corners of his eyes and one corner of his mouth. It turned a conventionally good-looking man into an extremely attractive one. Interesting. If she was Annabelle, she'd make strings of jokes so he'd smile more often.

Henry, on the other hand, going on what little she'd seen of him, smiled quite a lot. She did hope he'd manage to get in touch.

After Flora had negotiated the crowded High Street, got through a very narrow lane with cars on both sides and parked in an awkward spot in the yard behind the auction house, circumnavigating two removal vans as she did so, Charles said, 'I'd like to see you do all that with a trailer.'

'I'm sure you would.' Flora smiled sweetly. 'But unless you lend me the Land-Rover, you're not going to get the opportunity.'

'For that reason alone you can consider it yours until your car is ready.'

Flora got out, mentally thanking her father for letting her back his Land-Rover, with a trailer and boat attached, on to a crowded car ferry. It wasn't that Flora was over-confident, she just loved to see strong men with their mouths open.

'Thank you, Charles,' she said, coolly. She made to hand him the keys.

'No, they're yours now.'

She dropped them into her bag with a little skip of glee. They were her independence. She would no longer be marooned on her own, miles from anywhere.

The salerooms were seething with people and furniture and Flora followed Charles through the wardrobes, sofas, tables, chairs and rugs, all of which seemed to be on the move in contrary directions, to where low tables were set up to make an office area. Two women sat at computers and Annabelle stood between them, a clipboard in her hand, dealing out instructions.

'Oh, hi,' she said coolly to Flora, ignoring Charles. 'Good weekend? Lovely,' she went on without waiting to hear Flora's reply. 'I'm afraid, as you see, I'm far too busy to deal with you. Would you like to hang out with the porters? You may be able to help them shift furniture or something.'

Charles frowned. 'Couldn't she go through some of the boxes? Or there are the pictures – she could divide them into prints and paintings, watercolours and oils.'

'I did work in an art gallery once,' put in Flora. 'I could do that easily.'

'No! Looking decorative in an art gallery is not sufficient qualification for this job. I'd just have to do it all again. She'd be better out of the way with the boys.'

Flora suppressed a sigh, but it was her first day. Annabelle might trust her a bit more when she'd had a chance to prove herself. 'Hanging out with the boys sounds fun,' said Flora, glad that Geoffrey had told her to wear old clothes and bring gloves. He'd warned her that Annabelle wouldn't let her do anything except the most menial manual work.

'Annabelle is in charge of the saleroom on sale days,' said Charles.

'That's fine. I want to learn all about the family business, and, as I said, bottom up is best.' Flora delivered Annabelle a dazzling smile designed to disconcert her. 'I'll go and find Geoffrey, shall I?'

Annabelle frowned. 'He's not really the best person. He thinks he knows everything.'

'He was very kind to me over the weekend,' said Flora.

'Oh. Yes, I'm sorry we couldn't get over.' Annabelle didn't look as sorry as all that. 'Family commitments, you know.'

The insincerity in Flora's smile matched Annabelle's. 'That's OK. After all, I'm not very *close* family, am I?' She held back from suggesting that owning half the business strengthened the tie somewhat.

A few wrinkles appeared in Annabelle's otherwise smooth brow, fully exposed by the Alice band she used to keep her hair back. 'Well, go and see if you can help Geoffrey then. I'm certainly too busy to supervise you.'

'I'll take you to him,' said Charles.

'No, no, I'm sure you've got lots to do. I'll find him myself.' Flora smiled and waggled her fingers in a way guaranteed to make Annabelle want to shoot her. Unable to do this, Annabelle turned her irritation on one of the two women beside her, who produced the required piece of paper with admirable calm.

As she made her way through the furniture she wondered if it was worth trying to get on with Annabelle. Would she ever be able to drink instant coffee at a kitchen table with her, or share a bottle of wine in an overgrown garden and talk until it was too cold to stay outside any more? It seemed terribly unlikely, but she did so want to get her hands on Annabelle's wardrobe. Today she was wearing a shirt-waister that was just the wrong length, and not quite on her waist, with a Puritan collar. And in spite of the heat she was wearing quite thick navy blue tights. As for the navy blue velvet Alice band – was the woman stuck in a time warp? Perhaps that was it, Bishopsbridge was in a time warp where people still made 'good marriages' to people chosen by their parents, and fashion never dared encroach in case it frightened the horses.

Flora tracked Geoffrey down in a kitchen off a side hall. He was making tea for, it appeared, about twenty. With him were several people she vaguely recognised.

'Hello, Flora,' one woman said warmly. 'Do you take sugar?'

'Hello. Sorry, I don't think I know your name.'

'We're in the choir,' the woman explained. 'Several of us work as porters, part time. Not like Geoffrey, who's full time.'

'I thought porters were men, on the whole, so they could shift things.' Flora then blushed, worried in case she'd said something enormously politically incorrect.

'There's lots more to portering than moving furniture,' said another familiar face. 'We spend hours sorting the boxes, sticking on labels, making lists. You don't need brute strength for that.'

'While we're on the subject,' said a woman wearing a badge with 'Jenny' printed on it, 'don't forget that Dennis likes the bag left in his tea.'

'Come and help us up on the stage,' suggested the woman from choir who Flora was fairly sure was one of the subversive second sopranos. 'That's where the smaller stuff is: valuables, collectables, things like that. There's a mountain of things which need labelling. If you get confused about which vendor sent what, you're in real trouble.'

'Annabelle said I should be with Geoffrey—'

'Don't take any notice of her. She doesn't know what she's talking about.' Jenny leant in confidentially. 'She's not qualified, you know, or even working for her exams.'

'Oh?'

'She just thinks she knows everything because she did a bit of china mending at a course she went on once, when she was a girl.'

'She's still quite young,' protested Flora. Annabelle was almost certainly a bitch but she was probably still in her twenties, early thirties at most.

'And because she's got Charles twisted round her little finger. My name's Virginia, by the way,' the woman from the choir added. 'I was standing behind you in choir. I don't know what Charles sees in that woman.' She sighed.

'Oh, you know it's because their parents were such friends,' said Jenny helpfully, 'and then Charles's parents died – were they related to you, Flora?'

'Oh yes. Can't quite remember how,' said Flora. 'It was awful when they died. I was very young, but my mother was really upset.'

'So they've known each other all their lives.'

'Ah,' said Flora, trying to imply she thought this was sweet, when actually she thought it was a shame to miss the fun of the chase. Of course one often went chasing off down blind alleys, but it was fun all the same.

'We'll take our teas now, Geoffrey, save you carrying them up the stairs,' said Virginia. 'Flora, grab that packet of biscuits, will you?'

Flora exchanged glances with Geoffrey, to check with him that this plan was appropriate, and he nodded. 'The girls will look after you,' he said.

'Geoffrey!' they chorused. 'That should be "pre-women"!'

'Away with you,' said Geoffrey, unchastened. 'Or I won't make you tea again.'

Virginia flapped her hand, obviously not remotely concerned by political correctness from Geoffrey. '"Girls" is OK among friends.'

'Are you lot going to do any work today?' Geoffrey demanded.

Up on the stage, amid piles of boxes, crumpled newspaper and more extraordinary items than Flora could have imagined existed, she was given a sheet of stickers. Virginia, who seemed to be loosely in charge of the others, said, 'All these items need a sticker with "KGC" on it. Make sure nothing gets left out. Charles will come along later and do the lotting, and we can put things together in boxes, but until we know which of this rubbish is valuable and which isn't, we mark everything.'

'But can't you tell what's worth selling?' Flora regarded a box with a stuffed and mounted Jacob's sheep's head in it. The horns had fallen off and were lying next to the glassy-eyed face.

'We have a fair idea but there's often a jewel among the junk and we can't take chances. Imagine if you're the vendor, wanting every penny from the sale. It would be awful if something really valuable got missed and sold in a miscellaneous box.'

'I see.'

'And of course we have to make sure there's something tasty in every box, not just rubbish, or no one will buy it.'

'I see.'

'And you can't mix up the vendors, even if there is the missing jug from the tea set from another lot. The

73

buyer just has to buy both lots and make up the set himself.'

'Do you ever buy anything yourselves?' Flora asked, putting a sticker on to a plastic cuckoo clock.

'Oh yes. My husband says I get paid in antiques. You develop an eye, and if you wait long enough you'll get your bargain. Then you can do it up and sell it, if you don't want it for yourself.'

'I can see the attraction,' said Flora, spotting a very pretty little tea set with only five cups. 'Are you allowed to bid?'

'You tell Charles if you're interested in a lot and then he'll know to look up here when it comes up. Annabelle won't though. She's just awkward.'

'No one seems to like her, poor woman,' said Flora.

'Poor woman indeed! She comes from a very wealthy family and runs Charles into the ground.'

'Silly Charles for putting up with it!'

Virginia shook her head knowingly. 'She had her eye on him since she was nine years old. The poor man didn't have a chance.'

'He must have done,' said Flora briskly. 'He's free, white and over twenty-one!'

Virginia shrugged.

Flora forgot Charles and his marriage plans when she spotted a small leather case. 'Ooh! Can I play with this jewellery? It looks like a treasure chest, with it all spilling out.'

'You can just put a sticker on it. Annabelle's been through it already. It's all junk – or "costume" as we say in the trade.'

'Oh, let me play, just for a second,' pleaded Flora. 'I

just want to look at that brooch of a cat. My cat had kittens at the weekend.'

Virginia allowed herself to be distracted by this news. While describing the little bundles, with their flat ears and slits instead of eyes, Flora tipped out the box of jewellery on to a table and sorted through it.

'Of course you can come and see them when they're a bit bigger,' she said. 'Geoffrey's Edie is having one, and I might want to keep one myself, but there's still two more.'

'And they were born on top of your shoes?'

'Yes! And we'd made her such a nice bed. She's on it now, of course, and seems perfectly happy. I've used all the towels, though, and have to keep washing them by hand. Just as well the weather's fine. My shoes needed a bit of cleaning, too.'

'You should get a washing machine. Pick one up here for a song.'

'I'll speak to Charles about it. Oh look, these pearls are real.'

'They can't be. Annabelle would have spotted them.'

'They are.' Flora pulled out the long string of small, uneven pearls. 'They're gritty when you bite them. That's the only thing I know about anything.'

'Tell Annabelle when she comes round. She'll be cross that she missed it.'

Annabelle took some convincing. 'They can't possibly be real. They're far too long a string.'

'I really do think they are,' Flora said, agonised by the thought that she might not be believed.

'It's terribly unlikely. If anyone had a string that long they'd keep them separate and they were just jumbled together in all that diamanté and glass.'

'Well, you test them, then,' said Flora, beginning to doubt herself.

Annabelle shook her head. 'I can't do that thing with the teeth. So unhygienic.'

'Let's ask Charles,' suggested Virginia, as he appeared on the stage. She waved at him to come over.

'Are these pearls real or not?' she asked.

Charles raised them to his mouth. 'Yup. Freshwater pearls. Well spotted, Annie-bee. They should definitely go on their own.'

Virginia opened her mouth to say it wasn't 'Annie-bee' who spotted them, but Flora. Flora frowned and shook her head. Annabelle had enough problems with her without being shown up by the downsizing bimbo.

'You should have said something,' said Virginia when Charles and Annabelle had gone.

'There's no point in antagonising her any more. She already hates me.'

'She hates everyone she thinks stands in the way of her grand plan.'

'Oh? What's her grand plan?' Flora carefully put a label on each of three broken pieces that had once been a Toby jug.

Virginia regarded the pieces and frowned. 'She wants to close the place down.'

'But why would she do that? It's a good business, isn't it?'

'Could be better, and this building alone is fantastically valuable. There's a nursery school round the back, the rent from that is quite high, and it's used by the locals – drama groups, WI, Cubs and Brownies, Guides

– between sales. It would be a real loss to the community if it was sold.'

'So what does Annabelle want to do with it?'

'Divide it up into executive flats and sell them individually for a fortune.'

'Oh my goodness.'

'And then there's the house next door. At the moment there's a flat there that Charles uses sometimes, and the offices. But it would raise a lot of money if it were divided and sold off.'

'I can see it is quite extravagant keeping it, if it's not all being used. But this place is different. It's like a public space.'

'Exactly!' Virginia frowned suddenly and said, 'Who are you again? Apart from being Charles's cousin?'

Flora wondered if she should keep her exact identity secret, but decided that secrets were a luxury no one had round here. 'I've inherited a bit of the company. Annabelle wants to buy some shares from me.' It wasn't the entire truth, but it should be enough to satisfy Virginia. It wasn't fair to Charles that the whole town should know all his private financial affairs, even if they did know most of them already.

'Well, don't you let her, if you can avoid it. So you're learning a bit about the business?'

'That's the idea. Annabelle and Charles think I'll be a liability, but I'd like to prove them wrong.'

'They're not so good at it themselves. Oh, Charles is a good man, knows everything about anything that's likely to come through the doors and beyond, but he's too old-fashioned in many ways. Marketing is not his bag.' Virginia spotted Geoffrey coming up the stairs with a box. 'Over here, Geoffrey. Is that all the same vendor?'

While they discussed who owned what and what list it should be on, Flora resisted the temptation to go through the other boxes of costume jewellery, and hoped, very hard, that Virginia wouldn't have forgotten what she was telling her by the time she and Geoffrey had reached a conclusion.

'No,' Virginia said when they were alone again. 'My daughter offered to do them a website, for nothing, for practice, and Annabelle wouldn't hear of it. Said it was quite unnecessary. They put the better items on the Internet, which does get people down here, but they haven't got a website as such.'

'So how do they advertise?'

'The *Yellow Pages*, and of course the sales are listed in the local papers, but that's not going to get them much new business. All auction houses have websites these days. It's essential. My daughter could do them one very reasonably.'

'Hmm. I'll have to look into that,' said Flora. 'Do you want to do that box or shall I?'

'There's some jewellery and I can see you're keen. You go ahead.'

78

Chapter Five

While Flora was more than competent to drive the Land-Rover, she was a little less sure of the way. However, after finding herself in a village that was definitely not the one with the village shop and the pub which were currently her nearest civilisation, she managed to find her way back to what she now regarded as her cottage.

It was a heavenly summer evening, and Flora longed to have someone to share it with other than Imelda and her four little kittens. She parked the Land-Rover and got out, enjoying the sudden quiet after the noise of the engine.

'It would be different in winter,' she told herself. 'You wouldn't want to live here then.'

As she unlocked the front door she realised how tired she was. She'd been on her feet all day and done more physical work than she'd ever done in her life. But she'd loved it. The people were what made it, she decided. Apart from Annabelle, who'd been relentlessly unfriendly and dismissive, and Charles, whom she'd hardly seen, everyone had been so kind and helpful. And more than that, they'd made her feel one of the gang, not like an irritating outsider.

After she'd dumped her bag on the table she went upstairs to see Imelda and the kitts, who seemed to have grown since the morning.

Imelda was very pleased to see her, obviously thrilled to have some adult company after a long day alone with the kids. She purred and purred as Flora stroked her, and then went hungrily to her empty food saucer.

'All right, darling, I'll be right up with a sachet of cat food. I got you some new flavours today!'

Flora ran downstairs, all her tiredness forgotten in her delight with her cat and kittens. Perhaps she should become celibate and just live with animals from now on. Animals didn't do stupid things like marry people because it was assumed they would. Although, as she ran Imelda's saucer under the tap to wash it, cats in particular did seem to pick owners who'd spoil them. So perhaps men weren't as different from cats as all that.

She squeezed the food out of its pouch, thinking about her cousin. He was dyed-in-the-wool stuffy and she didn't like him, but unless Annabelle stopped being so controlling about the business, she didn't think he should marry her. What Virginia had told her about Annabelle's plans for Stanza and Stanza had really got to her, and as Flora didn't feel she knew Charles anything like well enough to tell whether he would let Annabelle bully him, she wasn't going to take the chance. She was staying, at least until the old family firm – if not the whole of Bishopsbridge – had joined the twenty-first century.

Imelda joined her in the kitchen, rubbing against her legs in an attempt to make the food come quicker. Flora sighed, recalling Annabelle's bossiness at the saleroom. With or without control, it would take something cataclysmic to turn Annabelle into a nice person. And she wasn't entirely sure Charles deserved the effort –

although everyone else around her probably did.

Flora opened a bottle of wine and a packet of nuts and then went upstairs to run a bath. Aware it was probably hugely extravagant, she had left the immersion heater on all day rather than risk there being no hot water when she got home. She'd been warned she'd be filthy.

She found herself nodding off in the bath and decided to abandon supper. She brushed her teeth in a cursory manner and tumbled into bed, the damp towel still around her. And, very quickly, she slept.

In fact, she overslept. When she woke, still tangled in the towel, she realised it was past eight o'clock and Charles was expecting her at the saleroom at eight-thirty.

She hurled herself out and started dragging clothes out of the wardrobe. She put on her knickers but clutched her bra and her dress to her, planning to put them on while the kettle was boiling. She was halfway down the stairs when she screamed. There was a man standing in the sitting room, looking at her.

'Please don't be frightened,' he said, a startled look on his face. The speaker was extremely tall and lean and was wearing clothes so faded it was hard to tell what colour they'd started life as. He had long curly hair and the bluest eyes Flora had seen for a long time. His nose was aquiline and his mouth beautifully curved. And his voice was low and melodic with no discernible regional accent.

Flora screamed again briefly and fled back into her bedroom to put on her dress. She abandoned the bra. She could run out to the Land-Rover without that. She went back to the top of the stairs.

'I won't do anything to hurt you, I promise. I've been here all night,' he said anxiously.

Flora was tempted to scream retrospectively. All night she'd been sleeping, naked, on her bed with the door half open, while this completely strange, although she had to admit not particularly threatening, man slept on her sofa. It was an outrage.

Imelda came to rub against her legs, probably wondering what the delay with breakfast was.

'Hello, puss,' said the man, and Imelda, the traitress, tripped down the stairs towards him. She allowed him to rub her ears for a moment and then looked up as if to say, 'Perhaps you'll give me breakfast?'

'Look,' said Flora, 'you can't sleep here. I live here. This is my home. You must leave! Immediately!'

'I've been sleeping here on and off all year,' he said apologetically. 'The window in the kitchen is very easy to open and I spent most of the winter here.'

'Oh God!'

'And I've boiled the kettle. Would you like some tea?'

'No! I mean, you can't offer me tea in my own house!'

'I realise it's not quite usual, especially when we haven't met, officially, but it seems the least I can do in the circumstances.'

Flora came down the stairs. She was dying for tea. She was desperate to feed Imelda so she could go to work, but there was this man. 'The least you can do – in fact the most you can do – in the circumstances is to leave. Now. So I can get ready to go to work. And feed my cat.'

'I could do that for you.'

'But I don't want you to! I want you to go!' The whole

situation was ridiculous and Flora just wanted it to be over.

'I will go, if you're sure, but wouldn't you like tea first?'

Flora came further into the room and could see through the kitchen door two steaming mugs. She remembered that she'd had two glasses of wine and no water the night before. No wonder her mouth felt stuck together with glue.

He saw that she was tempted and went to fetch one of the mugs. 'Do you want breakfast? I could rustle you up a couple of scrambled eggs in no time.'

'No!' She sipped the tea. It was heaven, but it was an impossible situation. And she *had* to get to work or Charles would think he'd been right about her all along. She just didn't have time for this.

Imelda, having given up on Flora's ability to move, miaowed at the man, making her needs clear.

'Hello, you. Oh, you've had kittens,' he said. 'You must be hungry.'

'She is. I usually give her something last thing at night, but I fell asleep and she's only had a few cat biscuits to keep her going.'

'Are the kittens here?'

Flora nodded. 'Upstairs. Not that it's anything to do with you, of course.'

He smiled. 'I'm William.'

'Flora. Listen, William,' she said firmly, 'you must realise how impossible this is.'

'I do see that it's difficult, but not impossible. After all, I haven't murdered you, have I? Shall I feed the young mother? What's her name?'

'Imelda. Yes please, do feed her. But . . .' She hesitated. She was so late. 'William? I've got to rush now, but could you please leave by the time I get home? About half past six or seven? This isn't my house and if the owners found out you'd been using it, they'd die of shock and have you put in prison for ever.' She took another sip of tea.

'You should eat. You obviously didn't eat last night.'

'Obviously?'

'No dishes, no sign of cooking.'

'Well, I haven't time now,' she almost snapped, horribly reminded of how she'd been with her mother sometimes when she'd tried to press breakfast on her before school. She sighed. 'I must find some shoes. And then I must go. And then you must go. But do, please, feed Imelda first.'

She ran back upstairs and found her sandals. She took a deep breath and reminded herself that he'd had all night to murder her in her sleep if that was his intention, and then ran back down again. Imelda and William were in the kitchen. He was putting food into a bowl and she was tucking into it before he'd even finished.

'I like feeding people, too,' he said.

Flora found herself smiling and tried to stop. She ran out of the door, scrabbling for her keys as she did so, and shouted, 'Go!'

It was only when she was in the Land-Rover and had started the engine that she remembered she wasn't wearing a bra. 'I'll have to buy a cardigan, or a T-shirt or something. Charles would die of shock if he caught the outline of a nipple through my dress.'

As she drove, she thought about William and his silent

invasion. It was awful, of course, but somehow not as terrifying as it might have been if she'd been living in London. There the thought of finding a strange man in the sitting room when she woke up was so horrifying, she shivered just thinking about it. Here, it was decidedly odd, but didn't have the same stomach-churning effect, even if she had been frightened at the time.

Thinking about the differences between town and country life made her realise that if she survived her stint in the country she could set up the very course she was looking for herself. 'Living without Sushi! How to survive Country Life.' Or she could get sponsorship from magazines. 'The *Country Living* guide to Country Life.' Or the other way round: 'The *Country Life* guide to Country Living.' Honestly, she was wasted on an old-fashioned, family-run auctioneers!

She didn't feel wasted when she got there, however; she felt needed. Now people had got used to her, had begun to trust her a little, she was sent all over the place on errands. Stickers to put on here, a piece of jewellery that had been mislaid to be hunted for there, vast numbers of cups of tea to be made and distributed, and learning, all the time.

She loved it. There was no other word for it. She found it interesting, exciting and hugely companionable. Charles and Annabelle might not have run the most cutting-edge auction house in the country, but it could be the most friendly one.

Virginia took her to buy sandwiches at about half past one, when there was a slight lull in proceedings. They found a bench in the park opposite the saleroom and ate them, and Flora commented on the family atmosphere.

'We do it for Charles,' said Virginia through a mouthful of chicken and mango wrap. 'Most of us knew his father and it was he who made the business like it is. Before they got engaged and Annabelle came, Charles was running it along the same lines. Then Miss Green-wellies-and-pearls decided to smarten us all up. She wanted us to wear nylon uniforms! Aprons are sensible, they keep the dirt off your clothes. But uniforms! We refused, of course.'

'Of course. Nylon! Yuck!'

'The firm does need updating, of course, but not how she's planning to do it, which, basically, is to maximise the property: turn all the buildings into executive homes.'

'I'll talk to Charles about the website. We should have one. Does your daughter still do them?'

'Oh yes, but she'll want paying now. It's her business.'

'Of course she'll want paying. I'll get on to Charles straightaway. There are a few other things I need to see him about, too. Where's he been all morning?'

'Doing a valuation, I expect.' Virginia leant in confidentially. 'The story is that when Annabelle did them, apart from not knowing very much about how much things were worth, she used to offend the customers. They're often recently bereaved, you see. A certain amount of tact is required.'

'And they get that from Charles?'

'Oh yes. He's wonderful with people.'

'Are we talking about the same Charles? My cousin?'

Virginia laughed. 'He may seem quite reserved, but he's very good at what he does.'

'I'll take your word for it.'

'It's Annabelle you want to watch.'

'If you don't mind my asking, how do you know so much about it all?'

Virginia laughed. 'Well, I keep my ear to the ground – in self-defence really. We all do. And Annabelle doesn't exactly make a secret about what she wants.' Virginia took another bite and chewed thoughtfully. Flora wanted to hurry her but knew she couldn't. 'I don't suppose this business makes very much money,' she said eventually, 'even though we get paid by the buyers and the sellers, but it would be a shame for it all to disappear.'

'Yes, it would. I'll have to see what I can do. After all, I'm the one with the stake in the business, not Annabelle.' Now it was obvious why Geoffrey didn't want Annabelle to have even a small share of it financially.

Driving home at the end of a long day, very tired and filthy dirty, Flora had time to consider how much money she stood to make herself if the buildings were all turned into flats and sold. She was too weary to make a very accurate guess but it was surely a great deal of money. What would she do with over a million pounds? Maybe it was the fatigue, but at that moment she couldn't think of anything she wanted except a hot bath, a packet of crisps and a glass of wine.

She had turned the key in the lock and opened the door before she remembered William. A wonderful savoury smell wafted out from the kitchen, and the cottage looked very cosy. There was a fresh bunch of wild roses on the mantelpiece that she hadn't put there, and a fire laid in the fireplace. Not that you'd need one in this weather, but it looked nice to have it there.

There was no sign of William, however – he'd clearly

seen that Flora was serious about her instructions to leave – so when she had dumped her bag she ran upstairs to see Imelda and the kittens. They were fine, and Imelda's litter tray had obviously been changed. The joke about the gay burglars who tidied the house and left a quiche in the oven came into her mind and made her smile. It must be William – who else could it be? But was he gay? She couldn't possibly tell.

She dragged herself away from the little furry bundles, which were making little swimming movements to get about, and went back downstairs, aware how hungry she was, thrilled that there was something in the oven.

She had just taken it out when there was a knock on the door. 'William,' she said, smiling in spite of her resolutions not to, 'you'd better come in.'

'I just came to check you'd come home roughly when you said you'd come, and that your supper wasn't burning.'

'It was very kind of you to make me supper.'

'It was very kind of you not to call the police and make an awful fuss.'

'Would you like a glass of wine?' She was desperate for one herself and realised that she would enjoy it more in company. And he had cooked for her, after all.

'That would be very nice. Shall I check on the pie?'

'If you like. You might as well share it with me. What is it?'

'Cheese and onion and tomato pie. I'm not a vegetarian, but you didn't have any meat. A bit of bacon goes well with it.'

'I'll get some tomorrow, if I have time to slip out to the shops.'

'I'll find some knives and forks.'

'William,' she said once they'd settled down with steaming plates on their knees, 'how much time do you spend here usually?'

'It varies, but I spent most of the winter here.'

'Is that why it smells of wood smoke?'

'Probably. The fire did smoke a bit when the chimney was cold.'

Flora swallowed a mouthful of pie. It was delicious and, she thought prudently, probably very cheap. 'Do Charles and Annabelle have any idea that you exist?' Then she realised that of course they didn't know, they'd be apoplectic at the thought.

'Who are Charles and Annabelle?'

'They own this cottage. Or at least, Annabelle does. Charles is my cousin.'

He shrugged. 'I don't care much about that sort of thing. If a house is empty, I don't see why I shouldn't use it. I didn't do any damage, after all.'

'I only have your word for that!' declared Flora, laughing. 'It could have been a palace before I moved in.'

William regarded her seriously. 'It was a cottage, it is still a cottage and will be a cottage until some Philistine puts a huge extension on it.'

'You're a fine one to talk about Philistines! Taking over houses without a by-your-leave. What are you doing around here, anyway? Are you a poacher or something?'

'I'm a poet and a portrait painter, but I do take the odd rabbit or pheasant if I need it.'

'And you squat in empty buildings?'

89

'Do you know why Marxists drink herb tea?' William took a sip of his wine.

'No.' She took a sip of hers.

'Because all proper tea is theft,' announced William. 'Only, of course, it wasn't Marx who said that.'

Flora laughed. 'Can I tell you what joke I thought of when I went upstairs and found you'd changed the cat litter?'

'That was to ingratiate myself with you.'

'I'm sure it was, but it made me think of the joke about the gay burglars, who tidy the house and leave a quiche in the oven.'

He laughed and shook his head. 'I'm afraid I'm not gay, but I'm completely trustworthy and, if it makes you feel any better, although I think you're very pretty, I don't fancy you.'

'That's all right then.' Curiously it did make her feel better. 'Is there any more of this pie?'

She was at the saleroom again at eight-thirty in the morning, and so was nearly everyone else. The sale started at ten. There was another chance to view from nine o'clock, and Virginia had told her that they allowed people to go on viewing on the stage, where the smaller, more stealable items were, until half an hour before the sale got to their lot numbers.

As always, she found a huddle of people in the kitchen, dunking tea bags in and out of mugs. 'Hi, Flora,' said Geoffrey. 'Ready for your first sale?'

'I hope so. I'm really looking forward to it. After you've spent days handling and looking at all this, you almost feel like it's yours.'

He chuckled. 'Well, if you want to bid on anything, let Charles know, and get a card from the office. It's a good way to furnish a house cheaply.'

Flora took a moment to consider how much fun it would be buying things for the cottage and then remembered it wasn't her cottage and that the London flat didn't really need anything extra – it was cramped enough already. 'Not at the moment, Geoffrey.'

'It's how Edie and me got most of the stuff for our daughters. If you work here long enough you'll see everything you could ever want or need pass by. I bought most of the furniture for our place when I was a dealer.'

'That's why you never made a mint when you were a dealer, Geoff,' said another porter. 'You couldn't resist hanging on to the best stuff.'

Flora remembered that Geoffrey and Edie's house had some very nice pieces in it. He laughed. 'You may well be right there, lad. Now, are we going to do any work, or are we just here for decoration?'

Flora was in the yard, helping Geoffrey make a collection of garden gnomes look attractive, when he looked at his watch. 'Five minutes to kick-off. I expect Charles will start but Annabelle should do out here really, get these small lots out of the way.'

'Why won't she then?' Flora felt it might be quite fun persuading people to part with hard cash for these cute little gentlemen who seemed to have fallen on hard times, judging by the state of their pointy hats.

'Because it's beneath her. She only likes doing the posh stuff. Not that she's any good at it, mind.'

'Poor Annabelle! No one has a good word to say for her.'

Geoffrey snorted. 'She's a rubbish auctioneer. She can't get the crowd on her side for one thing. You'll have to learn how to do it. You wouldn't have that trouble.'

Flora sighed. She acknowledged that she might very well be able to get the people on her side, but even her short time at Stanza and Stanza had told her that there was a little more to it than that. And it involved sums. 'I don't think I'd fancy it. When you watch it on television it seems terribly complicated.'

'Once you've learnt the steps you go up in – you know, five, eight, ten, or three, five, eight, ten, whatever is appropriate – you'd be fine.'

'Geoffrey, I have difficulty with my two times table, I don't quite see myself with a gavel in my hand. Do you do it ever?'

He shook his head. 'Very rarely. Only if Annabelle doesn't want to. She doesn't like me doing it because she thinks I'm only a porter, although I reckon I could get more for this lot than she could. Not that she'll try, of course.' He paused. 'Are you going to leave them like that?' He was referring to the gnomes.

'I thought they looked rather sweet standing in a circle,' said Flora. 'Ah, here comes the boss.'

Everything happened extremely quickly. The stuffy Charles Flora had come to know disappeared and turned into the star of the show.

'Good morning, ladies and gentlemen,' he said with a smile, 'and a very lovely morning it is. Now, lot number one, a very appealing collection of garden gnomes who appear to be peeing into a pond. Who'll start me then, twenty pounds? No? Ten? Five? Think how charming they'd look on your patio. Five, thank you, eight? Ten, twelve, fifteen . . . thank you. Sold! And the next . . .'

Flora looked on in awe, aware that she was due to go and guard the small stuff on the stage but unable to tear herself away. It went incredibly quickly, lot after lot was knocked down and yet Charles never appeared to hurry. He had his audience enthralled, twitching their cards, eager to buy what he was selling. He seemed even taller than usual and infinitely more charming. She began to get an inkling of why all the porters seemed so fond of him: apart from the business side, he was good at his job.

But there was no time for Flora to stand and stare at her cousin. At last she stopped watching and hurried through the crowd and the furniture to the stage, where she stood by a table full of tea sets – some beautiful, some mismatched, some frankly bizarre – and apologised to Virginia for being late.

'We've managed fine. Annabelle wanted to tell one of us regulars to go home because of you being here, but Charles wouldn't let her.'

'Virginia! You can't possibly know all that. You're making it up because you hate Annabelle.'

'Nonsense! She was asking me which porter to lay off when Charles overheard. Honestly.'

Flora grinned. She really liked Virginia but felt she was wasted as an auctioneer's porter and a subversive second soprano. She should have been in espionage.

When all the lots on the floor had been sold and many of them removed by quietly working porters with trolleys, the attention of the room turned to the stage.

'We've got some quite valuable lots up here today,' said Virginia. 'I expect Annabelle will sell it. I think Charles lets her in the hope that she'll get to like it, or at least get a bit better.'

Virginia was proved right and Annabelle took over from Charles. She settled herself at the desk, cleared her throat and then took a sip of water. The room waited for her to be ready. Flora could hear Virginia, clutching a huge Staffordshire ornament, tutting at the waste of time.

Even Flora's very limited experience of auction sales was enough to tell her that Annabelle was not good at it. Her voice was high and shrill and she behaved less like someone encouraging people to buy things and more like an irritable headmistress demanding answers to questions. It was little wonder that few people put their hands up.

At first Flora felt self-conscious, standing at the front of the stage holding strange items above her head, but that didn't last long and she spent the time, while Annabelle laboriously sent items under the hammer, looking at the crowd.

There were quite a lot of them. Virginia, next to her, ready to show the lot after Flora's, indicated the people she knew, talking out of the corner of her mouth.

'The man in the hat is a dealer. He buys loads of glass and sells lots of it on. We see the same stuff time after time. He puts quite high reserves on sometimes so it often doesn't sell. But he makes a good living so it must be worth it.'

Flora spotted the private buyers for herself. There were a couple of women who were having a day out together and had obviously had a glass of wine at lunch. They were thoroughly enjoying themselves. The porters enjoyed themselves too, and kept going on sweets and chocolates. Although they urged each other to take proper breaks no one liked to leave the action.

Charles took over from Annabelle quite soon. Flora had seen him at the desk, dealing with customers, and hoped he'd had time for a sandwich, at least.

'They need another auctioneer,' said Virginia to Flora, who was trying not to drop a very valuable lead crystal decanter that was attracting a lot of interest. 'You should train.'

'Not on your life,' said Flora through her smile.

Before the sale was over people came up to collect their purchases. One woman took charge of the pink slips that stated the items had been paid for and found the items, while the others carried on ferrying glass, crystal, and silver from the back to the front of the stage.

With Charles back in charge the lots whistled by and before Flora had seen it coming, the sale was over. The crowd of people wanting to collect their treasures built up. Now the selling was over everyone dealt with customers, helping them pack and finding newspaper for wrapping.

Flora really liked this part. Now the bidding was over the hardest-bitten dealer could appear pleased with what they'd bought, although they always muttered that they'd paid too much for it.

The pair of women were now extremely giggly, thinking up extravagant stories for their husbands as to why they felt they needed so much when they'd only come to buy a wedding present for a niece.

Virginia and the others knew many of the people and laughed and joked with them. Flora, as a new face, received a few curious glances. After a hurried consultation, Virginia introduced her as a new porter. Flora didn't want everyone knowing she was a family member, until it was either impossible to keep secret or politic to announce it.

She could have gone home; the others encouraged her to do so as it was her first sale. But Flora wasn't going to go until Charles and Annabelle did and she felt fairly certain Charles wouldn't leave until the floor had been swept and every last cup washed. She didn't want him accusing her of slacking.

'Is there anything else for me to do?' she asked Charles when it was only him, Annabelle and Louisa, the secretary, left. It was the first time she'd had an opportunity to speak to him and she wanted to congratulate him on being so good at his job.

'I don't think so.' Charles regarded her with his usual, barely-concealed contempt, all remnants of the charming auctioneer vanished. 'How did you enjoy your first sale? It's not quite like it is on television, is it?'

Hurt that he should still be so stuffy when she had seen him be so different, she said, 'Oh no. It's much better in real life than it is on television.'

'Oh!'

She had the satisfaction of knowing she had surprised him.

'It's not so bloody tiring on television,' said Annabelle. 'Or as dirty. I'm filthy. I'm going straight home for a bath, Charles. You don't need me?'

'I just want to let Louisa know what's going on. We're

doing a valuation over at a house in Churchfields tomorrow, Lou.'

'Oh, Charles!' Annabelle broke in. 'Do I have to? Can't you do it on your own?'

'I could, but it will take me ages. The tape recorder's broken. I need a note-taker.'

'Take Flora, then.'

Charles regarded his cousin, obviously debating who was preferable, a reluctant Annabelle or a completely inexperienced Flora. He pursed his lips.

'Really, darling, I can't.' Annabelle decided to help him in his decision. 'I need to go over to the cottage and take a proper inventory. You don't mind, Flora, do you?'

Flora did mind, for lots of reasons, principally William. 'But, Annabelle, Imelda and the kittens! You're allergic to cats.'

'Oh, I'd be all right for a bit. As long as I don't touch them or anything.'

'But do you really need an inventory? I'm hardly going to steal the furniture. And you can get Paris goblets at the local supermarket if I break any.'

'Yes,' Annabelle replied, 'but I'd like to list what I've lent you. When you go in a couple of months, I might have forgotten what we'd taken out when we decided not to rent this year.' She smiled. 'It would be awful if I blamed you for losing something that had never been there, wouldn't it?'

Not quite as awful as Annabelle discovering William in the cottage, Flora thought, but of course couldn't say.

'Do you know what time you'll be there?'

'No, but you'll be out with Charles, anyway. It won't make any difference.'

'Annabelle! I really don't want to take Flora. She's only just got here. She knows nothing.'

'I learnt a lot today, Charles,' said Flora in a way she hoped would both convince him and warn him that he couldn't treat her like an ignorant townie for ever.

'Flora! I don't mean to be insulting—'

'Then don't be.'

'But you are as much use to me as a chocolate teapot. Or the novelty ones that you collect.'

'But they are useful. You can make tea in them. And I can take notes, or do whatever it is you need me to do. You shouldn't believe all those blonde jokes you know. Blondes are no stupider than anyone else.'

'Oh, all right then! You can come with me. But for goodness' sake put some more clothes on!'

It was only then that Flora remembered she was not wearing a bra.

'You won't be wearing an apron tomorrow,' Charles reminded her.

Flora slipped away feeling surprisingly chastened. And she'd have to warn William to stay out all day. Poor Imelda would have to survive on fly-blown Kittikins and her litter tray. Life was never simple.

Chapter Six

Not having to be at work until half past nine seemed like a lie-in to Flora – although she would have enjoyed it more if she wasn't worried about William turning up at the cottage while Annabelle was there.

The previous evening when she'd got home there had been a note from him saying that he'd seen to Imelda and pointing out the salad he had made. He seemed to have used some lettuce and tomatoes that she had in the fridge and a lot of very strange bits of plant which he must have gathered from less orthodox sources. She recognised tips of hawthorn and what might have been some sort of wild sorrel but nothing else. After she'd spent a time-wasting half-hour with Imelda and the kittens, she had eaten it. Either the bits of plant tasted very good, or the vinaigrette, which he'd also made, disguised any unpleasant taste.

Grateful though she was to come home to a delicious meal, she would rather have actually seen William so she could have warned him about Annabelle. She could hardly leave him a note telling him to keep out of the way – Annabelle was far more likely to find it than he was.

Still, at least she had a television now. Charles had bought one for her from the sale the previous day. He'd put it in the back of the Land-Rover for her and said, 'I suppose you might as well have this. No one else seemed to want it.'

She had thanked him in a manner appropriate to such a grudging gift but a tiny part of her wondered if he was actually being quite kind, but didn't want her to know. The porters all seemed to like him well enough, but then they would, wouldn't they? He was good-looking in a conventional sort of way and if they'd known and liked his father, they were bound to feel motherly towards him. And, of course, he wasn't trying to force any of them to leave.

After she had got the TV to work, she settled down in front of it. But instead of concentrating on six young women from very sheltered homes struggling through the desert carrying Kalashnikovs and backpacks the size of small cars, which appeared to be the latest in reality television, she found herself thinking about the business and Charles.

Yesterday she had noticed that he had been constantly following on Annabelle's heels. Was he soothing ruffled feathers, or checking she'd done things right? If she'd been Annabelle and Charles had done that, she'd have killed him. Annabelle seemed oblivious. Did she not know? Or not care? It was hard to believe that Annabelle was really as bad at the job as she appeared to be, but going on what the porters said, she was worse, and bossy with it.

Flora yawned, aware that if she didn't go to bed soon, she'd wake up in the middle of the night on the sofa, cold and stiff. As she sleepily locked doors and windows, brought up more food and water for Imelda, and unplugged the slightly dodgy electric kettle, she decided that Charles and Annabelle were nothing to do with her and went to bed. They had certainly gone way past the 'in love' stage of their relationship.

So was their relationship purely for practical reasons? It was none of Flora's business of course, she told herself firmly, but she was a compulsive people-watcher and couldn't help but be fascinated by this oddly distant couple set on marrying. Why on earth were they together? If Annabelle wanted control of a business, why didn't she use her money to start one she liked, instead of muddling about with furniture and knick-knacks that gave her no pleasure at all?

Unless, of course, it wasn't that way round. Maybe she wanted to be financially involved in Stanza and Stanza so that when she persuaded or bullied or convinced Charles to sell the buildings, she would get her cut. Or even just be married to Charles to share his bit.

Charles was possibly hoping that Annabelle would invest some of her money in the business so he could improve things, do a little marketing, some proper advertising. But that seemed terribly cold. Maybe Flora was barking up the wrong tree completely. The trouble was, their private life could be a sea of endless passion but they were both so buttoned up and conventional the rest of the world would never know. And if they'd known each other from childhood, perhaps they'd never shared the white heat of a new relationship.

Thinking of new relationships reminded Flora of Henry. She liked Henry; he looked as if he could be fun. The twinkle in his eye was such a relief after Charles's disapproval, and in a town this small she was sure she'd run into him again. She was rather looking forward to it.

'I might just have to get one of those stickers saying "I Love My Landy",' declared Flora as she and Charles got out of their vehicles at roughly the same time. 'It's such fun being able to see into the gardens. And being so high up makes me feel empowered, sort of. Strong,' she added, in case the word 'empowered' was too frighteningly feminist for him.

Charles raised an eyebrow, possibly a little surprised at being greeted in this light-hearted way. 'Well, there's no reason why you shouldn't carry on driving it. It's a firm car – they're still waiting for that part for yours, by the way.' He frowned, and carried on. 'As long as you don't mind us using it to collect odd bits of furniture from time to time.'

'I would have thought a big old Volvo would be better for things like that?'

Charles held the door open for her. 'It would, actually, but Annabelle had her heart set on a Land-Rover.'

Flora had told herself she was going to see the positive in Annabelle at every opportunity. 'I expect she likes being able to see into the gardens, too.'

'No. She said it made her feel safe.'

'I can understand that. The roads round here must get quite icy in winter.'

Charles looked down his nose at her – probably by accident, he was so much taller. 'Not really. It's very mild here.'

Flora really wanted to go to the Ladies' but felt that

this conversation should be finished first so she followed him into the office. 'But I thought you said she found it difficult to drive. Where is she, by the way?'

'Going to your house, later. She does find the Land-Rover awkward to park.'

'Then why are you keeping it? It's quite new.'

'I think we need to have this conversation sometime, but not now,' said Charles. 'Can you pick up a notebook and a reliable pen and we'll be off? I don't want to keep these people waiting. They've travelled a long way to get their uncle's estate settled.'

It was very frustrating. Flora couldn't exactly accuse him of being secretive, but he simply wasn't telling her anything.

They were both silent as they set off in his old but roomy Citroën. Flora was wondering why the firm bought a Land-Rover it didn't really need when Charles was driving such an old car. Surely it couldn't just be Annabelle's whim?

Eventually Charles said, 'We mostly use tape recorders to do valuations these days, but ours has broken and it'll be good training for you. In the old days they were always written out by hand and typed up later. You had to have two of you doing it.'

'Doesn't Annabelle like doing them?' Annabelle had said as much herself, but Flora wanted to prod a little deeper.

'Not really. We don't do all that much fine furniture these days and she's not really into everyday household effects, which are the bread and butter of our business.'

Flora filed away the snippet about the fine furniture and stuck to her questions about Annabelle. 'Tell me to mind my own business – I'm sure you will – but does Annabelle really like working for – in – an auction house?'

He was silent, as if thinking about his answer.

'If she doesn't,' went on Flora, trying not to show her impatience, 'why does she want to buy the shares so you have the majority shareholding?'

'She likes to be in control,' he said slowly. 'She's very organised.'

'But she wouldn't be in control,' said Flora. 'You would.'

'Annabelle and I are going to be married. It's more or less the same thing.'

'Charles! It's not the same thing! Marriage doesn't bind you at the hip!' She thought of how her mother would react if anyone suggested that getting married gave either partner 'control'. And remembered, rather uncomfortably, Virginia's comments about Annabelle's plans.

'I really don't want to discuss my private life with you, Flora,' Charles said coolly, at his very stuffiest.

'You brought it up! I just wanted to know why Annabelle wanted to get involved with a business she didn't like. After all, she could run her own business. She doesn't have to be linked to yours.'

'She could but she feels . . .' He paused, drumming his fingers on the steering wheel, apparently going through a mental thesaurus for the right words.

Flora gave up trying to hide her frustration with his reserve. 'She feels that it's a failing business and that you'd be better to sell it?' This was probably far too far too fast but she was fed up with gossip and wanted to know the facts, straight from the stuffed-horse's mouth.

'Who told you that?' the horse demanded.

'All the porters know, Charles, and they are not at all happy. I don't know if you were trying to keep it a secret, but you've failed.'

Charles sighed deeply. 'I suppose it's inevitable that it should get out. The thing is, we may not be able to stay in business even if Annabelle did want to. We haven't made a profit for a couple of years.' Flora bit her lip, knowing what he was going to say. 'If we liquidated our property, we – you included – could make an absolute fortune.'

Flora thought about the enormous house, only partly used, the huge hall next door where the day before she'd experienced her first auction, and where the local community put on plays and flower shows and held discos, that also housed a nursery and a playgroup. With the amount of executive housing they would provide, the fortune probably amounted to millions.

'I can see why you're tempted,' she said.

'I'm not tempted!' Charles sounded really angry. 'I love the business. But if it doesn't make money, we can't keep it on like a family retainer or an aged pet!'

'If you feel like that about it,' said Flora quietly, 'don't sell.'

'Aren't you tempted by the money yourself?' He glanced across at her, genuinely curious.

She had had time to think about this already, but she considered the matter again, to check her feelings. 'Not really,' she said after a while. 'I haven't any dreams unfulfilled because of lack of funds. Besides . . .' She paused. What she was about to say sounded so sentimental, but then she said it anyway. 'I'd prefer to see Stanza and Stanza succeed. I haven't been here long, but I see why you love it. I think if you gave me a chance I could come to love it too. So, what we have to do,' she went on quickly, before Charles could possibly comment, 'is to make the business work, make it make money, then Annabelle won't put you under pressure to sell.'

Charles sighed. 'We could never make as much money as the property would raise.'

'I know, but if it was more profitable, very profitable, possibly, she'd feel happier about it. And as I said before, she doesn't have to work in it if she doesn't want to. You've got me now.'

He frowned. 'You're just here for the summer. The moment the lanes get muddy and it gets a bit chilly you'll be back off to London before you can say Jack—'

'I never, ever say Jack Robinson,' Flora interrupted. 'It's an absolute rule of mine. Come to think of it, I've never heard anyone else say it, either.'

He pursed his lips, possibly suppressing a smile – but, thought Flora, more likely suppressing irritation.

'Tell you what,' she said, 'as your far-off cousin and your partner in this firm, I will undertake to get this business on a better footing. Of course I can't promise to put it into profit, but before the lanes get muddy and I'm even tempted by the thought of bright lights and sushi bars, we'll be doing better. I give you my word.'

'That's very kind of you, Flora,' he said quietly, 'but how on earth are you going to do that when you hardly know more about it than you can have picked up on the *Antiques Roadshow*?'

'I know a lot more about it now,' she said confidently.

'I've been at my first sale, don't forget.' She became thoughtful. 'The *Antiques Roadshow*,' she murmured. 'Hmm.'

The house where they were to do their valuation was on what had once been a council estate. It was a very tidy, well-ordered estate where many of the houses were now privately owned, but as it wasn't a gated community, full of large, detached properties with professionally mown lawns and indoor swimming pools, Flora thought she knew why Annabelle hadn't wanted to come.

'It's unlikely that there'll be anything of huge value here,' Charles said, 'but it's important to remember that these are the effects of a much-loved relative. You must be tactful. In fact, it would be better if you didn't say much at all.'

As Charles had no reason to think she'd be anything other than the soul of tact, Flora realised he'd probably suffered from being with a less-than-sensitive Annabelle. 'Of course,' she said. 'And there might very well be a Steiff teddy about to be thrown out.'

Charles frowned at her. 'Very unlikely.'

The door was opened by a well-dressed woman in her fifties. 'Oh, hello. Was it difficult to find?'

'No, not at all,' said Charles, smiling at the woman with a mixture of kindness and charm which Flora couldn't have imagined directed at her. He didn't have to be so stuffy, Flora noticed. He could unbend if he wanted to.

'It's my uncle's house,' the woman went on, still holding the door open, but not letting them in. 'It's in a bit of a state, I'm afraid. He didn't like to throw anything away.'

'Don't worry about that, Mrs Jenkins. I'm Charles Stanza and this is my colleague Flora – Stanza.'

'Oh, are you married?' asked Mrs Jenkins.

'Heaven forbid!' said Flora, laughing. 'We're distant cousins. Very distant. I'm just helping Charles out today.'

'Oh, sorry,' said Mrs Jenkins, slightly embarrassed to have jumped to the wrong conclusion.

Charles and Flora hovered on the doorstep, waiting to be allowed across the threshold.

'I was expecting a Spanish or Italian gentleman,' said Mrs Jenkins, not asking them in, possibly for a reason.

'It's an Italian name but our branch of the family has lived in England for generations.'

By now Mrs Jenkins had stepped back sufficiently for them to get into the little hallway. Charles and Flora did so, then waited patiently.

'It's the most awful mess, I'm afraid. I've done what I can, but . . .' She put out a hand and opened the door to the living room, deliberately not looking inside. 'I suppose you'd better know the worst.'

The smell was appalling and at first Flora couldn't tell where it was coming from, it was so dark. Thick curtains covered the windows and there was so much furniture piled up in front of them what little light penetrated the curtains was blocked off. Then she saw the mountain of take-away food cartons littering the floor and a row of half-empty milk bottles.

'We had to stay in a bed and breakfast last night,' said Mrs Jenkins, obviously greatly distressed. 'I was going to try and make a start on it this morning but my husband told me it was better not to, not without proper equipment.'

'Quite right,' said Charles. 'This is a job for professionals.'

'My uncle got a bit eccentric towards the end. He was always a hoarder, and towards the end he wouldn't even throw away rubbish.'

'I can recommend a very good firm who'll deal with all this for you, Mrs Jenkins.' He smiled again. 'But don't worry, I've seen much worse than this.'

'So have I,' said Flora, 'when I lived in student accommodation.' It wasn't true, and she suspected that Charles was lying, too, but it was in a good cause.

'Some rubber gloves might be a good idea,' said Charles.

'I'll pop out and get some,' offered Flora. 'I spotted a shop on the corner. Is there anything you need, Mrs Jenkins? Air freshener? Milk? Chocolate biscuits?'

Mrs Jenkins laughed. 'Some chocolate digestives might make it seem less awful. I'll fetch my purse—'

'I'll pay for them,' said Flora. 'It's all part of the service. And don't worry about all this, we're here now.' Flora gave Mrs Jenkins an encouraging smile and went.

Aware that Charles couldn't do much without her, she was as quick as possible. When she got back, Charles, Mrs Jenkins and a man who was presumably Mr Jenkins were in the kitchen. It was a little less like the town dump than the first room they had seen and Mrs Jenkins had made a pot of tea.

'He never ate in here,' she explained, 'and the hot water's going, so I could wash a few cups and things. But it's so dreadfully sordid. It's like one of those television programmes I can't bear to watch.'

'You would come down here,' said Mr Jenkins. 'I said you'd be better just getting someone in to clear the house.'

'But there might be valuable antiques in among this filth!' This was obviously a well-worn argument. 'We can't afford just to pay someone to take it all away.'

'I'm sure there'll be enough in this room alone to pay for that,' said Charles.

'Really?' A spark of hope brightened Mrs Jenkins's anxious expression.

'I can see there is without even moving,' Charles re-assured her. 'All that enamelware, it's very collectable.'

'I would so hate to have wasted your time.'

'You won't be doing that, I assure you,' said Charles. 'Got your notebook, Flora?'

'Let the poor girl have her tea first.' Mrs Jenkins smiled at Flora and offered her a biscuit, obviously relaxing a little.

'The village is very pretty,' said Flora, blowing crumbs.

'It is,' agreed Mrs Jenkins. 'It would be nice to have a little walk, but I don't suppose there'll be time.'

'There's no reason at all why you can't just leave us to it,' said Charles. 'At least to begin with. Why don't you two go and have a stroll and enjoy summer while we've got it.'

'Good idea,' said Mr Jenkins. 'This place gives me the creeps.'

When their clients were safely out of the way, Flora looked at Charles.

'I'm sorry,' he said. 'I had no idea it would be as bad as this . . . but on the other hand,' he went on after a pause, 'it's as well to know how bad the job can be.'

'Yes,' agreed Flora, aware that her reaction was a sort of test. One little wrinkle of her nose and she'd be castigated for being squeamish.

'I'm glad Annabelle didn't come. She'd be retching and heaving and having a fit.'

'It is a bit gag-making,' said Flora, who was breathing through her mouth so as not to have to endure the smell. 'Have you really seen much worse than this?'

Charles shook his head. 'I don't suppose so, although you do get used to some pretty dire situations.' He sighed. 'It was nice of you to buy the biscuits.'

'It was nice of you to tell them to go for a walk.'

'We'll get on much quicker without them.' He shrugged off her compliment as if it were a cobweb.

'Shall we make a start, then?' said Flora, a little hurt, but determined not to show it. She had just started to warm to him, because he'd been so nice to the people, then he went cold on her again. 'Here are your rubber gloves.'

'Right,' said Charles, when he had pulled them on. 'A collection of enamelware. Twenty to fifty pounds. A nineteen-thirties kitchen cupboard, it's in fairly good condition under the grime, possibly fifty to seventy.'

Flora started writing, hoping she'd be able to read it later.

Charles took Mr and Mrs Jenkins to the pub for lunch, an expense Flora was quite sure would never be claimed from petty cash.

'We're going to need to go back in there this afternoon,' he explained, 'but I suggest you stay out of the way. When we've done our valuation and you've decided what to keep, I'll contact the removal firm, the house-clearance people and the cleaners.'

'I'm sure we don't want anything from there.' Mr Jenkins put his glass down with a shudder. 'It would never feel clean.'

'There are some quite valuable pieces,' said Charles and Flora remembered removing half a dozen bottles of sour milk so he could inspect a sofa table. She had retched but Charles had carried on with the work.

'It would be wonderful if you could arrange all that,' said Mrs Jenkins. 'My husband's right. I'm sure we don't want anything and I just can't cope with the mess. It's so squalid, I feel ashamed.'

'We all have eccentric relations,' said Charles, casting a quick glance in Flora's direction so she was in no doubt about whom he was referring to. 'They often have eccentric wills, too.'

'We're spared that,' said Mrs Jenkins. 'I'm his only surviving relative. Really, Mr Stanza, you've been very kind. I don't know how we're going to repay you.'

'Well, there's a seller's premium and a small lotting fee,' said Charles with another of his charming smiles. 'So I'll be making lots of money out of you.'

Seeing the way he was with this upset, embarrassed woman made Flora warm to him. He had a stuffy and conventional veneer but not far beneath it was a man who could be very kind and very tactful. He would just never be like that with her.

They were on the way home, both exhausted and in need of steam cleaning and sterilisation (or at least, that was how Flora felt), when Flora's phone went.

'Is that you, Flora?'

'Annabelle? Do you want Charles? I'll just wait till he's pulled over and pass him the phone.'

'No! It's not him I want, it's you! But not when Charles is there, I want to speak to you alone.'

She sounded rather odd and Flora's stomach churned. What could be the matter? Had Imelda taken a fit and ruined the cottage? Or worse, and much more likely, had she discovered William? But if so, why would she want to talk to her on her own about it? Surely Annabelle could rant and rave on that subject in Charles's hearing. 'Of course, Annabelle,' said Flora meekly. 'When would be convenient?'

'What does Annabelle want?' asked Charles. 'Hang on, I'll pull over.'

'No, it's me she wants.'

But it was too late. A handy lay-by had appeared and Charles had swung into it before Flora had finished speaking. He took the phone from her. 'Darling? What is it? Ghastly valuation. I'm so glad you weren't there.'

Flora harrumphed in her seat. He wouldn't want Annabelle having to deal with sour milk and filth, rat droppings and cockroaches, but for her it was considered good training.

Charles handed back the phone. 'She wants to discuss the inventory with you. She'll meet you in the Coach and Horses. It opens at six. I'll drop you off and she can take you to the office to pick up the Land-Rover.'

'Hang on! Annabelle?' But Annabelle had disconnected. 'I'm filthy, Charles! Besides, it's choir night.'

He frowned. 'Is that so important to you? You've only

113

just joined, after all. You can't be making such a huge contribution yet.'

This hurt, but she ignored it. 'Maybe not, but they welcomed me in. I can't just not turn up.'

'And you can't leave Annabelle at the Coach and Horses. I do think you should make some effort to get on with her, Flora.'

'But I'm filthy! I probably stink! Wouldn't Annabelle understand if I told her I needed to go home and change?'

'I'm sure she'd understand but I'm not sure she'd appreciate it. Give her a call and say you can't be long. Shall I find the number for you?' He made to take her phone from her.

'No, it's OK,' she snapped, 'I've got it. Annabelle? I won't be able to stay long because I'm really grubby and must check on my cat. It's choir tonight or I'd do that all first and meet you later.'

'In my experience you always get dirty doing valuations,' Annabelle said loftily. 'It's one of the reasons I hate doing them. OK. We'll sit in the snug. There won't be anyone we know in there.'

If Flora hadn't been suffering from a guilty conscience about allowing William to stay, she would never have agreed to meet Annabelle.

'It looks like it's my turn to cook tonight again,' said Charles a few moments later, making what would qualify for anyone else as polite conversation.

'Oh.' In spite of herself, Flora was surprised. 'Do you cook often?'

'Oh yes. Annabelle always cooks if we entertain, but the humdrum stuff gets left for me, mostly.'

Flora felt an unexpected pang of sympathy. He'd had

a very long day. He probably didn't want to start cooking the moment he got home. 'If I were you, I'd get a take-away, or go out.'

Charles sighed. 'I probably will. I've got a lot of phoning to do when I get in and I won't have time to do much in the way of cooking.'

'You went the extra mile for those people today, didn't you? You could have just given them the names of the house-clearance people, and the removal firm. You didn't have to say you'd arrange it all.'

He shrugged. 'I felt sorry for them, that's all.' He brightened up. 'Although there's quite a valuable estate underneath the squalor.'

Flora did the best she could in the pub's Ladies', but apart from getting the streaks of dust off her face, there wasn't much she could do. Already her standards had slipped, she thought, turning up at a pub wearing clothes she'd been doing a mucky job in all day.

Annabelle had already ordered two glasses of mineral water and was looking quite untidy too. She was fiddling with her hairband, trying to put it back in, but not doing very well, for some reason.

'Here,' said Flora, taking it from her. 'Let me help.' She put the Alice band on the table. 'Much better.'

'Oh, but . . .' began Annabelle, and then said, 'Perhaps you're right.'

'What did you want to see me about?' asked Flora.

Annabelle sat forward in her seat. 'Well, when I was at the cottage, taking the inventory, I saw a man.'

'Oh no,' said Flora nervously, unable to decide if she should admit to knowing William or not.

'He was in the garden, doing some sort of exercises. He was stark naked.'

'Oh my God!' Flora was genuinely shocked this time. 'Did you call the police?' Really, William was the giddy limit! He had the whole damn forest to prance about naked in, why did he choose to do it in her garden?

'No!' said Annabelle, leaning closer. 'He looked – I mean, he didn't look like a criminal, or anything. He wasn't doing any harm. It was just very odd.'

'Oh,' said Flora again, surprised. She hadn't expected Annabelle to discriminate – any naked man in the garden was trespassing, surely?

'Flora' – Annabelle gave her a hard look – 'do you know him?'

Flora took a long sip of her mineral water, wishing for a minute that it was something stronger, like a magic potion that would spirit her away. 'I may do,' she said cautiously. 'Of course, I don't know for sure.'

'Flora! How could you?' Annabelle looked furious. 'I lend you my cottage, and within a week you've got strange men moving in!'

Flora flushed angrily. 'Well, that's not exactly—'

'I'm honestly shocked, Flora, I really am.' Annabelle was clearly determined not to let her get a word in. 'And I can't imagine what Charles will say!'

'Oh, for God's sake, Annabelle. Stop over-reacting,' Flora snapped, and then took a breath to regain her temper. She couldn't quite imagine what Charles would say either – and didn't particularly fancy finding out. 'I think,' she said in a calmer tone of voice, 'that he may be . . . er . . . a friend of a friend,' she improvised. 'Perfectly harmless,' she added in what she hoped was a reassuring way.

'Well, I don't know, Flora.' Annabelle didn't look reassured. 'Will he be back?'

'It's possible,' Flora admitted. 'But I'm not at all sure Charles needs to be bothered with something like this. I know he's terribly busy, and . . .' Her voice trailed away as Annabelle gave her a long stare which made it perfectly clear that she knew full well that Flora wasn't thinking about Charles's best interests.

'OK then,' Annabelle said after a moment's thought. 'But if you're going to have a strange naked man hanging around my cottage I need to meet him. I'll have to check him out.'

Flora frowned. 'Check him out how, exactly?'

Registering Flora's confusion, Annabelle erupted into a peal of nervous laughter. 'Oh, don't be ridiculous! I don't want to check him out like that! Just check he's not a burglar.'

Flora was very tired. She wanted to go home, see her cat, have a proper drink and something to eat before she had to rush out for choir. 'I'll see what I can do, Annabelle, as long as you promise never to wear that Alice band again.'

'Don't you think it suits me?'

'I think it makes you look like a horse.'

Chapter Seven

❦

'You don't really think I look like a horse, do you?'

Annabelle's expression of horror filled Flora with compassion and guilt. She shouldn't have been so outspoken, and if Annabelle hadn't been so annoying about William, she wouldn't have let her mouth get away with her like that. But the truth was out now and nothing Flora could do could put it back in again whole. She'd just have to backtrack as best she could.

'Well . . . not really. No, of course not, Annabelle, I'm just awfully tired. I spoke without thinking.'

'Oh.' Annabelle still sounded despondent; it was strangely pathetic.

'And I was a bit – surprised – by you telling me there was a man in my garden,' she added.

'A naked man,' said Annabelle.

'That's it. A naked man. Very shocking. I'll do my best to—'

'Although he was rather beautiful, in an aesthetic way.'

'Was he?' Flora squeaked. She would not have put Annabelle down as someone who saw men's bodies as aesthetic.

'Mm. The thing is, what am I going to say to Charles about him?'

'Well, I definitely wouldn't mention you thought he

was beautiful,' said Flora, knowing this was not the right answer.

'You know what I mean, Flora. Charles is already very unhappy about you being here. If I tell him I saw a naked man in your garden, he'll pack you off to London before you have time to put on your lip-gloss.'

Flora took a deep breath, then a sip of mineral water. She needed time to think. 'Charles could hardly blame me if – the man – is nothing to do with me. Just a friend of a friend.'

'Charles could blame you if there was a cyclone and the crops were ruined.'

This was the plain truth, there was no denying it. 'Unless you didn't tell him,' suggested Flora, not at all happy to find herself at Annabelle's mercy.

'Exactly.'

Flora frowned. 'But why wouldn't you tell him? You don't want me here either, do you?'

Annabelle flapped a hand. 'Look, shall we get proper drinks?'

'I shouldn't.' Flora got to her feet. If she really hurried, she should have time to get back home to feed Imelda and throw another layer of clothes on top of her dirt. 'It's choir night.'

'Sit down, Flora.'

Flora sat.

'I won't say anything to Charles because relations are already bad enough between you, but you must arrange for me to meet this man so I can check him out. If he's a bad lot, I'll have to report him to the police.'

'But supposing when I get back I find out he's not this friend's friend. Suppose he's nothing to do with me?'

Annabelle looked her firmly in the eye. 'I think what would be a good idea would be for you to arrange a little dinner party, so Charles and I can meet this man under civilised circumstances.' She paused, to make sure Flora knew that any stories she might come up with of finding no trace of anyone when she got home would not wash with her, then she said, 'I'm going to get us both a glass of wine now.'

She certainly went in for straight talking, thought Flora, while she waited. You had to hand it to her.

When Annabelle came back with the wine and sat down again she said, 'Now, there's something else I'd like your help with.'

Although her words were her usual 'order-poorly-disguised-as-a-request' type, there was something a bit more tentative in her manner than usual. Flora sipped her wine.

Annabelle sipped hers, too. 'I wouldn't usually ask you about anything as you're obviously much younger and completely . . . I mean, well . . . Anyway, you are quite pretty.'

'Yes?' Flora wasn't going to waste time arguing about her looks.

'I've been invited to a school reunion.'

'Oh.'

'And' – Annabelle looked momentarily embarrassed – 'and I really want to look my best. I wonder if you could give me some tips on how to improve my appearance?'

Flora translated this as: 'You're a complete nit-wit but men seem to fancy you – tell me your secrets.' She sighed. She was often dismissed as being pretty and blonde as if these two things combined precluded any ability in any sphere except shopping.

'Well . . .'

'I was just wondering if it's a bad thing that I always go shopping with Mummy?'

Flora thought how best to phrase her reply. 'I don't think it's a bad idea in principle. I quite often go shopping with my mother when we're in the same country, but the difference may be that she always takes my fashion advice, not the other way around.'

Annabelle sighed. 'I've never much cared about fashion. I just want to look tidy and reasonably smart. But . . .'

There was a horrible pause while Flora waited for what she knew would follow.

'I think men may like women to be pretty, don't you?'

'There won't be any men at your school reunion, will there?' If Annabelle had gone anywhere that wasn't a clone of Benenden or Roedean, Flora would eat her filthy dress.

'Well, no, but women are more critical, don't you think?'

'Well, yes, but Charles obviously likes you the way you are. You don't need to change anything for him.'

'I know that!' Reassuringly, Annabelle reverted to type. 'I just don't want to turn up at the school reunion looking . . . like a horse.'

Flora resigned herself to missing choir. She would go and ring Geoffrey in a minute. 'I only said that—'

'I know, but many a true word spoken in jest, or something. I have become aware, since you've been here, that perhaps I dress a little . . .' She paused again.

Flora waited, not daring to fill the word in for her. 'In a rather old-fashioned way and if you could see your way to helping me, I would be very grateful.'

'Of course, I'd be happy to help.' Particularly, Flora added to herself, if that stops you telling Charles about my houseguest.

'Would you?'

Mischievously, Flora was suddenly struck by a vision of Charles's face, confronted with an Annabelle decked out in strappy dress and kitten heels. 'But you don't think Charles would mind if you looked completely different?'

'Well, I won't look completely different and even if I did, our relationship is very solid, you know. It's not likely to be affected by mere clothes.'

That was clothes put in their place! 'Oh?'

'Our relationship is based on all we have in common: companionship, a business we share. Well, nearly share,' Annabelle added.

'What about love?' asked Flora rashly. Possibly love was too frivolous an emotion for the likes of Charles and Annabelle.

'Of course I love Charles,' said Annabelle. 'And I know he loves me, very much.' She paused for a moment. 'Look, Flora. I know you think Charles is stuffy and old-fashioned, and I know you think I'm far too uptight.'

Flora started to protest, but Annabelle was on a roll.

'I can see it in your eyes every time we talk, and it's fine. Really. I can't imagine being you, and you can't imagine being me. You can't appreciate what Charles sees in me or what I see in him. But I have to tell you, Charles and I are completely committed to each other. We've been

122

friends for ever – I can't remember a time I didn't plan to marry him – and knowing that we're going to be together for the rest of our lives makes us both very happy.'

Flora didn't think they looked very happy, but Annabelle's little speech was the most passionate thing Flora had ever heard come out of her mouth. She felt rather guilty over her musings about whether their engagement was almost a business arrangement.

'And so I don't think a few new clothes and a haircut are going to change any of that, do you? Charles has been in love with me his whole life.'

Flora finished her wine. She hadn't the heart to go to choir now, even if she would just make it if she ran.

'So shall we make a date to go shopping sometime, then?' went on Annabelle, unaware of Flora's low spirits.

'If you really want me to, of course I will.' She could hardly refuse a few fashion tips. Charles might well appreciate a less horse-like Annabelle. Those pie-crust collars must irritate any sensible man.

'In that case, I'll press on. I think I might cook Charles something rather delicious for supper. Oh, and you won't forget about the dinner, will you?'

William was making a stir-fry when Flora got in. She didn't know if she was delighted to see him because he'd cooked and taken care of Imelda and was a friend, or furious with him for letting himself be seen by Annabelle.

'I have had such a day!' she told him, gratefully accepting the chilled glass he handed her.

'You're back late,' he said mildly, looking into his glass as if for portents of the future.

'I had to go and have a drink with someone after work and miss choir.' She frowned at him. 'It's all your fault.'

'My fault? Why?'

Flora sank on to the sofa and pulled a cushion into the small of her back. Considering how many sofas must go through their hands, she thought, you would have thought they'd have provided their holiday cottage with a more comfortable one. 'Because Annabelle, who's sort of my boss, engaged to my cousin, saw you here today.'

'But I didn't come into the house. I heard a car and kept out of the way.'

'You were doing exercises in the garden, naked.'

'T'ai chi. And I was not in the garden. I was only just out of the woodland. I really didn't know anyone could see me. I am so sorry.'

Flora sighed. She knew she should be angry, but just didn't have the energy. 'I think you're the one who may be sorry. Annabelle wants to meet you. Just to check you're not a sinister person she should report to the police. And I warn you, she's terrifying.' Annabelle on the prowl would daunt anyone, even laid-back William.

'Is she really? Why is that?'

'She just is. She's very businesslike and efficient.'

'Is she pretty?'

Flora felt very tired indeed. 'Not yet.'

'How do you mean?'

'She wants a few tips on style and stuff. She's asked me to help her. She's got a school reunion coming up and wants to look her best.'

'Well, I'm sure you're just the girl.' His gaze flicked

over her, with, she noted, a certain amount of approval, but no real desire.

It was odd, Flora realised, but she didn't fancy him, either. It was probably why they had become so relaxed with each other so quickly – sex hadn't reared its ugly head between them.

'I'm sure I am. Once I've got her underwear sorted out we can get somewhere.'

'Underwear's important, is it?'

Flora nodded. 'If you've got substantial breasts, definitely. Annabelle's currently wearing what is known in the trade as sheepdogs. They round them up and point them in the right direction, but they do nothing for shape.'

William was starting to look more interested and Flora wondered idly if perhaps she shouldn't have mentioned Annabelle's breasts. Partly to change the subject, she said, 'And now I've got to think up who you should be.'

'What on earth are you talking about?'

'I mean, I'm supposed to try and find out about you and invite you to dinner, so she can give you the once-over.'

'Couldn't you just tell her there was no trace of anyone when you got home?'

Flora shook her head. 'She didn't put it in so many words, but she made it pretty clear that she'd tell Charles about you if I didn't let her check you're not a psychopath.' She bit her lip for a moment. 'I suppose I could say I found a note from you, that you're a friend of a friend come to call, who obviously just took the opportunity to do a bit of t'ai chi in the buff when he was in an isolated spot.' She paused. 'I'm really surprised Annabelle didn't call the police.'

'Why should she? I wasn't doing any harm.'

'Annabelle would consider trespassing harm, and I would have thought she'd have considered nakedness a police matter, too.'

'But she didn't.'

'No, but we still have to explain your presence without them finding out you've been living here all winter. I'll say you're a friend of a friend who lived near and came to look me up. That suit you?'

'I have been living on my own for a while, but do you think someone looking up the friend of a friend would be likely to take off all their clothes and do a spot of t'ai chi while they're waiting?'

'Well . . . yes, if that's your bag. After all, there can't be many opportunities for doing stuff like that.'

William nodded, conceding this point.

'Let's eat, William. I'm starving.'

When supper was disposed of, the kittens had been marvelled over, and William had decided to go to his shack in the forest, Flora found a spot in the garden that had reasonable reception and called Emma.

'Is this a good moment?' she pleaded, when Emma picked up the phone.

'Yes. Dave's out. I'm just watching a movie and it's not very good. It's a perfect time to ring.'

'Thank goodness. I need advice, Em!'

'Really? Well, on the whole green is considered the best colour for wellies but you could get away with blue at a pinch.'

'What are you talking about? Now listen, Annabelle, who's engaged to my cousin Charles, and wants to buy me out of the business, well, not completely, but a bit . . .'

'Go on.' Emma was obviously on the move. 'I'm just going into the kitchen to make a cup of tea.'

'Anyway, she saw this man William, who's been living here in the holiday cottage all winter, and is still around.'

'Nice?'

'Very.'

'Fit?'

'Well, I suppose so but definitely not my type. Although Annabelle tells me that upside down and naked he is – what did she say? – aesthetically beautiful.'

'He sounds extraordinary. If you want him, I'd take him.' Emma sighed a little wistfully.

'I don't want him. I want you to listen to me. You see the thing is, Emma, Annabelle has more or less ordered me to have a dinner party so she can meet him.'

'And?'

'Well, should I introduce Annabelle to William?'

Emma thought for a moment. 'Sorry, Flora, I don't see the problem. I really don't see why you shouldn't have a little dinner party and introduce this Annabelle to the naked man.'

Flora sighed. 'That sounds so easy in theory, but you don't know Charles! Having him, Annabelle and William round for dinner would be torture. No one would have anything in common, it would be ghastly!'

'Well, invite some other people then! That way you won't notice Charles so much.'

Flora felt that however many people she asked she was bound to notice Charles. He took up quite a lot of space. But it would certainly dilute him. 'That is a good idea. I could invite Henry.'

'Who's Henry?'

'Oh, someone I met in the supermarket when I first arrived. We haven't actually been out yet, but he's very nice.'

'You met him in the supermarket? You're so jammy! The only people I meet in the supermarket are other wild-eyed singletons looking for low-fat Chardonnay. We bond over the fromage frais.'

'I may not be jammy, he may not turn out to be any good at all, but it's nice to have someone to think about. The trouble is, I haven't got his number. But with luck, I'll run into him soon. Annabelle didn't give me a date for this dinner party, after all.'

'I should check him over for you,' said Emma. 'Make sure he's not another Justin.'

'You can't tell just by looking. And do you know, Justin was at school with Charles! But I've just had a brilliant idea! If you came down for a weekend, you could come to the dinner party. That would make it much more fun.'

Emma laughed. 'A dinner party with your stuffy cousin and his ghastly fiancée does sound tempting, but on the other hand, we could wait for you to come back to London and have a really nice time.'

'I'm not doing that! I've only been here five minutes and I'm beginning to love it. The whole auction house thing is so exciting, even though I spent all day today in a filthy house looking at furniture. It's terribly hard work but so fascinating.'

Emma spoke in tones she normally used when confronted by a psychopath on the tube. 'Well, honey, if that's the way you feel about it, I don't think I can help you. You need a professional.'

Flora ignored this slight on her sanity. 'I've just had a thought.'

'Go on.'

'If you came down for the weekend, I could say that William is a friend of yours.'

'I don't think I'd have a friend who took off their clothes in other people's gardens.'

'Well, no, but you wouldn't necessarily have known about his passion for naked yoga, or whatever. I think that's a very good idea. Now, when can you come?'

Emma sighed. 'I'd quite like to come down. I don't suppose Dave would be able to get away.'

'That's perfect! I mean, it's a shame, but it's perfect from my point of view. You and William could be a couple.'

'I don't quite understand what your thinking is on this one, Flo.'

'I don't either, but come down, one weekend some-time soon, and we can make a plan when you get here.'

'I'll see what I can do. It's not easy at the moment.'

'Oh darling!'

'But don't worry, I'll try to sort something out.'

'Annabelle tells me she saw a man at your house yesterday.'

The wretch! Annabelle had definitely said she wouldn't tell Charles if Flora agreed to have a dinner party! Determined to keep her cool for as long as possible, she said, 'Hi, Charles, I'm fine. Yes, it is a lovely day, but it looks like rain later. Though we do need it.' Bloody Annabelle! And bloody Charles! He might have said hello before he confronted her about William.

'Who is he?'

'Well, when Annabelle first told me about him, I hadn't a clue, but when I got back I found a note. He's a friend of a friend in London. He lives quite near here. Not sure where,' she went on quickly, before he could ask her awkward questions. 'The friend thought I might be lonely and asked him to look me up.'

This sounded feasible as long as Annabelle hadn't mentioned the naked t'ai chi.

'Oh. Right. So you didn't meet him yourself?'

To lie or not to lie? 'No. He might be calling again tonight. He's going to give me a ring on my mobile. Talking of which, any chance of that land line? The reception's not good there.'

He frowned. 'Sorry, yes. I'll get on to it. And would you mind making a start on typing up that valuation we did yesterday? Louisa is off and I want to get it done as soon as possible. I realise it's not what you do, but I would really appreciate it. Louisa can do it properly next week, but it would save her some time.'

'No probs, Charles,' said Flora, keen to be helpful. 'I'll get started just as soon as I've hung up my jacket. Is the computer on? There is a computer, isn't there? Not just an ancient Underwood typewriter that didn't sell in an auction?'

Charles almost smiled. 'No, there is a computer. Just

do as much as you can. Annabelle said something about you wanting to go shopping.'

Trust Annabelle to make her out to be the one in need of retail therapy. 'I don't want to sound patronising, but to me shopping means London, Paris, New York, Milan if you're in Italy, not some jumped-up market town. It's Annabelle who wants to go, for her school reunion, but if I've got work to do, she can go on her own. Or with her mother.'

'Keep your hair on. You're perfectly entitled to take time off whenever you like, you don't work for us.'

'Oh yes I do, Charles,' she replied, somewhat disconcerted that he seemed to have forgotten. 'Now point me in the direction of the computer and I'll get on.'

By the time Annabelle arrived to take her shopping at about two o'clock, Flora had not only typed the valuation, but she'd taken advantage of being entirely alone to have a good prowl round the building.

Annabelle came in looking prettier already, partly because her hair was loose and clean. It still needed a good cut, though. 'Charles told me I'd find you typing. I expect you hunt and peck?'

'I don't hunt, Annabelle. I think it's cruel.'

'I didn't mean that sort of hunting. I meant typing, but never mind, you can leave it now. Louisa will do it later. There's no great hurry, after all.'

Flora picked up her jacket, not disclosing that she was in fact a very fast touch typist. Her mother had once told her, 'Learn to type, it's useful, but don't tell anyone or you may not get to do anything else.'

'Where are we going shopping, then? Bristol?'

Annabelle looked shocked. 'Do we need to go so far?'

'I think we do. Now, shall we lock up?'

'I'll do it.'

'And, Annabelle,' said Flora as she watched her set the burglar alarm and memorised the numbers, just in case, 'you said you wouldn't tell Charles about . . . the man, and you did.'

'I know,' said Annabelle breezily, making the building ring with the sound of the alarm. 'I changed my mind. He was surprisingly cool about it,' she went on, as they came out into the street, all safe and quiet behind them. 'I think he's coming round to the idea of you.'

Flora softened. Annabelle really was being very good. 'If you think it's wasteful to have a clear-out we could have one of those parties where everyone prices up their old clothes and then buys them from each other. Most of the money goes to charity, but you can take a cut if you like. You have wine and nibbles. It's a great evening out, usually. One person's expensive mistake may well become another woman's favourite outfit. Someone's mother is bound to like pie-crust collars and navy blue.' Flora frowned. 'The trouble is I don't know anyone round here, really, and I don't suppose your friends . . .?'

'No.' Annabelle was very firm. 'My friends would not enjoy buying second-hand clothes.'

'Even from each other? For charity?'

'I don't think the Conservative Party needs us to go to quite those lengths yet.'

Flora laughed. 'OK, no need to sound quite so head-mistressy. It was only an idea. But I do want those pussy-cat bows out of your wardrobe. They can go to the charity shop.'

Flora would really have preferred to go home, but she stuck with Annabelle not only to continue with the revamping process, but because she wanted to find out what really excited Annabelle, something that would take all her time and attention. Annabelle needed a hobby of her own, something to replace the auction house that she would enjoy and be good at, so that Flora could get on with dragging Stanza and Stanza into the real world, and from there, with luck, into profit. And she also wanted to see the look on Charles's face when he saw his new fiancée.

It was the first time Flora had been into Charles and Annabelle's house. Having parked the Land-Rover in the little street next door, she followed Annabelle up the front steps with strangely mixed feelings.

What she saw was partly a relief and partly a disappointment, it was so predictable. She should have been able to predict the pale, safe colours, the polished wood floors, the textbook good taste that had no individuality. Everything was smooth and immaculate, and although some of the things were obviously old – the fire basket and the chimney-pot-turned-vase – they were all restored to within an inch of their lives. She scanned the walls for something, a picture, a photograph, which indicated the personalities of the inhabitants, but found nothing. A few old maps of the county, an enormously fat pig, which on inspection proved a modern reproduction, and a portrait of a lady in pearls, was all there was. Flora, depressed, felt she already knew the answer to her first question. 'Do you and Charles own this house together? It's lovely.'

'No, it's mine.' Annabelle kicked off her low-heeled loafers. 'I'm glad you like it. Would you like something to drink before we go upstairs? Come on, let's open a bottle of wine. I'll get Charles to run you home later.'

'Or I could take a taxi. Charles could pick me up for work tomorrow.'

'No! Don't be silly. Charles won't mind.'

'He might want a drink himself when he gets in.'

'Well, he can wait.'

Flora wished she had the strength of character to stick to mineral water herself and so be able to drive home, but the thought of a glass of wine was far too tempting.

'So, what have you bought her?'

'A nightie – it's what she said she wanted. Do you think she'll like it?' He held up a rather mumsy white nightie which would certainly leave everything to the imagination.

'It's . . . er . . . lovely. I'm sure she'll be thrilled.'

'Oh good. I'm just not sure of her size.'

'Oh my goodness! Don't tell me you're buying her clothes and you don't know her size!'

'Is that very bad?'

'It's a disaster! Have you any idea at all?'

'Well.' He regarded Flora for rather a long time. 'She's probably about the same as you are.'

Flora took hold of the offending item and checked the size. 'This is a sixteen. If she's my size it'll be much too big.'

'I'll go and get a couple of sizes down then,' he said meekly.

'Sorry, Henry, but just think how horrible your sister would feel if she thought you thought she looked two sizes bigger then she is.'

He shrugged. 'It seemed sort of roomy, but I thought it'd be OK.'

'No. OK is not good enough. Off you go.'

'I will if you give me your telephone number,' he said with the twinkle she remembered from the abbey card shop.

Flora smiled and let the lady standing behind Henry, who'd been enjoying their exchanges, go in front of her. 'Only if you give me yours.'

'It's a deal.'

* * *

Chapter Eight

'Yes, you do have to be fitted. It's the most important thing. Get measured properly. My mother taught me that.' This last accompanied a shove in the back which finally got Annabelle into the changing room.

The kindly sales assistant added, 'I'll check your size and then go and find some bras I think might suit you.'

'And I'll be back when you're in one of them,' said Flora. 'Now I'm going to buy knickers.'

In fact, having forced Annabelle to be measured, Flora picked up a few bras that were in the sale and didn't even think of trying them on. Her mother had indeed given her that sound advice and Flora believed it wholeheartedly. She just didn't think her size 34 B needed quite as much attention as Annabelle's double D cup.

She was queuing up to pay for them when she became aware of a man behind her. It was Henry. She laughed.

'I know, I know, what's a man doing in the lingerie department?' he said.

'Obviously shopping.' Flora indicated the pile of cotton in his hand. 'For you?'

'No! My sister. It's her birthday tomorrow. I was buying a card the other day but I didn't find anything in the abbey shop that she would want that I could post.'

After the day she'd had, she felt she deserved it. Annabelle was very hard work, and might be less so if both their senses were a little dulled by a nice, crisp Chardonnay.

When Annabelle, showing a generosity Flora hadn't suspected, had filled two huge glasses to the brim with wine, she said, 'Come on then. Let's go upstairs and carry on with this.'

Flora, following her, aware that if she drank even half that amount of wine driving herself home was out of the question, decided that abandoning the Land-Rover was the only answer.

Annabelle led the way into a thickly carpeted bedroom that was as bland and tasteful as the sitting room. She pulled open the door of a row of mirror-fronted cupboards.

'Oh Annabelle! What a fantastic wardrobe!' Flora, who had taken a hefty sip of wine on her way up the stairs, sank on to the bed and stared at the masterpiece of space-saving, categorising and colour co-ordinating before her.

'I thought you'd come to trash my wardrobe,' commented Annabelle, taking a deep drink from her own glass.

'The contents, not the thing itself. It's completely fab. I want one.'

'Not in the holiday cottage you don't.'

'No, but where I end up eventually.'

'I got a firm in to do it for me. Charles was all for getting a little local man to do it, but I felt I wanted a professional. It's an investment, really. It will add value to the house.'

'Quite right,' said Flora, not sure she agreed with herself. 'Now, let's get started.' If they hung around too long they would both fall asleep and Charles would find them on the bed together, possibly snoring lightly, which would worry him in all sorts of ways. Besides, she was beginning to miss her kittens. 'All round-necked jumpers, out.'

'But—'

'They make your boobs look like bolsters, even with the new bras. You can try one if you don't believe me. Oh, and polo-necks.'

'But it gets so cold in winter!'

'OK, keep the polo-necks, but just remember they won't flatter you.'

The super-de luxe wardrobe system meant a pile of unsuitable sweaters were soon placed neatly on the floor.

Flora now got off the bed and started going through the rail designated for shirts and blouses. 'Pie-crust, pie-crust, pussy-cat bows.' A pile of Liberty prints hit the floor. 'And any of these that go straight down should go really unless you promise to tuck them in. They should be a bit fitted, or you get too much bulk in your waistband. Those have to go anyway. Those flowers are too busy.'

'I always wear that under a jumper, so you only see the collar.'

'Would that be a jumper with a round neck?'

Annabelle nodded ruefully.

'Then you won't be needing it any more, will you?'

'But it's smart and comfortable. I like it.'

'It looks like a school uniform, only not in a sexy way.'

Flora fixed her with a steely eye as she added the shirt to the discard pile. 'I'm not sure the flowers are quite right with your skin. We really should get your colours done.'

'No, that's fine,' said Annabelle, obviously reluctant to submit to more tyranny. 'I trust you, Flora.'

'Good! Now, skirts. Oh, this is wonderful! They're all neatly together. This is so easy. Knee length box-pleats haven't come back yet, Annabelle, and I don't see it happening soon. Out! A kilt?' She looked at Annabelle who was looking a little pathetic as all her favourite outfits were cast aside. 'OK, you can keep the kilt, but promise me you'll only wear it in Scotland. Anywhere else it will make your hips look enormous.'

'But not enormous in Scotland?'

Flora chuckled. Perhaps Annabelle did have a sense of humour in there somewhere. 'In Scotland, they're allowed.'

In celebration of this dispensation, Annabelle went downstairs for the rest of the bottle.

'Shall I make some pasta and salad? I've got one of those fresh sauces we could have with it?' Annabelle tore open a packet of nuts with her teeth.

'It's sweet of you, Annabelle, but I'd like to get back. My cat and kittens, you know. But the nuts are lovely. Oh, look, a whole section for ball gowns. You are a party girl.'

'Hunt balls, mostly. Things like that. Oh, can't I keep that?'

'Royal blue is quite a difficult colour, Annabelle, and look how high cut it is. It won't show off your boobs and will cling to your stomach. You want something low cut, but with sleeves. No frills, though,' she said, extracting something reminiscent of Princess Diana's wedding dress. 'When you're over thirty it's better to stick with something simple and sexy.'

'OK.' Glum but obedient, Annabelle put a handful of peanuts into her mouth.

'Now, shoes.'

'I have to be comfortable, Flora. It's no good trying to make me teeter about on high heels. I can't do it.'

Flora was merciful in defeat. 'Well, just promise me you'll buy one pair of black court shoes—'

'I have three pairs of black court shoes.'

'With heels. Even small heels. Just something. And remember, the more you pay for shoes the more comfortable they are.'

'Your mother's advice again?'

Flora tried to remember. 'I think it was more something she told my father after she'd spent a lot of money on some shoes. But it is true.'

They sank back on the bed and both dived into the nuts at the same time.

'This has been quite fun,' said Annabelle. 'I didn't expect it to be, but it has.'

'I think you'll enjoy the new you. I should take you up to London to get your hair cut, really, but I expect there's someone down here who's quite good.'

'You're positive I must have it a bit shorter?'

Flora nodded. 'And a few layers. It looks lovely now, for instance, when it's all mussed up from you trying on jumpers. And I was right about the bolster, wasn't I?'

'I suppose so. Now I want to go out and show off my

new look. When can you arrange that little dinner party? The one you're giving so I can check out the naked man in your garden.'

Flora giggled. 'You make it sound like there's always one there.'

'I suppose they do mostly come in bronze.' She sighed, and it occurred to Flora that she was probably very tired.

'I thought I'd do it when my friend from London, Emma, comes down for the weekend. She was at university with William.' The wine had gone to Flora's head a little and she couldn't remember if she was supposed to know William's name or not. She blundered on. 'It's more fun if there are several people there, don't you think?'

'Yes . . .' Like cats, they both became alert as they heard a key in the door. 'There's Charles.'

Flora shifted to the edge of the bed and got up. 'I'll run down and see him, tell him not to have a drink until he's driven me home, while you make sure you're looking completely fab.'

Annabelle got up off the bed and smoothed her top down over her skirt. 'OK, but there's no need for you to hurry down. We're up here, darling,' she called, hitching up her breasts. 'In the bedroom. Can you drive Flora home?'

Charles came up the stairs and stood in the doorway, half embarrassed, like a father at a teenage sleepover. He didn't know quite where to look. 'Oh my God!'

Flora felt a bit like a cross between a Fairy Godmother and a gooseberry. Annabelle was looking surprisingly sexy, and any normal man would want to do something about it. But not, apparently, Charles, who just stood and stared at her.

'Well, doesn't your fiancée look stunning in her new clothes?'

'She certainly looks different.'

'In a good way,' said Flora, determined to force him into the right reaction. 'Do a twirl, Annabelle.'

Annabelle twirled and Flora felt her hard work had paid off.

'The girls at the reunion will be very impressed,' said Flora. 'Fancy frumpy old Annabelle turning out to be so sexy.'

'The reunion?' said Annabelle. 'Oh, I'd forgotten about that for a moment.'

Charles was frowning. 'I think I liked you better the way you were before, pumpkin.'

'Oh, for goodness' sake!' said Flora, exasperated. 'She hasn't changed her whole personality! Just her clothes! And she looks gorgeous! Admit it.'

'Well, yes. I suppose she does.' Charles came further into the room and kissed Annabelle on the cheek and then on the lips. 'But beauty is only skin deep. It's what's inside that counts.'

Flora rolled her eyes. 'We all know that, we've been hearing it since we came out of the egg, but the point is, the inside is still the same! Annabelle is still Annabelle, she just looks younger and prettier and sexier.' It was certainly uphill work teaching Charles not to judge by appearances.

'Flora's right, you know,' said Annabelle. 'It's only my clothes and the way I wear them that's different. I'm still your little pumpkin inside.' Flora shuddered. 'By the way,' Annabelle went on, getting into the role that went with her new look. 'Flora needs a lift home, sweetheart.'

'Oh.'

Flora didn't bother to check Charles's expression. He was bound to be looking like there was a poker fused to his spine. 'No, really. I'll order a taxi. I don't want you love-birds to be kept apart for another minute, and it's a good half-hour to the cottage, and then another back. Annabelle, cook Charles something delicious, and Charles, order me a cab. Please?'

Charles moved away from Annabelle and came to look sternly at Flora. 'I'm perfectly happy to drive you.'

This was a bit of a surprise. 'No, honestly. I'd much rather take a taxi.'

'Are you sure?'

'Of course she's sure,' said Annabelle. 'She's not a child, even if she does look rather young. And do you know, sweetie? Flora's going to invite us for dinner when her friend comes to stay. Such fun.'

Oh God! She'd have to do it now Charles knew about it. Why did she drink all that wine? Look at the trouble it was getting her into. Perhaps Emma was right, and living in the country had got to her, and not in a good way.

'You will have to get me a dining table first, though. I couldn't have you eating on your laps.'

'I can certainly arrange that,' said Charles. 'Come down and we'll phone for a taxi. Are you coming, darling?'

'I just want to tidy myself a little,' said Annabelle. 'My hair's a mess.'

'Annabelle,' said Flora warningly. 'You're not to put that headband back on!'

'You see, Charles?' she said to him as they walked down the stairs. 'She may have changed on the outside, but she's still tidy Annabelle underneath.'

'I'm very relieved to hear it. I wouldn't like that aspect of my life being turned upside down, too.'

'What do you mean?' She turned to him as they reached the hallway.

'You've caused quite enough upset in my life without messing about with my perfectly satisfactory fiancée.'

Flora took a breath and then saw that Charles was almost smiling. 'Oh. You're teasing. I wish you'd warn me when you're going to. It's so unexpected, coming from you.'

'You could make me a little sign that I could hold up when I'm going to do it, like the bidders.'

Flora chuckled. 'It's a good idea, but it's unlikely to happen enough to make it worth my while.'

'Oh, I don't know about that. So, you girls have done some shopping?' He flicked through the *Yellow Pages*.

'Some. We've also done a lot of sorting out. But I want you to tell me if Annabelle doesn't make a trip to a charity shop very soon.'

'You're not telling me you've been shopping in charity shops?'

Flora couldn't tell if Charles's horror was his own, or on behalf of Annabelle. 'No,' she said coolly. 'We haven't. But a lot of Annabelle's current wardrobe is quite wrong for her and she should get rid of it. It's all in a pile. Well, a heap, really.'

146

'Oh.' Charles found a number and started pressing buttons.

'Do we advertise in the *Yellow Pages*?' she asked him while he was waiting to be connected.

'Just a small entry. Large ads are very expensive.'

'I really think you ought to have a proper advertisement, you know.'

'Most of our business comes from local people, who know about us.'

'But think of that valuation we did the other day. They weren't local, even if their uncle was. How did they know to ring you?'

'A friend of the uncle's recommended us.'

'But if he hadn't, and they came down here and wanted an auctioneer, what would they do?' As Charles seemed to be being rather slow, she answered for him. 'They'd look in the *Yellow Pages*.'

'Ah, yes. Can you take someone out to Fiddler's Wood, please?'

When the taxi was arranged, Flora continued, 'I want to have a talk about the business, Charles. I've had some ideas.'

'Have you?'

He was obviously very tired. His usually immaculate shirt and tie was looking a little rumpled. A strand of hair had fallen away from the rest. Flora had a sudden, almost irresistible urge to smooth it away. Only the fact that she couldn't have reached it unless he had bent down a little stopped her.

'I have. But we won't talk about them now, you look tired.'

'Oh, I'm all right. It's been a bit of a long day, that's

all. You won't want to come into the office tomorrow as it's Saturday, but I'll drop the Land-Rover off. Annabelle can follow me in her car and give me a lift back.'

'Are you working tomorrow then?'

'I have got a few bits and pieces to tie up, yes.'

'Then I'll come in too, at least for the morning. Apart from anything else, it'll save Annabelle having to come.' She frowned as she realised that she'd only achieved half her goals regarding Annabelle – she still hadn't found out what sort of business she would really like to go into. Though probably not anything connected with fashion.

'Are you sure?'

Something in Charles's tone made Flora vehement. 'Yes! It's my business too! Besides, I haven't got anything else on, much.'

'You wouldn't like a day to relax?'

'I'll do that on Sunday.'

'That's showing great dedication to duty, Flora.'

'Did you expect anything less?' She couldn't help teasing him just a little.

'If I did before, I certainly wouldn't dare now. Oh, and your car is ready, by the way. I'd collect you in it tomorrow, only there's something I want to deliver for the cottage that you might find useful.'

'That sounds exciting. It's not a dining table?'

'Alas, no.'

'And it's good about my car. I hope it wasn't horribly expensive.'

'Don't worry about that. And you can go on using the Land-Rover if you like.'

'I do like it.'

At last they heard someone coming up the front steps and ring the doorbell.

'I'll say goodbye, then,' said Flora.

'Goodnight, Flora.'

The following morning, she saw Charles's car come slowly down the lane and went out to meet him. She was feeling oddly jittery, although she didn't know why. He got out of the car and stood there while Flora came up to him.

'Hi, Charles, how are you?'

'Fine.'

'Did Annabelle give you a fashion show? She got some lovely things.'

'I think you've finally proved to me that it's not a good idea to try and judge a book by its cover, yes,' he said, with a twinkle oddly reminiscent of Henry's.

Flora smiled and bit her lip. 'Good!'

'Come and see what I've brought you. Not a dining table, but something a bit similar.'

It was a white painted metal table and two chairs for the garden.

'Oh, that's lovely! It will be perfect in the corner by the roses. I can just see myself sitting there with a glass of wine.' She frowned a little. 'Wasn't this, or something very like it, at the last sale? I seem to remember it went for a reasonable sum.'

'Yes, it did. I bought it. Geoffrey bid for me. I thought it was just what you needed here.'

'Is that legal? Buying stuff when you're the auctioneer?'

'As long as your bid is the highest, yes.'

'That's really kind, Charles, thank you.'

'I will make sure there's also something to eat off before . . . when is it?' It was his turn to look thoughtful. 'I hope Annabelle hasn't railroaded you into having a dinner party. She seemed very keen to come for some reason. I was very pleased, though,' he went on, 'I would really like Annabelle and you to become friends. She doesn't have many close women friends.'

'No?'

'It would be good for her to get some young company.'

'She's not that much older than me, Charles.'

'No, but currently her best friend is her mother, which is all very well, but I think you need friends your own age, don't you?'

'Absolutely!'

'So we can come for dinner?'

Flora found herself nodding. 'Of course! It'll be fun.'

'I'll just put these things where you want them and we'll be off. How's Imelda?' He carried the table to the corner of the garden where some rambling roses made a natural arbour.

Flora picked up a chair. It was unexpectedly heavy. 'I didn't think you cared about Imelda, or her kittens.'

Charles looked surprised. 'I did, but I didn't want to ask if I could come and see them in case she ate them, or something.'

'Oh. Well, you could come and see them now, if you're interested.' Perhaps she'd misjudged him a little.

He glanced at his watch. 'I'm meeting some people at eleven. I shouldn't really.'

Flora was disappointed. 'Perhaps you could come and see them another time.'

'I'd love to.' He put the second chair down by the table.

'It looks wonderful,' said Flora. 'Like something out of a magazine. It only needs a bottle of wine, a loaf of bread, some olives and a book.'

'*A book of verses underneath the bough, A jug of wine, a loaf of bread – and Thou,*' he quoted softly.

'What's that?'

'Oh, just a bit of poetry. Now, have you got everything? We should be off.'

When they got to the office, Charles said, 'What are you going to do?'

'I'd like to get on with sorting out those old filing cabinets. There's stuff in there no one's looked at for years. I'm not going to destroy any of it, just put it into document boxes and label it, so you can throw it away later.' She was quite looking forward to a day of getting on with things together in companionable silence. And perhaps they might even have a proper chat about the business without everyone else around.

He smiled. 'That doesn't seem a very nice way to spend a sunny Saturday.'

'Well, you're working, so I should be, too. And once those filing cabinets are empty, we can put them somewhere else and have much more room in the office.'

'Um, I'm only working until eleven. The people I'm meeting, with Annabelle, are friends.'

'Oh.' Flora felt suddenly put out. 'Well, I'll only work till twelve then.' Then, worrying she sounded a bit dependent, she hurried on, 'I've got a friend I've been trying to meet for lunch for ages.'

'Oh?'

151

This was obviously an invitation to tell him who the friend was. Flora decided to refuse it. It was none of his business, after all. 'We'd better get on, then, if we're only working for a couple of hours.'

When Charles was out of the room, doing whatever he had to do, Flora decided to ring Henry. She didn't usually ring men until the relationship was fairly well established, but this was an emergency. She couldn't be seen as Flora-No-Mates when Charles and Annabelle were going to be all couply and have lunch with friends.

'Henry? It's Flora Stanza.' For all her confidence, Flora always felt a little shy telephoning people she didn't really know.

'Flora! How very nice to hear from you!'

His enthusiasm was a great relief. 'I'm working this morning, but as I'm in town, I wondered if we could meet for lunch, or a drink, or something.'

'That would be delightful. Shall I pick you up from the office? I know a very nice little pub we could go to.'

'That would be lovely. About twelve?'

'Great. See you soon. Cheers.'

Charles was standing in the doorway when she put the phone down. 'So you're going out for lunch too?'

'Yup. Something to look forward to after all this sorting out.' She smiled at him, sensing that for some reason he was dying to know whom she was going out with.

'I heard you say the name Henry. Would that be Henry Burnet?'

Flora had to think for a moment. 'Yes, I think that would be him.'

Charles frowned. 'I should tell you, Flora, that he's

not someone I would wish any relative of mine to go out with.'

'Isn't he? Well, never mind, we're not that closely related.'

Charles pursed his lips and strode off.

Chapter Nine

They left Flora's Land-Rover in town and drove to a charming pub with a sloping garden that was full of people with their dogs and children.

'I was so glad you rang me,' said Henry as he delivered a glass of Pimm's to her. 'I was going to ring later, but I never thought you'd be free for lunch today.'

Flora felt rather guilty, aware that she'd arranged a date with Henry almost as much for Charles's benefit as for the pleasure of his company.

'I was really lucky you were free, but I was in town already, and it's such a lovely afternoon, I wanted to take the chance.'

'Well, here's to you,' said Henry, picking up his own Pimm's and looking down into her eyes.

Flora met his eyes for only a second, but then inspected the fruit salad floating in her drink. She didn't want Henry to get too keen until she'd decided how much she liked him. If he did get too eager for her company, she'd go off him immediately. In fact, she rather hoped Geoffrey was right about him being a philanderer – the last thing she wanted right now was a complicated relationship.

Fortunately, he seemed to take the hint. 'Now, what do you fancy for lunch? They do excellent home-cooked ham and a particularly good salad dressing.'

Flora chuckled. 'And I thought I'd left all the gourmet flesh-pots behind in London.'

'Seriously, the ham is outstanding.' Henry was laughing too. 'You should definitely try it.'

'I will then. And the particularly good salad dressing.'

While Henry was away, placing their food order, Flora thought about him. He was good looking, and laughed at her jokes, which was a definite plus – she'd had enough of people not getting her jokes all day. He would definitely do for the time being.

Later they went for a walk along the canal tow-path and Flora kept asking Henry about the various wild flowers growing along the path.

'I'm afraid I know nothing about any of them. Flowers have never interested me that much.'

Flora was disappointed. 'I think, because of my name, I should know more about them. I'll get a book.'

'So do you think you'll stay around for a while?'

It was the first remotely serious question he had asked her and Flora considered how best to reply. For some reason she didn't want to reveal her passion for her family business too early in their friendship.

'Oh yes, for a bit, anyway. I'll probably go back to London when the weather gets horrible, but I'm definitely here for the summer.'

'Oh good,' said Henry, 'then so am I.'

Henry kissed Flora's cheek when he dropped her back at her car. It was very pleasant. She liked Henry and she could tell he liked her, but not in an oppressive way. He seemed very relaxed and laid back about things, and that was just what she needed.

* * *

Flora was in the garden pulling up the goose-grass that covered everything with a sort of green mist. She had taken her breakfast out and eaten it at the little table and then felt inspired to do what she could to make the garden look better. She was surprised at her enthusiasm but even more surprised when she heard a car, looked up and saw that it was Charles.

'Good morning,' she called. 'I didn't expect to see you again so soon.'

'I've got some garden tools for you. Annabelle wanted you to have them,' he said through the window. 'But I see you've started without them.'

'Just this green stuff. It comes out easily, although it's given me a bit of a rash.'

Charles got out of the car. 'You need long gloves.' He went round to the back of the car and opened the boot. 'I've got a fork, a trowel, some fairly ancient gardening gloves and a bucket with a hole in it. To put the weeds in.'

By this time Flora had joined Charles at the boot. 'Where did these come from? Another sale?'

'No, I think these are throw-outs from Annabelle's parents. They're great gardeners. Annabelle's keen, too, although of course there isn't much garden with her house in town.'

'She didn't want me to have an idle Sunday, obviously,' Flora said wryly.

'Actually, I offered to bring them over. Not because I want you to get stuck into clearing out the bindweed . . .' He paused.

'What?'

'I couldn't just have a peep at the kittens, could I?

I've been dying to ever since they were born.' He appeared a little embarrassed by this request. 'As I said, I didn't like to earlier, in case it upset Imelda.'

Flora was strangely touched. And since William had left a note saying he was off for the day and wouldn't be back until suppertime, she didn't have to worry about him suddenly appearing.

'Come on then.'

As Flora led Charles through the house she worried briefly in case William had left some trace of his presence, but if he had, Charles didn't notice. And she had at least made her bed, so if her room was a bit untidy, it didn't look too slutty.

Charles knelt down on the floor in front of where Imelda was ensconced, feeding her babies, purring loudly. Seeing his large form hovering over the tiny bodies, who were pumping their mother for all they were worth, was surprisingly touching.

'Can I pick one up?'

'Take that one who's stopped feeding for a minute. Aren't they heavenly?'

He put the kitten next to his neck and stroked it with a long finger. 'Mm. I do wish we could have one, but . . .'

'It's all right. I know. Annabelle's allergic to cats.'

'And she doesn't like them, either.'

'I suppose if they make you sneeze, or itch, it would put you off them a bit.' Flora was trying to be generous. How could anyone not like cats?

He shook his head. 'Her mother's the same. She's not allergic, she just doesn't like them.'

'Is Annabelle like her mother in other ways? You know

what they say,' she went on playfully, wishing she could shut up, 'you should always check out the girl's mother before you commit yourself, because that's who you'll end up married to.'

'She's a very fine woman.' He frowned slightly. 'I think I remember meeting your mother once.'

'Oh?'

'Yes. She looked very like you, Flora. Very pretty.'

Usually Flora would have accepted this compliment with grace and aplomb. Now she felt embarrassed. It was probably because Charles didn't usually say things like that: it made her feel awkward. 'Well, it's a shame neither of them like cats. But some people like dogs better.'

'What about you, Flora?'

'Oh, I like both. They're like men and women – although not actually like men and women. I don't think dogs are like men and cats are like women, or anything like that. I just think they offer you different things.'

'Yes?' Charles had helped himself to another kitten and put it in the same place as the first one.

'Dogs build you up, make you feel better. Cats keep you in your place. They love you but they don't need you. Dogs are needy.'

'When we get married we might get a dog. A nice black Labrador.'

'Mm. I can see Annabelle with a Labrador.'

'They are very sensible dogs.'

Flora didn't comment. For her Labradors were on a par with flat shoes, knee-length skirts and Hermès head-scarves: pleasant enough in their place, but not very exciting.

Charles went on. 'Now *you* I can see with something

much more frivolous and decorative, like a poodle or a Cavalier King Charles spaniel.'

Flora, content with his choice of breed for her, replied, 'You, on the other hand, should have something stately and enormous, like an Irish wolfhound.'

He turned away from the kittens for a moment. 'Is that how you see me? Stately and enormous?'

Flora nodded. 'And kind. You can be quite kind when you're not being bossy. Wolfhounds are very gentle. I used to know one when I was a child.'

Charles detached the kitten and sighed. 'I can't see Annabelle putting up with anything that size.'

'Well, I suppose if you're both working, it would be difficult. Just the same for any dog, though.' She found Charles being in her bedroom, within touching distance, too intimate, somehow.

'Do you worry about leaving Imelda during the day?'

She was just about to say that William came in and checked on her at lunchtime when she remembered that Charles didn't know about William. 'I leave lots of food and the kitchen window open. She's fine.'

He got to his feet, putting himself safely out of reach again. 'I must get that cat flap organised. Annabelle would not be happy if she knew about you leaving the window open.'

Flora glanced at herself in her dressing-table mirror but resisted the temptation to pick up her lip-gloss and add a layer. As a reward for this restraint she allowed herself to dig about Annabelle a little. 'Annabelle doesn't seem that happy about working in an auction house either,' she said.

'No,' said Charles as he followed her down the stairs, making Flora feel like a midget pursued by a giant. 'She prefers proper antiques to the house-clearance stuff we mostly get. Poor girl. I don't think she realised how much of the things we handle would be so run-of-the-mill.'

'Would you like a cup of coffee?'

'I should be getting back, really. Lunch with the in-laws.'

'Are they coming to you, or are you going to them?'

'We're going to them.' As he showed no signs of leaving she went through to the kitchen. He followed her and watched while she put the kettle on.

'Um.' He cleared his throat. 'How was your lunch with – Henry Burnet yesterday?'

'Oh, lovely! He took me to a really nice pub and we ate ham and salad. He's great fun.' Flora displayed a little more enthusiasm than she felt, although she had enjoyed herself. Something about Charles's cosy lunch with his in-laws made her want to seem a bit attached too.

'Good. But I do think I should warn you, as your cousin, that he hasn't got a very good reputation with women.'

'Hasn't he?'

'No.'

'I'll watch my step, then,' said Flora.

'I hope you don't mind me saying.'

'Not at all!' She smiled. 'So you will have coffee?'

'Oh, go on, then.'

'No need to be so gracious, Charles. I had an idea.' She opened a jar of coffee and found a teaspoon.

'About what?'

'About the business. How to improve the quality of the lots.'

'Yes?'

'I got it when you mentioned the *Antiques Roadshow* the other day. Why don't you do them?'

'What on earth are you talking about?'

'Put on a roadshow. You'd have to advertise, of course, but you could ask people to bring in their antiques, stuff they have lying around and don't really want or need, and then, if they're valuable, they might want to sell them.'

'Well—'

'You could do it in all the small towns nearby. Hire a room, or something. People would love it, I'm sure. And it would be a good advertisement for you anyway.'

'It would be terribly expensive. And if people didn't want to sell their stuff, it would all be for nothing. There's no slack in this business for mistakes, Flora.'

'You need some capital.'

'I know that.'

She bit back her question about Annabelle's capital. She'd been happy to use it to buy Flora out, so why wasn't she happy to use it to invest in the business in other ways? Annabelle by herself had been quite fun on their shopping trip, but as far as Stanza and Stanza went she was a disaster.

Instead she said, 'You have a huge house which you only use a very small part of as your offices. If you sold it you'd have plenty of capital. You wouldn't have to sell the hall.'

'You mean I could buy you out?'

Flora smiled weakly. 'You could, if I was willing to sell, of course, but that's not the point. What I'm saying is, if you sold that building, dividing it up into flats first if you like, you could afford to do lots to make Stanza and Stanza work.'

'I don't know what Annabelle would think about that.'

Flora got the impression that this was just an excuse. 'Annabelle is not your partner! I am! And if she's not really interested in the business, why should she worry about what you do with the house?'

'It's not that she'd worry about selling the house. In fact, I think she's had some idea of doing that, too. It's what we did with the money that would worry her. And Flora, she's been involved for a while. She does have a right to her opinions.'

'Oh.' Crossly, Flora poured boiling water on to the coffee. 'I could do with a coffee grinder if I'm going to have a dinner party. Or a cafetière, or something.'

'I'll see what I can do. I'm sure Annabelle's got a spare one.'

Neither of them were really thinking about coffee or how to make it. 'Shall we use the table and chairs and take it out into the garden?' suggested Flora.

'I really mustn't be long. Annabelle will be expecting me.'

'We'll stay in the kitchen then.' Flora sat down and picked up her cup. It must be hard for Annabelle, being engaged to a man whose life was so taken up with a business she was part of but didn't enjoy.

'That house has been in the family a very long time,' said Charles.

'I know,' Flora replied, although she hadn't known, really, but only guessed.

'But we can't afford to be sentimental, I suppose. If Annabelle is . . .'

'Is what?'

'Unwilling to put capital into the business—'

'She was willing enough when she wanted to buy shares from me.' Flora felt a rush of indignation.

'That was different.'

'Why?'

'Because Annabelle would get something tangible for her money. She's helped a bit in the past but just putting money into the business generally wouldn't be the same at all.'

Flora sighed and sipped her coffee, which wasn't very nice. It wasn't that she wanted Annabelle investing in her family business – she might have to become a director or something. But if Annabelle could invest enough to make Stanza and Stanza profitable without selling the house, she should be encouraged to do so.

'Why don't you tell her about the *Antiques Roadshow* idea? If she could see that having a bit more capital, to advertise further afield, would make better stuff come in, it would be more interesting for her.'

'But if we sold the house or raised money from it, we could buy up a couple of auction houses owned by people who want to retire. Someone asked me only the other day if I'd be interested in buying them out. I had to refuse, but it would be a good way of getting more business.'

'Talk to Annabelle about it. And while you're on the subject, let's get a proper website. It's ridiculous not having one in the twenty-first century. And don't forget the proper ad in the *Yellow Pages*.'

Charles looked exhaustedly at Flora. 'We'll have a meeting soon. You, me and Annabelle.'

'Fine.' It wasn't fine, really. Annabelle wasn't a partner and had no real right to be there. But if Charles wanted his fiancée present, she could hardly complain.

'Changing the subject . . .'

'Yes? This coffee's disgusting, isn't it?'

'Yes, but I wasn't going to say that. I was going to ask if I could bring an old friend to your dinner party.'

'A male or a female friend?'

'Male. It wasn't my idea, I have to say.'

'Annabelle's?'

'Yes. She thought it would be nice for you to have someone to show you about the place.'

'It's a kind thought. And of course he can come, but I do have Henry.'

Charles stiffened. 'Oh yes. So you do. But Jeremy would be far better than Henry.'

'Really?' She was longing to tell her mother about this. Her mother knew that this sort of statement was destined to send Flora catapulting away from Jeremy into Henry's arms.

'Yes. He's a good, steady chap.' He frowned, as if he wanted to say something else, but then thought better of it.

'Yes?'

'Nothing.' He got to his feet. 'I should be getting along. Annabelle will be waiting.'

Flora smiled. 'Thank you for bringing the gardening tools.'

'That's all right. Have a pleasant Sunday, Flora.'

Later, she rang Emma and told her with satisfaction that things were going much better with Charles.

* * *

Monday morning found Flora awake early and full of energy, if a little stiff after her gardening. William had not appeared the night before so she had had a bath and gone to bed early with her book.

'I must have early nights more often,' she told Imelda, as she gave her a last cuddle before leaving for work. 'I feel great!'

It was only when she reached town and realised there was very little traffic about, that she looked at her watch. 'It's only seven o'clock!' she squeaked to herself, horrified. 'I must have got up at about half past five! I'm such a dilly – how could I not have realised? Still' – she swooped the Land-Rover round in a generous curve – 'it gives me the whole yard to park in!' Thank God she had a key and didn't have to sit on the doorstep waiting for someone to let her in.

By the time she had got into the building, unset the alarm, and put the kettle on, she decided it was time to stop talking to herself and do some work. There was no point in turning up hours early if there wasn't anything dramatic to show for it.

Sipping her tea, she went back to the files she was sorting out, but after she'd consigned several years' worth of garage bills to a file, she decided it was too lovely a day to spend among ancient dust. She went into the main office and looked around.

The first day she had arrived she'd thought the place looked dingy. And while there was no spare money for major refurbishment, surely a little decorating was not out of the question? There was a piece of peeling paper on the ceiling that had been driving her mad since she got here.

Determined to be safety conscious, she carefully cleared the computer off one of the desks and put a chair on it, so she could easily reach the paper. She was glad she'd put on a pair of loose linen trousers today. She couldn't have done this if she'd been wearing a little strappy dress and frivolous shoes.

The first piece came away beautifully and Flora started to think about colours. A subtle yellow, to bring sunshine into the room? A pale straw, stylish and light? Or a fresh green? She dug her fingernail under the next strip and found that too was easy to remove.

She was making good progress and tugging away merrily when suddenly there was a crash followed by what felt like a minor landslip. Dust, plaster, paper and quite large chunks of stone showered down. It felt as if someone had emptied a rather lumpy bag of flour over Flora's head. Coughing, she stood still until everything stopped. 'Oh my God,' she said aloud. 'The paper must have been holding everything else up.' She looked around her as the dust slowly settled, and took in the chaos. What on earth had she done? A large chunk of ceiling had come down and a substantial part of the wall was bare. And a thickish layer of dust covered everything – including the computers. Oh no, the computers! Please let them be OK.

She glanced at her watch. Half past eight. Her heart sank. Charles could appear any time from now. She had to do something. She felt a rising panic, and tried to swallow it.

First, she clambered down and ran to get a dustpan and brush, then she swept up as much as she could easily. The place had to stop looking like there had been an earthquake before anyone else arrived. She dumped the debris in the bin, then she regarded the paper, hanging from the ceiling in a way that no one could possibly avoid seeing – or indeed bumping into. However much she swept and dusted, that paper would betray her. What a disaster.

Drawing pins? Could she pin it up out of the way? No, they would never hold in all the crumbling plaster. Then she remembered seeing a tub of Copydex in a drawer. That would be perfect! She could stick the paper back up, stuff what she'd already pulled down in the bin, and then wipe and polish away all traces of her abortive attempts at decorating. Fingers crossed Charles wasn't in too early.

She was just standing on the chair, teetering a little as she reached up, holding the glue in one hand, the brush in the other when the door behind her opened.

'What the blazes are you doing?' Charles demanded loudly, making Flora jump and dislodge the chair.

He caught her before she fell but before she could thank him he took a deep breath and started. 'What the bloody hell do you think you're doing? You could have broken something if you'd fallen!' Thinking he was concerned for her, she was about to reassure him, but he thundered on. 'The place is covered in rubble! Is that you thinking you'd move on from *Bargain Hunt* and play at *Changing Rooms* or something?'

'Charles! Calm down! I—'

'For God's sake, Flora. Those computers aren't paid for yet! If anything happens to them, we're stuck, we can't buy new ones.'

'I was just trying to help!'

'Trying to help? Trying to sabotage the whole caboodle more like! Honestly, Flora, I've had enough. The sooner you go back to London and leave us to get on with our work, the better!'

As she'd slithered through Charles's arms on to the floor, Flora had felt guilty. She had been foolish, she could have damaged the computers with falling dust and detritus and she had been quite willing to apologise. But not now.

'Leave you to rot in your own failure more like! There are breweries round here that haven't had piss-ups for years because you couldn't organise them! This business is going from bad to worse because you have less business sense than my cat!'

'Less business sense than your cat! Grow up, Flora. You're being infantile. You—'

'Infantile!' Now Flora was really furious. 'How dare you? From the moment I walked in here, you've behaved appallingly. You took one look at me and decided I was just young and silly and pointless.'

'Well, if the cap fits—'

'And you were determined not to listen to a word I said. You're so stuck in your ways that you can't even imagine that a fresh pair of eyes can see something you can't. Yes, I'm younger than you, but I'm not a child! And I do have something to contribute.'

'Don't be ridiculous. You're playing at country life and country living. You're just a spoilt little princess used to getting her own way and as soon as you get bored you'll run off back to London.'

Spoilt little princess? Flora couldn't believe it. 'What on earth makes you think you know me so well? You know nothing about me – because you and your bloody fiancée can't think further than getting rid of me. But you're destroying Stanza and Stanza in the process!'

'You have absolutely no right to say that!'

'Oh yes I have, because in case you've forgotten, I'm the senior partner here!'

A look of shock passed across Charles's face and Flora herself felt rather shocked that she'd been so blunt. She hadn't meant to say that. 'You're nothing of the kind!' he shouted. 'You just happen to own more than me owing to the blundering of a poor old man who must have been suffering from senile dementia when he left anything to you, let alone half a business!'

'He had not got senile dementia, he was perfectly lucid and perhaps he left it to me because he knew what a crap job you were making of it!'

'I doubt that! I expect he was just seduced by your big brown eyes and pretty ways. He was just manipulated by you, same as every other sucker you get your claws into!'

'What the hell are you talking about?'

'You know perfectly well what I'm talking about. Don't try and play the innocent with me, because unlike most of the people round here, I'm not fooled!'

'And nor am I! Just because you're your father's son, the women round here seem to think you're God Almighty. Well, not me! I know what a hopeless businessman you are.'

They confronted each other, both breathing hard. Flora felt a little dizzy, possibly because she'd used up so much breath shouting at Charles. Charles was flushed; his usually ordered hair was falling over his forehead.

'I may not be Richard Branson but at least I never pulled the building down about our ears! Now could you try and get this lot cleared up before Annabelle gets here.' And he stormed past her out of the door.

Flora shook her head to clear it. Anger lent her wings and very quickly she got the office looking more or less as it had been. She turned on both computers and, much to her relief, they both worked. But once the adrenaline faded, she felt exhausted and horribly near tears. She went into the Ladies', to wash, and then slipped out to the shop to buy a bar of chocolate. There was something in chocolate that made it good for you, she told herself.

She met Charles in the passage. He looked down at her, as frosty and far away as Everest. 'I apologise if I said anything inappropriate,' he said formally.

If? 'I accept your apology, if that is what it is,' she replied, thinking that 'I apologise' is what you say if you're not remotely sorry. 'I probably said things I shouldn't have, too.'

He nodded, and then stalked out of the back entrance to the car. Flora suddenly longed to go home to bed.

Chapter Ten

Flora spent most of the rest of the day in a mild state of shock, with her files, where she could do no damage. She left promptly, while Charles was out, and said goodbye to people briefly. She was fairly sure she'd hidden the fact that anything was wrong, but when she got home, she saw that there was still quite a lot of plaster in her hair. 'This job can turn you white overnight,' she said to her reflection, in an attempt to cheer herself up. It didn't work, she still felt rotten.

The following day she crept in, but was pleased to see Louisa, who didn't work on Mondays. At least she could be normal with her.

'Hi, Louisa. Nice weekend?'

'Lovely, thanks. My husband takes my children swimming and to the library on Saturday mornings so I got a lot done in the garden. You were in on Saturday?'

'Only in the morning. I went out for lunch with a friend in the afternoon.'

'Well, you did a very good job on that valuation. Are you a typist, then? No one told me.'

Flora checked to see if anyone else was in earshot. 'Well, I can type. It's useful, but I wouldn't want to do it for a living. I temp from time to time if I can't get anything more interesting to do.'

'So what did you do, actually?' Louisa settled herself at her desk. 'Before you came here, I mean.'

Flora shrugged. 'Nothing specific. I just had jobs, really, not a career. The longest I've ever stayed in a job was two years in an art gallery. This is the only thing so far that I've really enjoyed. It's hard work but it's so varied. You're doing a valuation one day, being a porter the next, and typing up stuff the day after.'

Louisa smiled enthusiastically at her. 'You can help me type the next catalogue. They were supposed to be getting me an assistant but nothing ever happened.'

Flora bit her lip guiltily. 'Oh, I think I'm supposed to be doing that. When I first came, Charles didn't want me to be here at all, so I applied for the job as assistant so he couldn't send me back to London. And I haven't really assisted you at all.'

'Well, be around for the next catalogue and I'll forgive you. And you did do the valuation.' Louisa got up out of her seat and peered out of the window. 'Here's Annabelle. Goodness, she's looking very . . . different.'

Flora rushed to see what Annabelle was wearing. It was the long, slim-line fuchsia skirt and the black V-neck top. Her hair was held back by a black velvet band, which was against the rules, but on the whole she didn't look at all bad. 'We went shopping the other day,' said Flora. 'I was doing a Trinny and Susannah on her.'

'My God! That was brave! Did she kick up a lot of fuss? And why on earth did she agree to let you?' Annabelle disappeared through the front door at that moment and they knew she would be with them in seconds. 'Oh, here she is.'

'Annabelle, what is that thing on your head?' asked Flora, on the attack.

'My hair kept flopping all over the place, it distracted me.'

'What's wrong with her hair?' asked Charles, who came into the room a few steps behind, looking daggers at Flora. He obviously hadn't forgiven her.

'It's lovely hair,' said Flora, realising that she was not going to win this one. 'It's just that Alice bands aren't usually a good idea for anyone older than Alice in Wonderland was.'

'I'm sorry, Flora,' said Annabelle briskly. 'I've got to be able to see.'

Flora sighed, 'OK. It does look quite sweet, I suppose,' reluctantly relinquishing her position as the style Nazi.

'Charles says you want a meeting?'

What else had Charles said, she wondered? And how much of it would have been repeatable? 'Well, I have got some ideas I'd like to discuss.' Although she'd much rather discuss them when Charles was actually speaking to her.

'Oh God,' said Annabelle with an exasperated sigh. 'Your ideas are so expensive. I spent a fortune the other day.'

Flora gave a tense little smile. Annabelle had asked Flora to help her with her clothes, and she herself had donated two very expensive pairs of knickers to the cause. 'You have to speculate in order to accumulate,' she said, more breezily than she felt. 'So, when can we have our talk?'

Charles glanced at his watch. 'I have to go over to a farm a bit later. If we're quick, we can do it now.' The heat in his expression made it very clear to Flora that if she said anything he didn't agree with, he'd be down on her more heavily than the office ceiling had been.

Annabelle smoothed down her new top, revealing a well-defined waist. 'I wish you wouldn't do those farm sales! They're so dreary! All that plastic binder twine and fertiliser sacks, and there's never anything remotely valuable in the house.'

'Annabelle, you're going to love my idea.' Flora took hold of Annabelle's arm, prepared to bully her even more thoroughly than she'd bullied her before. If Charles was more set against her than ever, Annabelle was her last hope.

'Let's talk about it in the boardroom,' said Charles, sounding impatient, and led the way to the room where Flora had been interviewed what seemed like a lifetime ago.

'I thought,' said Flora, anxious to cut to the chase and wondering if Charles would let on that she'd told him her plans already, 'that if we had our own antiques road-shows, got people to bring in their forgotten treasures for a valuation, they might be willing to sell them some-times. It would get a better class of item to the auctions.'

'Flora, that's such a romantic idea!' For 'romantic' Annabelle really meant 'ridiculous'. 'What you'd really get is hundreds of people with car-boot finds and Barbie dolls without their boxes, wondering if they're collec-tors' items yet.'

Flora had watched enough afternoon television shows to know this was true. 'Well, yes, there would be a bit of that, of course, but it would raise our profile.'

'But if we got any amount of people, they'd be queuing

for hours,' went on Annabelle. 'Charles is the only one who can do valuations. I'm not qualified.' She managed to say this with the air of someone who declares they don't smoke, or drink, or anything else dubious but fun.

'On the other hand,' said Charles, carefully addressing Annabelle rather than Flora, 'I suppose I could ask Bob Butler – he's been an auctioneer for years – if he'd help.'

'Why would he do that?' demanded Annabelle. 'He hasn't retired yet has he? Although he's about a hundred. We're in direct competition.'

Charles hesitated before answering. 'There's something else we need to talk about, darling. Flora and I had a discussion.'

If he was calling it that, he couldn't be referring to their row, thought Flora with some relief.

'As I said, if Flora's involved it'll be expensive,' repeated Annabelle, as if to make quite sure Charles saw her as an extravagant dilettante who was bound to cost the firm money.

'Or, a much cheaper idea, we could ask Geoffrey to help with the valuations,' suggested Flora, biting her lip.

'But he's just a porter!' protested Annabelle.

'Not "just a porter",' Flora contradicted her. 'He used to be a dealer and is extremely knowledgeable.'

Charles pursed his lips, clearly reluctant to agree with anything Flora said. 'If we used Geoffrey, we could get going on the roadshows right away,' he conceded reluctantly.

'Well, if you insist on employing him full time, he might as well do something for his money,' said Annabelle.

'So you think the roadshows are a good idea?' If she

hadn't still been reeling from her row with Charles she might have clapped her hands with glee.

'How would they work, exactly?' asked Annabelle, oozing scepticism.

'Well,' said Flora, 'we'd rent a room somewhere, if we weren't in Bishopsbridge, advertise, and people would flock to us with their valuables, which we would then sell.'

'I think "flock" might be putting it a bit strongly, Flora,' said Charles.

'Oh. Well, yes. I suppose it's the television that brings all those people.' She fell silent, but the word 'television' had lodged itself in her brain. No idea concerning it had come to her immediately, but she was prepared to be patient.

'It's not a bad idea, I suppose,' said Annabelle.

'Flora also wanted to discuss rethinking the buildings,' said Charles, apparently leaping in to prevent Annabelle thinking any good of Flora.

'What do you mean?' Annabelle suddenly sat up very straight.

'Flora thinks we should sell the house and use the money to put some capital into the business.'

Annabelle was silent for a few moments. 'Of course, I can see that having this whole house for just the office does seem a bit wasteful, but there is Charles's flat at the top.'

'Or we could divide it up into flats and he could keep it. Anyway, why does he need a flat? You live together.'

'That's Annabelle's house,' said Charles firmly. 'I like to have somewhere that's mine.'

'If we did that,' said Annabelle, who hadn't noticed

Charles's statement, 'we could buy another house and do the same thing. Bishopsbridge is such an up and coming town – practically commuting distance from London, the music festival—'

'I thought we should invest the money in the business, the auction business,' snapped Flora.

Annabelle took a sharp breath. 'Which would just be throwing good money after bad. It's about time you faced that. There's no money in auctioneering.'

'There isn't a lot of money, I admit,' said Charles, forced to come over to Flora's side. 'But we employ a lot of people and the hall is used by all of the local community, in one way or another.'

'Oh, wake up and smell the coffee, Charles! You can't really keep a failing business going just because a few old-age pensioners and children use the hall! That building would be worth an absolute fortune if it was divided up and sold off! It would raise even more money than this house would.'

Flora opened her mouth to wonder how many flats in large houses a town like Bishopsbridge really needed, but closed it again. This was between Charles and Annabelle.

'Stanza and Stanza is a very old, established business, and while I'm prepared to consider selling this house, or dividing it into flats to raise capital, I am not even going to think about selling the hall and converting that to flats.'

'Well, I think you're mad. You're letting sentiment rule you,' said Annabelle.

'I'm sorry you think that, but I'm not budging on this one.'

The two confronted each other. Flora felt she should have left the room a few minutes before, but was far too interested to do anything of the kind. Now she let them stare at each other for a few moments before clearing her throat.

'Well,' she said. 'We could have the first roadshow without having to sell anything. An ad in the paper isn't going to break the bank, is it?'

'I suppose not,' said Annabelle.

'And nor would getting a website,' Flora added, while the going was good.

Annabelle turned to Flora. 'Haven't you got any money you could invest in the business? After all, it's half yours.'

'I'm afraid not.' She didn't think now was the time to remind Annabelle that she owned slightly more than half.

'What about your father, couldn't you ask him for some?'

Flora was outraged. 'No, I could not! I've just become an heiress, for goodness' sake! I'm not going to ask Dad if he could put money into a business which should jolly well be able to afford to pay to market itself!'

'Oh,' said Annabelle. 'I know for a fact that if I asked my father for a bit of capital he'd be only too keen to let me have it.'

'Well, I'm thrilled for you, Annabelle,' said Flora, still furious. 'But I'm still not going to ask him.'

'So we'll go ahead with the roadshow idea,' said Charles, attempting to smooth things over. 'Flora, you write the advertisement and I'll speak to Geoffrey about helping with the valuations.'

'And Bob Butler?' asked Flora. 'In case he was willing to help, too?'

'I hardly think that will be necessary, Flora,' said Annabelle nastily. 'It'll only be two damaged Staffordshire figurines and a fake Steiff bear.'

Flora pulled back her lips in a fake grin. She would get people there in their hundreds, if she had to sell her body to do it!

'Well,' said Charles tensely, looking at his watch. 'I must go.'

When the two women were left alone, Annabelle said, 'I'm really looking forward to your dinner party. Have you got a date yet?'

Flora couldn't believe the way Annabelle changed track so fast. 'I need to check when Emma can come down,' she said cautiously.

'And have you found out anything else about that man? Why he was in your garden?'

'Actually, I have! Well, I was right – he's a friend of Emma's from university. She told him where I was and he came to look me up, only of course I wasn't in.'

'But he didn't leave a note or anything. I checked.'

'No. Emma explained he couldn't find anything to write with, or something.' Flora regarded Annabelle firmly. 'It wasn't as if he was in the house, or anything.'

'No,' Annabelle admitted. 'Have you seen him again?'

'He's gone away, but he should be back for the dinner party.'

'Oh good.'

'But I must get a dining table before then.'

'I'll see to it,' said Annabelle. 'And did Charles ask if he could invite Jeremy?'

'Yes, but I'm not sure—'

'Good.' She smiled, suddenly refreshingly girlish. 'I must think what to wear for it.'

'What? The reunion?'

Annabelle's forehead wrinkled a little. 'Oh yes! I must think what to wear for that. But the dinner party comes first.'

Flora nodded vaguely. Either she or Annabelle seemed to be losing the plot a bit, and she had a horrid suspicion it was her.

The next fortnight flew by. The kittens seemed to grow daily and would be killing their own prey and dragging it back to the lair any day now. And Flora'd been for drinks with Henry twice after work. The more she saw of him the more she liked him, although in spite of his obvious attractions – and he was a very attractive man – Flora wasn't convinced there was sufficient spark between them for it ever to be much more than a bit of fun. And she was pretty sure he felt the same. He was always wildly flirtatious and certainly quite persistent, flatteringly persistent in fact, but she thought it more than likely that he was like that with a lot of women, which was a relief, in a way. But she'd played it safe by always keeping things low-key: she'd refused all his dinner invitations, sticking to casual drinks and suppers in the pub where she could pay for herself and it didn't feel too much like a date. The last thing she needed was him misreading her signals. Plus, if she was really honest with herself, the degree to which her appearing to date Henry annoyed Charles was part of the pleasure of seeing him.

Charles, unfortunately, had still not forgiven Flora. The little glimpses of a nicer, more human Charles she'd seen at the auction and at the valuation had completely disappeared. Or they disappeared the moment Flora walked into the room, anyway. He only spoke to her when absolutely forced to either by extreme necessity or politeness – he was always icily, meticulously polite – and so Flora, inexperienced as she was, was reduced to trying to organise the roadshow pretty much single-handed. If they'd actually been on speaking terms she might have been able to persuade herself that his leaving her to it was a gesture of faith, but as things were it was quite clear that he wanted her – expected her – to fail. Worst of all, Flora was feeling horribly guilty about everything she'd said in their row. How could she have thrown the fact of her owning more shares at him? It was a terrible, childish thing to have said and Flora felt desperately ashamed of herself.

And now the dinner party loomed. The date was set, although Emma was still not definitely coming.

Flora was writing Emma another begging email from the office computer when Annabelle who, self-involved as she was, had remained blissfully unaware of the tension between her fiancé and his cousin, came into the room.

'You type awfully fast! No one told me you could do that.'

'No I don't! I'm not typing! I'm just exercising my fingers. It's good for the nails.' Flora checked her nails to see if in fact they'd survived her flurry on the keyboard.

'Oh, Flora! You're so vain!' said Annabelle, pleasingly

gullible. 'I just came to remind you to write the advert for the paper about the roadshow. They have to have it in by today, or it won't make this week's paper. Charles and I decided that Wednesday the week after next would be good. Almost two weeks' notice should be enough, don't you think? Do you think we'll need the big hall? Or just the small one at the back, where the playgroup is? If so, we need to tell them.'

'Don't they meet on Wednesdays then?'

'Oh yes, every day, unless there's a sale on. This would count as a sale. It's in their lease that they can't use that room if we need it.'

Flora thought of all the mothers and children who would be inconvenienced if they couldn't go to play-group and said, more grandly than she felt, 'Oh, we'll definitely need the big hall. No one uses that on a Wednesday, do they?'

'Not during the day, no. But that shouldn't make any difference. We own the hall. We should use the space we need.'

'You seem quite keen on the idea, anyway,' said Flora, pleased that her idea had proved popular even if it was unacknowledged as hers.

'Quite keen' wasn't part of Annabelle's vocabulary when connected to the auction house but she shrugged. 'Well, you never know. Doesn't hurt to try. Don't suppose many people will come.'

'I'd better get on to it,' said Flora. She turned away from Annabelle and laboriously started a new document. When she was alone again she thought guiltily about the advertisement she had already written and dispatched to every local newspaper in the county. She had also made posters which she had gone round the town begging shops to display. She was determined to fill that hall with people desperate to sell their family heirlooms.

Her phone rang as she drove back home. She knew it was Emma without even looking, and pulled into a convenient lay-by to answer it. The reception was better there, anyway. Emma was initially full of reasons why it was out of the question for her to come and stay the weekend after next, but eventually she said, 'Sounds quite fun, anyway. Dave won't like it when I tell him he's not invited.'

'It'll do him good for you to do something on your own for a change,' suggested Flora hopefully.

'Mm,' said Emma. 'I wonder what I should wear.'

'I wonder what I should cook!'

'Oh, don't worry about that yet. It's a fortnight away. But clothes – they take thinking about.'

It occurred to Flora, as she made the rest of the journey home, that country life had already changed her. Not long ago she'd have shared Emma's priorities. But not long ago she had shared Emma's access to wonderful little shops that sold food it was easy to pass off as home-made. Down here, 'entertaining-lite' was not an option. Here it would have to be hard-core cooking.

When she got home, she rang Henry. He'd left two messages on her phone and she wanted to ask him to the dinner party. He'd be jolly, open the wine, see everyone was happy and if Charles didn't like it, well, too bad.

'Hello, you,' he said when he heard her voice.

'Hello, you, too,' she said, smiling. He had a nice voice and was soothingly non-confrontational.

'Do you fancy coming out for a drink?'

'I'd love a drink. I need some cheerful company. It's been so hectic at work lately.'

'Well, why not make it dinner, then?'

'Oh, I'm glad you mentioned dinner,' Flora replied, gaily side-stepping the invitation. 'I want to invite you to come to a dinner party at mine. The weekend after next.' She crossed her fingers.

'Oh Flora, I'm going to be away.'

Flora's heart sank. 'How can you be away? Can't you change it?'

Henry chuckled. 'I'm afraid not, but I could take you out to dinner tonight, instead.'

'That is not at all the same thing!' Flora said grumpily, knowing she was being unreasonable.

'No. It's better from my point of view.'

Flora suddenly felt very tired. 'Are you sure you can't come to my dinner party?'

'Quite sure. Big meeting in Switzerland; I can't possibly miss it, or change it. I am sorry.' He paused. 'But I could take you out for a very nice steak and hand-cut chips.'

'It sounds very tempting, but I'm just too tired to go out tonight.'

'You weren't too tired a moment ago.'

'I know, but I am now. Can we do it tomorrow?'

'What, steak and hand-cut chips? Certainly.'

'I meant the drink. I'm better at going out if I haven't gone home first. It's like the gym.'

'What?'

'Oh, never mind. Shall I meet you in the Fox and Grapes at six?'

'Great. And I'll try and talk you into dinner, too.'

'We'll see, shall we?'

When Flora had put the phone down she wondered if her reluctance to have dinner with Henry was her subconsciously punishing him for not coming to her dinner party. But then she decided she didn't have enough emotional energy for a deeper relationship just now. He was good company, though, and it was lovely to spend time with someone who didn't disapprove of her all the time.

Flora hadn't envisaged life in the country being quite so busy, but now she was wondering how she was going to get everything done, what with choir rehearsals, Henry, and everything that needed doing at work – which included a little light decorating. She did it after work one evening, very carefully.

Charles caught her yawning, the morning after she'd stayed on into the evening to redecorate, and said sourly, 'Henry keeping you up late, is he?'

Flora delivered a very sarcastic smile but said nothing, perversely pleased that he hadn't noticed either the repaired ceiling or the paint on her nails.

Choir had suddenly sprung voice tests on everyone, too. Geoffrey had to physically drag Flora to the rehearsal they were taking place in.

'Every choir has to do this from time to time,' he insisted. 'It's only sensible. It'll be very low key. James won't make you do anything terrifying, honestly.'

Although she wasn't asked to leave (in fact her small but tuneful voice received a grave compliment from James), Flora's palms sweated for days afterwards, just thinking about it.

If it hadn't been for William, who had come back to his place on the sofa, Imelda and the kittens would have almost been neglected. The following Friday Flora went home, planning to have a very quiet weekend – organising the roadshow all by herself on top of everything else had left her exhausted – refusing even a Sunday lunchtime drink with Henry. She would do a little light gardening if the weather held, lots of reading and have plenty of little naps.

Geoffrey had other ideas. He rang her up on Saturday night.

'There's a good car-boot sale on tomorrow.'

'Is there?' Flora said without much enthusiasm.

'Edie and I are going and we're planning to take you.'

'Are you?' Flora was still a novice at country life but even she knew that car-boot sales started very early and that Geoffrey would probably want to be one of the first people there.

'Can you get here by seven? We'll go in my car.'

Flora felt even more exhausted just thinking about it. 'Geoffrey, I'm awfully tired. I was hoping to have a lie-in. Sleep a little,' she added, in case the concept of staying in bed was so foreign to him that he didn't know the jargon.

'It's a valuable part of your training, young woman. There'll never be time for me to teach you much when there's a sale on. A car boot, a good one, is a very good place for you to get your eye in. We might even buy some things for the next auction. Make a bit of money.'

Flora sighed deeply. 'OK. At your house, at seven. Tomorrow. Sunday morning. When every sensible person is asleep.'

Flora went to bed extremely early, leaving William washing up downstairs – as the weather was still fine he planned to go and sleep in the woods later. Flora no longer cared what he did. Although mostly she was grateful for his company and more so for his cooking, part of her felt he had unwittingly caused her a lot of work. If Annabelle hadn't spotted his naked antics, Flora might not be contemplating a dinner with a lot of people she didn't know, without a dining table.

Chapter Eleven

On Sunday morning Flora dragged herself out of bed at six o'clock and saw that the weather had changed. Instead of the misty dawns that had lit her little garden, the fields and woods beyond with the promise of gold, it was cloudy and looked as if it would rain. She decided to wear jeans and a pair of loafers. Car-boot sales were bound to involve a lot of walking.

'How are the kittens?' asked Edie, the moment she saw Flora. 'Have they opened their eyes yet?'

'Yes. They're quite wide open now, but to begin with they were just little black slits. The book said it would happen at about twelve days and I was terribly worried they wouldn't open them on time' – Flora, listening to herself, had a sudden flash of how neurotic mothers felt – 'but then I woke up one morning and there they were, squinting at me. They're very sweet. You must come and see them.'

'It must be a worry for you, having to leave them alone all day.'

'Mm. It is a bit. But Imelda's a very good mother. She goes straight back to them the moment one of them squeaks.' While she wasn't lying to Edie, really, she felt dishonest, and hoped, once the dinner party was over, that she could be more honest about William's presence and role as co-carer for Imelda.

'Stop gossiping, you two, and get in the car,' said Geoffrey.

'Flora was telling me about the kittens,' said Edie.

'But if you want real gossip, have you heard about the roadshow?' Flora clambered into the back of the car.

'No. What's a roadshow?' asked Geoffrey.

'I can't believe Charles hasn't told you!' she said, when she'd explained. 'You're going to be one of the valuers! Charles said so.'

'Really! I bet that didn't please her ladyship,' said Edie.

'Well, no,' Flora admitted. 'But she did say it would make Geoffrey better value for money and that we probably wouldn't get many people. I think we might, though. I've already got Virginia's daughter to put an ad on the web somehow, as well as to make us a website of our own.'

'Hm. I expect that's a good idea,' said Geoffrey, sounding dubious.

'Oh, it is. Trust me. And can you stop at a cashpoint machine? I need some money if I'm going to buy anything.'

Flora tapped in her pin number and waited for a balance, trying to remember which day of the month her tenants paid their rent. She had deliberately made it a few days before her standing order to her parents went out. When her balance came up on the screen she frowned and decided she needed to have it printed. Apparently she was within a whisker of exceeding her overdraft limit. How had that happened when she had hardly had a moment to breathe, let alone spend money?

Aware of Geoffrey and Edie waiting for her in the car, she couldn't make major financial decisions immediately, and just took out the thirty pounds that she had left before incurring massive charges. When the ATM obligingly gave Flora her card back, she murmured a heartfelt 'Thank you' under her breath. Only when she was confronted by the news in print did she remember how near her limit she had been when she first came down here. That little spending spree with Annabelle had taken her dangerously near the edge of poverty.

She got back in the car with a sunny smile to cover her dismay. Then she started making frantic plans and rejecting them all, equally frantically. The first, to find something wonderful for nothing at the car-boot sale and put it into the next auction was fine, except there wasn't a sale for some time. It was a long-term plan. Putting up the rent on her flat didn't seem like an option, either. Emptying the contents of the holiday cottage and taking it along to the car-boot sale to see how much she could get for it wouldn't work because she couldn't fit it all in the Land-Rover and the stuff was mostly Annabelle's anyway. Her last idea, which seemed the most impossible, the most unacceptable, was apparently her only option. She would have to ask Charles for the wages she would have earned had she really been an office assistant. He'd said himself that they were crap, but they would have to do.

If it wasn't for the dinner party, she wouldn't have been so worried. Flora bit her lip. 'I wonder if Mum's got a recipe for rabbit she could give me?' she wondered aloud.

'What's that, dear?' asked Edie from the front of the car. 'Did you say something?'

'No, nothing really. I was just wondering how far away we were.'

'Not long now. You don't feel sick, do you?'

Flora did, a bit, but she didn't think it was anything to do with the motion of the car. 'I'm fine,' she said breezily, feeling anything but.

'It's obviously a popular boot sale,' said Geoffrey as they glided to a halt behind the last car in a long string of traffic. 'The change in the weather hasn't put people off.'

'It's not actually raining,' said Edie. 'That does deter them a bit.'

'Well, I hope it's not all just housewives clearing out their bits and pieces,' said Geoffrey.

'What's wrong with that?' asked Flora.

'Nothing wrong with it in itself,' Geoffrey amended, sensing Flora's defence of people wanting to declutter. 'But they tend to have modern stuff, not anything with any antique value. You want the small-time dealers for that, people who pick stuff up at jumble sales for a few pennies and are happy to sell it on for a couple of pounds.'

Edie sighed. 'Geoffrey says all these programmes about antiques are spoiling it for the professionals. Everyone knows to look on the bottom of things to check for hallmarks and makers' names.'

As those very programmes were the source of what little knowledge Flora had, she didn't reply.

The airfield was already bustling with activity by the time they had finally parked the car and walked the long distance to where the action was. 'We have to be methodical,' said Geoffrey. 'Make sure we visit every stall.'

'Good thing I put on comfortable shoes,' muttered Flora, suddenly wishing she could go back to bed.

The first stall they reached was a burger van selling coffee and tea as well as hot food.

'Let's have a cup of tea now,' said Edie. 'We can drink it while we look.'

Geoffrey shook his head. 'You can't have a good root through a box if you're holding a cup of coffee.'

'Well, Flora and I will have a cup and you can do what you think best. I know I need a cup of something.'

Geoffrey made a growling noise, but when Edie got to the front of the queue and looked enquiringly at him, he nodded. Flora was very grateful for her cup of tea. Her anxiety about money was colouring her enjoyment of the day out, and she hoped the tea might help.

'Now come along, Flora,' said Geoffrey, halfway down his cup of tea. 'You're here for your education.'

Flora wandered over to where a cheerful-looking woman stood behind a table selling, among other things, a climbing frame and a skateboard. Reluctantly, Geoffrey followed.

'Those ramekin dishes look useful,' she said to him.

'Ten pence each,' said the woman quickly. 'There are six.'

'Sixty pence for six ramekin dishes!' said Flora, fishing for her purse. 'That's a bargain!'

'What do you want those for?' asked Geoffrey. 'You can't sell them on at the auction.'

'I know, but I've got people coming to dinner. Almost anything looks better in a little dish, doesn't it, Edie?'

Edie was inspecting an electric grilling machine advertised by a boxer and didn't answer.

'Well, I like food in proper dishes,' grumbled Geoffrey, and moved on.

Flora paid for the dishes, put them in her bag and hurried to catch Geoffrey up. Already she was feeling better as her first little hit of retail therapy took effect.

Then she spotted the most wonderful teapot. She'd almost forgotten about her collection of novelty teapots, which she'd started when she was twelve, and now rarely added to. But this was perfect! It was supposed to be a ball of wool. A coil of it was used to form a base for the pot, the handle was the sleeve of a half-knitted jumper, and the spout was the other half. It was studded with kittens, clawing their way over the wool in a way that was so delightfully vulgar Flora knew that money shortage, or no money shortage, she had to have it.

'Look!' she called to Geoffrey as Edie, who would have appreciated it more, had gone off in search of plants.

Reluctantly, he came back and saw what she was exclaiming over with such pleasure. 'Hm, not bad. There's a market for kitsch. How much?' he asked the vendor, a businesslike young woman who was mostly selling children's toys.

'That's ten pounds. It's a genuine Carter.'

Geoffrey sucked his teeth. 'Ooh, I doubt that it is. Doesn't have the quality. I'll give you three for it.'

'Sorry. Can't do that.'

'Four pounds?'

She shook her head again. Geoffrey sighed and pulled

a five-pound note out of his pocket. 'Here you are then. Call it a deal.' He handed the note to the woman in such a way that she had to accept it.

She sighed, picked up the teapot and started wrapping it in newspaper. 'You've robbed me, but it's not to everyone's taste, I don't suppose.'

Geoffrey handed Flora the teapot as they walked away. 'Here you are.'

'Hang on, I've got a five-pound note here,' she began.

'Nonsense. It's a present. On a good day it could fetch fifteen quid at auction.'

'Oh, I want to keep it! I collect teapots. Thank you so much.' Privately the thought of how much Charles would hate it made her quite skippy inside.

'It's a pleasure. But I do think you should consider selling it next time we have a sale.'

Flora stood by Geoffrey as he went through boxes of old tools. She was watching the groups of people as they inspected the bottoms of pots, no doubt still hoping to find an undiscovered Clarice Cliff. Clothes fluttered on rails and she wondered if her own clothes would fetch enough to make any difference to her financial state. While Geoffrey's attention was elsewhere, she took the opportunity to inspect the nearest rail. She found a dark brown suede skirt.

'How much for this?' she asked the stallholder, a young woman who had two small children with her and was obviously not entirely focused.

'Oh, I don't know. Make me an offer.' She looked longingly at the skirt in Flora's hand. 'I loved that skirt. I just don't think I'll ever fit into it again.'

'Of course you will!' said Flora, who instantly rejected

the idea of buying it now she knew it was so precious to its owner.

'Give you a couple of quid for it,' said another woman, who obviously lacked not only Flora's sensitive nature, but also her figure.

The young woman started to take the skirt off its hanger. 'No!' Flora interrupted quickly. 'I'll give you a fiver.'

The young mother looked hopefully at the woman who had offered two pounds.

'No way,' she said disgustedly and moved away.

'She wouldn't have got into it,' muttered Flora, watching her move through the crowd.

'She'd sell it on,' said the skirt's owner. 'Do you really want it for a fiver? I'd like you to have it. I wouldn't feel so bad about selling it if I knew it was going to a good home.'

Flora found her purse again, cursing her sentimental nature. The ramekins she could justify, but spending five pounds on a skirt she didn't really need, when she was so broke, was just silly. Perhaps she would have to put her teapot into the next sale.

'I don't think I'll bother to sell my clothes,' said Flora as she caught up with Geoffrey, forgetting he was unaware of her financial straits. 'I wouldn't get much for them.'

'Why would you want to?' he asked.

'Oh, I was just wondering, you know, what I might get for them.'

'I think you'd be better off buying than selling, if it's clothes you're interested in. What have you got there?' He indicated the plastic bag containing the skirt.

'Oh, a dear little skirt. It was only a fiver.'

'A fiver! You were robbed, my dear. Did you haggle?'

'Er . . . not really,' Flora admitted. 'I thought it was a good price.'

'You should always haggle. I could have got that for you for no more than a couple of quid.'

'Oh.' Flora smiled, feeling foolish. It wasn't that the skirt wasn't worth what she'd paid for it, it was just that she was unlikely to want to wear it before the autumn and it had cost a sixth of all the money she had in the world at that particular moment. 'I felt sorry for the woman,' she said quietly.

'You're daft, you are,' said Geoffrey. 'Now come along and I'll show you how it's done. There's a tool stall up there. Some of them sell very well at auction, and the sellers aren't always so aware of what's valuable. Ceramics, collectables, people know can be worth a bit. There won't be the margin in it.'

Geoffrey and Flora walked slowly along the tables. Although Geoffrey was looking for tools he allowed Flora to pick up things and examine them. Some things seemed to be wildly overpriced to Flora, but she had learnt her lesson and didn't let herself get involved with the sellers. 'Who wants an old Tressy doll with no hair?' she asked Geoffrey when they were out of earshot of her owner.

'Some little girl with a few pennies to spend. But if she was in good condition, with her box, she'd be worth money.'

'And what about those ghastly china ornaments?'

'The little ones probably aren't worth a lot, but some of those big heavy horses will fetch quite a bit. They have to be undamaged, though. Ah, here we are.'

Finding herself quite unable to be interested in a jumble of carpenters' tools, old planes, files, chisels and saws, Flora had a little wander on her own. Her mind was not on the job. She was supposed to be learning her craft but she was too concerned with her financial situation at the moment. Her parents wouldn't let her or Imelda starve, but ever since she'd left home Flora had been extremely independent and wouldn't take subsidies, except in the form of the fare to whatever country her parents were residing in and, of course, free board and lodging while she was there.

Determined to snap out of her despondent and unhelpful mood she went over to yet another stall run by a young woman who looked vaguely familiar and also rather despondent. She was selling children's toys and clothes, some handbags and a few bags of cakes. She was perched on the tailgate of her car and perked up a little when Flora approached.

'It's Flora, isn't it? I'm Amy, from the choir. Alto.'

'Hello! I thought you looked familiar,' said Flora. 'Do you do this often?'

'Never by myself before. I'm hopeless at it and I forgot to bring anything to eat or drink.'

'Well, I could go and get you something, if you liked.'

'No, it's all right. I'll manage. It's really the chance to have a wander round that I'm missing.'

Flora glanced up and down the aisle of tables and spotted Geoffrey, deep in conversation with someone. Edie, miles away, appeared to have bought a tree. 'Well, if you like, I could mind your stall while you have a look. My friends – oh, it's Geoffrey and Edie – they seem occupied and wouldn't mind if I was here for a little while. Of course, you don't really know me. You might not trust me.'

'Of course I trust you!' The young woman became enthusiastic. 'Would you mind? I find selling terribly difficult. I'm only here because there are a few things we must make space for, and if my friend had come with me, we'd have made a bit of money. Enough to buy a bit more stuff with, anyway.'

'I thought the idea was to make space, not fill it.'

'It is. It's just different space. Would you really mind my stall for a bit?'

'Sure.' The saleswoman in Flora awoke. Amy would never sell anything as things were, she needed a bit more enthusiasm for the task. 'Would you mind if I played with the things? I'd quite like to test my selling ability. I want to know if I could ever have a stall at a car-boot sale myself.'

Amy shrugged. 'Help yourself. I've hardly sold anything so far.'

'You go off then and I'll see if I can sell anything for you. What about prices?'

'Oh, just get what you can for it. I'm hopeless about prices.' Amy hitched her bag over her shoulder and, looking far more cheerful, set off into the crowd.

Flora set to work, using skills developed during a holiday job in Bond Street when she'd worked for a friend of her mother's.

She took the toys out of their plastic bags and grouped them together in a way that made them look as if they were already being played with. She forced the Barbies to sit around under a toy umbrella, with outsize cans of lemonade in their hands. A teddy bear she made read a book, miniature to a child, enormous for the teddy. A tea set was set out with plastic cakes and hot dogs and a toy cart was filled with two plastic apples. Everything was the wrong scale, but Flora still enjoyed herself.

Once the toys were dealt with, she turned her attention to the handbags. Under the dust, she discovered that a couple of them were very good makes. She found the napkin she'd been given with her cup of tea and wiped them down. Then she plumped them up and made a little display of them. Everything that was for sale was regrouped, rearranged and made to look more appealing.

Her first customer was Geoffrey. 'What are you doing here? I only left you alone for a minute.'

'This is Amy's stall. From choir? She asked me to mind it while she had a cup of coffee and a look round. I thought it would be good practice for me, selling stuff.'

'I have no doubts about your selling abilities, dear. It's whether you know tat from quality that I'm concerned with.'

'Oh, don't worry about that now. I've got plenty of time to learn all that stuff. You go and see if you can pick up some bargains while I look after the stall.'

She didn't want any witnesses to her barrow-boy antics, that's if she had the nerve to perform them.

Flora decided to target the buyers rather than depend on what she was selling to attract them. She spotted a father with two little girls. He was obviously entertaining them while his wife got on with things at home.

Flora came out from behind her stall and said hello to the little girls. 'Do you like Barbies?'

'We have a million Barbie dolls at home,' said the father, looking weary.

'But have you got these Barbies?' Flora decided that flirting was allowed when she was doing it to help someone, and smiled. 'They're extra special and an absolute bargain. Look, they're having a picnic,' she turned her attention to the girls again. 'Fifty pence each. The food is extra,' she added, glancing up at the father with a sideways grin.

'Oh, Daddy! Can we?'

'It's up to you. You've got your own money to spend.'

Flora handed over three Barbie dolls for one pound fifty pence, hoping she hadn't sold them far too cheaply. 'And do you need the food as well? Look, you get all this too.' She shook the plastic bag that contained the more battered toy boxes and tins of groceries. 'Twenty pence. Now, what about the picnic set? Then you could have a big party, with all your dolls.'

Having screwed every penny out of the two little girls, but given them, in her opinion, very good value for their money, she turned her attention to their dad.

'What about a nice bag for your wife? This one is a very good name. Not quite Prada, but getting there. You have heard of Prada, have you? No? Obviously a serious-minded person, but let me assure you, your wife has heard of Prada, and a bag like this, while obviously not Prada, or it would be worth about a million pounds . . . '

The words poured out of her. She smiled, she flirted, she made him laugh, and by the time he'd gone away he was laden with plastic carriers of toys, a handbag, and a set of Mr Men books. Although fairly satisfied,

Flora was disappointed that she hadn't managed to convince him that a rabbit hutch was a pleasing garden ornament, even if you hadn't got, and didn't want, a rabbit.

She was just counting the money she'd made, hoping Amy wouldn't be furious with her for selling so much so cheaply, when a man came up and asked about the rabbit hutch. 'How much for the hutch, love?'

'Twenty pounds.'

'I'll give you five.'

'Five pounds! Are you trying to rob me? Do you know how much they are new?' As Flora didn't know this herself, she was rather hoping he'd tell her.

'I don't want a new rabbit hutch. It's only for my ferrets. Five pounds. All it's worth to me.'

'Fifteen then. I'm practically giving it away.'

'Six pounds, that's my absolute top offer.'

'Twelve. Cheap at twice the price.'

'Ten. And I'm being robbed. I could keep them in an old crate for nothing.'

'But then they'd escape. Ten pounds is fine. Thank you very much.'

'I've had a brilliant time,' said Flora, when Amy came back. 'But I expect I've sold everything far too cheaply.'

'You've sold it, that's the main thing. And that looks like loads of money.'

'A fiver of it is mine, I'm afraid. I sold a very nice suede skirt I'd bought by mistake.' She frowned slightly. 'I hope the man was right, and his wife was a size ten.'

Once back at the cottage, when she'd seen to her brood and shown them the teapot, which now had pride of place on the mantelpiece, Flora lay on the sofa, contemplating the prospect of a dinner party with no money. Having too little money to buy posh ready meals was bad enough, but barely having enough to buy basic ingredients was worse. The rain was pouring down outside and, she reflected, a less buoyant personality than her own could get pretty miserable.

William came in through the back door, shaking his hair, sending water flying off him. 'I'll sleep here tonight if you don't mind, Flora.'

'Don't blame you. The kittens are so adorable! I could hardly bear to leave them. Go up and look.'

'I will in a minute. Tea?'

'I'm already on the wine, I'm afraid. What am I going to feed these people on, William? I've hardly any money.'

'Vegetarian then. Far cheaper.'

'But I don't know how to cook any vegetarian dishes. Isn't it all goats' cheese and aubergines and that bean curd stuff?'

'Tofu? Not necessarily, but aubergines are good.'

Flora winced at the thought. She felt too tired to think about big shiny vegetables she never knew what to do with. Didn't they require something complicated to do with salt? 'I'll see if I can get some recipes off the computer.'

'I could cook for you,' William offered amiably.

Flora opened her eyes. 'Could you?'

'I've worked as a chef and I used to cook in the Buddhist centre where I lived for a while. Vegetarian dishes are my speciality.'

'That would be fantastic! But wouldn't it look a little

odd, you doing the cooking? Did I tell you that you have to pretend to be Emma's partner?'

'No! Why do I have to do that? Why can't I just be another friend?'

'Because where would you sleep?'

'On the sofa, where I always sleep.'

'Yes, but no one's supposed to know that! And although I could put a guest up, I suppose, you're meant to be Emma's partner, calling on me, while I'm down here!'

William frowned. 'This is all far too complicated.'

'I've got to explain your presence somehow, for your sake as much as anything.'

'It would be much better if I were just Emma's friend. Far less complicated.'

Flora thought about this. Having a handsome, heterosexual male as a regular caller was not going to do her any good in the eyes of Charles and Annabelle. 'You wouldn't pretend to be gay?'

'No.'

'There's no stigma—'

'No, Flora. I'll be pretend to be Emma – is it Emma? – Emma's old friend from university, who she got back in touch with, and told that you were living down here and didn't know anybody.'

Flora nodded slowly. 'That could work. That could explain why you were doing t'ai chi naked on the lawn. Emma doesn't know you very well and you've changed over the years.'

'That part at least is true,' he said with a grin. 'I'll have a think about what to cook and give you a shopping list.'

'And I'll make chocolate mousse for pudding. I can use my new ramekin dishes. Oh, and I must ring Henry. I'm still hoping he'll cancel his conference in Switzerland and come.'

But Henry resisted all blandishments.

Chapter Twelve

'I can't believe you've joined a choir!' said Emma as Flora drove her back from the station on Friday evening. 'It's such a – well – you know . . .'

'What?' asked Flora defensively.

'"Old person" thing to do.'

'Nonsense! I love it! It's very soothing, singing. You have to concentrate, really hard, all the time – or at least I do because I'm not very good – and that means you can't think about work. We're going to do a concert. You must come down for it. Now, how are you?'

Emma knew that this meant 'how are you and Dave?' 'Well, OK. He's just lost interest in me, I think. All the little things I do that he used to think were sweet now just irritate him.'

'Oh, I do understand! That happens to me all the time!'

'What?'

Realising that she was about to say how she got irritated by the little habits that used to enchant her, Flora hurriedly inverted her statement. 'About how they sigh when you do things wrong when they used to do them for you, in a really sweet way.'

'Exactly.'

'Well, what you need is a new man, sweetie. And I've got just the one.'

'You mean William, the naked tae kwon do expert?'

'T'ai chi. It's quite different. And he mostly wears clothes.'

'Still don't fancy it, Flo.'

'It's him you have to fancy. You probably will, no problem. He's gorgeous.'

'So why don't *you* fancy him, then?'

Flora had thought about this, and presumably so had William. 'Don't know. The chemistry's not right, I suppose. But he's really nice, funny, cooks, everything a girl wants, really.'

'Perhaps you fancy someone else. Henry?'

Flora wrinkled her nose and then remembered it would give her lines and stopped. 'Yes, I do fancy him, sort of, but not in a gut-wrenching way.'

'It doesn't always have to be gut-wrenching. It can creep up on you slowly, from behind.'

'Well, if it does, it does, but it hasn't yet, and quite honestly I have no emotional energy left to spare for a relationship, just at the moment. The business is my obsession.'

'So do you fancy your business partner, then?'

'Charles! What? No way!'

'Why not?'

'Apart from the fact that we had a blazing row, he can't wait to get rid of me and I hate his guts, you mean?'

'Never stopped anyone fancying anyone before.'

Flora laughed. 'True, but not in this case. He's too stuffy to live. I mean, when I'm not hating him, I do admire him, for the way he does his job, but definitely not the way he runs his business.' She thought for a moment. 'And he is good-looking, and I suppose his sternness could be sexy, but no!'

'Why not?'

'Come on, Em, he's spoken for, for one thing, and even if he wasn't, it would take years to get him to unbend.'

'You've always liked projects before. A challenge, someone who doesn't just fall in love with you immediately they see you. Treat her mean and keep her keen was always the way to get you interested.'

'No, it wasn't,' Flora denied, wondering if what Emma said had any truth in it. 'Anyway, Charles would be more than a project, he'd be like climbing Everest without any training. Or oxygen.'

'Hm.'

'Anyway, even if I did fancy him, which I *so* don't, he loves Annabelle. I couldn't disturb that.'

'Are you sure he's happy with Annabelle?'

Flora thought about this. 'I think so. I don't know he's not. They're very well suited and they've known each other for a long time.' Before her huge falling-out with Charles she'd probably have said that Annabelle didn't deserve him. The Charles she'd seen when Annabelle wasn't around, the Charles who was passionate and knowledgeable about his business and great with the people he employed, deserved better than a woman who wanted nothing more than to sell up and get out. And although Flora had warmed to Annabelle a bit when they went shopping together, she was still incredibly self-centred and utterly self-obsessed, which couldn't be fun to live with. But since the collapse of the ceiling, Flora rather thought they were perfect for each other:

the strict, austere Charles she saw when Annabelle was in the room was clearly the real one, and Annabelle was welcome to him!

'Sounds terribly boring,' said Emma, and Flora realised she hadn't been listening properly, off in her own little world. She laughed.

'It does, doesn't it? But I don't suppose it is really. So, let's talk about Dave or your work or something metropolitan.'

'Oh no, don't let's. I'd like to forget about Dave just for a weekend.'

Flora glanced at her friend, worried, but the look on Emma's face told her now wasn't the time. 'Fair enough. Shall we call in for some chips?'

'Haven't you prepared a gourmet meal for me on my first night with you?'

'No.'

Emma laughed. 'Chips it is then. I do miss you, Flo. I'm really looking forward to you coming back to London.'

'You'll have to ring him,' Emma insisted the next day, putting down her tea towel. 'He's your landlord and you need a dining table. Now.'

Flora smoothed on some hand-cream. She and Emma had just done the washing up after lunch and William was scooping the insides out of aubergines.

'It's Annabelle's cottage. She's responsible,' Flora pointed out.

'Ring her then! I'm sure she'd understand about having people to dinner and not having a table.'

'OK. But it'll have to be quite a big table. It'll take up all the space in the cottage.'

'Not if it folds down or has leaves or something. I don't know why you didn't get it sorted out earlier.'

'I told you, Charles and I had this awful row, and although we did both apologise, it was in that way when you know you have to say sorry, but you're not.' It had been nearly two weeks since they'd had a civil conversation.

'I do understand but we still need a table.'

'I was busy, Em! I'll do it now,' Flora snapped, feeling more harassed by the minute.

'We'd have much more room it we ate outside,' offered William. 'The rain's cleared up and it could be a really nice evening.'

'Weather wise, you mean,' said Flora, who didn't think it could possibly be nice in any other way.

'Yes. Why don't you ask your cousin—'

'His name is Charles,' said Emma, who wasn't getting on with William quite as well as Flora would have liked.

'If he's got a large picnic table we could put a bit of board on,' William went on.

'How many people are we going to be?' asked Emma.

'Only six,' said Flora. 'It's not a huge number. An ordinary table would be fine.'

'As long as it doesn't come on to rain and we have to rush indoors with it,' William explained.

'Oh no, you're right. Annabelle would freak if inside furniture got wet or anything. I'll suggest something like that,' said Flora. 'But I'll go and get it. We want to get the table set in plenty of time. If we're going to eat out it would be nice to decorate it with wild flowers and things.'

'Aren't you getting just a little too rural, Flo?' suggested Emma.

'Not at all. It's just nice to appreciate nature's bounty.'

'Pick up the phone,' ordered Emma, not impressed.

'There isn't a phone. I'll have to take my mobile outside, for the reception.'

Flora went into the front garden, glad to be on her own for a minute, but not relishing having to ring Charles. At least if she got Annabelle, she knew she'd understand the problem.

Charles answered. Although she knew he was perfectly likely to pick up the phone, hearing his voice panicked her. 'Er hello, it's me.' Flora always forgot her name when she was nervous.

'Flora,' he said.

'Yes, sorry. I'm just ringing about the table. For tonight?'

'Oh. Yes. You'll be needing one.' Flora heard Annabelle's voice in the background. Then she snatched the phone.

'Flora? What's the matter? You're not cancelling, are you?'

'No. I'm just asking if there's a table we could use. We don't want to eat on our laps.'

'Oh God, I forgot we'd sold the table. I'll organise Charles to do something about it immediately. When do you want it?'

'Well, I would like to have time to set it before you all come, but I suppose—'

'Of course you must have it sooner than that. Don't worry. Um, did your friend arrive all right?'

'Oh yes. I picked her up from the station last night.'

'And – um – the man I saw . . . ?'

In her slightly frazzled state, Flora couldn't remember

quite what she'd said to Annabelle about William, but decided to stick to William's suggestion that he was an old friend of Emma's. 'Oh yes, he's here too. He's doing the cooking.'

'OK. I'll send Charles over with the table, then.'

Now they'd convinced Flora that they couldn't possibly pass as a couple, William and Emma began to get on much better. They'd gone off to the woods together quite happily. Whether they were intending to gather the makings of a starter, Flora wasn't entirely sure. She was making chocolate mousse when Charles arrived.

She saw him drive up and went out, wiping her chocolatey hands on the tea towel she had tucked into her belt as an apron. She was in some ways relieved to see him – it would have been such a bore if they'd had no time to set the table nicely – but she wished Emma and William were here to diffuse things if it got heated.

'Hi, Charles,' she greeted him neutrally. 'This is very kind of you.'

'Not all that kind. You should have had a table all along. I'll bring it in. I've got some wine, too. Save bringing it later.'

'Lovely. Emma and William have brought some too.' A thought occurred to her. 'It's not a very precious table, is it? We thought we'd eat outside. It would be a bit cramped in the cottage for six.'

'No. It's an army surplus one. But it would have been for the officer class,' he added.

Flora was taken aback. That was definitely a joke. 'That's all right then. I wouldn't want my guests sitting at anything that wasn't worthy.' Flora smiled, deciding that as Charles was obviously making an effort at being more civil, she should too.

'Have you enough chairs? I brought a couple of plastic stacking ones, in case.'

'Chairs.' Flora mentally trawled the two bedrooms and the bathroom. 'Actually, a couple of chairs would be very useful, thank you,' she added, making proper eye contact for the first time since the fight.

'Where are your other guests?'

'In the woods. Picking something, probably. I hope you like nettles.'

'Oh, absolutely. My favourite.'

'You think I'm joking, but I'm not,' she said solemnly.

He nodded, equally serious. 'Flora . . .' He looked oddly embarrassed for a moment. 'I've also got a cheque here for your back wages. If you give me your bank details we can do it by standing order in future.'

Flora regarded him quizzically. That was definitely the last thing she'd expected, but maybe he was as daunted as her by the idea of a hideously uncomfortable evening, and was trying to engineer some kind of truce. 'You've forgiven me for pulling the ceiling down, then?'

Again, he looked a little shame-faced. 'You did put it up again, very neatly. And while I do think you're a liability, you're quite a hard-working liability, and deserve to be paid something, even the pathetic wages we're offering. And . . .' He paused again, clearly feeling awkward. 'And Geoffrey said something to me.'

Flora flushed. She wasn't entirely sure she wanted to be the subject of discussions between Geoffrey and Charles.

'He said there were relatively few people who'd give up a job in London to come and work for the minimum wage in a small business in a small town, and we were lucky to have you – and to be honest it was only then that I realised that actually you've been working very hard for us for several weeks for free. Which, even though you're a shareholder, obviously isn't on.'

'Oh.' Flora felt inordinately pleased at this grudging approval.

'I'll get the paperwork.'

While he was gone she did a quick check on her feelings for him. Perhaps he wasn't the most horrible man on the planet. Perhaps he was almost human. It took a bit of work to make the mental adjustment, but hell, she was flexible, she could do that.

When he came back he had a stern, businesslike expression and he gave her a look which seemed to draw attention to the amount of chocolate smeared over her. She reverted to disliking him. Life was simpler that way.

He produced a cheque. 'Is there somewhere I can put this where you won't lose it?'

'I won't lose it! But if you're worried, you can put it on the mantelpiece.'

He crossed the room and then caught sight of the teapot. 'Oh my God!'

'It's lovely, isn't it? Geoffrey gave it to me. We found it at a car-boot sale.'

'It's the most revolting piece of kitsch I've seen in a long time. I'm surprised Geoffrey let you have anything to do with it.'

Flora grinned. 'Well, to be honest, he wouldn't have,

only he could see I had my heart set on it and thought I'd pay too much if he didn't do the deal for me.'

'So how much did he pay for it?'

'A fiver.'

'Hmm. That's not bad, actually. I should sell it, if I were you.'

'But, Charles, it'll fit in so well with the rest of my collection!'

He rolled his eyes. 'Sell all of it. On a good day you'd get quite a lot of money.'

'I may be a bit hard up, but I'm not ready to sell my precious teapots, yet.' Although it was a good idea, she acknowledged silently. She could do it on the Internet, and get her mother to pack them off to eager buyers.

'You're hard up?'

'Did I say that? No! I'm fine, now you've paid my wages.'

He frowned. 'I'm sorry that our rather sticky relationship meant you couldn't tell me something like that.'

She shrugged.

'On the other hand, our sticky relationship is entirely your fault.' He smiled, and for a second Flora caught a flash of the charm which all other women seemed to get all the time. 'I don't suppose I could have another peep at the kittens? I wouldn't like to ask in front of everyone else or they'll all want to see them too and it might be a bit much for them.'

'That's very considerate of you, and of course you can see them. They've opened their eyes since you last saw them, I think.'

As he followed her upstairs she felt suddenly anxious at the thought of him being in her bedroom, it was so untidy. Still, it was too late now. She could hardly bring the whole caboodle downstairs, Imelda would hate it.

'You'll have to excuse the mess,' she said as they reached the landing, getting more anxious by the second.

Her bedroom did indeed have that 'just burgled' look and he glanced around it, trying and failing to disguise his horror at the clutter of make-up and beauty preparations on the dressing table, and the heap of clothes on the bed.

'I'm a bit short of clothes storage and I'd put a lot of my things in Emma's room,' Flora explained hurriedly. 'I had to bring it all back here when she came.'

'I see.'

Then, because in spite of everything she was annoyed by his silent disapproval, she added, 'And some of them are waiting to be washed. I can't decide if I should just wash them all by hand or take them to the launderette.'

This little dig went home. 'I did promise you a washing machine, didn't I? I promise I'll get on to it. Now I've seen how great your need is . . .' He paused. '. . . I'm less likely to forget. Now, are the kittens still where they were before?'

Flora nodded. 'In the cupboard with my shoes. Imelda and I are almost psychically in tune, you know.'

He chuckled and knelt down.

'This little black one is my favourite,' he said, plucking it up from the others.

'He's very shy. He usually squeaks like mad if you pick him up.'

But the little bundle didn't squeak, it purred, snuggling into Charles's neck.

Flora felt a pang of irritation at the sight of her kitten

215

taking so well to someone else. 'He likes you.'

'Is it a boy?'

'I think so. It's quite hard to tell. No, don't look! He's happy where he is.'

She stood up too quickly and, swaying slightly, put her hand on his shoulder to steady herself. 'I'll leave you to it. I must get on.'

'Yes, sorry, I must get back.' Charles put the kitten back in its box and got up. 'Things to do. Jeremy's really looking forward to it.'

'Is he? I don't know if he should. I think we're having nettle quiche to start.'

'It wasn't the food I was thinking about when I was giving him details.'

'Oh?'

'It was the company.'

Charles started downstairs, Flora behind him, suffering from mild shock. He was being nice. Or polite, at least.

'Are you going to wear that dress?' Charles asked.

Flora glanced down at the little slip dress covered with a tea towel. 'No. It's got chocolate on it.'

'Oh, so it has.'

Flora became thoughtful. She was sure she'd seen him looking at the chocolate smears with distaste. Perhaps she'd got it wrong.

When he'd gone she went back to the kitchen and started whipping egg whites, wishing there was an electric beater in the cottage. Charles really was a law unto himself – talk about inscrutable! He made the sphinx seem like easy reading.

* * *

216

William, the cook, in charge of it all, was the calmest during an afternoon of preparation. He just stayed in the kitchen, doing his thing, while Flora and Emma cleaned and tidied and panicked. Flora was nervous for so many reasons that they'd merged into a single mass of anxiety. Loyally, Emma picked up on her feelings and did her best with the downstairs, which wasn't too bad, while Flora attacked her bedroom.

The disadvantage of having kittens in your bedroom, she realised, was that people were likely to go in there and look at them. Thus it had to be tidy. She was still blushing with embarrassment about how it had been when Charles came, although they did seem better friends now than before, which was definitely a good thing.

Now her bedroom was a picture of ordered simplicity. Her bed was made so perfectly it looked as if no one had slept on it, ever. The clothes and shoes, which had been strewn everywhere earlier, were packed into suitcases and hidden in the Land-Rover. The fact that even the clean ones would now have to be ironed again, possibly even washed, had not deterred her. She had a travel iron, after all, and she was aiming for the nun's cell look.

To this end, all the detritus of womanhood had been swept from sight, put into shoe boxes and hidden under the bed, and a simple bouquet of wild flowers adorned her dressing table in their stead. If she could have persuaded Imelda and the kittens to stay in their current, artistically arranged positions, she would have been completely satisfied, but as they'd look beautiful whatever they did, she wasn't too bothered. Annabelle wouldn't go up to see them anyway. That Jeremy might, though, and now she wanted Charles to admire them again, so he could see she wasn't always a slut. She could do minimalism, she just didn't, often.

They had spent hours decorating the dining table. Emma, after scoffing at Flora's ideas initially, had become particularly enthusiastic.

'I want it to be very French,' Emma said, 'like a picture out of a posh cookbook. You know, when they have really pretty children in white dresses with garlands of flowers in their hair, and the mums are all really thin and gorgeous, even the cook.'

She had gathered tiny bouquets of wild flowers and pinned up the corners of Annabelle's double sheets that were doing service as tablecloths.

'You don't think it looks a bit – bridal?' said Flora when Emma had finished. 'It just needs a big white cake in the middle and a priest.'

'It's totally how I want my wedding to be,' said Emma. 'Only with champagne, of course.'

'Sorry about that,' said Flora. 'Have some frascati instead.'

Emma took the glass without thinking. 'I wonder if Dave would like a wedding like this?'

'Darling,' said Flora seriously. 'Don't think about the wedding, think about the man. It's not worth going through all the hassle of getting married to end up with . . .' She paused.

'Dave?' suggested Emma.

'Well, yes. Sorry, Em. I just don't think he's good enough for you.'

'He doesn't want me, anyway.'

Flora glanced at her watch. Sympathetic as she was to Emma's feelings, and usually very willing to let people talk about their problems, she just felt there wasn't quite time for it all now. 'He probably does, but you have to think really carefully about whether you want him. Now I want you to take time this evening, when we're all chatting and laughing – please God we do all chat and laugh – and think about whether he makes you happy. Not necessarily all the time,' she went on, reasonably, 'no one can expect that, but most of the time. Now, I'm just going to get a cloth and polish the cutlery. It still looks smeary. And the glasses.'

'Let's have another glass of wine first,' said Emma. 'Then I'm going to change.'

Both women were in the kitchen, getting in William's way, when they heard a car drive up. They both rushed into the sitting room so they could see who it was before Flora went to the door.

'Do you think they'll all come together?' she asked Emma.

'How on earth would I know?'

As the doors of Charles's car opened and a large man emerged, they exchanged glances. 'Don't fancy yours much,' murmured Flora to Emma.

'Oh I don't know,' said Emma. 'I think he's OK. Now let's have a look at this Charles.'

Fortunately for Flora, her hostessly duties meant she had to go out and greet her guests and not listen to her friend's opinion of her cousin and business-partner, who she had recently discovered was not quite as loathsome as she'd once thought.

Jeremy, whom Flora would have paired with Annabelle, had she been playing Happy Couples, a card game she had yet to patent, was pleasantly tall, with slightly sparse curly hair, and wore a striped shirt and the sort of corduroys that look good in the country.

He was also the kind of man who kissed everyone, even on a first meeting. This set the tone for everyone else, otherwise Charles would never have kissed her, possibly fearing that such an action might turn him to stone. Not that you'd've noticed before, she added, with a secret chuckle. But he had loosened up a bit that afternoon.

After the initial introductions were over, and they had moved inside to the sitting room (William was still in the kitchen), Flora murmured to Annabelle, 'Just come upstairs a minute.'

'Going to see the kittens, sweetheart?' said Charles.

'No,' said Flora briskly. 'Emma, can you and William do drinks?'

'Why have you dragged me up here?' demanded Annabelle. 'I must say, it looks very sweet. Oh, there are the kittens.'

'Never mind the kittens, it's your hair! What's with the hairband?'

Annabelle crouched down and regarded herself in Flora's dressing-table mirror. 'I used to get house points at school for having tidy hair.'

Flora tugged off the hairband and ruffled Annabelle's glossy locks. 'Why not go for some life points and muss it up a little?'

Annabelle, surveying her newly tousled hair and accepting its attractiveness, turned to Flora. 'It's very kind of you to do this.'

'Yes, isn't it?' Flora said wryly. 'I hope Charles has noticed the improvement.'

'Charles loves me no matter how I look,' Annabelle announced rather smugly. 'This – er – change, is just for me.'

'And the school reunion?'

'Yes, and that. Now let's get back down and join the others.'

Imelda yowled suddenly from her space in the bottom of the wardrobe. Flora stayed to comfort her so she could have a few moments alone.

Chapter Thirteen

Downstairs, Flora found that Jeremy, Charles and Emma were still standing round drinkless. William had just emerged from the kitchen and introductions were being got through. She took over in time to say, 'Right, well, Emma, this is Annabelle, and Annabelle, this is William, an old friend of Emma's.'

William took Annabelle's hand. 'I believe you saw me the other day. I'd come over to look up Flora, on Madam's instructions' – he glanced at Emma – 'and as she was out, I thought I'd do some t'ai chi.'

Jeremy regarded William with suspicion. 'Is that one of those martial art things?'

'Sort of.'

'I don't think he's remotely dangerous,' said Flora, and Jeremy smiled.

'I hope not,' said William. 'I'm a pacifist – and a portrait painter, and a bit of a poet, too.'

'All the p's,' murmured Emma.

'I'm ex-Army, myself,' said Jeremy.

Seeing what could become a problem, Flora rushed to save the situation. '"Ex", you say? What a shame. I do love a man in uniform.'

'I prefer men who don't need clothes to give them status,' said Annabelle, horribly against type.

Flora, rather thrown, rushed on, 'Shall we all have a drink? What would everyone like? Wine, red or white, elderflower pressé, apple juice . . .'

'I've got a glass of wine in the kitchen,' said William, 'and if you'll excuse me, I'll go back to the cooking.'

'Can I help?' asked Annabelle, quick as a knife. 'Did you say you were a portrait painter?'

'Among other things, and thank you,' said William, 'I could do with a hand.'

Flora knew perfectly well that if it had been she cooking, Annabelle wouldn't have dreamt of offering help, but she seemed peculiarly intrigued by William. Then again, the whole point of the evening was for her to make sure William was safe to trust around her cottage. 'Better take a drink then, Annabelle. White wine?'

'Marvellous, thank you.'

'What about the rest of you?' asked Flora, hoping that William needed Annabelle to tear up raw nettles.

'White wine for me, too, please,' said Emma.

'Right.' Flora tipped the bottle up to pour the wine and realised it was empty.

'Here, let me,' said Charles, and took the corkscrew from Flora's hand.

Usually she would have protested and opened the bottle herself, but the corkscrew was the kind that required you to put the bottle between your feet and pull like mad, nearly cutting off your fingers in the process. She surrendered the bottle and the corkscrew.

'I'll have red,' said Jeremy. 'If that's open already.'

Flora smiled at him as she handed him his glass and saw his response. Oh, don't do that, she thought. This dinner party is complicated enough already.

'Let's go outside,' she said instead, leading the way out of the front door. 'It's such a lovely evening and we're eating out there. Besides, you might have noticed, there's nowhere to sit here. All the furniture's in the garden.'

'It looks very pretty,' said Jeremy, who had followed. 'Did you decorate the table, Flora?'

'No, Emma did, actually. She's very artistic. She's got a real flair for design.'

Emma, following him out, looked appropriately modest.

'So, are you in that sort of business, Emma?' asked Jeremy. 'You're obviously really gifted.'

Flora watched with satisfaction as Emma drew Jeremy away to where the wrought-iron table and chairs that Charles had brought had been pulled into a little area by the hedge. There was a cloth on the table and, on that, a vase with a single sprig of honeysuckle and a small dish of pistachios. The garden, untidy as it was, was still extremely pretty with rambling roses scrambling over the hedge, honeysuckle scenting the air and poppies spilling their petals shamelessly on to the grass.

'What are you having, Flora?' asked Charles from behind her. She turned, unnerved, to see him with his hands full of bottles.

'Oh, I think I'll just have elderflower. Emma and I had a glass of wine earlier.'

'Well, it's not stopping me,' called Emma, hearing this. 'I'm surprised it's stopping you, Flo. It's not as if we've got to drive anywhere.'

'I have to drive,' said Charles. 'I'll have elderflower, too.'

'So, tell me all about what you do now you're no longer in the army,' said Emma to Jeremy, turning back to the matter in hand. 'I've learnt far more than I want to know about auction houses from Flora. She's totally hooked.'

'Is that true?' asked Charles quietly, following Flora, who'd gone to perch on the arm of the sofa.

'Well, I probably have chewed her ear off a bit,' she admitted.

'I mean that you're hooked on auction houses.'

'I wouldn't put it in the plural, but I am hooked on our auction house, yes.' She looked him in the eye. 'But you did know that, Charles. I have told you. On more than one occasion.'

'I suppose you have.'

Flora took a breath, thinking about their row and how it still hung between them. She badly wanted to just sit in silence, enjoying the beautiful summer evening and not say anything about anything, but she couldn't.

Did he mind about Annabelle disappearing into the kitchen leaving him to make polite conversation? Was he fighting the urge to go storming in there, demanding that Annabelle rip off her rubber gloves and come back to the party? Would there be a fight? The thought made her smile slightly – it was so unlikely.

'What's making you smile?' asked Charles.

'Oh, nothing really!' She, who could chat for Britain, was totally at a loss. It might be that she was tired, but she feared it was because that she knew she had to apologise properly for the terrible things she had said to him during their row. She took another sip of her drink, wishing she hadn't been so abstemious and had allowed herself another glass of wine. She couldn't apologise when anyone was likely to overhear her – she didn't want the whole thing common knowledge.

'Do you think Annabelle's all right in the kitchen?' she said awkwardly. 'Perhaps I should go and see?'

Charles was standing in her way, and would have to move if she did want to escape back inside the house. 'Annabelle's perfectly capable of leaving it if she's not enjoying herself, I assure you,' he said.

Was there something a little cold in Charles's voice when he said this? Perhaps they'd quarrelled on the way over. Except they'd had Jeremy with them in the car. That would cramp Charles's style, if not Annabelle's. 'I'll try not to worry about it then.'

She wasn't really worried, just a bit uncomfortable. She racked her brain for a neutral topic of conversation.

'Just relax, Flora,' said Charles, putting a hand on the small of her back for just a second as he came round to sit on the sofa next to her. 'I know entertaining is stressful, but I'm sure William's got it all under control. And if not, Annabelle's very capable.'

Flora sighed again. If only it was William, Annabelle and nature's bounty that was worrying her. Fortunately, William and Annabelle both appeared just then, carrying plates.

'A few little nettle quiches to keep you going,' said William.

'He's so clever!' said Annabelle enthusiastically. 'He's created the whole meal out of things he'd gathered from the hedgerows. Oh, and some aubergines.'

Flora, who knew this, had been hoping to keep the information from her guests and had sworn Emma to secrecy. Still, the cat was out of the bag now.

'I hope that doesn't mean we're having hedgehog,' said Jeremy, guffawing in a way Flora feared would put Emma off for ever.

'Oh no. It's strictly vegetarian,' said William. Flora had vetoed rabbit pie, although William had said he had a wonderful recipe for it. The thought of the skinning and disembowelling was all too disgusting.

'Oh!' said Jeremy.

'But not vegan,' added William, by way of reassurance. He and Flora had agreed that while they were keeping costs down, as Emma had brought a hunk of very nice Parmesan cheese with her, it would be a shame not to use it.

'It's nice to try something different,' said Emma, who'd had a sample quiche earlier and knew they were nice. 'Mm! These are gorgeous.'

'Here goes, then,' said Jeremy, putting one into his mouth whole. 'Actually,' he said a moment or two later, blowing crumbs. 'These are excellent.'

'Don't sound so surprised, Jeremy,' snapped Annabelle. 'William's a brilliant cook.'

'The secret with nettles,' said William, 'is to only pick the top two leaves, like you do with tea.'

'Have another quiche, Jeremy,' said Emma, seeing his slightly horrified expression. 'And don't worry about the food. I happen to know that the pudding's quite normal.'

'I'm sure it will be delicious,' said Jeremy, looking at Emma. Emma looked back.

Observing this, Flora felt pleased. It would do Emma's ego so much good to be admired and it would do Dave good if he discovered that Emma wasn't above a little extra-relationship flirting. Maybe he'd start to appreciate her.

'So, what are we having?' asked Charles.

'I think it should be a surprise,' said Annabelle. 'Then we can all guess!'

'As long as none of it's poisonous,' said Jeremy.

'Of course it's not poisonous!' said Annabelle, who obviously found Jeremy irritating, in the way that women often found their partner's male friends irritating. 'William's been doing this for ages!'

'And I think I should go back and check on it all,' said William. 'I'm not used to having to leave my cooking and make polite conversation.'

'I'll come with you!' declared Annabelle and dashed after him.

Flora looked up at Charles. He didn't seem remotely bothered. 'Don't you mind Annabelle spending all her time in the kitchen?'

'No. It'll make a nice change for her.'

And so, with Emma and Jeremy deep in the exchange of information that goes on when people meet and fancy each other, Flora was left to entertain Charles. She still couldn't think of a word to say to him. Her guilt loomed between them and she couldn't get past it. She'd have to find an opportunity to do it. This was too painful. She put her glass down on the coffee table, which was a bit wobbly on the grass, and sank back into the sofa, wishing she could go to sleep, then wake up and find that everyone had gone home.

'So, what are we having to eat?' Charles asked. He was sitting on the arm now.

'Do you really want to know?' Flora wasn't quite sure of the details, having blanked out a lot of what William had said about the rules of picking from the countryside and what you could eat when. He could get a bit obsessive.

'No. I was just making conversation.'

Flora chuckled. 'We could talk about work.'

'We could, but I don't think we should.' But he did smile as he spoke.

'No. And I can't show you the kittens because really, they haven't changed at all since you last saw them.'

'They were very sweet. I wouldn't mind seeing them again.'

'Well, you could pop up and have a look. You could see how tidy my bedroom is now. But I won't come with you. I must stay down here and see to things.'

'What things?'

'Oh, you know, just unspecified "things".'

'Then I won't bother with the kittens again.'

Flora wondered briefly if this was a good moment to get her apology out of the way. She and he could nip up, she could say sorry, and they could nip down again. But Emma would notice and perhaps say something embarrassing.

'I think I need another drink,' she said. 'And I'll make it wine, this time.'

He took her glass. 'Red or white?'

'White, please.'

He was back with it in an instant. If Flora hadn't known better she'd think that Charles was being gallant. It couldn't be, it was impossible. Charles couldn't be gallant with her any more than she could hang-glide, but he was doing quite a good impression of it.

'Here's to us, then,' she said, taking a gulp, realising too late it was probably quite the wrong thing to say. 'To Stanza and Stanza, I mean.'

'To Stanza and Stanza.' Charles raised his glass and looked down into her eyes. 'Which is comprised of "us".'

Fortunately, before Flora succumbed to her desire to scream and go running out into the woods, William and Annabelle emerged bearing between them a basket of bread rolls and a pile of soup plates.

'It's ready,' said Annabelle. 'People should sit down. Have you a *placement*, Flora, or would you like me to do one?'

'No, I've worked out where everyone should sit,' said Flora, grateful for her mother insisting that this was an essential part of entertaining. 'Now, as William did the cooking, he should sit at the end, as host.' She sent him a smile she hoped conveyed her gratitude for this. 'I'll go the other end, of course. Emma and Annabelle, you go next to William, and Jeremy and Charles sit next to me.'

'As long as I don't sit next to Charles, that's fine by me,' said Annabelle.

Jeremy managed to hide any disappointment he felt in not sitting next to Emma and everyone sat down except William and Annabelle.

'Shall I see to the wine?' asked Charles.

'Yes, that would be lovely. I should go and help William bring stuff out, really.'

'I think Annabelle's doing that,' said Charles.

Flora subsided, deprived of her duties as a hostess. She fiddled with her cutlery. 'The little garlands round the napkins look very pretty, Emma,' she said.

'It must have taken you hours,' said Jeremy.

'I really enjoyed myself.' Emma looked across the table at Jeremy, obviously still enjoying herself.

'I hope it won't get chilly later,' said Flora, more anxious about the food than the weather, but unable to express that. 'I've got a couple of pashminas upstairs if it does.'

'Are you cold now, Flora?' asked Charles, putting his hand on her upper arm, as if to check.

'No, I'm fine! It's just later it may—'

Before she could blunder on with more boring prognostications about the temperature of the glorious summer evening, William appeared with a tureen that Flora and Emma had bought that morning from a junk shop. Annabelle was holding a butter dish.

'Right,' he said. 'We're having cold watercress soup to start with, and some rolls I made earlier.'

'Wow,' said Emma. 'Home-made bread! You are good!'

'Then what are we having?' asked Jeremy, still a little anxious. 'After the soup?'

Annabelle glowered at him, but William said, 'It's a sort of pudding made with—'

'I thought you weren't going to say until they'd tried it, William,' said Flora briskly, glad the meal was actually going to start at last. 'William, you serve the soup. How's everyone's wine?'

Charles got up and refilled glasses, including Flora's. She knew perfectly well she should have put her hand over her glass, but she didn't.

'This is fantastic!' said Jeremy, when everyone had been served and were taking their first tentative sips.

'It is, William,' said Flora. 'Thank you so much for doing it all.'

Her anxieties about the meal subsided a little. A good bowl of soup, which was full of cream and therefore filling, with bread and butter, should keep people going until the chocolate mousse, if the main course was disgusting.

'William was telling me he's been hearing nightingales in the wood,' said Annabelle excitedly.

'But not recently. They've pretty much stopped singing now.'

'But I thought you said you heard one last week,' said Annabelle.

'How long have you been down here?' asked Charles. 'I thought you came with Emma for the weekend.'

'Oh I did,' said William smoothly, 'but I live quite near. I know this wood well.'

'No need to stay the night then, really,' muttered Jeremy, looking at Emma possessively.

'So, where do you live, exactly?' asked Charles.

Flora got up. 'Excuse me, I've just forgotten something really important.' She almost ran into the house.

Once there, she went upstairs to her bedroom. What on earth would William say? If it was the wrong thing, it would be worse for him than for her, but she still didn't want to witness his lies. She glanced out of the window. Everyone seemed to be chatting, and just as she peeked out further, laughter broke out among her guests. A moment later, she rejoined them.

'Sorry,' she said, as everyone regarded her questioningly. 'I realised I hadn't put any lip-gloss on for hours. More soup, anyone? Jeremy, you'd like some. And another roll.'

As Flora took the soup plates into the kitchen and put them down on the floor, the only surface available to her, she consoled herself with the fact that everyone was almost full already. She met William coming in with the empty tureen followed by Annabelle with the empty bread basket.

'Annabelle! You shouldn't be helping still. Go and sit down and enjoy yourself. William and I can manage fine, now.'

'Oh no, I insist. I find this whole "food for free" thing fascinating.' Annabelle giggled, positively girlish.

Flora went out to join her guests.

'So, Jeremy, what do you do now you're not in the Army?' she asked.

'Computer consultant,' he replied.

'Oh! Emma's in computers, too. What a coincidence.'

Jeremy leant forward a little. 'What does William do again? I'm sure someone's told me, but I seem to have forgotten.'

Flora swallowed. 'He's a poet and a portrait painter. Did he do art at university, Emma?'

Emma opened her mouth as if seeking extra oxygen. 'No. Something to do with the environment, I think,' she said eventually. 'You'll have to ask him yourself, Jeremy.'

'I was just wondering what sort of a living you could make painting people's pictures.'

Both women hoped passionately that Jeremy wouldn't ask William this as he'd probably just tell the naked truth, which in his case could be very naked.

'Ta da!' carolled Annabelle as William put a plate on the table. On the plate was something resembling a cloche hat swathed in green material.

'Now will you tell us what it is!' Jeremy was half pleading half impatient.

'Dock pudding,' said William.

'And salad, all picked from the hedgerows,' announced Annabelle proudly.

'I'll just go and get the potatoes,' said Flora, who'd insisted on a nice substantial dish of them, cooked in the oven with cream and onions. It may have been mostly 'food for free' in a financial sense, but certainly not in a calorific one. There was also a tomato salad, that Emma had made, which added a little colour to the table.

'More wine, anyone?' said Charles.

'Well, that was super!' said Annabelle, sitting back in her chair and looking extremely relaxed. 'Now I want to hear the nightingales.'

'It's really very unlikely you'll hear any. They stop singing at the end of May.'

'But you said there might be a rogue one. Oh, do take me, William. It's such a heavenly evening.'

Annabelle, Flora thought sourly, had clearly decided William wasn't a criminal.

'What about you?' Jeremy asked Emma. 'Would you like a walk in the woods?'

Emma obviously would like one, judging by the look she gave Flora.

Flora felt like the head girl. Was she to forbid the expedition? Or condone it? Personally she didn't care what anyone did, but she found she didn't want Charles to be upset.

Although he was the only member of the party who was not now on the drunk side of tipsy, he seemed quite

234

relaxed. As the driver, he could have announced it was time to go home.

'I really don't feel like a walk myself,' said Flora. 'But I'll pop up and get a couple of shawls for you two. It is getting chilly. What about you, Charles?'

'I don't need a shawl, thank you. But I'll help you clear up if the others want to go.'

'Thank you.'

When the others had set off into the trees Flora started to clear plates. Charles put his hand on her arm and stopped her. 'Why don't you just sit down and look at the stars while I clear up?'

'I couldn't possibly do that. Besides, I can't recognise any of the constellations.' In spite of her protest she sank on to the sofa and stared up into the heavens. 'Why don't you sit down too, or I'll worry about you washing up without me.'

He remained standing. 'I don't mind doing it.'

Flora shifted herself to the edge of the sofa so she could confront him. 'No, don't. I really want to talk to you.'

'Oh? I didn't realise I was your favourite agony aunt.'

'This is no time to develop a sense of humour,' she said sternly. 'I want to apologise.'

'What for? You didn't step on my foot, did you?'

'Charles, please! You've never been funny before, please don't start now. I want to say how sorry I am for saying those dreadful things. The other week, in the office, when I pulled the ceiling down.'

'I thought you knew that I'd forgiven you for your attempts at decorating.'

'Yes, but that wasn't what I wanted to apologise for.

235

It was for saying you couldn't run a piss-up in a brewery and that you were hopeless, and that I was the senior partner, things like that. I do think we should work hard to advertise and all that stuff, but I don't think you're bad at your job. At all. I was just angry and said the most hurtful things I could think of.'

'I was angry too,' Charles said quietly. 'I probably said unforgivable things.'

'Well, not totally unforgivable, but I was a bit upset that you thought I was heartless and manipulative.'

'I don't think that now. And I must say, I'm glad not to see Henry here. He's not the sort of man you should be spending time with.'

'Oh.' Flora was a bit thrown by that. 'Well, I did invite him, but he couldn't come.'

'Oh.'

Flora wondered if she should have admitted this as Charles reverted to his normal state of buttoned-up inaccessibility. She sighed. 'So why did you think I was a heartless bitch?'

'I didn't say that.'

'Not in so many words but it's what you meant.'

It was his turn to sigh. 'It was Justin.'

'Justin?'

'Justin Mateland. You broke his heart, you know. Or at least, that was what he told me.'

'I don't think Justin's heart was remotely involved,' Flora said crossly. 'He just got annoyed because . . .'

'Why?'

'Because he obviously expected me to . . . Well, he'd bought me dinner and assumed . . . I really don't want to go into details.' Flora shuddered at the memory; it had been so sordid. She'd had to fight him off and she'd been extremely frightened.

'Oh.' Charles blanched as he suddenly realised what she meant. 'I didn't realise. I had no idea. When he got in touch with me he was very upset. Now I realise he was angry.'

'He was certainly angry when he left my flat.' And bleeding, she remembered.

'God, I'm sorry, Flora. I shouldn't have made the assumption that he was right without getting to know you first.' Charles did, to his credit, look genuinely abashed. 'What Justin had told me about you, that you were a . . .' He coughed, unable to think of a polite way to put it. 'Well, anyway, what he told me about you meant that I'd made up my mind before you even arrived. I suppose I didn't want anyone new arriving and sticking their nose into what, I'm afraid, I do still think of as my business, and particularly not a spoilt little girl who would come in and mess everything up and then disappear off as soon as she got bored.' He shook his head. 'Annabelle and I didn't exactly give you a warm welcome, did we?'

Flora smiled. 'No, not exactly. But you're not the only one guilty of going on first impressions. I should have seen beyond the "at-a-glance taxidermy".'

'The what?'

'I thought you were so stuffy that one look from you and any living creature would become glassy-eyed and full of sawdust.'

'Good God! I hope it's not how you see me now.'

'I can't see you at all, Charles. It's too dark.' She opened her mouth to ask him again to come and sit

237

down on the sofa next to her, but shut it again. The summer night was having a strangely sensual effect on her and it wouldn't be a good idea to have him sitting next to her, in the near-dark, when she'd had too many glasses of wine.

He came and perched on the arm of the sofa. 'Perhaps we should clear up. Or at least, perhaps I should.'

'No, don't. There's nowhere to put anything.'

'The kitchen's not really designed for entertaining.'

'No. Would you like some more coffee or anything?'

'No, thank you.'

The silence hung between them for a moment. Flora struggled to think of something to say. 'They must have gone for quite a long walk. I wouldn't have thought Annabelle was the sort to go trudging through the woods in the dark.'

'She has hidden depths.'

'And have you and she been engaged for long?' She didn't really want to know, but it gave them something safe to talk about.

'We've been engaged officially for about a year, but it was always understood that we would marry. We've known each other from the cradle.' He paused. 'I did fall in love with another woman, briefly, while I was travelling. But it didn't last. I was very glad to come back to Annabelle.'

With anyone else, Flora would probably have asked if this woman had broken his heart, but not with Charles.

'Will you let me wash up, now?'

'No—'

'I just don't think it's a very good idea to go on sitting here in the dark with you.'

'I'm not a vampire, Charles,' said Flora, strangely pleased.

'You're a lot more dangerous than that. Come on.'

Charles and Flora were still drying up when the others came back. They all seemed a little more dishevelled than when they went out and Emma had goose-grass draped over her shoes.

Flora put down her tea towel and picked it off. 'My mother calls this "wild sellotape". Did you hear any nightingales?'

Annabelle sighed. 'No, but it was so beautiful. We should all walk at night more often, it's a forgotten pleasure.'

'Well, I think I'm going to take you home now,' said Charles. 'Flora, thank you for a lovely evening.' And he kissed her cheek, disturbingly near her ear.

'Yes, it's been great,' said Jeremy. 'A really splendid meal.' His kiss was quite hearty. 'Emma? I'll be in touch.'

'Yes, do,' said Emma, with a smile that was only just short of a smirk.

'Flora!' Annabelle took hold of Flora's shoulders and kissed her. 'Fabulous meal and everything.'

'I didn't cook it, Annabelle.'

'I know, but you did set it up and it was all super.'

'I'm so glad you enjoyed yourself.'

Annabelle turned to William. 'What can I say? That walk was magical.'

'I'm glad you enjoyed it.'

'You know so much about the countryside and everything.'

'Well, I spend a lot of time in it.'

'Come on,' said Charles. 'It's late.'

Charles at last got Annabelle and Jeremy into the car and Emma, William and Flora watched them drive away from the doorstep.

'I think that went really well,' said Flora. 'What did you two think?'

'Jeremy was very nice,' said Emma. 'Annabelle was a bit scary, though.'

'Did you think so?' said William. 'I thought she was very friendly and she has really interesting features, in that strong, Pre-Raphaelite way. I'd really like to paint her.'

Flora took this in for a moment, wondering if her make-over could possibly take any credit for Annabelle's strong features, and deciding that it couldn't. 'Well, anyway, you were a star! And so economical!'

William shrugged. 'Why pay for food when you can get it for nothing?'

Later, while Flora was brushing her teeth, she reflected that she and Charles seemed to have moved on. Now she knew why he was so wary of her, assuming she was a bitch because of Justin, things should go much better. She was surprised to realise quite how relieved she was that the atmosphere between her and Charles had been cleared. It had obviously been getting to her more than she'd known, and if she was back in his good books then they could both stop treading on eggshells and get on with getting Stanza and Stanza back on track.

Yes, things had definitely changed between them tonight, but it wasn't just that they'd gone back to how they were before the row – it felt more as if they were actually becoming friends, rather than polite partners, and she was surprised again to register how much that meant to her. Perhaps if the roadshow went really well, he might stop thinking of her as a dumb blonde and see her as a really useful person.

Chapter Fourteen

❦

'Thank you so much for dinner,' said Charles on Monday morning.

He and Annabelle were getting out of their car. Flora had just parked the Land-Rover and waited when she saw them arrive. She felt strangely excited to see Charles again and put it down to their new, improved relationship.

'Yes, it was wonderful! Imagine! All that lovely food for free!' said Annabelle.

'Well, add a couple of pints of double cream and some parmesan,' said Flora. 'Any old weed tastes nice if you know what to do with it.' She smiled, hoping she hadn't sounded churlish.

'The chocolate mousse was delicious,' said Charles.

Flora suddenly remembered him looking at the smears of chocolate on her and found herself blushing. She cleared her throat. 'Well, I'm really glad you both enjoyed yourselves.'

'So did Jeremy,' said Annabelle. 'He seems very taken by your girlfriend. You must tell me all about her sometime.'

By now, the three of them had reached the back entrance to the office, so Flora was spared having to respond to Annabelle's request for information about

Emma. It was Monday morning and she wanted to focus on the week ahead. She was feeling much more optimistic about everything now things were better between her and Charles. It would surely be easier to get Stanza and Stanza profitable now Charles realised she was on the same team. And she was rather hoping for some help with the roadshow.

'Where's Louisa?' asked Annabelle as they all arrived in the office. 'I'm desperate for a coffee. Oh, of course, it's Monday!'

'I'll make it,' said Flora. 'How do you like it?'

'Black, two sugars.'

'Charles?'

'The same, please.'

She brought a tray of coffee through to Charles's office where Annabelle and he were ensconced.

'Have you brought coffee for yourself?' asked Charles. 'We need to discuss this roadshow on Wednesday.'

'Ah yes. So we do,' said Flora, thanking God he'd decided to get involved. 'I'll run and make myself a cup of tea.'

She was putting off the moment, she knew. By now someone, probably Charles, would have read the various advertisements she'd placed and found out what she'd done. Or at least, some of what she'd done. She hadn't paid for all her sins by the word – some of them would come to light later.

'Right,' said Charles, when Flora had pulled up another chair to the desk. 'I've spoken to Geoffrey. He's on side. And I've got Bob Butler and another couple of retired auctioneers to come along.'

'Darling, we won't need all those people,' said

Annabelle. 'What on earth were you thinking of?'

'I think it's good to have plenty of people there to help,' Charles went on smoothly. 'We don't want to keep people waiting too long.'

'For goodness' sake! We'll be lucky if anyone comes at all. No way will there be enough people to form a queue.'

'You never know,' said Flora brightly, realising that Charles had seen the advertisements but that Annabelle hadn't and he hadn't told her about them. It seemed to give them a sort of solidarity. 'Do you think we should have somewhere where people can get drinks and snacks?'

'Excellent idea,' said Charles. 'The porters will organise that if I ask them.'

'They'll need to be paid, don't forget,' said Annabelle, 'and this is all very speculative. It's probably far too short notice for them to organise anything, anyhow.'

'Actually, I spoke to one or two of them at choir,' said Flora.

'What?' Annabelle frowned.

'Because I see them at choir, I took the opportunity to ask them if they could do something at short notice, should it be necessary.' This wasn't quite how she'd put it to the Subversive Second Sopranos, but the general effect was the same.

'Good idea,' said Charles.

'I know, why don't you ask William if he'll come along and help with the refreshments?' suggested Annabelle who, Flora had noticed, was wearing her hair in a pleasantly untidy way.

Flora felt a bit confused. Why on earth did Annabelle think William might like to help? 'I don't think it would be quite his thing, Annabelle. I know he's a fabulous cook, but selling chocolate bars and ham rolls isn't really what he's into.'

'Besides, I expect he's gone home by now, hasn't he, Flora?' asked Charles, rather stern.

'But he lives quite near,' said Annabelle. 'He said. It's why he knows the wood so well.'

'I haven't got his address,' said Flora firmly and, at last, truthfully.

'Oh,' said Annabelle. 'But you could get in touch with him via Emma?'

'Possibly, but Emma's away for a few days,' she improvised, and rapidly changed the subject. 'Now, what other preparations do we need to make?' Really, she was far too busy to think about William and his availability. Annabelle must have approved him by now, or why did she go wandering around a wood with him at night? 'What else do we need to organise?'

'There's only so much we can do before the day, but we'll get the tables set up and the chairs put out. Please remember there might not be thousands of people, Flora. I don't want you to be disappointed.'

'Definitely not!' said Annabelle. 'I don't know why you two are making all these preparations. It's not the *Antiques Roadshow*, after all!'

Flora and Charles exchanged glances. 'No,' said Flora. 'It's not.'

'Well, if you two don't mind, I want to go and get some things for Mummy. You don't need me for anything, do you, Charles?'

'Not at the moment, no,' said Charles.

Did he really love her? Flora wondered as she and Charles watched Annabelle leave the room. Surely some sort of endearment would have been appropriate just then? But there was nothing, not even a 'darling'. They both professed to be in love, but from where Flora was sitting there was something strangely cold about the whole relationship.

'So,' said Charles when he and Flora were alone, 'how many people do you think will turn up?'

'Well, thanks to Geoffrey, almost everyone at choir will bring something. Edie's got the WI and various other local groups interested.'

'And then there's the advertisements,' Charles said levelly.

Flora nodded and confessed. 'Which I put in every local paper for miles around.'

'So I noticed.' Flora couldn't tell if he was pleased at her initiative, horrified, or just accepting.

'And there's one more thing I should tell you,' she said.

'Yes?'

'You know all those antiques programmes on telly have really lovely young male presenters?'

'Flora, I don't have time to watch daytime—'

'Of course, sorry. Well, they do. And one of the tenors in the choir looks really like one of them. He's going to wear the right clothes and hang around.'

'Are you saying you've hired a television presenter look-alike, when the genuine article probably doesn't know anything about antiques, let alone the fake version, so people think they might be on television?'

Charles didn't seem nearly as annoyed about this as he would have been last week, Flora realised. 'Those presenters have all been in the antiques trade for years,' she protested.

'That's not the point I'm making, Flora.'

Emma had hinted there was something sexy about a man being stern and Flora now had to agree with her. 'It's just a bit of set-dressing. I'm not really deceiving anyone.'

The sternness continued just long enough to make Flora genuinely anxious, and then he said, 'Actually, there's something I ought to confess to you, although why I should when you didn't tell me any of what you've been getting up to . . .'

'What, Charles? God, you're so maddening sometimes!'

'I know one of the experts those programmes use. He's coming down to help. And he might bring a small television crew with him. It depends on what else is on.'

Flora got past the furniture and into his arms without knowing how she'd done it. 'Charles! You are such a star! I love you!' She kissed him hard on the cheek and then stepped away. 'Only in a cousinly, co-director sort of way, of course,' she added.

'Of course,' he said after a second or two. 'I would never imagine you meant it in any other way, ever.'

'Oh, I don't know, Charles,' said Flora, made reckless by his news and her recent encounter with his smooth cheek and subtle aftershave. 'If you weren't already spoken for . . . No, only joking,' she added hurriedly, not sure which of them she was teasing, Charles, or herself. 'Now, given what you've just told me – have you told Annabelle, by the way?'

He shook his head. 'She's still expecting a man, his dog and a rickety kitchen table the dog will probably fall in love with.'

Flora smiled delightedly. 'You have got a sense of humour – that's so nice!' She frowned suddenly. 'How do you think she'll react?'

'I think,' he said carefully, 'we might find she does some dressage on Wednesday, so she need only find out about it when the Sheraton chairs come flooding in.'

'But you don't think they will.'

'Actually, I know they will because Bob Butler's got a very nice set he's bringing, just in case the film crew turn up and the whole thing becomes real.'

'Is he the one who asked if you wanted to buy him out?'

'Actually, there are two of them. They've both been in business for ever, but can't quite bring themselves to retire if no one will take on the business.'

Flora sighed. Bearing in mind they hadn't been speaking for most of the last two weeks, she couldn't believe he'd done so much to help make sure her road-show was a success. Perhaps he didn't think it was such a silly idea after all. 'This is fantastic! I do hope the caterers can cope. I only asked a few of them to come.'

'Don't worry. The WI will spring into action if the need arises.'

'They're more into making sexy calendars than sand-wiches these days, aren't they?'

'I promise you, most rural women have been making tea out of urns and buttering baps since they were in short socks. With a blunt knife, and at speed. Trust me on this one.'

'I trust you on everything, Charles.' She bit her lip. 'We'll need loads more fliers. Shall I do them on the computer, or get them printed? I could buy some coloured paper, so they look a bit more interesting.'

'Fine. It will save time just to print them off, and then we can do more if we run out.'

'I'll organise that then. Anything else?'

'It might be as well to contact the local paper. They might like to send someone along. It is a first, after all.'

She skipped out of the room, inexplicably happy. Her mock *Antiques Roadshow* was going to be a stunning success thanks to Charles. And to her, of course, but mostly Charles. A real 'television' expert would mean more to the punters than any number of people who just knew everything there was to know about antiques. It was a cynical thought, she realised, but true.

The days before the sale merged into a blur of activity, and Flora had never felt so happy and fulfilled. Annabelle didn't seem to be around much, but Flora and Charles became a team. They were not quite equals, thought Flora, but she was no longer the idiot child.

'Thank God it's not raining!' said Flora as she looked out of her window very early on Wednesday morning. 'We don't have to worry about people not turning out because of the weather.'

Now all she had to worry about was what to wear. It was important, what she looked like. Should she be businesslike in a suit? Practical in jeans? Or pretty in the dress that Charles had complimented? No contest, really. She plugged in her travel iron and found the dress, hand-washed the previous Sunday and now a crumpled mess. She arrived at the hall an hour later, a little chilly, but confident that the sun would soon warm her.

Charles appeared shortly after she'd let herself into the building and had started putting white sheets on the trestle tables that had been put up the day before.

'Good morning,' he said.

'Hi,' she said, suddenly feeling incredibly shy and wishing she'd worn jeans.

'You'll get your dress dirty. Why don't you put on an apron? There's a drawer full of them in the back room.'

'Good idea.' She left Charles with the tablecloths and found herself an apron. Someone had once told her that there was something very sexy about a woman in an apron over a pretty dress.

When she came back Charles was talking with two men in tweed jackets and flannel trousers. They were both elderly and distinguished-looking.

'This is Flora Stanza. Flora, this is Bob Butler, and this is George Woodman. They've both been in the business since Noah was a boy, but they're rivals, not friends.'

They both laughed. 'And we've neither of us been going quite that long, but long enough.' Bob Butler took Flora's outstretched hand. 'You look far too young to be a co-director of an old established business, if you don't mind my saying so.'

'I am quite young, but I like to think I'm picking it up. What do you think, Charles?' Although she was only making conversation, she found she was pathetically eager to hear his answer.

'Oh yes. Flora's doing very well. This was all her doing, you know.'

George Woodman looked around sagely. 'Well, there's no saying how many people will turn up, but it's a good idea.'

'I must get on,' said Flora. 'I'm going to put the kettle on when I've done the cloths. Tea, coffee?'

The men told her what they wanted. 'Nice to have a pretty girl to make you tea, Charles,' one of them said as Flora left.

'We all make tea from time to time at Stanza and Stanza, even the directors,' said Charles. Flora felt very pleased: Charles had referred to her as a director – yes!

At five to nine Flora peered out of the window to see if anyone she knew had turned up, terrified she'd be greeted by an entirely empty street. 'Argh!' she shouted.

'What?' Charles came running.

'About a million people! All queuing up outside, clutching things.'

'You'd better let them in then,' he said with a broad grin. 'They're all there because of you, you know. It's a good thing I told the local television news team about it. This'll be very good advertising for us. Do you need a hand with those doors?'

'It's just like it is on television,' said Virginia a couple of hours later. She was now in charge of the snack bar.

Flora, just back from the supermarket, put two four-litre containers of milk down on the counter. 'Here you are. That should keep you going for a bit, anyway. It's amazing! We'll have made a fortune on the snacks alone.'

'A man was telling me that he and his wife had driven

251

all the way over from Trowbridge. They were so excited to have their pot examined by Eric Someone.'

'Oh, you mean the expert? He's awfully nice, isn't he. A real charmer.'

'They were certainly very happy. Now, have you had anything to eat, Flora? You've been running about since the moment you got here, probably at sparrow's fart, looking after everyone else. Let me make you a nice ham roll.'

Flora had been dreaming of ham rolls since about ten a.m. when she'd remembered she hadn't had breakfast. Now she hadn't had lunch, either. 'That would be lovely. I keep seeing people coming away from here with their trays and I've had to stop myself mugging them. I'd love a cup of tea, too.'

'I'll make you a fresh one. Oh my goodness, look who's just come in.'

Flora turned round. 'Annabelle!' She instantly felt guilty, convinced Annabelle was going to tell her off, although it was obvious the whole event was a stunning success.

'It's all right, she's not coming over,' said Virginia. 'She's seen Eric Someone and has gone over to him.'

'Phew. I'm sure I should still be writing down people's names and addresses and getting them to sign up to sell their treasures, or something more director-like.'

'Keeping us supplied is very important, and Louisa's doing a great job, now her mother's come to take her little boy home. Don't you worry about Annabelle.'

Flora didn't know her mixed feelings about Annabelle were quite so apparent. 'It was really kind of Louisa to come in on one of her days off.'

'It's all hands to the pump at Stanza and Stanza – or it is now you've joined us.'

'Virginia! That's the nicest thing anyone's ever said to me!'

'It's only the truth. Annabelle, on the other hand, doesn't show anything like your commitment.'

'But it's different for her.' Flora tried to be fair. 'It's only her fiancé's business, not hers.'

'She knew what she was taking on when they got engaged, though.'

'When you're in love, you don't always take practical things into consideration.'

Virginia frowned. Flora was aware that all around them people were busy and felt guilty for wasting time, but she really wanted to know what Virginia had to say about Charles and Annabelle – because, personally, she found them rather mystifying. 'I don't think Charles and Annabelle were ever in love, really,' said Virginia after a moment's thought. 'Or if they were, it never showed when they were in the office together.'

'I would think they're both quite private people, really. They wouldn't canoodle in public.'

Virginia giggled. 'Canoodle! That's a nice old-fashioned word. But I didn't mean that, really. On the other hand, how can you tell what goes on in anyone else's relationship? It's hard enough to keep track of your own, sometimes. But with Charles and Annabelle it always seemed more like a sort of business relationship than anything else.'

'Oh.' This tied in with what Charles had told her at the dinner party – not in so many words, but it gave the same impression.

'Well now,' said Virginia, 'if you've had your tea, you'd better take some over to Eric Expert. He's about due for another cup.'

Flora nodded. 'I'll find Charles first, and check on his name.'

'Oh, he's got a huge queue. Take him some tea, too.'

Flora set the cup and saucer at his elbow and Charles glanced up from the cow-creamer he had just described as 'having a nice touch of antiquity about it' and smiled. She felt inordinately pleased for a moment and then realised it should have been Annabelle who was supporting him, not her.

Flora hadn't realised she knew so many people in Bishopsbridge, or that they knew her. So many people came up and said hello, all thoroughly enjoying themselves. 'That man off the telly told me my old pot's worth thirty pounds! Can you believe it! It was the dog's water bowl. Better buy him a plastic one instead.'

'Well, my aunt died a couple of months back. I was going to get one of those house-clearance people in, but I reckon I'll get one of your lot over to value the furniture.'

'That's the best thing to do,' said Flora. 'There's bound to be a few valuable things there.' Flora wasn't sure if she knew this woman or not, but as she seemed to know her, she carried on as if she did. 'Have a leaflet.'

She'd gone back to the office to print off more fliers twice already, and had nearly run out again.

Flora saw that Charles had handed his queue over to Geoffrey. The crowds were thinning now and he came over, carrying his cup and saucer.

'I've asked Annabelle to open up the office to use as

254

a temporary store. There are people who don't want to come back with stuff they've agreed to put in the next sale.' He looked at Flora, particularly at her dirty face and feet. 'We'll have to put on an extra one. We didn't have anything scheduled until the autumn.'

'You must be thrilled, Charles,' said Virginia. 'This was a brilliant idea of Flora's.'

Annabelle joined them. 'Yes, it was an amazing success. Who'd have thought it? How did everyone know they were going to be on television? Eric only agreed to come at the last minute. And then the local TV news turned up. It must have been pure fluke.'

'Not quite a fluke, Annabelle,' said Charles. 'I did contact the news office.'

'Yes, but why did all those people come?'

'Flora put a very attractive advertisement in all the local papers,' said Charles.

Flora looked down at her feet, which were now very grubby. She should have worn jeans, or a suit, not a skimpy summer dress and sandals.

'I must say, Flora,' said Annabelle. 'You've turned out to be surprisingly useful.' She put her hand on Flora's shoulder. 'Come and have a little word. There's something I want to ask you.'

'Don't keep her too long, Annabelle,' said Charles. 'She's been here since before dawn and must be exhausted.'

'Not before dawn,' said Flora. 'I think Dawn and I arrived at about the same time.'

He laughed, showing his teeth, which were very straight and white, either the product of good genes or good orthodontics.

'I won't keep her long, you don't have to worry. There's just a little question I want to ask her about clothes. School reunion?'

Trust Annabelle, thought Flora, to have ducked out of all the work involved in the roadshow and then just expect Flora to put her mind to what she should wear to her school reunion.

Annabelle checked that the little room they had squashed themselves into, full of child-sized chairs and tables, plastic ride-on toys and space hoppers, was far enough away from the main hall to be safe from anyone listening. 'First of all, it's lovely that you and Charles are getting on better. He was so annoyed with you at first.'

'I know.'

'And I was thinking of wearing a navy suit, but' – she raised a hand in mock reproof – 'I knew you'd tell me off if I didn't add a scarf or something. What colour, do you think?'

Aware that outside everyone was clearing up and sharing in the aftermath of their success, Flora tucked a strand of hair behind her ear. 'I really wouldn't wear a suit, Annabelle. Terribly matronly, unless you wear it with nothing underneath and show a lot of cleavage.'

'Oh.'

'And navy? It sounds more suitable for a Conservative Party meeting than a girlie night out.'

'The Conservative colour is royal blue, you know.'

Flora slumped in her tiny chair. 'So it is.'

'So I won't wear the suit then, but there was something else I wanted to ask you.'

'Yes?' Virginia and some of the others were going to

the pub afterwards. Flora was hoping that Charles was going too. If Annabelle kept her too long, they might all go off without her.

'Can you give me William's mobile number?'

'He hasn't got a mobile.'

'He hasn't! How on earth does he manage?'

Flora shrugged, as mystified as Annabelle. 'Why do you want it, anyway?'

'I've had an idea. It's a bit of a secret.'

'What?' Annabelle didn't seem a 'secret' sort of person, really.

'I want him to paint my portrait. As a wedding present, for Charles! Do you think he could do it by November?'

It seemed terribly soon, somehow. 'Is that when the wedding is? What a funny time of year.'

'Yes, it is, rather, but the abbey gets terribly booked up in spring and summer. It's also when Daddy's insurance policy matures, to pay for it.'

'You're all practicality, Annabelle.'

'I know, and a jolly good thing too. But I do think a portrait of me would be something Charles would really like. Don't you?'

Flora thought. Her father had had a pastel done of her mother when they were first married, and it *was* a lovely thing to have. 'Yes, I do. And William did say . . .' Should she tell Annabelle what William had said? She decided that she should. 'He said he'd really like to paint you.'

'Did he? Oh, that's so cool.'

Flora laughed. It was nice to hear Annabelle using contemporary language. 'Mm.'

Annabelle appeared inordinately pleased, but then, thought Flora, it was a nice thing to hear about oneself.

'But how can I get in touch with him if he hasn't got a mobile?' said Annabelle, all practicality again.

'I'll try and see if I can get a message to him.' She didn't want to say she could just ask William to ring her, as she didn't think Annabelle knew that William was more or less living with her.

'Could you do that? He could ring me. But it would have to be on my mobile as I really wouldn't want Charles to find out. It would spoil the surprise,' she added.

'I'll see what I can do.'

'Do please try quite hard, Flora.'

'I will!' Honestly, once Annabelle decided she wanted something, she wanted it immediately. Flora got to her feet, longing to go back to the others.

Annabelle got up too. 'Tell me, Flora, rumour had it that you were going out with Henry Burnet?'

'Oh, well, sort of.'

'I just wondered why you didn't invite him to your dinner party, or was that because of Charles?'

'I did invite him but he couldn't come. But why would Charles care? Don't he and Henry get on?'

'No, not really, and I don't think he'd like it if he knew you two were going out.'

'Why not?'

'Henry's a bit of a bad lot, actually. Charles knew his ex-wife Natasha a little, and I think Henry treated her quite badly – I know Charles ran into her shortly after she'd found out about the affair and she was utterly distraught. He was horrified. And he feels quite protective towards his baby cousin.' She smiled, in case Flora was in any danger of misinterpreting the word 'protective'. 'Come on. Let's get out of this hell-hole. By the way, Flora, do you really think that dress is suitable for an event like today?'

Chapter Fifteen

❦

The hall was nearly empty when they got back to it. Charles was there, looking impatient, and all the euphoria seemed to have evaporated. They were just in a dusty hall, waiting to go home.

'The others have all gone to the pub, Flora,' he said. 'They wanted you to join them, but I thought perhaps we three might go out for a meal.'

'That's a lovely idea,' said Flora, keen to celebrate their success. 'I'm starving.'

'Oh good.' He seemed very pleased. 'Then let's think where to go.'

'But, Charles,' said Annabelle sharply, 'have you forgotten? We're having dinner with Clarissa and Benjamin.'

'Oh. I'd completely forgotten.' He looked at Flora, who instantly felt like a remnant from a jumble sale that no one wanted. 'Could we bring Flora with us?'

'Don't be silly! They don't know her. And she wouldn't want to be dragged along and make things difficult for them!'

'No, I wouldn't,' Flora agreed, suddenly feeling near to tears.

'You go to the pub with the porters,' said Annabelle. 'Have a nice drink with them.'

Flora knew she had to get out of Charles and Annabelle's presence very quickly or make the most awful fool of herself. 'Actually, I'm quite tired. I might just go home. Goodbye, both of you!'

'Flora?' Charles called after her, but she didn't stop.

Once in the car park, Flora took some deep breaths and thought about what she wanted to do. She could ring Henry. He'd already rung her during the sale and asked her out, but she'd hoped – assumed, possibly – that she'd be going out with the people she'd been working so hard with for the past few days.

But if she went out with Henry now, while she was feeling so anti-climactic, she might drink too much and get maudlin and depressed. So, should she join Virginia and the others?

No. She'd go home, have a glass of wine, and tell William that Annabelle wanted her portrait painted. Then she remembered she hadn't actually got Annabelle's mobile number. Oh well, she could always get it tomorrow.

As she drove home, summer seemed to gather its skirts, and prepare to leave. Thunder began to rumble and in the distance, sheet lightning lit the darkening sky. It had not yet started to rain, but the air smelt of it, and even London-bred Flora, who wasn't so aware of the signs, knew that when it came it would be torrential.

The first spots of rain hit the windscreen as Flora turned the Land-Rover into the lane that led to the cottage. They were the size of pound coins and after the first few seconds, they became a waterfall. She slowed right down and swore mildly. As she negotiated the car through the rain the events of the day ran through her head. It would have been so nice to have gone out for a cosy meal with Charles and the others, and that hadn't happened, but otherwise it had been a huge success. People had come in droves and, according to Geoffrey, who was the only person she'd been able to ask, the quality of the items had on the whole been reasonably high.

And there was Henry. She hadn't accepted his invitation for that evening, but when she'd said no, he hadn't sounded too fed up: he'd ask her again.

It was only when she thought about Charles her spirits got low, which was silly. They were getting on much better and had really worked together well. That's all she wanted, after all. She was inordinately pleased to see William.

After she'd had a hot bath and come down again in her dressing gown, he handed her a glass of wine.

'I expect you deserve that,' he said.

'Oh, I definitely do!'

'How did it go?'

'Wonderfully. We had loads of people, the local paper sent someone and we might even be on the local news on telly.'

'So, what's bothering you?' He handed her a bowl of sunflower seeds and cashew nuts that he had roasted in the oven and sprinkled with soy sauce.

'Nothing. Why do you ask?'

'You're just not your cheery little self, that's all. And if something you've organised has gone really well, you should be on cloud nine.'

Flora took a sip of wine. She'd been trying hard to convince herself that she was perfectly fine, but she wasn't, really. 'I expect I'm just tired. And I did think we might all go out for a meal together, afterwards. But Charles and Annabelle had plans. Oh! Annabelle! I nearly forgot. She asked me about you.'

'I thought she'd done all the checking out and I came out with top marks.'

'You did! That's the point. She wants you to paint her portrait.'

'Oh? A commission? That's nice. We were talking about it a bit the other night, but I didn't realise it was a portrait she had in mind.'

Flora frowned. 'What did you think, then? Beautiful as it is, I don't think she can be after you for your body. She's engaged to my cousin.'

'The estimable Charles. Well, if you say so.'

'I do say so! Annabelle is just not the type to cheat, it would all be far too messy for her. She wants a portrait as a wedding present for Charles, which I think is a very nice idea.'

'It is.'

'The only problem is, I forgot to get her mobile number to give you, but I can get it tomorrow.'

'Hmm. I wonder what sort of portrait she had in mind.'

'Oh, very conventional, I should imagine. Possibly like the old photos they used to put in *Country Life*, when they looked naked but for their pearls.'

'That would be a good choice for Annabelle. She has lovely arms and shoulders.'

Personally, Flora thought Annabelle's arms were on the large side, but she didn't comment. 'You'd be happy to do it, then?'

'Oh yes. Definitely. The only thing is, I was thinking of moving on tomorrow.'

'You're abandoning me?' Flora hadn't expected that.

'Flora, if you remember, you weren't at all keen on my being here when we first met.'

'But since then I've got used to your little ways. And your cooking.'

He laughed. 'I've got some things I need to attend to over the other side of the wood. A friend is building a house from straw bales and wants my advice. I'll probably be back in a week or two. If you'll let me come back.'

'Of course I'll let you. Especially if I can smell some wonderful smell coming out of the oven.'

'More quiche. And I've made soup and a salad. That suit you?'

'Oh, fab! Thank you so much.' And she gave the most enormous yawn. Later, she only just got up the stairs and into bed before she fell asleep, Imelda purring in the crook of her knees before her family needed her again.

It was still raining hard the following morning. The lane resembled a small river and Flora got soaked just running out to the Land-Rover for her wellingtons.

'You won't go off today, will you, William? You'll drown.'

'It will ease off a bit later. Bound to. I'll be gone by the time you get home tonight.'

Flora felt bereft. 'You don't really have to go, do you, William? If Annabelle wants her portrait painting, she'll want you to do it soon. They're getting married in November.'

'You don't need to worry about that, Flora.'

'I'm not worried, but Annabelle will be. She likes to get ahead with her life!'

'Really, it's time I was moving on. I'll be back soon.' He smiled. He had a very kind smile. 'I've been getting awfully soft, living here with hot running water and electricity.'

'And me,' added Flora.

'Of course,' he said, 'but so far it's been me pampering you, not the other way round.'

Flora chuckled. 'I must say, I could not have managed that dinner party without you, even cooking normal food.' Flora picked up a slice of toast that he had made, and buttered it.

'Well, don't have any more dinner parties until I'm back, then.'

'No way! Far too much stress. Although I did enjoy it.' The memory of sitting on the sofa under the stars flickered into her mind. Then she snapped herself back to the present. 'I'd better go.' She looked at William who was crunching into a piece of toast. 'So will you really not be here when I get back?'

'That's it. I really won't be here when you get back. Not even a ghost of me.'

Flora laughed and came round the table. 'I'll kiss you goodbye then. I'm really going to miss you.'

'It'll do you good to cook your own meals for a bit. Make you a bit more independent.'

'It's not as if I can't cook my own meals! It's just that you've been here and simply done it.'

William put his arm round her and gave her a hug and then kissed her cheek. 'Go to work, Flora.'

*   *   *

At the office, everyone was very buoyant about the previous day's activities, especially Geoffrey. 'Charles is talking about me doing a bit of selling. I've done it before, of course, years ago, but it's been a while.'

'And Virginia's daughter is going to put the better items up on the website,' said Louisa. 'When she's created it, of course. But she says it won't take too long because she'd done a bit of work on it before.'

'I can't think why you haven't had a website long since, Charles,' said Flora, feeling a bit flat in the face of everyone else's optimism.

'It's hardly been worth it up till now. We're just a small country auction house, after all,' said Annabelle, deputing herself to speak for her fiancé. 'But we got some good stuff in yesterday, didn't we, Charles?' She paused.

'Yes. One old lady had about a dozen carrier bags of silver. All completely black, but Georgian, some of it.'

'And there was that wonderful Art Deco tea set with triangular handles that Eric valued. He was really enthusiastic. Are you OK, Flora?'

Flora hadn't been aware that she'd been less than sparky. Honestly, first William and now Annabelle thinking she was miserable – she must remember to smile more. 'I'm fine!'

'You just seem a little . . . flat. Doesn't she, Charles?'

Flora did not want to have to listen to Charles speculate on the state of her spirits. 'I'm fine, really, it's just that William – you know, from the dinner party?'

Charles nodded. Flora didn't look at Annabelle. 'Well, he's been staying with me and he's going today.'

She laughed, hoping she didn't sound shrill. 'I'll be fine on my own, of course, but he's company and a great cook.'

'Oh,' said Annabelle.

Flora regarded her and wondered if her low spirits had instantly affected Annabelle.

'Can I have a word, Flora?' Annabelle asked.

Flora suddenly remembered about Annabelle's mobile phone number not being in William's possession and why. Luckily she knew of a portrait painter in London she could offer as a substitute for William, if one was required. She followed Annabelle out of the room, taking her handbag with her.

'So? Did you – um – manage to give William my number?' Annabelle asked, sounding anxious.

'No. Unfortunately, I didn't have it. I suppose we both thought I already had it. But I hadn't.'

Annabelle tutted with irritation. 'You'd better put it in your mobile now.'

Flora produced her phone and Annabelle recited the numbers. When Flora had them stored she said, 'I'm not quite sure when I'm going to be able to give it to him, but don't worry, I know a portrait painter in London, who's really good and not expensive.'

Annabelle considered. 'I would feel happier sitting for someone I knew, even if only a little.'

'He's only gone for about a week.' William had been slightly less specific, but Flora thought a week's delay might be considered bearable.

'You don't understand! Portraits take ages. He'll have to start very soon if he's to get it done.'

'I did tell him about you wanting a portrait.'

'Oh? What did he say?'

'He was keen. He said you had lovely arms and shoulders.'

'Really?' Annabelle's expression became almost dreamy. 'That's so nice. So, he hadn't left yet?'

'No. He was going to wait for it to stop raining.'

'Right. OK, then.' Annabelle swallowed. 'Um . . . I wonder if you could give me the keys to the Land-Rover? I've got to go and deliver something to a farm and will need it. My car isn't awfully good in mud.'

Flora clutched her handbag to her. She thought of the Land-Rover as hers. 'Are you likely to be long? It's choir tonight. I want to get away on time.'

'Take your car then. It's fixed and it's just sitting in the yard waiting for you.'

'But the lane! I won't be able to get my car up and down it. It isn't awfully good in mud, either.'

'Oh, Flora, I'll bring it back in plenty of time. I'm only going to be a couple of hours.'

Reluctantly, Flora burrowed about in her bag and handed over the keys. 'You will be careful, won't you, Annabelle?'

Charles opened the door. 'What are you two gossiping about?'

'We're not gossiping!' Annabelle was very indignant. 'I'm just getting the Landy keys from Flora. I'm going up to Stringers Farm, and then I might pop in on Mummy.'

'Oh. I was going to do that. They've got a pair of rather fierce collies, don't forget.'

'I'll be fine! I'm not frightened of dogs. Bye, you two!'

Flora felt all this was a bit odd, but as Charles seemed

to think it was perfectly normal, she supposed it must be.

At five o'clock there was still no sign of Annabelle.

'I'm so sorry, Flora,' said Charles. 'I'll run you home now, and pick you up in the morning.'

'That's not necessary, really. It's choir tonight. I'll pop across the road and get a sandwich, and work until it's time for choir. If you could leave the Land-Rover keys somewhere obvious, I'll just pick them up and drive home.' She smiled brightly. Ever since the roadshow, when he'd tried to drag her along to the dinner party he was going to with Annabelle, Flora had decided that now he no longer hated her, he felt a bit sorry for her.

'That doesn't sound much fun.'

'Or I might give Henry a ring! We could have a drink,' she said before remembering how Charles felt about Henry. But honestly, she was perfectly capable of looking after herself – and Charles should realise that.

'Oh. Very well,' he said stiffly. 'I'll put the keys under the dustbin by the back steps.'

'Fine.' Flora smiled more genuinely. Ringing Henry was a very good idea. It would do her good to see him.

When Geoffrey heard that Flora was stuck in town and was planning to go for a drink with Henry, he shook his head, very disapproving. 'You could have had some tea with me and Edie, Flora. It would have been no trouble.'

'You're very kind. Do you think it will matter if I turn up without my music? I had actually put it in the car, but Annabelle's got it.'

'No one will mind sharing. I'm just not all that happy about this Henry Burnet.' Geoffrey obviously considered himself *in loco parentis*.

Because it was Geoffrey, whom she loved, rather than Charles being bossy, Flora found this rather sweet. 'This way I can finally keep a date with him, but not spend a whole evening, or have to get him to drive me home or anything. And really, you don't need to worry.'

Not entirely pacified, Geoffrey went home and Flora made her way to the pub.

'It's good to actually see you, Henry,' she said, kissing his cheek. 'I've been so busy lately, and then you couldn't come to my dinner party.'

'I'm flattered you could find the time to see me now.' He raised a slightly cynical eyebrow that tweaked at Flora's conscience.

She patted his hand. 'And I'm really flattered you still want to bother with me. I know I'm far too busy to be any fun.'

Mollified, Henry smiled. 'Better the occasional drink together than none at all. Now, what would you like?'

'These drinks are definitely on me. And do have a bar snack with me. I've got to be at choir in a couple of hours.'

Henry sighed. 'I'm lucky you could fit me in.'

'You are! But now the roadshow's over things shouldn't be quite so frantic. I'll make it up to you, I promise.'

As she carried the drinks over to where Henry was sitting she reflected that she had treated him very badly and that she must do something nice for him soon. As long as he didn't expect anything she wasn't prepared to give, he was good company. And good for her slightly bruised ego.

Flora arrived at choir slightly late, having had one and a half glasses of wine. She apologised profusely, but luckily Moira had brought in a very nice station clock the day before, which had been valued for five hundred pounds; Flora was definitely in her good books.

Afterwards, she was surprised to see lights on at Stanza and Stanza as she approached. Geoffrey, who had insisted on walking with her, hurrying through the pouring rain, was too.

'Charles does keep very late hours, sometimes,' he commented, 'but half past nine is later than usual.'

Charles greeted them at the top of the steps. 'I'm afraid Annabelle didn't get back.'

Flora felt suddenly sick. 'My God, how awful! What could have happened?'

'She's all right. She rang, but I'm afraid she put the Land-Rover in the ditch. She's spending the night with her parents.'

Relief mingled with a Cassandra-like feeling that all would have been well if she hadn't given Annabelle her car keys. 'As long as she's all right. What about the Land-Rover?'

'It's all right, too. We'll get it pulled out in the morning. In the meantime, I'm going to drive you home.'

'As I see you're in good hands now, I'll be off,' said Geoffrey. ''Night, Flora, 'night, Charles.'

When he had gone, Flora said, 'There's no earthly need for you to take me home. I'll drive myself. My car's just in the yard.'

'It'll never get down the lane in this.'

'Then I'll call a taxi. You've been here hours. You must be longing to get back.'

'I'm fine, and I'm not having you waiting hours for a cab that will probably get stuck, too. We'll be fine in my car.'

Flora realised that Charles was annoyed and could sympathise, but she didn't really want him driving her home in that sort of mood.

'I'll call a cab. It's miles out of your way and you'd have to come and pick me up in the morning. It's silly for you to drive me. Logistically.'

'Don't use words you don't understand. Now come on.'

Flora opened her mouth wide with indignation.

'Only joking. Have you got everything?'

Chapter Sixteen

'It's still raining,' she said, aware that she was stating the blooming obvious for about the eighteenth time, but finding it necessary to break the silence. They were driving very slowly, the windscreen wipers going at double speed. 'Was Annabelle with her parents all day?'

'I don't know. Her mobile was switched off for most of it.'

'Well, there's not much point in wasting the battery when there's not much coverage.' Flora did her best to sound nonchalant, but she couldn't help wondering if William might have had something to do with her absence. But he hadn't had any painting materials with him, so they couldn't have actually made a start on the portrait, could they?

'No.'

'I haven't seen rain like this for a long time,' said Flora, a little later. 'The last time I did, I was in the Caribbean.'

'And it's been dry for so long, the water's all staying on the surface and the drains can't cope. Still, don't worry, I'll get you home all right.'

'I'm sure you will. And I can always get a taxi in tomorrow morning. You really won't want to drag yourself all the way out there to collect me.'

Charles gave her the briefest smile. 'There's always the kittens, Flora. They make any journey worthwhile.'

'But won't you have Annabelle with you? She doesn't like kittens, remember.'

'She can drive herself in, like she did today. It suits us better sometimes. She likes to come in a bit later and I'm not always ready to finish at five.'

Annabelle did not deserve such a hard-working fiancé. No wonder she was set on marrying him. In Annabelle's eyes, if she could only get Charles to give as much dedication and energy as he did to the auction house to something more lucrative, he would become the perfect husband.

'I know. I'm so sorry about you having to drive me back. You've been working so hard today, you must want to go home and pour yourself a large drink.'

'It's not your fault you can't drive yourself, Flora, and you've been working just as hard. The roadshow has put a huge extra load on everyone, although they're all really pleased about it,' he added, possibly aware that Flora might feel this was a criticism. 'But I must admit, at home there's a very nice single malt that's got my name on it.'

'Has it? That's very grand, Charles. I know you can have—'

'Not literally.' He took his eyes off the road for just a second. 'It actually has the name of an unpronounceable Scottish island on it.'

'I must say I might well change my name to Svetlana, or something. Emma brought some vodka with her. There's a bit left.'

'It won't be long now before you can get at it.'

Flora frowned. 'Not at this rate. We're only going about five miles an hour. How many miles is it?'

'I don't know. It's not far, really. It's such a nuisance about the Land-Rover. I probably wouldn't have let you drive alone, but I could have got you home safely.'

'You're not implying you can't get me home, are you?' The thought of spending the night with Charles in a roadside inn set up a feeling of panic she couldn't quite explain.

'Not at all. It would have been easier in the Land-Rover, that's all.'

'At least Annabelle is OK. That's the important thing.'

'Yes. And I don't expect the Land-Rover will have anything wrong with it either, once it's out of the ditch. I don't know what's got into her. She isn't usually so careless.'

'The road conditions are awful. She probably wasn't careless at all.'

Charles didn't answer and they sat in silence. The road was getting worse and, like Charles, she was concentrating on it, trying to see through the rain that the wipers couldn't quite keep up with, watching for flooding or obstructions.

'How was choir tonight?'

'A lot of people didn't make it. I probably wouldn't have come out in this if I'd gone home.'

'And what did you do beforehand?'

'I had a drink and a snack with Henry.'

'Oh yes.' Charles cleared his throat, fiercely focusing on the road ahead. 'So are you and he "an item"?'

Flora stifled a laugh. The words sounded so strange coming out of Charles's mouth. The inverted commas were almost audible. She was about to deny there was anything serious going on between her and Henry, but then remembered his original opinion of her. She didn't want him to think she was a hussy just when her hard work and dedication to duty had convinced him she wasn't. 'We're not an item yet, but who knows? He's very good company.'

'That rather depends on your definition of "good company". I don't know if I'd describe him like that myself. He's divorced, after all.'

'So are lots of people! It doesn't necessarily make you a bad lot! Besides, I define "good company" as someone who makes me laugh.'

'That rules me out, then.'

Flora allowed her chuckle to escape. 'You do make me laugh sometimes, Charles. But sometimes – like now, for instance – you can be awfully stuffy.'

'I think you've told me that before.'

'Well then. Stop being stuffy!'

'I'll do my best.' He took his eyes off the road again and smiled at her. 'But it's hard to go against nature.'

'It's not nature! It's habit. Anyway, did I tell you? We've got a concert coming up. The choir, I mean, not you and me.' Flora was aware that she'd suddenly become flippant, but couldn't decide if it was a good or a bad thing.

Charles ignored the flippancy. 'A concert? How nice. Annabelle and I should come.'

'I'm thinking of asking Mum if she'd like to come over for it. She hasn't been to England for a while and she really wants to see the cottage. She can't quite believe how I've taken to country life.'

Charles laughed. 'Well, I must say, you've surprised us all.'

'I don't see why!'

He laughed again. 'I know now that I was quite wrong, but when you first appeared you didn't look like such a hard worker.'

'I've told you before, you shouldn't judge by appearances. It's a great mistake.'

'It's not a mistake I'll make again. Not with you, anyway. So, how are the kittens?' he asked, as the road improved a little.

'Fine. They haven't changed much since the weekend.'

'I don't suppose they have. I was just making conversation.'

'Well, please don't on my account. I'm your work colleague and your cousin, not someone you need to charm.'

'Oh, I don't know about that.'

'Charles?'

'I sometimes wish I had your social skills, that's all.'

'But I'm always putting my foot in it!'

'You make people feel relaxed and good about themselves. It's a great gift. One I don't share.'

'Yes, you do!' Flora was indignant. 'Think how lovely you were with those people in that grisly house. You made out it was all perfectly normal and they believed you. Hell, I believed you! I was really worried that I'd be facing squalor like that every week!'

'That's different. That's work.'

'Well, as you work most of the time, that's OK. You probably don't have much time for a social life anyway. Talking of which, how's Jeremy?'

'He's fine. Very keen on your chum Emma, by the way. Is she available?'

'Yes and no. She's with someone but I don't think he's anything like good enough for her.'

'And what does Emma feel?'

'I don't think she knows, really. But she liked Jeremy, too. It would be good for her to be with someone who's kind to her.'

'I really brought him along for your benefit, Flora. I thought it would be nice for you to have someone to take you out while you're down here.' He scowled through the rain-drenched windscreen. 'But you didn't need my help in finding someone to squire you around.'

'That is a lovely, old-fashioned expression,' she said, refusing to be drawn on Henry. 'Only you would use it.'

'Don't change the subject.'

'I'm not, I'm just not willing to talk about Henry.'

'It's not my place to comment, but—'

'Then please don't comment. As you said yourself, it's not your place. And it's only been a couple of drinks and perhaps a lunch.' Just at that moment, Flora couldn't think how many times she'd been out with Henry. 'Like you, I'm far too busy to go out much.'

'Forgive me if I doubt that it's always like that for you, Flora.'

'Of course I'll forgive you, and no, it isn't always like that for me. It's just that this time it's half my business. It does make it a whole lot more interesting.' She frowned. 'Although actually, I think if I was just working for Stanza and Stanza I'd feel the same. It's so fascinating.

I'm seriously considering training, although I know it takes a long time.'

He glanced at her briefly before turning his gaze back to the road. They were still travelling very slowly. 'You could do it part time, while you work. Lots of people do.'

'Well, isn't that nice? That's the first time you've behaved as if I'm going to be here for longer than the summer!'

He chuckled. 'I must be beginning to believe your propaganda.'

'Propaganda, indeed.'

'You wouldn't think there could be so much rain in the sky, would you?' he said a little later.

'No. I expect the land needs it though, doesn't it?'

'Mm, if it doesn't all run off. Slow, steady rain that sinks in is what farmers like.'

'So Annabelle's father will be happy?'

'He's not really a farmer in a way most people would recognise. More an "agri-businessman". He makes most of his money from investments. Property, by and large.' He paused, as if debating whether or not he should pursue this conversation. 'I owe him a great deal, and he'd like me to join him.'

'Oh.' Flora stopped herself from saying more. It explained why Annabelle only liked Stanza and Stanza for the property it owned.

'But I can't really see myself getting interested in renting office blocks in London.'

'You could get interested in starter homes, though?'

'Annabelle's father doesn't do starter homes. He's not interested in anything other than the top end of the market.'

'Oh,' said Flora again.

'Besides, I have a business I love.'

'And I love it too.'

His sigh was audible over the sound of the engine. 'Annabelle and her parents think I should sell out to you. Let you take it over.'

Flora realised that for him it must be like them suggesting to a mother that they put their child up for adoption. They had probably tried to convince him that it would all be for the best.

'I'd never buy you out, Charles. Apart from the fact that I'd never have the money, I couldn't run Stanza and Stanza without you – even if I trained and had a bit more experience. It would take me years and years before I had even a tiny fraction of your knowledge.' She frowned. 'What on earth must they have been thinking to suggest something like that?'

'That you're very enthusiastic, you already own slightly over half of it, and could employ Geoffrey to help you.'

'They really have discussed it, haven't they?'

He nodded.

'They're talking absolute gibberish, aren't they?'

He nodded again.

'You wouldn't sell out to me if I offered you a million pounds, would you?'

He shook his head. 'Not to you, and not to anyone, unless I absolutely had to.'

'Well, you won't have to. Not if I have anything to do with it,' said Flora briskly.

Charles looked at her a little oddly, and she wondered why. Yet she didn't feel able to ask him.

'I won't be able to give you alcohol,' she said, 'but I can offer you a nice cup of tea when we get home,' she said. 'Possibly a biscuit.'

'I'd really appreciate that,' said Charles. 'Especially the biscuit. It's taking longer than I expected.'

'And we're not there yet. I'll ring Annabelle and tell her how slow we're being. We don't want her to worry.'

'Oh, I'm sure she's not doing that.'

'I think I'll stop here,' said Charles a little later. 'Before it gets too narrow. Will you be all right on foot?'

'Of course. But how will you turn round?'

'I should manage to turn here OK. But I won't take you up on your kind offer of tea.'

Flora couldn't decide if she was relieved or sorry. 'I'll stay with you in case you need a push.'

'There's no need—'

'Oh, shut up and do your three-point turn.'

He did. Perfectly. Flora was forced to get out into the mud. 'Thank you so much!' she said through the car window.

'I should have just taken you home with me.'

The words tugged at her heart in a strange way. 'I couldn't have gone. The kittens.'

'Oh yes. Well, goodnight, Flora. Don't stand there in the rain. Go home. And I suggest you take your shoes off and go barefoot.'

She grinned, already soaked down to her knickers.

It seemed a very long time since she'd left home that morning. She was completely drenched. She padded to the kitchen to wash the mud off her feet before going upstairs to feel the hot tank and check on Imelda and her brood. The tank was hot and Imelda and the kittens were all fine, and Flora began to relax. She turned on the taps and began to run herself a bath. While the water was running, she climbed out of the skirt that was sticking to her, and pulled off her top and then her underwear. She was chilly without her clothes and pulled on her dressing gown. What she needed was a hot cup of tea. She turned off the taps and went back downstairs.

The kettle had just boiled when she heard the knock on the door. It was either William or Charles, she decided, and went to answer it. It was Charles.

'I got stuck a bit further along the lane,' he said, dripping on the doorstep. 'Can I come in?'

Flora opened the door wide, finding a smile forcing its way past her embarrassment at being caught in her dressing gown when she wasn't expecting visitors. She found herself very pleased to see him. 'Oh dear. But never mind, I've just run a bath and the kettle will have boiled by now. Which would you like first, a bath or a cup of tea?'

'You must have run the bath for yourself. I couldn't take it from you.'

The thought that they could share it floated into Flora's mind from nowhere, like a wicked butterfly. She mentally brushed it off. 'Tea then? Or coffee? Will you ring the AA or someone?'

'No. I've rung Annabelle and told her I won't be home.'

'Oh! And she didn't mind?'

'She said you had a very comfortable sofa and it would be better to sort it all out in the morning, when the rain will have stopped.'

'Oh.' Almost too generous, Annabelle.

'I realise you probably don't want guests tonight, when you must be so tired.'

'You're tired too. And you don't need to sleep on the sofa. There's a perfectly good guest room. I'll make some tea.' Suddenly feeling very naked under her dressing gown, Flora retired to the kitchen and then turned in the doorway. 'Or there's the vodka?'

'Let's have the vodka and the tea.'

She found a glass and some tonic and made him a drink. 'I tell you what, I'll get in the bath, just quickly, and then you can have it after me. You must be chilly and it would take ages for the water to heat up again.'

'That sounds fine. In the meantime, I'll make a fire. Or is it too late to be worth it?'

Flora glanced at her watch. It was past eleven. On the other hand, the thought of a fire was so cosy.

'That sounds a lovely idea. I'll go and hop in the bath.' She almost ran upstairs. Supposing William had used all the logs Charles was expecting to find? She'd just have to hope he couldn't remember how many had been there. She slipped off her robe and got in the bath.

The hot water against her cold limbs was heaven. She closed her eyes. Strangely, she found herself thinking about Charles downstairs, lighting a fire. It was such a domestic thing to do. If they were a couple, he'd come up when it had got going and hurry her out of the bath so that he could get in it. She would go down and make a snack, which they would eat together, with the sofa pulled up to the fire.

'Flora?'

She stifled a scream as she heard Charles's voice.

When she opened her eyes she realised he was outside the door, not in the bathroom with her. 'Yes?'

'I thought you might have gone to sleep in the bath. The fire's going quite well now. There was more wood than I thought and lots of kindling.'

'Oh good. Yes, I think I had drifted off for a minute. I'll get out now and you can get in. If we boil a kettle we can make it a bit hotter. I think I used all the hot water.'

'I'll go and boil the kettle.'

When Flora joined him downstairs in the kitchen, her robe was so tightly belted it would have taken Houdini to release it. She hadn't gone so far as to get dressed, or even put on her nightie, but she had put on a pair of knickers, and was covered from neck to ankle in white towelling. She trusted Charles not to jump on her more than she trusted Imelda not to break into song, but she couldn't spend the evening with him without knickers.

'I've put a clean towel in the bathroom, and I found one of my father's old sweaters I stole from him once. It's a bit holey, but cashmere, and wonderfully soft.'

'It sounds perfect.'

'So you take the kettle up and I'll make some supper. Did you get something earlier?'

'Not very much, and it seems a long time ago. I'd love something, but don't go to any trouble.'

She ignored this. 'Can you put the kettle outside the door when you've finished with it? We might have to have Cup-a-Soup.'

He laughed. The vodka seemed to have relaxed him. 'Is that all you can offer me? I would have thought you'd done a cordon bleu cookery course at some time in your career.'

'I did, but for that you need ingredients. Now run along.'

On her mettle, Flora was determined to produce something half decent, but what? It was quite late to eat a big meal but, on the other hand, she was starving, and Charles was too. She had spaghetti and a jar of pasta sauce, but somehow she had to make it more special.

She'd learnt a lot from William, subliminally. First, she toasted seeds and nuts and splashed tahini on them. Then she cut up a crust of sliced bread, rubbed it with garlic, cut it into cubes and fried it in olive oil, glad that William had insisted that she bought a good quality one. With something to nibble ready, she started on the sauce. She ran out into the rain and found marjoram, then dug out some salami that Emma had brought and chopped it up. It would still be spaghetti and sauce, but it would be a bit better than just that. There was parmesan left from the weekend that Emma had stayed. Her greatest coup of all was a bottle of red wine that had somehow not been drunk at the dinner party.

She put another log on the fire, lit candles and turned off the lights, and, for a final touch of cosiness, she brought down the box of kittens and settled them by the fire. She fiddled with her hair but didn't put scent or make-up on. There was still a little smudge of something round her eyes. That would do. She wanted the room to be cosy and comfortable, but she did not want it to look as if she was setting out to seduce him. Because she definitely wasn't.

'Oh,' said Charles as he came down the stairs into the room. 'It looks – very cosy.'

'Good. Now come and sit down. Supper's nearly ready. Glass of wine?'

'Flora, I'm only staying over because I can't get home. You don't have to provide a romantic dinner for two.'

'I have to provide something to eat, and you lit the fire.' She suddenly felt slightly embarrassed. 'We might as well sit in front of it. And I've brought the kittens down for you to play with, so just stop being grouchy. And here, have a nibble.'

He laughed and the sound of it affected Flora somewhere in her breastbone. The timbre of his voice was one of the most attractive things about him, she realised, wondering how or why she hadn't noticed before.

Everything took a little longer than she had anticipated and when she finally went into the sitting room, with two plates of spaghetti and sauce, Charles had fallen asleep. A kitten, the little black one who was far shyer than the others, was nestled into his neck.

As quietly as she could, she set the two plates down on the low table that was in front of the fire. She went back to get her glass, the parmesan, and a jug of water. By the time she'd come back for the last time, he'd woken.

'I must say, this looks delicious,' he said.

'It's just spaghetti and sauce out of a bottle, you don't have to go overboard with the compliments,' she said. 'Tuck in.'

'I'm sorry. That remark obviously stung. What I meant to say was that you didn't need to go to a lot of trouble. A Cup-a-Soup and a bit of toast would have been fine.'

'That's what you'd've got if I'd had any bread,' she laughed. 'Not sure what I'll give you for breakfast. Nettle soup, possibly.'

He raised his glass to her. '*Slainte*.'

'What?'

'It's what they say on Scottish islands with unpronounceable names.'

'Oh. All right then.' She raised her own glass and then took a sip. The look in his eyes when he'd lifted his glass in her direction had done something strange to her.

'Oh, napkins,' she said, and hurried out to the kitchen. What was going on with her? Just because it was late, and the cottage was cosy, there was no need for her to go all girly. It was Charles she was with, not Mr Darcy.

Chapter Seventeen

'This is extremely nice!' said Charles, having taken a few mouthfuls.

'No need to sound so surprised. I did do the course. It wasn't cordon bleu, but it taught me a few basics.'

'But I thought you needed ingredients.'

'I had ingredients – well, a jar of sauce and some spaghetti. The rest is just . . . my special magic.' She laughed. She was glad it had turned out so well, but she knew the special magic was pretty much fluke.

'I'm surprised you're not married, Flora.'

'Oh?'

'You're lovely and you can cook. What more can a man ask for?'

Flora frowned, hoping he was at least in part joking. 'It's not what more a man can ask for, Charles, but what a girl can ask for. These days women are not prepared to settle for mediocre. There has to be a good reason to give up your freedom and independence.'

'That's me put in my place then.'

'Yes.' Flora didn't dare look at him. She knew he was laughing. She was trying not to laugh herself.

'Has this little chap got a name?' he asked. He had put his plate down and started stroking the little black kitten again.

'No. He's terribly shy, usually.'

'I think I'll call him Macheath.'

'Oh? Why?'

'Because I like the name, and because this is the one I want to keep.'

'But, Charles, you can't have a kitten. Annabelle is—'

'Allergic. I know. But I thought we could have an office cat. Everyone would love it.'

Flora coiled up her last forkful of spaghetti thoughtfully. Charles poured out the last of the wine.

'I was going to offer you tea,' said Flora, suddenly very drowsy.

'I'll make it. It's your turn to have a nap on the sofa.'

'I'll be fine with just the wine, I expect.'

Charles scooped up another kitten. 'This is so cosy.'

'Mm.' Flora closed her eyes. She wanted to ask if Charles had cosiness like this with Annabelle, but realised she didn't want to hear the answer.

She was aware of clattering in the kitchen but she allowed herself to doze through it. Eventually she was forced to open her eyes again. Charles was standing in front of her. He put out a hand and pulled her upright. Then he wrapped his arms around her and hugged her, very, very tightly, and rested his cheek against the top of her head.

She was buried in cashmere that confusingly smelt of both her perfume and of Charles. His arms about her were crushing, making it difficult to breathe, but she would quite happily have stayed there, quietly suffocating, for ever.

At last he released her. 'Goodnight, little one,' he whispered. 'Now go upstairs quickly. Please.'

She flew up the stairs and into bed, aware that the kittens were still downstairs, but so confused about how the evening had progressed that she didn't want to go downstairs and fetch them – because it would mean facing Charles again. And not the Charles she'd seen at work for the last few weeks, but a rather different man: softer, warmer and infinitely more sexy. A Charles who, as long as he was engaged, she was much better off not seeing.

She suddenly felt a rush of jealousy of Annabelle. No wonder she was so determined to marry him! Although somehow, she wasn't convinced that the man she'd just seen a glimpse of was the man who got into bed with Annabelle every night – he just didn't seem Annabelle's type.

How had things changed so fast? It must be the drama of the storm, the lateness of the hour and the vodka, she decided. In the morning, everything would be back to normal – and the strange man downstairs would have reverted to type and she'd be faced once more with the old Charles, who was definitely no threat to her sleep patterns. Although, frustratingly, there was a nagging part of her which hoped she was wrong. Complicated as it made things, the new Charles was certainly interesting.

Before sleep claimed her, which, in spite of her frustration, it was threatening to do, Flora wondered what she'd do if Charles and Annabelle broke up. She was asleep before she'd decided on an answer.

Flora got up early, and went downstairs to check on the kittens. They weren't there. The washing-up was all done, but she'd been vaguely aware of Charles doing that the night before. The kittens were a mystery. She realised as she went back upstairs that Charles must have taken them, and Imelda, into his bedroom, for safe-keeping. If she hadn't recently seen a side to him that was nowhere near as unfeeling as he'd appeared at first, that gesture alone would have brought her round. Although she was determined not to like him too much; she had felt rather too drawn to him for comfort last night. Luckily, she was sure it was only the circumstances. The fire, the food, the wine, the kittens, and the fact that they were both very tired, made them think of bed when normally it wouldn't have crossed either of their minds. Still, it might add a certain frisson to their working day!

She met him coming out of the bathroom. 'Good morning!' she said brightly.

'Are you a morning person, Flora?' Charles asked with a smile.

'I think so. Are you?'

'Not specially. I took the kittens and Imelda into my bedroom. I thought they would probably have been all right downstairs, but I knew they were used to human company and I didn't want them to get lonely.'

'That was very sweet of you. They would have been fine, but they are used to being with me. Or is it that I'm used to them?'

'Whichever. Shall I go downstairs and see what I can find for breakfast?'

'That's a good idea. I think it's stopped raining, but everything is still pretty soggy.'

'I expect it is. See you in a minute.'

Flora dressed with all her normal care, although now he'd seen her first thing without her make-up, and last thing when what make-up she had left on was all under her eyes, so it was a little late to impress him. She smiled at her reflection. To her relief, things seemed back to normal this morning. The cold light of day had brought back a rather less sexy, rather more cousinly Charles, which, bearing in mind the situation they were all in, had to be a good thing. She and Emma had once confessed to each other that wherever they worked, they tried to find someone they sort of fancied. They didn't do anything about it, or at least, only if everything else was right, but it sort of cheered up the working day.

This situation, however, was rather more tricky. If things worked out as Flora increasingly hoped they would, she and Charles would be involved in running Stanza and Stanza together for a long time. A crush, though entertaining, would be disastrous if unrequited – and she had no illusions about either Charles or Annabelle breaking off the wedding. It was only a few months away now, and Charles was hardly going to risk a ten-year relationship for the sake of someone he'd only known a few weeks. As Annabelle had pointed out, he'd been in love with her all his life.

Yes, Flora decided briskly, it was infinitely better that things returned to a businesslike, friendly but not too friendly footing.

She went into the spare room to retrieve the kittens and to feed Imelda. Everyone seemed fine after their night with Charles. Flora felt quite envious, and then chided herself. If anything had happened between them they would have hated themselves and each other now.

Charles had found some of the real coffee left over from the weekend with Emma and was making it. He had also found some bits of ciabatta, which he was toasting.

'Why is everything worth eating in this kitchen Italian?'

'Emma works near a really good Italian deli and brought a lot of stuff down,' Flora explained. 'I stuffed that ciabatta in the top of the fridge. It must be quite stale.'

'It'll be fine toasted.'

Flora suddenly longed for a corner shop where she could buy fresh bread and orange juice. 'I don't have much time for shopping, myself.'

'Nor you do.' He smiled at her, and for a moment Flora wondered if this having a slight crush was actually going to make things quite difficult. It couldn't, she decided. The business was far too important to jeopardise with random hormones.

She pulled up a chair and sat down at the little table. If he was happy making breakfast, she didn't want to interfere.

'You've made this cottage very homely, Flora. Even if you don't have much time to spend in it.'

'I made an effort before the weekend, when Emma and you all came. But it is very sweet. I could happily live here for ever.'

'I'm so glad. I would have thought you'd have got lonely.'

Flora shook her head and sipped the coffee he placed in front of her. She didn't like to tell him she usually had tea, first thing. Or that she'd had very little experience of living in the cottage alone.

'I hope Annabelle's all right,' she said, after a moment's mastication.

'Why shouldn't she be?'

'No reason. Some women might be a bit miffed if their fiancé spent the night with another woman.'

'Annabelle and I have far too good an understanding of each other for her to worry about things like that.'

Flora frowned. This sounded just a bit too complacent, in her opinion. It wasn't as if there hadn't been an undercurrent of something not quite platonic between them the previous evening. 'Oh. Very modern of her.'

'She knows she can depend on my sense of responsibility, in all things. Some things are too important to endanger.' He took a sip of coffee and looked across the table at her, as if making a point. 'Sometimes the grass appears a bit greener, but it never is if you do climb over the fence.'

'I can't imagine you ever scrumped apples, Charles!' said Flora, to lighten the atmosphere, but in spite of all her best intentions, Flora couldn't help feeling rather crestfallen. There was absolutely no ambiguity in what he'd said – he was clearly slightly embarrassed about the atmosphere the night before and wanted her to know she shouldn't read anything into it.

'You don't actually have to go into the lion's den to realise it isn't a very good idea,' he continued.

'Do you talk in riddles to Annabelle every morning?' Flora asked slightly irritably.

'I have to confess that Annabelle and I don't talk much in the mornings any more. We've reached that contented stage when you don't have to make an effort all the time.'

'But to begin with, you did? All women like to be romanced, Charles!' She couldn't help it – she was intrigued.

'One of the things that attracted me to Annabelle – when I was an adult, I mean—'

'I know you've known each other for ever.'

He nodded. 'Was that she was so practical.'

'A safe pair of hands,' said Flora. Of course she didn't know for sure but she was convinced that his heart had been broken by the woman he had met when he was travelling.

'What do you mean?'

'You saw Annabelle as someone reliable and steadfast.'

He laughed. 'You make her sound very boring.'

Flora laughed too. 'Of course not.'

'I'm a man who sticks to things.'

'Like chewing gum on the bottom of your shoe, you mean,' said Flora, not feeling nearly as flippant as she sounded.

'We'd better get going,' he replied. 'I'll just wash these few things.'

'Don't bother, I can easily do them when I come home, and you did all the washing-up last night.'

While Charles was brushing his teeth with Flora's spare toothbrush, Flora stacked the plates. The intimacy, the happy closeness of the previous evening had been spoilt, and she made a decision to put it entirely out of her mind. She and Emma had been wrong to think it was fun to have a crush on someone you work with. Sometimes it was a really bad idea. Just as well she had Henry to think about.

* * *

'At least we've got boots on this time,' said Flora as they walked back to the car through the mud.

'Yes. It was lucky for me that William left his behind.'

Flora wondered idly how William was managing without them, and why on earth he forgot them when it was raining so hard.

'Do you think the car will be all right?'

'If it isn't, I'll ring Annabelle's father and ask him if a tractor can come and get us.'

'I have got some Sunday papers, if we could do anything clever with them.'

'What we'd need would be old carpet, or something with some grip. I think it'll be the tractor or nothing.'

'Oh God! Supposing the tractor can't come?'

'We'll walk to the end of the lane and get a taxi or Annabelle to pick us up.'

Flora didn't think Annabelle would like that suggestion very much, but didn't say so. After all, she was his chosen one. It wasn't for her to comment.

'This may not be a good time to discuss it,' said Charles, 'but after the roadshow, Bob and George were both really keen that I – we – should buy them out. They're both well past retirement age.'

'And we could afford it if we sold the house?'

'We haven't talked money yet, but I should imagine so.'

'Well, let's do that then,' Flora said excitedly. 'We don't need a huge great building. We just need a little office somewhere.'

'And I would like a flat. It's useful and when Annabelle and I get married we might move further away.'

'Right.'

'And we should buy somewhere for you to live, too. We could buy the holiday cottage from Annabelle if you liked.'

'I'd have to think about it,' said Flora, wondering why the thought of living down here after Charles and Annabelle had got married was so depressing. 'Maybe somewhere a little nearer town might be more sensible.'

'Whatever.'

'On the other hand, how much is the building likely to raise? Buying out a couple of auctioneers, an office, a flat for you, a cottage for me – it's asking quite a lot of one building.'

'If we do what Annabelle suggests, and convert it into flats first, we should manage it. But I agree, it might be stretching our resources too far.'

'And it all takes time,' said Flora. If she did feel she had to leave, she wouldn't want to do it before Stanza and Stanza was on the way to profit, but she couldn't ask Charles and Annabelle to postpone their wedding. 'Although I'm quite happy in the cottage. Perhaps I should pay Annabelle rent.'

'Actually, you are. Or rather I am, on behalf of Stanza and Stanza.'

'Oh?'

'I have a tiny private income. I can't get at the capital, but the interest is useful. Annabelle likes to keep her books in order,' he went on, 'but that's something else we must sort out.'

'What is?'

'The financial situation. We should know what money is the company's, and therefore yours too, and what is mine.'

'I'm beginning to feel bad for not having a private income,' said Flora. 'It would make life so much easier.'

'On the contrary, it's much better you not having one. If I hadn't had any other money to keep me afloat, I might have gone on and got the business on a proper footing before now. Having you here, you needing to earn a living from it, has galvanised me, not before time.'

'But you love the business! And you work so hard!'

'Hard, but not smart,' he said thoughtfully. 'I've just kept doing it the way we always did it, making a loss year on year and taking no notice. That will all have to change now you're here.'

'Well, I'm glad I have my uses.'

'Oh, you do. Now, let's see if we can get this car to go.'

It took quite a bit of backing and filling and mud churning, but eventually the car was on the track and slowly they progressed along it. Once they reached the main road, Flora said, 'We're both quite muddy, actually. I expect you want to go home and get some clean clothes.'

'I'd better. Now, would you like to come back with me and drink coffee while I sort myself out? Or would you rather go back to the office? I'm afraid going home and getting a change of clothes isn't really an option for you.'

'Oh, take me to the office, please. I've got lots to do.' She didn't want to sit in Annabelle's drawing room sipping coffee, knowing Charles was showering on the floor above.

Flora did have quite a list of things to do, but before

she had done more than wash the flecks of mud off her face, Geoffrey came and found her.

'There's a bit of an emergency with choir,' he said. 'James rang me, quite late last night. It turns out that there's a problem at the house we were supposed to be doing our concert at.'

'Oh dear.'

'Yes. The valley guttering in the roof collapsed when it first started raining heavily. It so happened that James was on the phone to the woman who owns it shortly afterwards. She was in a terrible state.'

'And so is her valley guttering, apparently,' said Flora, wondering what valley guttering was.

'Yes. And it won't be fixed in time for the concert. We need a new venue.'

'Couldn't we just cancel?' This option was very attractive for Flora as she didn't know any of the work very well. She'd welcome an opportunity to learn everything more thoroughly before performing it in public.

'No!' Geoffrey was horrified. 'We've got an audience, practically ready made, and it's for a very good cause. We really can't cancel unless it's absolutely vital. Besides, the choir is getting paid and we need the money.'

'Well, let's ask Charles if we can have the hall. We could get chairs from somewhere, it would be fine, I'm sure.'

Geoffrey shook his head. 'No, Flora.'

Flora had sensed that no simple solution would do for Geoffrey and that what he had in mind involved her, somehow. 'What then? It seems a good idea to me. We wouldn't have to pay to rent it, I'll see to that. It's local, there's parking, sort of. What's wrong with it?'

'The concert has been advertised as "A Stately Summer: Music for a Summer Evening". The hall won't do. We need a wonderful house to have it in.'

'I'm awfully sorry, Geoffrey, I'm fresh out of wonderful houses. Now, had you asked me last week . . .'

Geoffrey ignored Flora's flippancy. 'We know which house we want. We just need you to go and ask if we can use it.'

'Why me?'

'Because apart from the fact that you weren't at the meeting to say you wouldn't, you know the owner of the house.'

'Do I?' She didn't think she knew anyone with a stately home.

'Yes. It's Henry Burnet.'

'Oh. Oh, Geoffrey, I'd much rather not.' It felt terribly awkward.

'Why?'

'You can't just bowl up somewhere and demand the use of a house to have a concert in! I would hate to make him think I was just using him.' She cast around for more reasons. 'He may not have a suitable room, for one thing.'

'James knows the house. He says there's an orangery which would be perfect and has lovely acoustics.'

'Then why doesn't he ask about it, then?' Flora asked tartly.

'He's far too busy. He's got so much on at the moment. He'll go and check it out if we get permission to go there, but you have to make the first approach.'

'But I'm busy! I've got a lot on, too! Why me? I'm not the only female member of the choir, you know.'

'Of course, I know that, but you work for yourself, Flora. You can take time off when you want to. And you know the owner.'

As things turned out, however, Flora couldn't quite take time off whenever she wanted. In the aftermath of the roadshow Stanza and Stanza was receiving an unprecedented number of enquiries, and before Flora knew it it was six o'clock and she hadn't had a minute to think about going to view Burnet House and charm Henry into lending her his orangery.

So it wasn't until the next morning, after a couple of hours of catching up with all the admin she hadn't had time to do the day before, that she got round to Geoffrey's mission. Annabelle had delivered the Land-Rover back to Flora the morning after the storm – once out of the ditch it had turned out to be fine – so Flora wasn't expecting to see her in the office on a Saturday. But just as Flora was about to leave, she materialised.

'Are you free for lunch, Flora? I feel I ought to take you out as an apology for putting the Landy in the ditch. Charles was furious.'

'Oh dear, there was no need for that. But I'm afraid I can't make lunch today, Annabelle. I've got to go somewhere. Tomorrow, perhaps?' It seemed a good idea to put a bit more distance between her cosy evening with Annabelle's fiancé and a girly lunch.

Annabelle seemed genuinely disappointed. 'Where have you got to go?'

'Somewhere Geoffrey told me about. It's a large country house, and I need to visit it personally.'

'Oh? That's interesting! Are they thinking of having a sale? Nothing could be better for us than a proper

301

country-house sale. Hen's teeth these days, of course, but it would be a brilliant feather in our cap. Shall I come with you?'

The thought gave Flora goosebumps. 'Better not. It's Henry's house.' Frantically she tried to think of a good reason why she should see it on her own. 'I haven't seen him lately,' she lied. 'Things might be a bit tricky.'

'Then better to have me with you, surely? I'd love a snoop round Burnet House. I hear it's lovely. Is it?'

'I don't know! I haven't been there before, but I should go if I'm going. Thank you for rescuing the Land-Rover.'

'It's all right. I was the one who put it in the ditch, after all. Was it all right having Charles to stay the other night?' Annabelle went on. She looked at Flora slightly questioningly. Was she asking if anything had 'gone on'?

Flora wasn't going to respond to unspoken questions. Besides, Annabelle might scratch her eyes out if she got the answer wrong.

'Oh yes. He did the washing-up and everything. You've got him very well trained, Annabelle.'

'Oh yes. He's very good. A perfect husband.'

Flora smiled. 'Now, I must fly.'

'We'll do lunch soon, Flora.'

Flora smiled and nodded absent-mindedly.

Sitting in the Land-Rover half an hour later, Flora had a road map borrowed from the office, she had a map drawn by Geoffrey, and she had a description of the house, but she still didn't know exactly where she was going. She rang Henry, to warn him she was coming, but there was no answer. He'd be surprised to see her turn up at his front door but, she hoped, not displeased. She couldn't quite decide how much Henry cared about her. Was he just after some fun and company, like she was? Or was his heart engaged? Either way, he was her only possible love interest, and should therefore be cherished.

She eventually found Burnet House. It was at the end of a long avenue of beech trees, and even in the aftermath of so much rain, looked beautiful. She turned the Land-Rover in between the open gates and made her stately way up the drive, which was heavily potholed. Before she'd even decided if she should park in front of the house, or try and find somewhere at the back, she'd become aware that the house was in desperate need of repair. She parked, got out, and then knocked on the door. The bell didn't work. She turned and regarded what had once been a lawn and was now a paddock. There seemed to be a ha-ha, but there was no stock to keep away from the house. If there was going to be a concert there, someone would have to do something about the grass. Perhaps a member of the choir had a ride-on mower.

Eventually, she heard footsteps approaching and braced herself, hoping it wasn't a stranger. 'Hello, Henry,' she said when the door opened.

Chapter Eighteen

'Flora! How lovely to see you! This is an unexpected pleasure!'

'Don't be too pleased, I'm on the cadge.' Flora felt hideously embarrassed.

His expression became quizzical. 'It's rather a long way to come to borrow a cup of sugar.'

'Don't joke. It's not sugar I'm after, it's your house.'

'My house?' Henry looked confused.

'Not all of it. Look, may I come in? I could explain better if I'm not on the doorstep.'

'Of course, but I should warn you, I don't usually do favours.'

His smile was mocking and very sexy. Flora smiled back. It was much more fun flirting with someone who wasn't engaged. 'Do something you don't usually do every day,' she said. 'That way life doesn't get stale.'

'Oh? Have you become a life coach, or something since Thursday?'

Flora frowned. 'No. I'm still an apprentice auctioneer, but that's not why I'm here.'

'Good. There's very little here of any value. Of anything at all, actually.'

'That's fine,' said Flora. 'You have got an orangery, haven't you?'

'Well, yes, but it's not for sale.'

'I know!' She smiled again. 'I – we – only want it for one night. Not too much to ask, is it?' Flora was beginning to get the feeling that visiting Henry in his house might turn out to have been a mistake. Still, she'd promised the choir she'd ask about the orangery, and they'd been so supportive of her with the antiques roadshow and things, she had to give it a go.

'We'd better go through to the kitchen.'

Flora didn't want to waste time being given coffee and biscuits. 'Could we cut to the chase and go to the orangery?'

'Flora! I thought you'd come to see me, as at least part of your errand.'

'I'm working today, actually, Henry. I can't be too long.'

He shrugged, possibly not used to having his hospitality dismissed so summarily. 'OK, but I warn you, it's in about the same condition as the rest of the house.'

The auctioneer and valuer in her (as yet a small, undeveloped part) still noted, as they strode through the house, that there were no antiques, no rooms stuffed with old toys, paintings or other apparent rubbish that would turn out to be worth a fortune when discovered by the cognoscenti. That meant Annabelle's country-house sale was a non-starter and Flora could concentrate on the challenge Geoffrey had set her.

'You may remember, I'm a member of a choir.'

'I do, but I don't think you look old enough.' He smiled. 'Or, for that matter, young enough.'

'You don't have to be old, or a choirboy, to enjoy making music,' she replied primly.

Henry shrugged and opened the door to the orangery. By now Flora was fully prepared to find it completely unusable, and then it would have to be the hall. At least she would be able to go back to Geoffrey and tell him she'd done her best.

'Ah,' she said. There was a puddle the size of a small lake on the floor. 'Why is that water there?' she asked.

'Possibly because there's a hole in the roof.'

Flora looked up. One of the rooflights was broken, but she could only see one damaged pane, not a whole slew of them. 'Is it fixable?'

'Sure. If you've got enough money. Unfortunately, I haven't. You need scaffolding, you see, and it's more than just a broken pane. The woodwork is rotten so the whole frame needs replacing. It makes it all prohibitively expensive.'

'I see.'

'So, what was the favour?' He regarded her with the faint, not unattractive, arrogance of a man who is confident with women.

Flora pulled her shoulders back and returned his gaze. Her confidence wasn't quite equal to his, but she wasn't going to let him know that. 'Oh, didn't I say? I'm a member of a choir—'

'You said that.'

'And we would like to do a concert in your orangery. If you don't mind. And if it's suitable.'

'Well, obviously it's not suitable. There's a hole in the roof and a puddle on the floor.'

'There is that, but I expect we could mop up the water and pray for a fine night.'

He raised an unconvinced eyebrow. 'Supposing your prayers aren't answered? It was like Niagara here last night.'

'I can imagine.'

'Although, to be fair, considering how hard it rained and how long for, it's not too bad.'

Flora regarded the village-pond-sized pool and didn't comment.

'I expect you're wondering what I'm doing, living here in a house that's a candidate for a television appeal. Why I haven't mentioned it.'

Flora raised her eyebrows. She had more than her fair share of human curiosity and now he had brought the subject up, she did want to know.

'I had been thinking about going abroad,' he said, 'but I can't sell the house in this condition, or at least, for only a fraction of what it would be worth if it was properly restored. I want to earn the money, do it up, and make a killing.'

'Thank you for sharing,' said Flora, realising that she was unaffected by the news that he might be leaving the country.

'You are unusual. Most women go gooey at the thought of a beautiful house in need of restoration, especially if it comes attached to a . . .' He paused.

Flora raised her eyebrows, unable to resist a chuckle. 'You've shot yourself in the foot there, Henry! You can't possible say what you're thinking without appearing to be unbearably conceited.'

He laughed back at her.

'You obviously are fairly conceited,' she continued. 'But possibly not unbearably so.'

He smiled apologetically. 'Sorry, but you can see why I don't invite women back. They're either horrified and run away, or get pound signs in their eyes and prowl.'

She chuckled. Annabelle would have prowled. 'I won't do that, I promise.'

'I don't think I'd mind too much if you did.' They exchanged glances. Flora knew he was interested in her, and was making an effort to summon up more interest in him. He was available, after all.

'Can I make you a cup of coffee?' he offered. 'To make up for being such a prat? Although now I think about it, it'll have to be instant which probably won't make up for anything.'

Flora had previously decided to refuse coffee as she was so busy, but she didn't want to be churlish. She'd be furious with any woman of her acquaintance who didn't maximise her opportunities.

'I'd appreciate a cup of something. Instant coffee would be fine.'

Flora followed him into a seventies-style ginger-pine kitchen which she yearned to take an axe to. 'So why did you get divorced, Henry? It's the one fact about you that everyone knows and talks about.'

He sighed. 'Very much as you'd expect, I'm afraid.'

'Philandering?'

He frowned. 'You could call it that, I suppose, but there was only one woman.'

'And you are properly divorced, not just separated?'

'Divorced. She took me for every penny.'

'Good for her.'

'What do you mean, "good for her"? I was a good husband.'

'Who cheated.'

'OK. I was a good husband who cheated. That doesn't make me all bad, you know.'

'But not all good either. I don't suppose you have a tea bag instead, do you? Or did your wife take those, too?'

'I managed to hide a box from her. You can have tea. I even have biscuits, of a sort.'

Flora helped herself to a seat and watched as he filled the kettle, found biscuits and was generally hospitable. She understood, now, why she had been sent. Henry was a bit touchy about his house and if someone else had gone, even a young and female member of the choir, they might not have got the right result. Indeed, thought Flora, there was no guarantee that she would be successful, but at least she was in with a chance.

'Here's your tea. Only dried milk, I'm afraid.'

'That's OK.'

He pulled round the bench that was on the other side of the table where Flora was sitting.

'So, where abroad might you go?' she asked. 'If you went, I mean?'

'The States. Or maybe Switzerland.'

'Oh. They both sound quite exciting.'

'Mm. Well, to be honest,' he said with a glint in his eye that left Flora in no doubt at all that he was about to be far from honest, 'I'm only planning to sell up and leave because I'm broken-hearted. I mean, I'm getting nowhere with you and—'

Flora blushed, even though she knew he was joking. 'But you're not getting nowhere! We had dinner—'

'Bar snacks. Not the same.'

'And it wasn't my fault you couldn't come to my dinner party.'

'Probably just as well. Charles Stanza doesn't approve of me.'

309

'Oh? What makes you say that?'

'I met him in town the other day. He was perfectly polite and all that, but I got the impression he didn't really like me going out with his baby cousin.'

'I'm not his baby cousin! I'm his business partner.'

Henry shrugged. 'So, you want my orangery for some sort of concert.'

'Yes. My choir needs an appropriate venue for a concert called' – what was it Geoffrey had said? – '"A Stately Summer – Music for a Summer Evening".'

'And you want to use the orangery?'

'Yes. We'd be terribly tactful about it. We would hardly annoy you at all.'

'But what about the lake in the middle of it? Anyway, why on earth would I let a whole lot of strangers use my house?' He seemed to be joking, but Flora couldn't be sure.

'Well . . .' She took a breath. 'It's perfectly possible that among the choir members there are people who could fix the hole in the roof. That would be a good pay off, wouldn't it?' She knew one of the basses was a partner in a firm that made fitted kitchens. It wasn't quite the same as one who repaired glass roofs, but he probably had connections.

Henry looked thoughtfully at her for a moment. 'Well, yes. It would. But what about the other stuff? I really don't like people in my house, snooping round, and there'd be cars parked all over the lawn.'

'Your grass hasn't been a lawn for some time,' said Flora bluntly. 'And you could go away for the weekend. Then you'd come back to a manicured lawn and an orangery without a swimming pool. And you'd have that much less to do up before selling it.'

'And of course I may change my mind about selling. I may do it up and live in it. If I get over my broken heart.'

'I'm sure you'll recover, but you'd have to earn lots of money to sort this place out. What do you do, again?' She knew she should have known this, but her mind just hadn't been engaged when they first exchanged all this information.

'IT.'

'Oh. That's all right then. You can earn lots of money.'

'But sadly, not enough. Not right now, anyway. This house would swallow up a hundred grand and still have room for seconds.'

The thought that Burnet House might be perfect for Annabelle and Charles had flickered through Flora's mind quite early. The thought of them living there made her uncomfortable for some reason and the fact that it would be so fabulously expensive to renovate was perversely cheering. She decided to be helpful.

'I bet there's something here, something that's valuable, that your wife didn't know about.'

'It wasn't my wife who was the problem. It was her solicitor.'

'Sorry. Solicitor. I bet though, if I had a look around, I could find something worth selling. I'm an auctioneer, after all.'

'Apprentice, you said.'

Flora laughed. 'Well, OK, but I'm not a complete idiot, and if I found anything even half interesting, I could get Char— someone to come along to give you a proper valuation.'

'Well, there's a library, but I think I'd have known if there were any first edition Dickenses in it.'

'Or James Bond. He's valuable too.'

'Only if the dust-jackets aren't torn and therefore in pristine condition.'

She laughed. 'We obviously both watch the same television programmes.'

He regarded her. 'Why don't you finish your tea and come and look,' he said.

She hesitated for a moment.

'I assure you there are no etchings involved. Although I might ask you out to dinner, later. We still haven't done dinner, have we?'

She inclined her head politely.

'Would you come?'

'I was brought up to wait until I was asked,' she sidestepped. 'Shall we inspect the library?'

'The solicitor did send someone to look at everything,' Henry explained as they reached a room lined with bookshelves, obviously a custom-made library. 'But he admitted he wasn't all that up on old books. He searched for anything that was obviously a first edition, but didn't find any. He put a blanket value of five hundred pounds on the lot, and then went home. I think he was tired by then.'

'Are these books precious to you? If you sold them, would you miss them?'

'No, not really. This is a family house, but I didn't inherit it from my parents, but from an uncle. Sounds a bit unlikely, I know, but it's true.'

'Oh, I believe you. I'm involved in the auction business because of an uncle who died, too.'

'You never told me that before.'

'Didn't I?' Flora was not willing to be distracted. 'There are a lot of books here. Even if there are no very precious ones, the value in each one would mount up, don't you think?'

He shrugged. 'I don't know. You're the apprentice auctioneer.'

'You'd have to get rid of them, anyway, if you were going to do up the house. Unless you stored them. That might be quite expensive.'

'I certainly wouldn't want to do that. Tell you what, if you get your cousin, or whoever, to come and have a look, and if they agree there's enough here to have an auction that will make a bit of money, I'll let your choir use the orangery.'

'I see.'

'But I'd want to pay a lower commission. I know auction houses, they take money from the buyer, money from the seller and add in a lotting fee as well.'

'I don't think you quite understand how many expenses are involved in arranging an auction,' Flora started.

'No, I don't. But you want a favour. Can you offer me a deal in exchange?'

Flora thought for a moment. 'No. Not off my own bat. I don't know if there's anything here worth a damn.'

'I want the books gone.'

'We could arrange a house clearance, that wouldn't be difficult, but if you want one of our experts' – Henry wasn't to know there weren't loads of them kicking their heels in the office – 'to come and give a valuation, to look at everything, we'd need all the commission we're likely to earn.'

'In which case, I'm not sure, Flora. I could get any auction house to do that for me. I want a bit more, in exchange for the favour.'

'I didn't realise that favours were exchanged. I thought people just did them out of the kindness of their hearts.'

'Not this people,' he said with a grin that contradicted his words. 'The kindness of my heart is all run out.'

'Well, that's a shame. But no matter. The choir can easily have their concert in our hall in town.' She batted her eyelashes just once and then looked at her watch, but didn't actually take in what it said. 'I'd better be going. Thank you so much for your time. I'm sorry to have wasted so much of it.'

'Hang on! Don't walk off in a huff! There's still room for negotiation.'

Flora had hoped this was the case. 'Oh?'

'Will you come out to dinner with me?'

She enjoyed flirting with Henry. He, like her, seemed to be a natural flirt – he flirted as naturally as he breathed – and that reassured her that he didn't have any particularly serious intentions towards her. It did seem to be delightfully free of complications, though as she was pretty sure she didn't want the relationship to develop beyond a few casual evenings she rather felt she should make her feelings clear. 'Well,' she answered, 'it rather depends. Would I be doing you a favour in going to dinner with you? In which case you're more in my debt than I am in yours. Or are you doing me a favour by feeding me, when I'm obviously so near starvation? Because I could only come to dinner if I was the one doing you the favour.'

He had a very sexy laugh, she decided. 'Don't worry,

Flora. I won't read anything into dinner. So shall we sort out the favours at a later date?'

'Could do,' she agreed.

'And in the meantime, could you ask one of your experts to give the library the once-over?'

'I could do that, too. But I can't make any deals about commission or anything. That would be up to my cousin.'

'Well, I could talk to him when he comes to look at the books.'

'No,' she said hurriedly. 'It won't be him, and our book expert isn't a company director. He won't have the authority to make that sort of decision either. But when we know if there's much of value here, we can sort it out.'

'I suppose I'll have to be satisfied with that.'

She put her head on one side. 'And with the pleasure of taking me out to dinner.'

'That is some compensation.'

'Also, the pleasure that the choir will repair your roof and cut your grass and very much enjoy singing in your orangery.'

'Did I agree to let the choir come? When did that happen?'

'When I said I'd go out with you.' She gave him her most provocative smile.

'I know taking you to dinner will be a pleasure, but I'm still not sure about the choir.' He did genuinely look a bit worried.

'Trust me. It will be a very positive experience. I'll get Geoffrey to come and give your library a thorough going-over.'

'Will you come too?'

'I might.'

'I'll walk you to your car.'

Dear Henry, he was a sweetie. And quite sexy too. She wished she could develop a crush on him. It would be much more convenient.

As Flora opened the door of the Land-Rover, he said, 'I might see if they've got a table at Grantly Manor. It's very good. They've got a chef down from London going for his third Michelin star.'

'Sounds horrifically expensive.'

'Oh, it is, but far less than it would be in London.'

'That would be lovely,' she said, and kissed his cheek.

'Well?' demanded Geoffrey, when Flora had tracked him down in the cellar of the house, sticking labels on the furniture that had come in via the roadshow. 'How did you get on?'

'Not bad, but not perfect, I'm afraid. The orangery has got a hole in the roof, and therefore there's a small lake in it. I suggested we could mop up the water and pray for a dry night but Henry Burnet wasn't too keen on that idea. I don't think he believes in the power of prayer.'

'I feel a bit bad sending you, Flora. It's why I thought I'd better come in and do some work.'

'It was fine! Henry's a friend, after all.'

'Just a friend, Flora?' asked Geoffrey, *in loco parentis* again.

'Well, maybe a bit more than that. He's going to take me to Grantly Manor.'

'Oh. Very grand.'

Flora was tired of talking about Henry. 'I did say the choir would fix the hole in the roof. One of the basses is a builder, isn't he?'

'One of them is a cabinetmaker, if that's what you mean.'

Flora made a gesture with her hands that asked Geoffrey to be a little more helpful. 'For the choir, do you think he'd go down a few grades and fix a hole in the roof? He must know people with scaffolding and stuff.'

'Now you're talking big money.'

'Well, if it's impossible, there's always the hall. But although I wasn't too keen on having to beg Henry to let us use it, I do think the orangery would be lovely to sing in.'

'I'm sorry, my dear. I wasn't thinking. I'll ask about fixing the roof.'

'He also wants you to go and value his library. He doesn't think there's much there, but you never know. Someone did give them a cursory glance before, when they valued everything when he got divorced, but they didn't look thoroughly.'

'I expect I can do that. If I'm not needed here. It'll be a real pleasure to use my knowledge and experience for once, instead of pretending I haven't any.' He regarded Flora seriously. 'Annabelle won't like it if she finds out. She's always been dead set against me doing anything except moving things from one place to another.'

Flora inwardly protested the waste of his talent. 'I'll square it with Charles. It'll be all right.'

Geoffrey smiled. 'Well, that's all looking very promising, Flora. You've done well.' Geoffrey was obviously very pleased at the notion of being a valuer again, instead of just a porter. 'If there's enough to give us a basis, we could do a specialist book auction. Put all the stuff up on the Internet.'

'Right. I'm glad you're pleased. I just hope it's not all just book club editions and Sunday school prizes.'

'Very collectable those, you know, especially if they've got good book plates in the front.'

'Yes, well, I'd better go and see if anyone's missed me upstairs.'

She met Annabelle in the hallway. 'How did you get on at Burnet House?' she asked.

'OK. He has some books that might be quite valuable.'

'That's good. But I have to warn you, Charles was livid! I told him it was very unlikely there was a house sale in the offing, but he was really cross about you going there alone.'

'But he knows I know Henry, that we've been out a couple of times.' Charles's over-protectiveness could be exasperating sometimes.

'It's the going to his house thing that so upset him.'

'Oh. Well, there isn't enough furniture for a house sale, but Geoffrey's going to look at the books.'

'Is he now. Well, do check with Charles first. He can be so bloody difficult at times.'

'I'd better go and find him, then. Do you know where he is?'

'He's out. Why don't we pop across to the pub and see if they'll make us a sandwich? I know it's late but we need to eat. You certainly do.' Annabelle eyed Flora's slim figure with envy. 'It is Saturday, after all.'

Flora thought about it. An angry Charles was possibly better not faced on an empty stomach.

'Oh, OK. Just quickly. I ought to stay and work, really, as I've been out all morning.'

'You don't want to get like Charles, and do nothing but work, work, work. Besides, I want to hear all about Burnet House.'

They sat in the pub garden. It was a bit chilly, the air having not yet warmed up after the rain, but it was rather smoky inside and neither of them wanted to advertise the fact that they'd been to the pub when they got back.

Annabelle had bought two white wine spritzers and ordered a couple of egg salad sandwiches. She took a sip.

'Now, tell me about Burnet House?'

'It's in awful condition. Henry says—'

'There you are!' Charles's voice suddenly declared behind them. 'Flora, I was worried about you!'

Chapter Nineteen

✦❧✦❧

'Why were you worried about Flora, darling?' asked Annabelle.

'I just heard she went chasing off to Burnet House. There's no earthly point. There's nothing there to sell.' Charles pulled out a chair, the metal grating horribly on the flagged courtyard.

'Can I get you a drink?' Flora got up. 'A pint? A spritzer?'

'Oh, just something soft,' said Charles, obviously not quite happy with a woman buying him a drink and still distinctly grumpy.

'A sandwich? Crisps?'

'Um . . .'

Flora retreated to the bar. She didn't know why Charles was in such an awful mood but she would have to tell him why she'd been to Burnet House. Learning that her visit wasn't even work-related might make him even crosser. On the other hand, he might prefer her asking to use the house for a concert to her having some mad idea about getting Henry to have a country-house sale when he knew there was nothing worth selling.

She came back with an elderflower pressé and two packets of crisps, having ordered another sandwich. He was possibly more bad-tempered than necessary because he was hungry. Her mother had always commented that her father was impossible to deal with if remotely peckish.

'I think I should tell you,' she declared, setting down her booty, 'that I went to Burnet House to see if the choir could use their orangery. I know we're frantic and I was going to work, but it was an emergency.'

'And now you're in the pub?'

'Charles! It's Saturday! And the girl's got to eat!' Annabelle said.

'Was Henry Burnet there?' Charles tore into the crisp packet.

'He was. He showed me the orangery. There's a huge puddle on the floor. I don't suppose you know of a good builder who could fix that?' She looked at Annabelle and Charles hopefully. This was really the choir's responsibility, but it would be useful to have a fall-back position, especially as it might divert Charles's mind from Henry Burnet.

'Oh God yes, I'm sure we do,' said Annabelle, helping herself to crisps. 'I'm starving.'

'He didn't . . . make a nuisance of himself, did he?'

'Who?' asked Flora, being deliberately obtuse, annoyed with Charles for being so old-fashioned, but oddly charmed by it as well. 'The builder?'

'Henry Burnet! He's got a bit of a reputation. I know you've been out with him a couple of times, but it's different you being at his house. You're my cousin and I feel responsible for you.'

'For goodness' sake, Charles! Flora is an adult, and I'm sure she's been round the block a few times. There's no need to be so stuffy.'

'Well?' demanded Charles.

Flora suddenly decided she liked Charles being so indignant about Henry, even if it was just in a cousinly way. 'He did say he'd try to get a table for Grantly Manor. I don't know if that counts as making a nuisance of himself.'

'Grantly Manor! Flora! How super! It's wonderful. We had a family party there for Mummy and Daddy's wedding anniversary. Henry must be really keen.'

Charles scowled.

'I think Henry's rather attractive,' Annabelle went on, either not noticing, or ignoring, Charles's reaction. 'And his wife made such a fuss. It was only one affair, after all. You could do a lot worse than him, Flora.'

'You think it's acceptable for a man to cheat on his wife, do you, Annabelle?' said Charles.

'Not if he made a habit of it,' Annabelle replied. 'I just think a marriage should be worked at, and there are worse things a man can do than have a little fling.' She smiled and put her hand on Charles's. 'Don't think I'm giving you permission to get up to anything, Charlie, I'm just saying I wouldn't break up a relationship for one misdemeanour. What do you think, Flora?'

'I don't know, really. I've never been in a relationship for more than a couple of years, but I suppose if you've got children, a home, all that stuff, it would be a shame not to make an effort to try again.'

'Well, don't think I'm so relaxed about extra-marital affairs,' said Charles, glancing at Flora, trying hard to relax.

Annabelle laughed and for a second Flora wondered if there was an edge of hysteria in it. 'Darling, I'd never cheat on you when we're married! As if I would!'

At that moment, the sandwiches arrived. As cutlery, napkins and seasonings were distributed, Flora hoped it would mean Charles would have to stop being grumpy. If I was his partner, she thought, I'd have fun charming him out of his bad mood.

'Oh, jolly nice sandwich,' said Flora, when the waitress had finally gone, managing to ooze quite a lot of the filling out as she took a bite. 'How is yours, Charles?' she mumbled.

'Excellent, thank you.'

'So tell us about the house,' said Annabelle, her mouthful not quite finished either. 'I'm dying to hear all about it.'

Flora chewed hard and swallowed. 'Well, as I said, it's in a terrible state. He – Henry – told me that it needed about a hundred grand spending on it.'

'As much as that?' Annabelle was shocked. 'Shame. I thought it might do for us, Charles.'

'It's enormous!' said Flora. 'You'd have to have about seven children to justify living in it.'

'Or you could just entertain a lot. And a yoga studio would be nice,' said Annabelle, becoming a little dreamy. 'Or t'ai chi.'

'A yoga studio?' said Charles. 'What would you want that for?'

'Oh, I just thought I could take it up. It's very calming and a good way of getting rid of negative karma.'

Flora glanced at Annabelle, momentarily distracted. 'And the kitchen is vile, it's that very orange pine, with too many small cupboards,' she said. 'You'd have to rip that out and start again.'

'Well, I said his wife was a stupid woman. No taste,' said Annabelle.

'No taste but a lot of furniture,' said Flora. 'She left Henry hardly any.'

'I suppose if he wanted to keep the house he had to sell off a lot of it to pay her off,' said Annabelle. 'I wonder who did the sale?'

'Not us, obviously,' said Charles. 'So did he say if he was likely to sell the house itself?'

'He said he wanted to earn some money to do it up, then sell it. Or he might keep it. I don't think he quite knows what he wants to do.' She took another bite of sandwich, for protection.

'Well, you could do a lot worse than him,' Annabelle repeated.

'Don't be ridiculous!' said Charles. 'Why on earth do you think Flora should go out with Henry Burnet, of all people?'

Annabelle shrugged. 'No need to get all worked up, Charles. He's quite good-looking and Flora needs someone to take her around, doesn't she? You told me she was a girl who liked to have lots of boyfriends.'

Flora blushed at being referred to in such terms. 'I've really been too busy for much of a social life since I've been down here, but it is nice to have a friend.' She looked at her handbag as it moved slightly and played 'Jingle Bells'. 'Oh, so sorry,' she said, embarrassed. 'That's my phone. Do you mind if I take the call?'

'Of course not,' said Annabelle.

Flora moved away from the table. It was Henry.

'I've got a table. Grantly Manor. Are you interested?'

'Yes. When for?'

'Tonight. Terribly short notice, I'm afraid.'

Flora considered. She'd lent her copy of *The Rules* to a girlfriend, but she was fairly sure you weren't allowed to accept an invitation for Saturday made later than Wednesday. There had to be three clear days in between the invitation and the date. No way were you allowed to accept a date for the same day.

'It's extremely short notice.'

'Sorry. I thought I should strike while the iron was hot. You're always so busy.'

'Next week would be better.'

'No tables available for next week. It's now or about three weeks away.'

'I was going to wash my hair . . .'

Henry laughed. 'That takes about five minutes. You can't use that old excuse any more.'

Flora considered. *The Rules* were made to be broken and she didn't want to marry this man, after all. 'I'll wash it anyway. Shall I meet you in town?'

'No, I'll pick you up.'

Flora hesitated for a second. 'OK. I'd better give you directions. Or do you have a fax?'

'I do.'

'I'll send a map from the office.' She didn't necessarily want Charles and Annabelle to hear her giving Henry directions to the cottage.

When she came back to the table she couldn't help a little smile of satisfaction tugging at her mouth. 'That was Henry. He's got the table at Grantly Manor.'

'Oh?' asked Charles, frowning. 'When for?'

Flora wished he hadn't asked that. It took the gilt off the gingerbread, somewhat. 'Tonight.'

'They must have had a cancellation,' said Annabelle, who obviously hadn't read *The Rules*.

'Well, it'll be fun, whatever. And now I must fly, I've got loads to do because I was out half the morning.'

Flora went back to the office in a buoyant mood. She was excited about the thought of going out with Henry, she told herself. If Charles was cross about it, then too bad. He was a silly old stick-in-the-mud. She reflected that usually when men were grumpy she just wanted to tip a bucket of water over them and tell them to snap out of it, but Charles's grumpiness was quite sexy in a Mr Darcy kind of way. And she was uncomfortably aware that at the back of her mind there was a small voice asking whether perhaps Charles was annoyed at her going out with Henry just because it was Henry, or whether he'd have objected to anyone she went out to dinner with. But no, mentally she gave herself a little shake, he'd made his position quite clear on Thursday night.

'Hi, Geoffrey,' she called when she got back. 'What are you up to?'

'Oh, Flora, I'm glad to see you. Virginia's daughter was on the phone. She wants photos of all the good pieces for the website. I wouldn't know where to start.'

'No probs. I'll borrow the digital camera. I'm sure there's somewhere in the cellar we could rig up an area with a white cloth to set the pieces off. Shall we go and look?' They went downstairs together. 'I've done this sort of thing heaps of times. When I worked in an art gallery.'

'Charles has put stickers on the ones to be on the

website,' said Geoffrey, opening a door. 'What about in here? Not too crowded. You're very cheerful.'

'Just back from the pub. Charles and Annabelle are still there. Charles was in a grump, but I expect Annabelle knows how to make him feel better. They're very well suited, after all. I think this would be fine.'

'Well suited, are they?'

'Oh yes. Both stiff as pokers, although at least Annabelle tried to stop him going on at me about visiting Burnet House. I'll borrow that cloth over there. It looks big enough.'

'Should be, it was a double sheet, once.'

Flora found a nail to hang it on. 'Henry wants a reduction in commission. I said I couldn't give him one, that I'd have to ask Charles. I wish I had the authority to do it myself. After all, I'm an equal partner, technically speaking, anyway. But not in any other sense. Anyway, what are you doing working on a Saturday?'

'I told you. And you know there's a lot on at the moment, and Edie's gone off to a plant sale with a friend.'

'Ah.'

'And you don't see Charles and Annabelle working on Saturday unless there's something very special on.'

'Charles does work very hard. He was at a farm valuation until late last night.' She knew this because she had seen the note he'd left for Louisa when she came in. She'd been tempted to type it up herself and might have done if she hadn't gone out. In a bizarre way the thought of sitting with ear plugs, listening to Charles, was quite pleasant.

'Shall we start with the chest-on-chest?' said Geoffrey. 'As it's in here already?'

'Good idea. Thank heavens there's two of us, Geoffrey,' she went on as they heaved the heavy furniture around. 'It's too much for anyone on their own. Do you think we can get it in front of the sheet, or shall I try to think of something else?'

'We'll manage it all right between us.'

Flora was breathing hard by the time they had eased it out from between a couple of commodes and got it in position. 'Now I'm going to have to practically climb out of the window to get it all in. Perhaps if I stand on this chair . . . It's all right, I'll put this bit of cloth on it – it's not an antique camel rug, is it? OK. You couldn't just pull out the corner of the white sheet. It looks a bit . . . That's better. Now smile, please. Look natural.'

Geoffrey chuckled.

'Well, it's important it looks its best. I think this is the piece Charles's genuine television expert was so enthusiastic about.'

'Television expert! Honestly, what do they know?' said Geoffrey.

'But it is a nice piece. It might go for three grand if it's properly advertised and the buyers turn up. George the Third, he thought.'

'Well, I'm not saying he's got the date wrong, but those are London prices, if you ask me.'

The chest-on-chest duly recorded, Geoffrey and Flora edged it back to its nook in the corner. 'So why is there such a hurry to get all this photographed?' he asked again, wiping his brow with a tartan handkerchief.

'It's partly so there's plenty of time for dealers to realise that Stanza and Stanza have decent stuff to sell. Because we've been a bit down-market in recent years, with few real antiques, we've got to build up our reputation. If the stuff is on the website, and all the links are right, the dealers will find out we're here, so to speak.'

'You're not going to be working all day, are you?' said Geoffrey, lifting a table with the skill that revealed his years of experience.

'Oh no. I've got a date tonight, with Henry. Grantly Manor. Charles was not pleased to hear about it. He seems to think Henry's some sort of Lothario and I won't be safe.'

'He's only looking out for you, as he should,' said Geoffrey, taking on the appearance of someone about to give a lecture.

'Don't you start, Geoffrey!' said Flora. 'A girl's got to have a bit of fun. Now, what's next? And don't let me forget to fax Henry a map.'

'It's always cheering, getting ready for a date,' said Flora to Imelda and the kittens. 'I'm determined to have a good time tonight. I deserve one! I've worked very hard lately, and Henry is fun.' She thought briefly of someone she would not describe as fun and then pushed him out of her mind. Henry liked her, he was very attractive and most of all he was available, so she was determined to give herself one more shot at developing a crush on him.

She put on her prettiest dress, did her hair and her make-up carefully, and put the shoes with the peony on them into a bag. Her mother, who was a fount of slightly dubious advice, had always told her to have running-away shoes to hand, in case. She'd also told her to keep enough money for a taxi home in her bra, in case she got separated from her handbag.

'So?' she asked Imelda, lacking anyone with more sartorial sense. 'Do I look OK?'

Imelda purred obligingly, and turned her attention to Charles's favourite kitten, who obviously needed a very thorough wash.

'I'll take that as a yes,' said Flora and sprayed herself liberally with scent, realising too late it was rather sexy, and was best applied sparingly. She shrugged and went downstairs to wait for Henry. She'd faxed him a map which Geoffrey, obliging but reluctant, had drawn for her.

She had barely had time to plump up the cushions and throw the dead flowers into the fireplace before she heard Henry's car drive up.

'The map worked OK, then?'

'Very well.' He kissed her cheek. 'Mm. You smell gorgeous.'

'You smell quite nice yourself. Shall we go?' She picked up her pashmina and her house keys, called 'Goodbye' to Imelda and they left the house. Henry's car was an old Jaguar XK120. 'Mm. Nice car,' she murmured, thinking that it was exactly the sort of car she'd thought Henry would own.

'A bit of a cliché, I'm afraid. I bought it in a fit of rebellion after Natasha left, taking most of my worldly goods with her. This represents most of what was left. Fifteenth-hand, of course.' He opened the passenger door and Flora slid in.

Grantly Manor was everything its name and reputation promised – a venerable old house set back from the road and arrived at via a carriage sweep. A good-looking young man arrived to park the car. Flora was impressed.

Henry was investing quite a lot of what he didn't spend on the car to show her a good time. Good for Henry!

'It would be better if they drove you home again afterwards,' he said, relinquishing his keys, 'but I suppose that would be rather expensive.'

'I could drive, if you like. That's a very nice car.'

'Not that I don't trust you, Flora, but it's only insured for me to drive.' His grin became rakish. 'Besides, this way, I can ply you with alcohol and stay perfectly sober myself.'

'Not that I don't trust you, Henry, but I won't drink too much, I don't think.'

He laughed, and ushered her into a panelled bar furnished with comfortable-looking sofas and small tables. Although it was summer, and not cold, a small log fire smouldered in the huge grate.

'This is gorgeous!' said Flora. 'I love having fires in summer. It's so decadent, somehow.'

'They do pay attention to detail. I think that's the secret of a really good hotel or restaurant. So, what can I get you? A glass of champagne?'

'Mm, that would be lovely.' Flora smiled and settled back into the cushions.

Henry brought menus with the drinks. Flora took hers.

'Why don't you have the oysters?' suggested Henry.

She looked at him over the top of her menu. 'I don't think I want an aphrodisiac.'

He laughed. 'I thought they only affected men.'

'I think I'll have the smoked salmon, as I don't want to leave room for pudding.' She regarded him. 'My mother has an old recipe book that says "Never trust a man who refuses apple dumplings".'

'I never do. Are they on the menu?'

'No, so I can't test you. I heard someone else say, "Never trust a man who owns a picnic set". Do you?'

'I don't think so.' Henry feigned anxiety. 'There may be one in the attic. I'm not sure.'

'Oh, if there is, put it in a sale. They sometimes go quite well if they've got all their fittings. My colleague Geoffrey was telling me the other day.'

'I didn't bring you here to talk about work, Flora. Think what you want to eat.'

'Guinea fowl sound interesting.'

'They don't, actually, they just make a quite boring clucking sound.'

'I meant to eat! Now don't get distracted. The girl will be back in a minute. It's such a bore when guests don't make up their minds because they're chatting. I've been a waitress,' she added, 'so I know.'

When they had eventually chosen, the waitress, who looked as if she was moonlighting from her day job as a model, so long were her legs and so short was her skirt, asked them if they'd like to sit outside. 'We've set a few tables at the end of the garden. It's very pretty.'

'It sounds lovely,' said Flora. 'What do you think, Henry?'

'If you'd like that, we'll eat there.'

They were led to a table by the French doors that opened on to the lawn that led down to the river. It was a glorious summer evening. The air was scented with jasmine and philadelphus, and peacocks strutted about, adding their raucous cry to the murmurings of people enjoying themselves.

Henry had ordered more champagne. 'I only want

one glass, so it might as well be the best. Here's to you.'

His eyes glittered down into hers as Flora raised her glass to his. He really was very attractive, in a rakish, obvious way, and, still determined to make an effort, she flicked back her hair with a slanting smile.

They were halfway through their starters when Charles and Annabelle drew to a halt just by them. Flora had her elbows on the table and was explaining to Henry how exciting working for an auction house was. She was very animated and slightly flushed, and the strap of her dress had slipped off her shoulder.

'Oh,' said Charles. 'Hello, Flora.'

Annabelle, slightly behind Charles, said, 'Surprise! We were so jealous to think of you both here, on this lovely summer evening, that we thought we'd treat ourselves. It was Charles's idea.'

'Oh really,' said Flora dryly, not at all pleased to see them. 'You just had a sudden urge to come here, Charles?'

'That's right,' he said rather woodenly.

'Tonight?'

'Yes, tonight.' He had the grace to look slightly self-conscious; he clearly knew she knew that he was there to keep an eye on his cousin and the philanderer he thought she needed protection from. Really, thought Flora, irritated, what century did he think he was living in?

Henry had already got to his feet and Flora leapt to hers, losing a shoe in the process. 'Fine. What a . . . er . . . surprise. Let me introduce you to Henry. Henry Burnet, Charles Stanza.'

'Actually, we have met,' said Charles, crushing Henry's hand in a trial of strength.

'Henry, this is Annabelle, Charles's fiancée,' said Flora, trusting that Annabelle would be more friendly.

'We know each other too, Henry.' Annabelle had followed Flora's instructions as to her appearance and was looking almost glamorous. 'We met at the Williams-Ellises – remember?'

'How could I forget?' Henry bowed over Annabelle's hand. Then he looked at Flora. 'Didn't you trust me?'

'Of course!' How embarrassing! 'Annabelle, I didn't ask you to come, did I?'

'Dear me, no! As I said, we just thought it was a perfect night for this place, and when we phoned on the off-chance they had a table.' She addressed Henry. 'I expect they had a large cancellation.'

'I expect so,' Henry agreed resignedly.

'Do you mind if we join you?' suggested Charles. 'You've only got as far as your starters.'

'Ooh, that would be fun!' said Annabelle, either oblivious to Flora's dirty looks or choosing to ignore them. 'It's quite dull going out when it's just the two of you, isn't it?' She pulled up a chair.

'Yes,' said Charles. 'After all, we know it's not a first date, so you won't mind.'

'Won't we?' said Henry.

Flora shrugged.

Seeing that he couldn't save the situation now, Henry said, 'You can join us on the firm understanding that next time Flora and I dine, it'll be on our own.' He smiled. 'She's a very difficult girl to get to go out with.'

'Is she?' said Charles blandly. 'That's reassuring.'

The waitress appeared. 'We could order another bottle of champagne,' said Henry, 'or would you rather not?'

'I don't want to drink too much,' murmured Flora.

'Oh, go on,' said Annabelle. 'Relax! Have another glass of champagne.' She leant in and whispered, 'If these two are going to be like dogs about to fight, we might as well get drunk and enjoy ourselves.'

Flora couldn't decide if having Charles to annoy would enhance the evening or not, but she silently agreed that a second glass of champagne might help things along a bit. 'Oh, OK. It's Sunday tomorrow. As long as Geoffrey doesn't make me go to a car-boot sale.'

'What?' asked the others in unison.

'Never mind. Here's to us all!'

Chapter Twenty

As she lowered her glass, Flora remembered her resolution to enjoy herself, and smiled warmly at Henry. His evening had been thoroughly mucked up – and her resolution to develop a crush on him wasn't exactly helped by Charles and Annabelle's presence.

'Well, Charles, are you the director of the firm where Flora works?' asked Henry, good-naturedly.

'The firm that Flora half owns, yes,' said Charles.

Henry frowned at Flora. 'You half own it? Why didn't you tell me? And why on earth couldn't you agree a lower percentage with me?' He turned to Charles. 'I wanted her to give me a special rate – a lower commission – and she said she couldn't.'

'I did say I was an apprentice,' Flora pointed out. 'That sort of decision is entirely up to Charles. And as it isn't his choir who wants to go and sing at Burnet House, he probably isn't open to offers.'

'Well?' demanded Henry, in a way that made Flora like him a little less.

'Oh, let's not talk about business,' said Annabelle, smiling at Henry. 'We're here to have a break from work. I'm part of Stanza and Stanza, too,' she added.

'Quite right,' said Flora. 'It's Saturday night. We're all in this lovely place – the food is wonderful, by the way

– we shouldn't sully the occasion with mere commerce.'
She took rather a large gulp of champagne.

'That's fine by me,' said Charles.

'So, Henry,' said Flora, touching his hand with her finger. 'How was your day?'

Flora found herself tuning out while Henry regaled the company with horror stories about viruses and worms and other IT disasters. She noticed quite a lot of it involved Henry saving various companies millions, but quite how he did it passed her by.

'Jolly interesting,' said Annabelle gamely. 'Now tell us about your car?'

That filled the conversational gap until Annabelle and Charles's food came, but as the evening went on, Flora began to wonder how much in common she actually had with Henry. He was very amusing, he told quite good, if slightly off-colour, jokes, but she couldn't help feeling that his conversation was rather vapid. Not that philosophy was exactly flowing out of her, it had to be said. Charles, on the other hand, was much more interesting. He'd travelled, to quite unusual places, and was widely read. Henry was a man who didn't read much unless he was on a plane.

The alcohol flowed, mostly between Flora and Annabelle, and there was never a ghastly silence, but Flora found herself faintly bored. She had really wanted to hear about Charles's experiences in Mongolia, but Henry seemed keener on telling stories about spotting stars at Cap Ferrat.

Eventually, it was time for pudding.

'Now, what would you girls like to drink with it?' said Henry.

Unusually for her, Flora found herself objecting to being referred to as a girl. She didn't say anything, though. 'I think I've probably had quite enough to drink, thank you.'

'Oh, go on, don't be a wuss. I'm sure Annabelle will have a glass of Monbazillac or something.'

'Oh, OK,' said Annabelle. 'I've drunk loads of water, after all. It's why I've kept going to the Ladies'.'

Flora had noticed that she'd popped out rather a lot. 'I still won't have any more to drink, thank you. Although I'd love some peppermint tea.'

'Peppermint tea it is,' said Henry, looking at her in a way which told her he was looking forward to the next part of the evening.

'Yes. I've got a bit of a headache,' she replied, suddenly deciding, rather recklessly, in view of the latest bank statement that she was definitely going to split the bill with Henry rather than let him pay for her. 'It's frightfully good for that.'

Henry behaved very well, considering, thought Flora, as she let herself into the cottage. He'd been expecting a dinner à deux, and possibly a little light lovemaking afterwards, and he got Charles and Annabelle and only the briefest kiss in the car afterwards. It was not unreasonable of him to expect to be asked in for coffee, she had led him on a bit even though her insistence on paying her half of the bill had made her caution clear, but the headache was now real, and she didn't want any more wet kisses.

She rang him the next morning feeling a bit guilty, and asked him if he wanted to go for a walk that afternoon.

'I'm sorry Flora, I'd love to, but I'm afraid I'm going out to lunch with some friends.' He did sound sorry, and Flora realised she really had to make her feelings clear to him. She liked him, he was good company most of the time, but hard as she'd tried to fancy him last night, the spark clearly wasn't there.

'Well, I'm glad I caught you,' she started. 'I wanted to . . .' God, this was awkward. How to put it? 'I just wanted to say how much I enjoyed last night, the place and everything, and that I value our friendship.' Oh dear, that sounded horribly formal. 'But—'

'But you don't want anything more than that?' Henry interrupted.

'No, I'm sorry. I just . . .' She paused to collect her thoughts, 'I'm just not in the right frame of mind, really. I don't know how long I'll be in Bishopsbridge anyway, and I'm so involved with Stanza and Stanza and learning about the business that I'm not sure I've got the energy for a proper relationship.'

'Yes,' he said dryly. 'I had noticed that you were . . . how should I put it? Distracted?'

'I'm sorry, Henry. I do want to be friends.'

'Me too.' He softened. 'But don't worry, I always knew your mind at least was elsewhere. It's been ridiculously hard even to organise a drink in the pub, so I was under no illusions about your priorities.'

'I really am sorry.'

'There's no harm done,' he said lightly. 'I do like you, Flora, but I'm not falling in love with you if that's what you're worried about.' It was, rather. 'So if you want to be friends, then we'll be friends. I might not give up trying to persuade you,' he added flirtatiously, 'but you

339

know I might well be selling up and leaving the area as well, so it doesn't make sense for either of us to get involved in anything terribly serious.'

'Thank you, Henry. It's good of you to be so nice about it.'

'I'm a nice man,' he replied with a smile in his voice, and then dashed off to his lunch.

Instead of a walk with Henry, Flora made rock cakes in a fit of domesticity and ate most of them herself, talking to Imelda, wondering why the little black kitten allowed Charles to pick him up, but still shied away from her.

Just under two weeks later, Flora was making up the spare room for her mother. She was so excited, and longing to see her. In many ways her life was perfect, but something was missing. She was fine when she was at work. She still found it all fascinating, and absorbed every scrap about the job that either Charles or Geoffrey let slip, but at home, she found she missed William. Or something. She still went out with Henry from time to time, but although she tried very hard, she didn't find him quite as fascinating as he seemed to find himself.

Her mother would know what was wrong. She was an excellent agony aunt – and also an excellent cook. Flora was looking forward to being looked after and cosseted, something her mother did particularly well.

Almost every hour had been accounted for since the bizarre evening at Grantly Manor. They had at last got the website going, and the date for the next sale was booked for early September. It was going to take one and a half days, and Henry's books, declared by Geoffrey to be sufficiently interesting to get a few collectors along, were going to start the sale. At work, everyone was buzzing with excitement and busyness, and even Annabelle had become more enthusiastic about life – not necessarily about work, but she was generally more skippy and happy.

The concert, the excuse for Flora's mother's visit, was tomorrow. Flora was beside herself with nerves, in spite of having had several private practice sessions with Moira, the unofficial head girl of the choir.

'If I mess up,' she explained to Moira, who had patiently bashed out the tunes of all the music on the piano until Flora knew them backwards, 'I'll ruin it for everyone.'

'You won't mess up,' Moira had said, sounding a little bored with having to repeat herself. 'You know the music, just concentrate, keep looking at James – he's the conductor, you know – and you'll be fine.'

'I think I just about know who James is.'

'Then you'll be fine! Enough panicking!'

Now Flora went into the garden to pick flowers for her mother's bedroom. She was driving down from London that evening and Flora wanted everything to be perfect for her. She had already found roses, lady's-mantle and mauve geraniums for the sitting room and bathroom. Now she wanted something extra sweet and tiny for the little mantelpiece in the bedroom.

'You're jolly lucky I'm not making you all wear bows round your necks,' she said to the kittens, who had grown up enormously and were tearing round the house like motorbikes out of control. Flora wasn't looking forward to explaining to Annabelle about the curtains. They were definitely taking on a hooked appearance from being swarmed up and down so often. Could she convince Annabelle that the curtains had always had that uncut-moquette look? The sofa she had protected with throws – a little too late, but she could leave the throws and Annabelle might never take them off.

She waded through the kittens to get to the garden. 'I'll have to find homes for you soon, those two of you who aren't going to live with Uncle Geoffrey and Auntie Edie. I might keep one.' She sighed. Charles had said he wanted the little black one, but he hadn't said anything about it recently.

As she climbed over the barricade she had erected to stop them getting outside, she wondered if talking aloud to kittens was on a par with talking to oneself on the guide-to-madness scale. Definitely not, she decided, kittens were animate. Mind you, so was she.

Having constructed the most perfect tiny posy, using forget-me-nots, tiny branches of yellow lady's-mantle and white ground elder, borage flowers, and a couple of spires of purple linaria, she came back inside. She had been tempted to add the little white flowers of the goose-grass which was currently weaving a net over the garden like something out of a sci-fi movie, but had decided she hated the weed too much. Early that morning, Flora had attacked it with a fork, winding it round and round the tines like spaghetti, but in parts of the garden it was still threatening to pin everything to the ground.

Now, she put the posy in the milk jug from a doll's tea set. She had bought the set from a recent car-boot jaunt. It wasn't complete, but it had only cost a couple of pounds; it was perfect for this purpose. Her mother would love it; she had a passion for tiny things.

In the kitchen, Flora had all the makings of a wonderful supper. Two bottles of Sauvignon Blanc from New Zealand, as recommended by the nice man in the off-licence, were in the fridge. To have with it, she had made lacy parmesan wafers, which had involved a lot of testing, they were so delicious. Smoked salmon on blinis with sour cream and pancetta were laid out on a very pretty platter, another car-boot find, and she had even sprinkled a few beads of lumpfish roe, in lieu of caviar, on the top, for decorative effect. As a main course they were going to have a William-inspired salad, enhanced with bits and pieces from the garden, chicken breasts poached in white vermouth with a lemon sauce, and accompanying it, in case it looked too much like diet food, was potato salad with home-made mayonnaise sprinkled with chives. For pudding she had made a raspberry pavlova, using the egg whites from the mayonnaise and raspberries given to her by Geoffrey and Edie when they heard her mother was coming. Everyone was looking forward to meeting her.

Restraining the kittens with difficulty, Flora climbed back out into the garden. It was such a beautiful evening she thought it would be nice to eat at the little table and chairs Charles had brought her, when she first moved here. It seemed a lifetime ago, and in a way it was – her life had changed so irrevocably since.

At last Flora saw a car appearing along the lane and rushed out so she was there the moment her mother got her first foot out of the car.

'Sorry, darling, I got a bit lost,' said her mother and crushed her daughter so tightly she couldn't breathe.

'Mummy!' said Flora, reverting to a form of address she hadn't used for years. 'It's so lovely to see you!' Flora hung on to her mother a little longer than she would have normally because she found herself weeping a little, and didn't want her mother to see. She wanted to be the adult daughter one hundred per cent.

'Let me take your bag. Oh, it's so nice having you here!'

Hermione Stanza looked about her. 'Isn't this pretty! Darling, no wonder you're so happy here.' She gave her daughter a quick glance and frowned a little.

Flora hoped her mother couldn't tell she hadn't been sleeping properly. She'd made such an effort to sound totally enthusiastic about everything in her emails and phone calls, she didn't want to reveal anything untoward when face to face. After all, her vague, underlying unhappiness was totally illogical. It wasn't fair to worry her mother with it when she couldn't do anything to help.

'Come on in. I've got a bottle of wine in the fridge. Goodness, this bag is heavy! What have you got in it?'

'A bottle of vodka, some gin and sweet Martini so we can cobble together some Pimm's and some lemonade, in case you didn't think to buy any. Oh and a dessert wine – Muscat and Flora, because it had your name on it.'

'Oh Mum, you're a star!'

Hermione needed a guided tour. She loved her bedroom, which Flora had made very pretty, and she adored the posy. She approved of the various unguents Flora had put in the bathroom, as well as the huge jug of cow-parsley that Flora put at the end of the bath.

'And this is my bedroom. And that's the cupboard where Imelda had her kittens.'

'But, darling! It's full of shoes!'

'I know. Imelda likes shoes. I had to clean out each one afterwards.' Her mother made an uncomfortable noise. 'Let's go downstairs and have a drink.'

They were both quite tipsy and had eaten the parmesan wafers and the smoked-salmon blinis when they saw a vehicle come down the lane. It was Charles.

'I'm so sorry to interrupt,' he said as he got out and saw them sitting in the garden, surrounded by plates and bottles, 'but I wanted to come and say hello to Hermione. It's been a while since we met.'

Flora's mother got to her feet in order to embrace Charles, who leant down and hugged her.

'It's been years, Charles,' said Hermione, 'but I'm going to resist the temptation to tell you that you've grown. Have you eaten? Come and join us. There seems to be masses of food.'

Flora smiled, feeling suddenly very shy. 'The trouble is, I can only do recipes for four people or over. I've never got the hang of half measures. There is loads.'

Charles looked at his watch. 'Well, I haven't eaten. I'll just give Annabelle a ring and see if she's cooked. If she hasn't, I'm sure she'll be glad not to have to.'

'I'll get some things,' said Flora. 'Will you have a glass of wine, or a home-made Pimm's?'

'The Pimm's is a bit strong, I'm afraid,' said Hermione.

'I couldn't quite remember how my husband makes it. And we've run out of lemonade.'

'A glass of wine would be lovely. Are you sure this isn't all too much trouble?'

'No,' said Flora. 'It's all too much food. You'll be helping us out.'

Charles came into the house to help. 'There's a chair there you could take,' said Flora, when he asked.

Charles wasn't showing much interest in chairs. 'I haven't seen the kittens for ages. They've grown up so much!' He picked up the little black one and inspected it while it chewed his finger.

'I thought you'd come to see my mother,' said Flora, feigning indignation. Her heart was warmed by the sight of him with the tiny creatures, although she was still a bit miffed about the black kitten cowering away from her, and yet going to him.

'I did, but the kittens were second on the list.'

Flora sighed, suddenly wishing she had a place on the list herself. If she had, it was probably about number seven, somewhere after the cottage, the garden and the state of the sitting-room carpet.

Once they had got back over the barricade with extra things, Flora piled Charles's plate with chicken and potato salad. 'There's another plate there you can put your green salad on if you like,' she said.

'It's wonderful,' mumbled Charles, his mouth full. 'You really can cook, Flora. Or did you do this, Hermione?'

'No, no. It's all Flora.'

'And has Henry sampled your cooking yet?' he asked Flora, once his mouth was empty.

Flora shook her heard. 'Not yet. We've both been

busy. I've been doing a lot of extra rehearsals with choir and with Moira. She's sort of head girl,' she explained. 'Although soon, maybe.' She added this for Charles's benefit as much as anything. Although neither of them had ever referred to it, she was still faintly embarrassed at the thought of the night he'd stayed in the cottage after the storm, and the thought of the long, close hug he'd given her as he'd sent her off to bed made her feel a bit peculiar. All of which meant that, inconvenient as his particular dislike of Henry was, it was far better that he thought she was occupied and in a sort of a relationship than that she was pining for him. Which obviously she wasn't.

'Have some salad, Charles,' said Hermione. 'It's really delicious. Full of all sorts of weeds.'

Charles heaped some on to his side plate. 'I've experienced Flora's salad before. She gave a dinner party soon after she first arrived.'

'Except William made that salad. I just copied his ideas this time.' She looked at her mother. 'Have you met William? Friend of Emma's?' she asked, wondering whether if you told a lie often enough, it would eventually become the truth, or only for the originator of the lie.

'I don't think so,' said Hermione.

'Oh, well, he's an excellent cook.' Flora went on, 'He's great on cooking food from the wild.' She regarded Charles's side plate. 'You don't have to eat all that if you don't want to.'

'Flora and I will eat the rest of the salad tomorrow. Possibly for lunch, before Flora goes to her concert rehearsal,' said Hermione. 'Are you coming, Charles?'

'Um . . . I'm not sure I knew about it.'

'Well, you should,' said Flora, suddenly indignant. 'Geoffrey and all your porters, or at least nearly all of them, are in the choir. And there's a huge poster in the window of the office. Anyway I did tell you, ages ago.'

'I've just never had it put in front of my nose, I suppose. And the poster would have its back to me.'

'I think you should go,' declared Hermione. 'Support your workers. And Flora.'

'Unfortunately, Annabelle and I have been invited out for dinner tomorrow night,' said Charles.

'Oh, OK,' said Flora, disappointed yet relieved. She wasn't really sure she wanted Charles watching her as she stood in the front row, trying to look as if she knew what she was doing.

'Next time, perhaps?' suggested Hermione.

'Definitely next time. You must give me plenty of notice, Flora.'

Flora indicated she would, knowing it was unlikely she would still be around to be in another concert. This was the choir's last event for a while and by the time the Christmas fixtures started, she would probably have gone back to London. The choir was one of the many things that she would miss terribly.

'Shall we move inside for pudding? I'm getting a bit chilly,' suggested Hermione.

'Good idea,' said Flora. 'I'll get it organised. Bring your chairs and your glasses. We can probably leave the rest.'

Hermione decided to rescue the salad and a few other bits and pieces as well. By the time they were all back in the house, most of the table outside had been cleared.

Hermione sat down on the sofa and picked up the nearest kitten. 'Aren't these just adorable?'

Charles found the black one. 'They are.'

'I haven't managed to stroke that one yet. He's very shy, but he seems OK with you.' Hermione frowned. She was good with cats.

Charles continued to stroke his kitten. 'It's very unfortunate that Annabelle, my fiancée, has an allergy to them. But I'm still hoping we can have one in the office.'

'You couldn't leave it alone at night while it's still young,' said Flora protectively, clearing a space on a little table.

'Oh, that's all right. I could stay in the flat for a while, until it's a bit older.'

'There's a flat in the office building?' asked Hermione.

'Yes. It's an old town house. We're thinking of putting it on the market, to realise some capital. Or possibly part of it, converted into flats. It was Flora's idea,' said Charles. 'She's been really innovative since she's joined us.'

'Flora always was an ideas person,' said Hermione, glancing at her daughter with pride.

'We were expecting a ditsy blonde,' explained Charles. 'Who knew nothing about auctions and antiques.'

Flora laughed, and handed him a plate of meringue, raspberries and cream. 'Well, you were right. I am blonde and I did know nothing about antiques or auction houses. I know a bit more now, though. And you hate my teapot.'

Everyone inspected the ball-of-wool-shaped pot, covered in ceramic kittens.

'Oh, darling, I'd thought you'd given up collecting

those,' said Hermione, obviously wishing that Flora had.

'I have to confess I prefer the real thing to the china variety of kitten, but those teapots do have a certain market,' said Charles.

Flora chuckled softly at this display of tact. He glanced at her and carried on, 'But generally you picked it up very quickly, and you have a great gift with people.'

'There!' said Hermione triumphantly. 'I told you that personal skills were more important than academic qualifications!'

'Thank you, Mother' – Flora handed her mother a loaded plate – 'for more or less telling Charles I didn't do too well in my exams.'

'Exams aren't everything and I'm sure Charles knows that.' Hermione smiled and Flora could almost see Charles softening under the warmth of it.

'Well, I do now,' he said.

Flora perched on the arm of the sofa where her mother sat. 'These are Geoffrey's raspberries. Dig in.'

'Delicious!' Hermione got to her feet after a short time when the scraping of plates replaced conversation. 'Can I get you some more, Charles?' She took his plate. 'Are you sure? I'll just tidy up the edges and start my diet tomorrow. Have you heard about it? You don't measure calories, just G. I.s or something.' She frowned. 'I haven't finished reading the book, but it's really good! Not that you need to think about anything like that, Flora. I'll go and put the kettle on.'

'Your mother is very like you,' said Charles.

Flora was used to hearing this. 'Is that good or bad?'

'Very good. She's delightful.'

Flora smiled. 'She's a fun mother to have, I must say.'

She fell silent, suddenly shy. Then she spotted the kitten, curled up on his neck, fast asleep. 'He really likes you. You must have him.'

'Annabelle might become accustomed to him. I've heard of people who are allergic to cats but are all right with their own.'

Flora sighed. 'But she wouldn't like the process of getting used to him.' She wondered if part of her sub-clinical misery was worry about how well Annabelle and Charles were suited. The thought of Charles spending the rest of his life with the wrong woman was deeply depressing. He deserved to be happy. He worked so hard.

As if agreeing with her, Charles sighed. 'No, I suppose not. I'll work something out.'

Flora slid off the arm and on to the sofa. She felt very tired. What she wanted more than anything else in the world was just to fall asleep, next to Charles. She let her eyes close.

Hermione came in with coffee and peppermint tea. Flora opened her eyes and accepted a mug. Her mother arranged the little table and put Charles's coffee near him.

'I need a shot of caffeine to wake me up,' he said. 'I was getting really drowsy just now. This is really good.'

'I brought the coffee with me. Flora said it isn't always easy to get good coffee down here.'

'Oh, you can't know the proper shops!' said Charles. 'There's a wonderful coffee shop. I must take you there.'

'That would be nice,' said Flora, in a small voice. Why did this casual, almost meaningless invitation mean so much to her? It was ridiculous. After all, Henry would take her to the coffee shop if she asked him.

Conversation ceased. They sat sipping their drinks, sleeping kittens on their laps, all perfectly content with the silence.

Eventually Charles got to his feet, detached the kitten and placed it where he had been sitting so it wouldn't feel cold. 'I must go. I've had a lovely evening. Thank you both, so much.'

He kissed Hermione on the cheek. Flora, he just waved at. For a moment, she experienced a horrid pang of jealousy and hated herself.

When he was gone, Flora's mother said, 'He's gorgeous! I can quite understand why you're in love with him.'

Flora burst into tears.

'I'm not in love with him!' she hiccuped. 'He's engaged to Annabelle.'

'I know, darling,' said Hermione sympathetically as she put her arms round her daughter, 'but it's not enough to stop you falling in love with him, is it? It should be, I know, but it doesn't work like that.'

'But really – I mean, he's so stuffy and—'

'He's not stuffy with the kittens,' Hermione pointed out sadly, 'and you told me he's really good at his job. There's something about him, Flo, and I can't blame you for responding to it.'

'Is that what's wrong with me, then? I've been feeling so odd, so discontented, when everything is going so well! I love it down here, and yet I know I can't stay here once Charles and Annabelle are married. Is that because I'm in love with Charles? How awful!' Ever since the storm Flora had done such a good job of

352

persuading herself that she felt nothing more than cousinly affection for Charles that suddenly facing up to the fact that she'd accidentally gone and fallen in love with him was quite a shock. Although she realised it had been true for quite a while now.

Hermione led her daughter back to the sofa and sat down next to her. 'Tell me everything. Things may not be as bad as they seem.'

Sadly for Flora, once she'd told Hermione the whole story, her mother agreed with her that things were just as bad as they seemed.

'You could seduce him away from Annabelle,' Hermione suggested tentatively.

'No I can't! He might be perfectly happy with her, and even if he isn't, it would have to be his decision or he'd blame me if anything went wrong. No, I'll just have to go away when the business is going really well, and forget him. I can't stay for the wedding, in November. It would kill me.'

Hermione sighed. 'It seems a shame.'

'It's a tragedy! But there it is.' She blew her nose on a by now much-used tissue. 'Although if I thought he was happy, I suppose I'd be OK about it. Sad for me but happy for him. Perhaps I could just go away for a bit, and come back.'

'Well, I'm bound to meet Annabelle while I'm here. I'll tell you if I think she's right for Charles, ultimately.'

'But even if she isn't, it's up to him to discover that. I can't do anything about it.' She thought back to what Charles had said the morning after the storm, about the grass only appearing to be greener on the other side and about being a man who stuck to his promises, and

353

realised that even if he did have doubts about his relationship with Annabelle, he'd feel obliged to do the honourable thing and at least give the marriage a very good chance.

Hermione sighed. 'That is a very grown-up way of looking at it. I think if it were me I might just go all out and seduce him. He obviously likes you.'

'No he doesn't, apart from in a cousinly way. He likes the kittens and feels protective of me, like a big brother might. Which is why he doesn't like me going out with Henry.'

'Tell me about Henry.'

'Oh, he's fine. Very good-looking. And free! Which is quite a major plus. I keep trying to fancy him, but somehow I just don't. Now I know why.'

'I think we should both go to bed. Things won't look so bleak in the morning.'

What Flora didn't tell her mother was that things always looked bleaker in the morning when, after a night of broken sleep, she awoke, and all her depression – now identified as heartbreak – came flooding back to hit her.

That night, however, whether because of the alcohol or her mother's comforting presence, Flora slept like a baby or, as her mother put it, a teenager. 'Babies don't sleep all that much,' she explained when they saw each other the next day.

They found themselves invited to have lunch with Edie and Geoffrey. 'It's only a salad and quiche,' explained Edie as she ushered them into the garden at the back of the house where there were chairs to sit on. 'Geoffrey wouldn't let me cook you a proper meal. He doesn't like to eat anything heavy before a concert.' Her glance at her husband implied she thought this was a bit prima donna-ish.

'You can't sing on a full stomach and we've got to be there for the rehearsal at five. Now, glass of sherry, Mrs Stanza?'

'Hermione, please, and sherry would be lovely.'

'Flora?'

'Yes, please, but could I possibly have a lump of ice in mine?'

'Of course you can, my dear. And there's only rasp-berries and cream for pudding,' said Edie, opening a packet of crisps and putting them in a bowl. 'Do you need a hand, Geoffrey?'

'Certainly not. You show Hermione the garden.'

While this was happening, Flora went into the house to find Geoffrey. 'Could I just check I've got my music in order?'

Together they went through their folders until at last Flora was convinced there was nothing missing and she wouldn't suddenly turn a page and find she was singing the wrong arrangement.

When Edie and Hermione had finished their patrol of the garden, Hermione had several plastic bags full of plants. 'We'll leave them here until after the concert,' she said, rather apologetically. 'And I'll put them in the garden tomorrow morning. Charles and Annabelle won't mind, will they?'

It was nice for Flora to go to Burnet House with Geoffrey. Apart from anything else, it meant that she would arrive at the right place at the right time. Edie had ironed her

355

scarf for her and Hermione had Geoffrey's clear written directions how to get to the venue.

'I'm so nervous I feel sick,' Flora said as she settled herself on the seat next to Geoffrey.

'There's no need for all that. A few nerves are good, because it means you'll concentrate, but you don't need to go overboard with them. You're not singing a solo, after all.'

'I know! But I'm afraid I'll mess it up for everyone else.'

'You won't. Not if you focus and look at James, all the time.'

'What about the words?'

'You'll know them by heart, almost, by now.'

Flora sighed. 'I haven't been in the choir as long as you, Geoffrey.'

Chapter Twenty-One

Flora was so focused on the choir and her nerves about singing in it that she had almost forgotten about Henry. He had not forgotten about her, however. He was in the field designated as a car park, theoretically telling people where to park, but in fact waiting for Flora.

She did not feel at her best in her long black skirt and black blouse, but she smiled brightly at him as he helped her out of Geoffrey's car.

'Hello, Henry. I do hope you don't regret this.'

He kissed her cheek and nodded to Geoffrey. 'I've had no reason to regret it so far. The hole in the orangery roof is fixed, the grass has been cut and I get to see you looking like . . .' He paused for the perfect metaphor. '. . . a nun without the wimple.' Something about him implied he did not find this look unattractive.

'You remember Geoffrey?' Flora found his slightly lecherous glance both unexpected and extremely unsettling. She grabbed Geoffrey's arm so he couldn't abandon her.

'Of course,' said Henry. 'We did spend an entire afternoon together. I was surprised there was so much value in that library.'

Geoffrey unhooked himself from Flora so he could lock the door of the car. 'There are a few nice early editions, and although I don't think there's anything there that's worth a huge amount of money on its own, put together, we should make you a tidy sum.'

'Oh, look, there's Euan! He's one of the tenors,' she told Henry. 'He breeds Cavalier King Charles spaniels and is a bit eccentric,' she explained. 'He seems to be going in the wrong direction. Perhaps you'd better chase after him, Henry, before he gets lost.'

'Euan never gets lost,' said Geoffrey after Henry had reluctantly gone to round him up.

'Doesn't he? Well, never mind. I can't chat just now, I need to focus. I'm so nervous.'

'You'll be fine,' said Geoffrey.

Flora thought she might very well vomit from terror, while those oft-repeated words were still echoing about her.

Carloads of choir members arrived in dribs and drabs. Almost everyone exclaimed at the beauty of the building and the pleasantness of the weather. They were all reluctant to leave the pleasantly cool summer evening to go inside to the orangery, which they knew was going to be on the warm side.

'These black clothes get awfully hot sometimes,' explained Virginia. 'We keep thinking we should have a different summer uniform, but we can never agree on what to have. We don't want anyone fainting. Have you got your scarf, Flora?'

'Yes, Moira gave me one. It's folded carefully in my bag. Edie ironed it for me. I don't think she trusted me not to burn it.'

'Well, you do have to be careful. And is your mother coming?'

'With Edie. They'll be along later. It's been lovely having her.'

'It must have been a bit lonely for you here, not knowing many people. Now, how do we get in?'

'This I do know. Follow me,' said Flora.

Henry came into the orangery just as they were going to start the rehearsal. He waved at Flora but she ignored him. It was hard enough to remember how they were walking in, where they were to stand so they could all see James, where the basses were going to be positioned so they could be heard by but not drown out the second sopranos. She fixed her gaze on James, waiting for the signal to start. How could people chat just before a dress rehearsal? Her palms were sweating and she still felt slightly sick.

But she couldn't ignore Henry in the break before the performance. Wine, soft drinks, tea, sandwiches and cake were laid on in a room off the kitchen. A woman in a black dress and white apron ushered them to it, saying Henry had arranged it.

The choir were thrilled and as they all wanted to thank Henry personally, it was some time before Flora could get to him. 'This is very kind of you, Henry,' she said. 'A few soft drinks would have been perfectly adequate.'

'I wanted to do something a bit better than that.' He looked down at her with a look that indicated he was hoping for some kind of reward.

'It's for the choir,' she said firmly, making it clear that no reward would be forthcoming. 'But it is nice of you.'

He appeared to accept this and shrugged. 'It seemed only fair to do something after they did all those repairs.'

'Roof OK now?' asked one of the basses who had access to ladders and window-repairing skills.

'Fine, thanks, David. Are you really sure I can't pay you?'

David shook his head. 'Nah. The materials didn't cost much and my boss gave me the time off work to do it.'

David had a wonderful voice and Flora loved it when they were arranged so she could hear it thrumming through her at the end of John Tavener's 'The Lamb', her favourite, but the most challenging piece they sang.

'It's a lovely venue,' said one of the other choir members. 'You should rent it out for functions. You could charge quite a lot, I should think.'

'Or get it registered so you could have weddings in here,' agreed another.

Henry became thoughtful. 'So I could. With the hole in the roof I never thought of it as being somewhere that could earn its keep.' He paused. 'So why am I doing it for you for nothing?' he asked, smiling at Flora.

'Because before we came along there was a field instead of a lawn and a puddle the size of Lake Windermere on the floor,' she said. When she had last seen Henry, this reply would have sufficed. Now, he seemed different. Or was it just Flora's nerves making her over-sensitive?

'That's a bit unfair. The puddle wasn't much bigger than the Serpentine.'

She laughed, to oblige him. 'You're doing it for the sake of charity and the good of your soul, which could probably do with improvement.'

'You're probably right.' This time his smile was less calculating and Flora recognised how attractive he was.

Come on, heart, she said to herself. He's nice, he's single! Be attracted to him! Why aren't you?

But she knew the answer and nothing she could tell herself could stop her wanting a rather stuffy man whose own heart belonged to another. Must try harder, she told herself firmly, and if you can't fall in love with Henry, find another romantic distraction.

Henry put his hand on Flora's shoulder and was about to speak when James said, 'The audience are beginning to come in. Could we get ourselves together, please? And can I tell you once more? Don't forget to smile! Flora?'

Flora found it very difficult to smile when she was so nervous. She tried a smile now, but her cheek muscles seemed to be made of plaster of Paris, and wouldn't let her. She found Moira, whom she was following in, and stood behind her. Moira adjusted her scarf for her and gave her shoulders a little hug of encouragement. 'You'll be fine! Got your music? In your left hand? That's right.'

Moira turned away and, a moment later, they processed in, the women in black with blue scarves, the men in dinner jackets with matching bow ties. Flora hadn't liked putting on black clothes and black tights on a lovely warm evening, but she admitted to herself that they were smart when they were all together.

The orangery looked magnificent. Although too nervous to look around much, Flora couldn't help recollecting how it had been when she'd first seen it: empty and dank, with a puddle on the floor. Now there were chairs arranged in rows in one half. Some huge plants, one of them a genuine orange tree in a huge pot, stood in the corners; someone had done something clever with the lighting and all the floor-to-ceiling windows were open, so the breeze wafted in. They had been rehearsing there not long before, but the addition of the audience, bright in their summer silks, added colour and excitement.

'Angela, in the altos, lent the plants,' Moira breathed to Flora out of the side of her mouth as they reached their places. There was no platform, but they had practised carefully where they were to stand so everyone had a good view of James, and could be seen by the audience.

Flora, terrifyingly, was on the end, in full view of everyone. 'Good luck!' whispered Moira as they settled in their positions.

Flora didn't reply. She could see her mother and Edie out of the corner of her eye. They were smiling encouragingly, but Flora realised she'd have felt happier if she hadn't known any of the audience. She wanted her humiliation to be kept private. There was Henry, of course. He was sitting at the back. She had no trouble forgetting about him.

James came into the room, turned to the audience and gave a short, witty introductory speech. The audience laughed. The choir laughed. Then he turned to his singers, regarded them all, then held up a sheet with a picture of a grinning face on it. Flora did her best to oblige him but didn't think it was a very good effort.

The accompanist played the opening bars of 'The Entrance of the Queen of Sheba'. The choir took a collective breath and opened their throats. 'Rejoice! Rejoice!' The orangery had lovely acoustics. Flora forgot her nerves and began to sing with joy.

*   *   *

'It's going awfully well,' said someone during the interval.

The choir were back in their room where a fresh lot of sandwiches and drinks had been laid on. Flora was sipping a glass of elderflower, not allowing herself wine until it was all over.

'And there's a very good crowd,' said Geoffrey. 'Someone's done really well with the ticket sales.'

'It's the venue, I'm sure,' said Moira. 'People are so curious. They'd listen to anything just to get the chance to get a look at a house like this.'

'And there's been a fair amount of scandal, hasn't there? Does anyone know any details?'

'Flora's going out with Henry,' said Geoffrey, to save Flora more embarrassment. 'It's how we've been allowed to be here.'

'It's just coincidence. We've only been out a few times.' Flora, aware that everyone was looking at her, found herself blushing. 'I don't know any scandal, I'm afraid, except that his wife left him and got most of the money.'

'Well, however we come to be here, we're very grateful,' said one of the altos whom Flora hadn't really got to speak to before. 'A "Stately Summer" from a church hall wouldn't have been the same.'

'The sandwiches are jolly good too,' said Euan with his mouth full. 'Egg and cress, my favourite.'

Eventually everyone stopped eating and drinking, James gathered his flock, and they filed back into the orangery. Flora felt much more relaxed now and felt she could get into the rather complicated version of 'The Lord's My Shepherd' with her mind totally on the matter in hand. Then she foolishly looked up to see if her mother was happy and saw Charles. He was sitting at the end of one of the rows. She felt herself go pink and looked hard at James, trying to concentrate. James caught everyone's eyes, saw Flora, and held up his picture of the grin again.

Just forget about him, she told herself and forced her lips to smile.

Like a tongue constantly seeking out a sore tooth, Flora found her eye go to Charles often. Dragging her eyes away she saw something that caused her to miss a couple of bars and, very nearly, her place in the music. Sitting next to each other, a couple of rows behind Charles, were William and Annabelle.

What on earth were they doing here? Together? Flora sincerely hoped that some sort of sense of performance meant that her shock was kept private. She didn't dare look at the audience again, and smiled in between songs with a vacancy she feared might be the fast track to the Asylum for the Bewildered. What was going on? Could she possibly avoid seeing any of them afterwards? No, she realised. After all, if William and Annabelle were there with Charles, in full view of everyone, she had nothing to worry about.

While they sang an English folk song with words so suggestive Flora was almost embarrassed, she concluded that guilt was like attraction, you couldn't just turn it on and off. If there was something going on between Annabelle and William, she was convinced it was all her fault. And no matter how much she tried to make herself fancy Henry, who had so much going for him, principally his lack of a partner, she couldn't. 'Riddle fol di ree!' she carolled, with feeling.

As the audience clapped enthusiastically, Flora tried to make a plan. James would say something, and then they'd do the encore. Then they'd file out, back to their room where they'd left their handbags and bottles of water and music cases. Could she dash out of the side door, steal a car and escape? No, she couldn't. Even if she delved into the handbags for a car key, it would take her ages to find out which car the key she stole belonged to. It was no good. She took a breath and prepared to sing 'Bobby Shaftoe', in parts, with complicated extras. Then after more clapping, she followed Moira out of the orangery, accepting her fate.

'Thank you, everyone,' said James. 'That went very well, I thought. Lovely venue, Flora. Thank you very much for getting it for us.'

'That's fine,' she said, hoping that the choir didn't all think she had had to sleep with Henry to get him to agree to let them use it.

'Oh, but if you hadn't asked so effectively we wouldn't have got it,' said James, confirming, in Flora's view, that he definitely thought she had slept with Henry. 'And the evening wouldn't have been quite so "Stately", would it?'

'I know Henry's very grateful for the repairs David did for him. He's done well out of it,' said Flora.

'Oh yes, it's been good for him, too,' agreed James. 'I gather he might rent it out for functions.'

Flora nodded, not knowing what to say. Geoffrey came up. 'Are you coming out to meet our audience, young Flora?'

'I suppose so.'

'Come on! You were fine. They'll have loved it. I

365

thought the Stanforth had never gone better, James.'

James nodded. 'I knew you could do it, if you all just concentrated.'

'Come on, Flora. Come and meet the crowd.'

Flora summoned up a smile and followed Geoffrey out of the room, clutching her music bag like a security blanket.

Long before they reached her mother and Edie, Flora spotted that they were chatting with Annabelle, William and Charles so there was no chance of avoiding them.

'Darling! It was wonderful!' Her mother gave Flora a huge hug as she reached them. 'Were you terrified? You looked a bit scared at the beginning, but I thought the standard was so high! It's a super choir!'

'The quodlibet went well, Geoffrey,' said Edie. 'You got it right at last.'

'Is that the one when the men sang one melody and the women another?' asked Hermione. 'The conductor explained it?'

'That's right,' confirmed Geoffrey. 'It's always a crowd pleaser.'

'You must have wondered why the audience suddenly got bigger after half-time!' Annabelle laughed. 'Charles said he'd promised he'd come along, and so William, Beatty and I thought it would be rather fun to come too. We were at dinner at her house. Beatty's gone home now.'

'To do the washing-up?' suggested Flora.

'No. She has staff!' Annabelle regarded Flora as if she'd gone mad. 'And Hugo. He's her husband.'

Flora nodded. The Asylum for the Bewildered seemed both nearer and more attractive than ever.

'You were awfully good,' said William, whom Flora hadn't seen for ages.

Flora smiled at him. He was very good-looking and seemed to have become very civilised since his days of living in the woods. And when had he become part of Annabelle's social circle?

'Have you met my mother?' she asked him. 'Mum, this is Emma's friend, William.'

'Who's Emma?' said Annabelle.

'You met her at my dinner party,' said Flora firmly. 'The dinner party where you and Charles met William.'

'Oh yes, I remember, the one Jeremy fancied.' Emma satisfactorily dismissed, Annabelle went on, 'Is there any chance we could get a look round the house, do you think? We did have that very jolly dinner with him. We're hardly strangers, after all.'

Henry was talking to James and a couple of other choir members, Flora could see. 'He's very touchy about letting anyone in. I was only allowed across the threshold myself because I knew him already.'

'He knows me already, too. We all had that dinner together,' she repeated. 'I'll go and ask him. Are you coming, Charles?'

'I want a quick word with Flora and if she says we wouldn't be welcome in the house, I'm not going to press the point,' said Charles.

'Then you come with me, William.' Annabelle took hold of William's arm and marched off.

Hermione drew Geoffrey and Edie to one side. 'I gather we can't see the house, but shall we go and get a breath of fresh air before we leave? I want to see if that's jasmine I can smell or someone's perfume.'

As they went off together, embarrassment, which had been ebbing and flowing over Flora all evening, suddenly flooded. She had no idea what to say to Charles.

'You were wonderful,' he said. 'I mean, the choir was wonderful. I had no idea my porters were all so talented.'

'It was nice of you to come. Oh, here's Virginia.'

'Charles! I don't think you've ever come to one of our concerts before,' said the ruler of Charles's saleroom, not unreproachfully. 'It must be Flora's influence.'

'I've seen the error of my ways, Virginia. I'll come to all of them now. I was very impressed.'

'So I should think. I'm not sure "The Lamb" was quite right, was it, Flora? I thought the tenors were a bit off.'

Flora shook her head. 'I'm afraid I was just concentrating so hard on my own bit, I couldn't pick out the other voices, really. My ear is just not good enough.'

'Never mind. You got us a lovely venue. Are you coming for a drink?'

Flora needed a drink, and certainly wanted one, but she wanted it in the privacy of her own home, where it went with a bath, and bed immediately afterwards. 'I've got my mother with me.'

'Oh, she's up for it! I've just been talking to Geoffrey and Edie.'

'I'll take you home if you're tired, Flora,' said Charles.

'That's settled then,' said Virginia. 'Your mother can drive your car home from Geoffrey's, can't she?'

Flora nodded. She ferreted out her car keys and handed them to Virginia.

'And Charles will take you home, so I'll just run and confirm which pub we're going to. You're sure you don't want to come?'

'Quite sure.'

Just as Virginia left and Charles turned to talk to someone he knew, Henry appeared. 'I thought I'd never get away from that lot. Come on, Flo.' He drew her away from the crowd a little. 'Let's go in for a nightcap. I'll drive you home later. I've got some very nice brandy. You certainly deserve some reward for all that hard work.'

'Actually . . .' Henry had never called her Flo before, and Flora wasn't at all sure she liked it. She only put up with it from close friends and family. '. . . I am quite tired.'

'Nonsense. You need something to help you wind down. And then, whenever you're ready, I'll take you back and tuck you up in bed. I'll even make you hot chocolate.'

As he came near her, Flora realised that he had been drinking, which was unusual for him. 'Really, Henry, I'd rather not. I'm exhausted.'

Henry was beginning to get belligerent. 'Oh, come on! I put my house at the disposal of your bloody choir and you won't even have a glass of brandy with me?'

Flora drew breath, not certain how to deal with the situation, and then suddenly Charles joined them. 'Actually, I'm taking Flora back,' he said smoothly.

'No need,' said Henry. 'You've got your fiancée – what's her name? Annabelle – to look after. Flora and I have things to attend to.'

By now there was no doubt about what things he had in mind and Flora started to feel very uncomfortable. She'd made it plain she didn't want to be anything more than friends, and had been careful not even to flirt with him since Grantly Manor.

'Flora's coming with me,' said Charles, ratcheting up his determination several notches.

Flora looked at the two men squaring up to each other and said nothing. She didn't know what to say.

'She's my girlfriend,' claimed Henry, beginning to get cross.

'She's my cousin and I'm taking her home.'

Flora began to feel anxious. This was by no means the first time men had competed for the privilege of taking her home, but they didn't usually get quite so tense.

'I think the relationship between us takes precedence over some distant blood link, don't you, Flora?'

'I—' began Flora.

'I don't think—' began Henry.

'Oh shut up,' said Charles, and punched Henry in the nose.

Flora's first thought was relief that no one was about to witness Henry clutching at his now bloody nose. Her second was a mixture of thrill and horror as Charles took hold of her elbow and marched her away from the scene of the crime.

'I'm so sorry, Flora,' he said when they were back at the car.

'Don't apologise to me! You didn't punch my nose.'

'I couldn't let him take you back. He'd been drinking and after what happened between you and Justin – well, I could see it happening all over again.'

'Me and Justin?' For a moment, Flora had forgotten all about Justin.

'Yes, when he – hit on you, I think the expression is, because he'd taken you out to dinner. Henry obviously felt you owed him something.'

Flora felt she owed him something, too, but not a free pass to her body. 'But what about Annabelle and William?'

'Oh Christ! I'd forgotten about them – I mean William – for a moment.' A thought passed across Charles's face that Flora couldn't identify.

'Well, you can't go back and look for them now,' said Flora, managing to conceal the nervous laughter that was beginning to erupt. 'But I can easily get a lift . . .'

'Hardly.' The corner of Charles's mouth began to twitch. 'I'll ring Annabelle on my mobile.'

As he pulled it out, Flora said, 'But what can you say?'

'Hi,' he said briskly. 'Flora's exhausted and I'm taking her home. Will you get home on your own? Or will you wait at the pub until I can come and collect you? Good girl. Fine. 'Night, 'night, sweetie.'

He disconnected. 'She and William will get a lift. Now we'd better get off the premises before Henry comes after me with a shotgun.'

Chapter Twenty-Two

❧

'This is silly,' said Flora, getting into Charles's car.

'I know, I'm sorry. I'll apologise in the morning. I don't know what came over me. I don't usually get into fights.'

'It wasn't a fight. Henry didn't hit you back.'

'Thank goodness. He probably could have pulverised me.'

Flora didn't respond. She doubted Henry cared enough about her to risk more damage – and at the moment Charles punched him Flora had been certain that Charles would have followed it up with more had there been an excuse.

'I'll send him a bottle of wine, or something, to apologise.'

'You realise he'll probably never want to go out with me again.'

'I can't say I'm sorry about that. I never did like you having anything to do with him.'

'In his defence, up till now, he never laid an unwelcome finger on me.'

'But he did just then?' Charles looked as if he was considering going back and punching him again.

'No! No, but he might have – I mean – oh, you know what I mean.'

'I know he fully intended to seduce you.'

'That's such a sweet, old-fashioned word.'

'There's nothing sweet about it, I assure you. You could have got into serious trouble if you'd stayed with Henry.'

'I am a grown-up, Charles,' she said quietly. 'Technically, at least.'

'I couldn't permit it. Sorry.'

Flora began to smile. 'I don't actually have to ask your permission.' She bit her lip to stop herself chuckling.

'I know that perfectly well.' Charles changed gear, driving rather fast. He sighed deeply, obviously making an effort to calm down. 'I admit I was in the wrong. I shouldn't have hit him. Violence is never the answer but I acted instinctively, as I would have done if you were my sister.'

'You haven't got any sisters.'

'That's beside the point! And really, there are plenty of good men out there. You don't have to scrape the barrel.'

'Well, thank you for that,' she said humbly. 'I'm so glad you don't think I'm so unattractive I have to go looking in seedy bars and gutters to find a companion.'

Charles bit his lip. 'You know perfectly well what I mean.'

'Are you suggesting I get you to vet any man who asks me out, then?'

'It wouldn't be a bad idea. After all, you're new to the area.'

Flora was giggling openly now. 'Perhaps I should tell you that my father didn't have much luck doing that when I was fifteen.'

Charles was forced to laugh, too, but Flora could tell he wasn't really amused.

'My father used to try and substitute suitable boyfriends for the unsuitable ones.'

'I did introduce you to Jeremy.'

'That didn't work, either. He fancied Emma.'

'I have other friends. Good men, who won't mess you around.'

'Not so long ago you were accusing me of messing your friends around.'

'I know you better now, Flora. I know you wouldn't do anything to hurt anyone, voluntarily.'

'Unlike you.'

'Unlike me.' He chuckled. 'Poor Henry. He just didn't see it coming.'

'Well, you're lucky I wasn't madly in love with him or I'd never speak to you again.'

'If you'd been madly in love with him you wouldn't have hesitated when he asked you in for a brandy. You'd have just gone.'

'I suppose so.' Flora tried to sound non-committal but she knew it was nothing but the truth. If Charles had invited her to drink brandy with him, however tired she'd been, she'd have just gone, too. But it wouldn't have worked the other way round. If Flora had invited him to drink brandy he'd have told her off, said she was far too young to drink spirits, and that she should go home and get an early night. 'I'm quite glad you haven't got sisters, younger ones at least.'

'Oh? Why?'

'Because you would have been a terribly bossy older brother.'

He laughed. 'I was Head of House at school. I probably learnt to look out for the younger ones then.'

That was her put in her place, then. He saw her as a sort of Smith Minor, in danger of getting into the wrong crowd, needing a steady, older boy to keep an eye on him.

He glanced at her. 'Do sleep if you feel like it.'

'It's all right. I don't feel so tired now.' She did actually, but was determined not to waste a second of this odd yet surprisingly enjoyable journey. 'So have you and Annabelle and William been socialising?' she asked.

'Yes. Annabelle needed a spare man for something and thought of him.' He frowned. 'I thought you knew that. I thought Annabelle said you'd given him her number.'

'Oh' – she hadn't, had she? Flora thought rapidly – 'yes, but I thought Annabelle just wanted some hurdles made or something.' Hurdles, that sounded suitably rustic and *Far From the Madding Crowd*. 'I didn't realise it was for social reasons.'

'We must have you and Hermione to dinner.'

Flora felt she'd rather sing a solo in a cathedral than endure an evening of watching Charles and Annabelle play Happy Couples. 'She's not here for long. Next time she comes, perhaps?'

'Do you know when she's coming back?'

'I'm not sure. Sometime before Christmas, I hope.'

'Annabelle and I might well be married, by then.' He stared ahead at the road.

'You might,' agreed Flora, discovering tears forming at the corners of her eyes. She wiped them away and yawned.

He saw her. 'You're shattered.'

'Yes.' People seemed to have been telling her that all evening.

'Nearly there, now.'

'Good.' The tears were falling faster now. In a few moments he was going to leave her at her door and then drive back to Annabelle, and probably (she forced herself to confront this thought) have passionate sex with her.

They turned into her lane. 'It's still quite muddy, isn't it?'

She cleared her throat. 'It's OK as long as you take it slowly.'

'Your voice sounds a little strange. Perhaps you've strained it, singing.'

She wanted to say, 'Actually, it's my heart. It's breaking and now the tear has reached up into my throat.' But she didn't, she just said, 'Mm,' in agreement. It was all she could manage.

At last he pulled up outside the cottage. 'If I came in and saw you were all right, made you a hot drink, would you think I was trying to seduce you?'

'No, Charles,' she said, in control at last. 'That is the absolutely last thing I would think.'

'I wouldn't ever do anything to hurt you, Flora.'

Not on purpose, no, she thought.

'Then make us some hot chocolate, if there's enough milk, while I get into my nightie.' She opened the door of the cottage.

'Actually, don't get into your nightie.'

'Why not? These black clothes are awfully hot.'

'I'm not a bloody saint, Flora!' He strode off into the kitchen and her spirits lifted, just a tiny bit.

* * *

Flora slept surprisingly well. The hot chocolate and the memory of Charles's chaste kiss on her cheek were very soothing. She heard her mother come in but didn't move. She needed her sleep.

Next morning, Hermione was full of praise once more. 'Well, darling, I have to say, I was very impressed. Very impressed indeed. And the choir are such a nice bunch. I had a lovely time at the pub last night.'

'I am glad. They are fun, aren't they?'

'So, did you find out what William and Annabelle were doing together?'

'Apparently William became part of their social life when Annabelle needed an extra man for something. He scrubbed up very well, I must say. I was shocked to see him with Annabelle, though. But Charles was cool about it.'

Hermione glanced at her daughter, who was crunching into toast and marmalade with enthusiasm. 'And Charles, he didn't tell you that he and Annabelle were a terrible mistake and he was going to break off the engagement immediately?'

'No. Though he did hit Henry! It was awful and yet really funny, at the same time.'

'Why did Charles hit Henry? It sounds very out of character.'

'It is, totally out of character. But he explained to me on the way home that he was Head of House at school and so he's programmed to look out for the younger boys.'

Hermione seemed confused. 'Are you telling me Charles looks on you as someone he has responsibility for?'

'Yup.'

'Oh, darling!'

'I'd be kidding myself if I thought any different, Mum. He does care about me, but only as a sort of older, terribly bossy brother.'

Hermione sighed. 'It's a pity. He'd make such a lovely dad. Think how sweet he is with the kittens?'

Flora laughed, as she was supposed to. They both knew that if they went any deeper into this conversation, Flora might get upset. Neither of them wanted that when she was just going off to work.

As Hermione was leaving a couple of days later she hugged her daughter. 'You will be all right, won't you?'

'Oh yes. The sale is coming up and we're really busy.'

'And will you see Henry again?'

Flora wasn't too sure. Henry had phoned, mortified, the day after the concert to apologise for his behaviour. It had been so completely out of character for him that Flora, once she got over her anger about the position he had put her in, was almost concerned for him – and it turned out she had reason to be. He'd apparently received a rather unpleasant phone call from his ex-wife earlier in the day to break the news, none too gently, that she was remarrying. That had come at about three in the afternoon and he'd stiffened his sinews with a shot of brandy, and never really stopped after that. By the time Flora arrived on the scene, his hurt pride at Natasha moving on and building a new family while he remained alone had swelled to such a point that he was determined to prove he had someone special in his life – and Flora had got in his way.

He was clearly horrified at his own behaviour, and Flora didn't think there was any reason to worry he'd do it again, but the incident still left a nasty taste in her mouth. And she rather thought their friendship had been soured by it.

'I'm not sure, Mum,' she said carefully. 'I'm not too sure Henry will want to see me, to be honest.'

'It's a pity in some ways. You need a distraction.'

'I'm working far too hard for distractions.'

Hermione shook her head. 'Working with Charles will not help! What about that nice William?'

'William and I don't fancy each other. We decided that ages ago.'

'What a shame!' Her mother hugged her again. 'Love can be such hell.'

Flora had expected to find meeting Charles after the concert at Burnet House embarrassing – he had behaved so extraordinarily, punching Henry – but he was completely blasé about it.

'I didn't mention the matter to Annabelle, but I did send some rather good claret to his house, and he was decent enough to thank me,' he said. 'But I do apologise again to you for involving you in a rather sordid incident.'

'Oh, Charles, you are so stuffy! Sordid incident, indeed! You punched him! Drew blood! But I'm glad you've made it up with Henry. It means I could see him again if I wanted to.'

He frowned. 'I don't think so.'

Flora sighed. 'No, I don't think so, either. Oh well. Now, do you want me to start putting numbers on?'

*   *   *

Everyone was keyed up on the first morning of the sale. It was one of those golden mornings in early September that make the passing of summer so poignant. As Flora drove through the countryside before the rest of the world was awake, she was struck by its beauty, and wondered if she had accidentally become a rural person when, by rights, she should be a City slicker. She got to the auction rooms by seven. Charles was there by half past, and even Annabelle turned up by eight-thirty. This was the sale of furniture and effects resulting from the roadshow. The sale that would prove if Flora was remotely useful to Stanza and Stanza or not – or that was how it seemed to Flora. But everyone felt it was a new start, a step forward.

Unusually for her, Annabelle helped Flora arrange the chairs. It amused Flora that all the chairs in any sale were put out for people to sit on. The logical conclusion to this would be to sell cups of tea in the Mason's Ironstone tea sets and seat the punters at the Sheraton tables, but she kept this thought to herself. Annabelle was unlikely to understand.

'These are pretty chairs,' said Annabelle. 'I might put in an offer myself. We've got some nice ones, but they're rather large, you can't fit many round the table.'

'And you could always put the ones you've got now in the next sale.'

'Of course. I don't know why I didn't think of that.'

Flora didn't know either, after all she'd worked in an auction house much longer than Flora had.

'It's exciting, having a half-decent sale for once,' Annabelle went on. 'There's been loads of interest. And I think that little item we had on the local news probably helped quite a lot. Several local antique shops have put in stuff that's been hanging around too long. You just need one or two items to attract a lot of attention, and people realise there's going to be extra interest and put their own stuff in. Charles has roped Bob Butler in to help as he can't do it all.'

'Well, I'm glad you see it my way at last,' said Flora evenly.

Annabelle was inspecting the underside of a Windsor chair. 'It's a bit wormy – still, caveat emptor and all that.'

Flora didn't speak Latin. 'As long as we don't imply it's perfect in the catalogue. Oh, I never asked you about the school reunion.' Flora had lost track completely of when it was and felt it must have happened by now.

'The school reunion?' Annabelle looked blank for a moment. 'Oh, that! It was fine, thank you. Caught up with some old chums I must invite to the wedding.'

'How are the preparations going? And the portrait?'

Annabelle smiled, looking a little dreamy, which was perfectly understandable. 'Fine for both. And by the way, I was going to ask you – it's a bit short notice I know, because dresses take ages to be made, but I wondered if you'd help me choose mine? I was originally going for something very traditional, but since you took me in hand, I thought I might have something a bit simpler. I've got the dressmaker all lined up, but she tells me I've got a week or so before she really gets going so there's time to make a few changes.'

'I'd be thrilled to help!' Manfully, Flora summoned up enthusiasm for a wedding that was going to end her chance of happiness for ever. 'I see you in something quite slim-fitting, oyster satin, something like that. Elegant and simple.'

'Great. We'll have a look at some mags together soon, but we'd better get this sale over first. I'm going to be on the phones most of the day. Will you and Louisa share the book for Charles? You know, make sure he doesn't overlook any commissioned bids? God! I hope I wasn't being patronising! I've had a lot on my mind lately.'

She strode off, leaving an amazed Flora dumbstruck. Annabelle apologising for being patronising! It was like the sea apologising for going in and out all the time, apparently never able to make up its mind. Annabelle had definitely improved lately, and not just because she'd had her hair cut shorter, and was emphasising her physical assets to the full. She had more enthusiasm for life. Flora decided it was because Stanza and Stanza was looking up at last, becoming more the sort of business Annabelle would like to be concerned with. And she was going to help Annabelle decide on a wedding dress . . . Flora sighed. Usually, she liked irony, but now, it felt like a poisoned dart.

There wasn't much time for further philosophical speculation as ten o'clock came and the public were let in for half an hour's viewing before the sale started at ten-thirty.

The sale had been going fantastically well, but now, at nearly four o'clock, it was almost over. Flora had been deputed earlier to apologise to the landlord of the local pub, whose car park had become full of buyers. Fortunately Flora had managed to convince him that the extra business would make up for some loss of local trade. It was something to think about. If they were going to become much bigger, parking space had to be considered.

Although the room was still quite full, earlier it had been positively heaving with people. A lot of bids had been left 'on the book' by people who had put in a bid but were unable actually to be present, and most of the day, Flora had sat next to Charles (or whoever was on the podium), just in case a bid got overlooked. It never was overlooked when Charles was there, but he had said it was good training for her.

Having been sent off for a break, Flora had taken her cup of tea to the back of the room, not wanting to leave the excitement of the saleroom. Or at least that was what she'd told Virginia when they'd met at the tea counter. Flora knew it was so she could watch Charles in action.

I'm sure it's not just that I'm in love with him, she decided, watching him hold the attention of the room with such skill and mastery. He's simply a fantastic auctioneer. And having the room so full and so busy was making him even better. It was brilliant! She found herself smiling with joy because he must be happy.

She shifted her position so she was standing in front of a complete set of Georgette Heyers, early editions and potentially very valuable. Charles and Geoffrey had been a little dismissive about them when they were discovered in Burnet House, but Flora knew they were special and her instinct was borne out by the interest in them shown on the website.

Her attention was distracted by a woman's striking, obviously home-made cardigan for a moment, but when she looked up again, she saw Louisa hand Charles a cup of tea and a home-made rock cake. He didn't usually drink tea while he was at the podium, but he'd been there a long time. Louisa probably felt he needed some sustenance. He acknowledged the tea, took a sip and a bite of the rock cake and then winced sharply, as if in pain. Louisa, having taken her seat beside the podium, stood up again and put her hand on Charles's arm. Her face as she looked up at him was worried, and he leant down and whispered something in her ear, at which she looked even more worried, and urgently whispered something back. Charles shook his head.

'I'm awfully sorry, ladies and gentlemen,' he said awkwardly, 'but I seem to have done something to my tooth. I hope you can hear me all right.'

He leant back to Louisa and spoke again, and she whispered to Virginia, who was on hand near the front. Then he carried on, appearing nearly normal, but Flora longed to get to him. She edged her way to the front. Then Bob Butler appeared. 'I'll now hand you over to Bob Butler for the last few lots,' he said, smiling through his obvious agony. 'I'll be back with you tomorrow.'

'Charles! Are you all right?' said Flora. She followed him into the little side room they used as an office on sale days.

'Broken a tooth. Bloody rock cakes.'

'Oh, I'm so sorry!' said Virginia. 'It was my fault! My sister made them.'

'Nonsense,' said Annabelle, 'he should have had that tooth sorted out ages ago! We'll make an appointment. They always keep a slot for emergencies.'

'I can't go to the dentist when there's a sale on,' Charles said with a panicked look in his eyes.

384

'If you're in pain, you must!' said Flora.

'I can't! This is the biggest sale we've done. I must be here.'

'That's just silly,' said Flora, aware she was being bossy, but too worried about him to help herself. 'Bob and George will do it for you. I'll catch Bob when he's finished and ring George at home. He's in the book under Woodman, isn't he? Bob's here tomorrow anyway, to finish off the furniture.'

Charles shook his head. 'No, that won't do. Bob doesn't usually do books and he's nearly eighty, his wife will never speak to me again if I make him do even more. He's got a bad heart, he shouldn't work when he's tired, and he'll be exhausted after today.'

'He loved it today. He'll be fine,' said Louisa.

'He won't,' said Charles forcefully. 'Look, I can't just abandon ship because I've got toothache! I'll just have to keep going.'

'You wouldn't be abandoning anything. It's called delegating, and it's a very good thing to do. You go to the dentist. We'll manage here until you get back.'

'I can't.'

'You can. No one is indispensable, Charles.' Still he remained looking at her. Flora decided it was time to pull rank. 'I am your partner. And I'm telling you to go to the dentist!'

He laughed, in spite of his pain. 'You're getting to be a very bossy woman, Flora.'

'I know. Good, isn't it?'

'God, Charles! You would never have agreed to that for me,' said Annabelle. 'It must be because Flora's the senior partner.'

385

Flora felt herself go white. She would never be the senior partner, even if she owned every share in the business and Charles owned nothing. She looked at him, aghast that he might think she valued herself so highly. 'Um, not really,' she murmured.

'Well, until Charles has got his tooth fixed anyway,' said Louisa, to Flora's enormous relief.

'Come on. I'll take you home and then make an appointment,' said Annabelle.

Watching them leave the building together forced Flora to confront the idea of them as a couple, to imagine them, years down the line, a happy, married twosome. Even with Annabelle's arm round Charles, she couldn't quite picture it.

Flora went to find Geoffrey, her prop and source of advice. Everyone had obviously heard the news and knew that, for the time being, Flora was in charge. She looked for Geoffrey everywhere except the Gents'. And then went back to ask Virginia.

'Have you seen Geoffrey, Virginia?' she enquired. 'I've looked for him in every logical place and several illogical ones.'

'I saw him go out the back with a huge armoire. I expect he was taking it to someone's van and will be back in a minute. Give us a hand while you're waiting.' Virginia at least was not treating Flora any differently. 'We'll spot him when he comes back in.'

Flora joined Virginia on the raised stage where Virginia was matching slips of paper to items stacked on and under the trestle tables.

Flora took a slip from a middle-aged man who looked like a successful dealer and saw he'd bought some glasses at a very good price. 'Would you like me to wrap them for you?'

'No, thank you, dear. Newspaper damages them. I'll do it myself with the proper stuff. If you just bring them over to me, a few at a time, I'll be fine.'

Flora, worried in case she missed Geoffrey while she was doing this, got the glasses to him almost too quickly for safety.

There was still no sign of Geoffrey, so she took another slip. She stared at it for a while and then said, 'I have no idea what a companion set is!'

Virginia pointed to a corner. 'Poker, tongs and shovel, over there.' Then she picked up a blue and white printed meat dish, which would have been worth a small fortune if it hadn't been damaged, and carried it carefully to its new owner.

'Oh, there's Geoffrey,' Flora said to the owner of the fire irons. 'You don't need me, do you, Virginia?'

'No, it's all right, Anne and I can manage. We know where stuff is.'

Dismissed, Flora followed Geoffrey into the kitchen, where he was eating one of the rock cakes that had caused Charles to break his tooth. He too had already heard about it.

Flora had decided that Charles was right about Bob: it wasn't fair to ask him to do more work tomorrow when they'd stretched his capacity to the limit already today.

'Geoffrey, I don't think we can ask Bob to stand in for Charles, but I'm sure George will, until Charles gets back after the dentist. And you could stand in too, if necessary, couldn't you?'

'Well, the thing is . . . Oh, you ring George. See what he says.'

'Flora!' George Woodman declared delightedly when he heard her voice on the phone. 'You can be the first to congratulate me! Our daughter's had a little girl! It was a difficult pregnancy and she's been in hospital for the past week, but now the baby's born and she's fine.'

'Oh, congratulations! You must be so thrilled!'

'We are. My wife's just throwing a few things together and we're off to see her. They've got a little boy already and her parents-in-law have been there, helping to look after him. Now they've got to go and we're taking over. Was there anything you wanted?'

'Nothing that won't wait until you get back,' said Flora. 'And congratulations again.'

She found Geoffrey again. 'He's just had a new grand-child and they were off to look after his daughter, so I didn't ask him.'

'Oh.'

'Bob's going to finish the furniture though. It's only the books. You can do books. They're your subject.'

'I can do them up to a point, Flora.'

'What do you mean?'

'Quite a lot of books towards the end of the catalogue are mine. I can't auction those. It wouldn't be ethical.'

Flora gulped. 'It's quite likely Charles will be back by then.'

'Quite likely.'

'And if he wasn't, you could do them. No one would know they were yours.'

'I would know,' he said firmly. 'If it got out it would damage the reputation of the firm irrevocably.'

'Oh.' For once, Flora was lost for ideas. 'So we'll just hope it won't come to that. I wonder what they'll have to do to Charles's tooth?'

'I couldn't say, but, Flora . . .'

'What?'

'If Charles isn't here, you'll have to do it.'

'Do what?'

'Auction the books.'

A fine film of sweat covered Flora as she realised what Geoffrey meant. 'Oh no. I couldn't do that.'

'Everyone's got to start sometime.'

'But . . . I wouldn't get the best price for you! This must be your pension, after all. You need to get the very best price for your books. So you don't want someone who's never done it before selling your life savings.'

'Flora, they're not my life savings, and you're just as likely to get a good price for them as I am. If Charles isn't back, you've got to bite the bullet and get up there and sell. I'll give you a bit of coaching tonight.'

Flora exhaled as slowly as she could. 'But, Geoffrey, I couldn't possibly! Think how nervous I was just singing in a choir with twenty other people! I couldn't stand up in front of all those people and sell things when I don't know what I'm doing!'

'Yes, you could,' he said in a broken-record voice.

'I couldn't!'

He sighed. 'Tell you what, you're tired and this idea has been sprung on you. You go and see to Imelda and the kittens, and then come back to me and Edie. Stay the night with us, and I'll give you a crash course in auctioneering. It's only counting in threes, fives and tens, that's not hard.'

'I can't count in ones! How am I ever going to be able to do that?'

'I'll train you. Now go home and sort out the cats and come straight back to me.'

'I can't go now, there's so much to do here.' She was aware that inside there was a mountain of paperwork and tidying and sweeping to be done. No one else would leave for a couple of hours, at least.

'They'll manage without you. They did before you joined the firm, didn't they?'

'And Charles, and Annabelle? They're usually here, aren't they?'

'I've told you, we'll manage. I'll explain what's going on. Now, shoo!'

Chapter Twenty-Three

Guilty, because she knew she should have stayed and finished the day's work with everyone else, but glad to escape, Flora climbed into the Land-Rover and set off for the cottage. The thought of a hot bath lured her like a siren; after it, she knew she'd feel much bolder about the prospect of standing up in front of a lot of strangers. It might not happen anyway. How long could any dentist appointment be?

But she was worried about Charles. Not just the dentist, he was probably one of those hardy types who could tolerate his teeth being filled without vast numbers of painkilling injections, but generally.

Was Annabelle really the right woman for him? Previously when she'd been in love (if you could call those girlish crushes love) her feelings had been very self-centred. She had wanted to go to Paris with him, she had wanted to share bubble baths with him, she had wanted to kick up dead leaves in autumn while they walked hand in hand through Richmond Park (or similar).

But this time, while she would have sacrificed anything to be the one with him while he experienced those pleasures, simple or otherwise, she wanted him to have them with a woman he truly loved and who truly loved him more than she wanted the happiness she would have gained herself.

She didn't consider herself to be a selfish person. She was kind to animals (Imelda was proof of that), to people (sometimes too kind, indeed), and she wanted to do good in the world. But never before had she wanted another person's happiness more than she wanted her own.

She kept on thinking like this until she turned into the lane that led to her cottage. Then she allowed herself to admit that if Charles wanted her, she would go to him, to hell with her pride. As long as he was honest with her, of course.

The kittens were a wonderful distraction for a little while. They were everywhere in the cottage now. Annabelle would probably never be able to go inside there again, because of her allergy, but then, she probably didn't want to anyway. Would she let Charles have a kitten? Would she cramp his style for the rest of his life? And, most likely, would marriage to her allow him to become set in his stuffiness? What he needed was someone a bit younger, a bit more frivolous, as committed to the business as he was, who really liked cats, to be with. He needed her, in other words. But, being a man, and sadly lacking in intuition, he might not ever realise that.

When she had fed the cats and made a cup of tea, about her tenth that day, Flora put on the television and curled up on the sofa so Imelda could have a proper cuddle. Watching Richard and Judy sitting on the sofa, bantering with each other and their guests, was very soothing. Imelda, who now had no time for her kittens, was very grateful for an opportunity to curl up on Flora's lap, hissing at any kitten that came near her. Flora closed her eyes. In a few minutes she would make sure there was enough food left to keep them going tomorrow, sort out the litter tray, pack a bag, and go to Geoffrey and Edie's house. While she was here, in her little cottage, she could pretend her life was both normal and happy. Once she arrived at Geoffrey's, she'd have to concentrate on learning to be a stand-in auctioneer. And all night she would pray she wouldn't have to perform.

'If only I'd practised when I first arrived. That first sale we had was quite little, with hardly any people, I could have coped with that! Oh, why did I meddle and make everything so busy?'

Imelda purred consolingly. Although she'd lost a little condition after having her kittens, she was turning into a very elegant cat. Flora had never seen her unpregnant and was pleased to see her filling out.

When Richard and Judy said goodbye, Flora got up and started her chores.

Flora wished she'd taken the opportunity to have a little nap while she'd been at home. 'I'm going to coach you until you're word perfect,' Geoffrey announced as she got through the door.

'But not until you've eaten, love,' said Edie. 'I've got a nice cottage pie waiting for you.'

'I love your cottage pie! You gave me one when I first arrived, do you remember?'

'Certainly. I know some people don't eat food like that in summer, but I think it's comforting. I've done peas and carrots with it. I'm afraid we've had ours. Cup of tea, Flora?'

'Give the girl a glass of wine,' said Geoffrey, pulling up the chair opposite Flora's.

'And how are my kittens?' asked Edie as she poured the wine. 'I can't wait to have them. Just let us get our fence sorted out so that next door's dog can't get in and menace them.'

'Edie, could you find us some paper and a pen? Flora might like to take notes.'

Edie went over to a drawer and produced a pad and pen. 'You should think about getting Imelda done, dear. You don't want her getting pregnant again, do you?'

'Certainly not, she's only young. Too young to be a mother, really,' said Flora. 'Although she's managed brilliantly.'

'Flora, we really should get on,' said Geoffrey.

'Let the girl eat her supper first, Geoffrey.' Edie set Flora's supper down in front of her. 'She's got enough on her plate without you giving her indigestion.'

Flora, confused as to whether Edie was referring to the food or the fact that she might have to conduct her first auction tomorrow, stuck her fork into a pile of mashed potato that had been browned in the oven.

'This is delicious, Edie. Comfort food – you're quite right. Just what I fancied.'

'Now, don't you worry about tomorrow,' said Edie, ignoring Geoffrey's frown and pulling up a chair so she could talk to Flora. 'It'll go swimmingly. Geoff'll be on hand to see nothing goes wrong.'

'I probably won't have to do it anyway. Charles will rush back from the dentist,' said Flora.

'And I keep telling you, Edie, that if it's my books going under the hammer, I can't have anything to do with it.' Geoffrey pulled the top off a pen and started fiddling with it.

'I hope they go for a good price,' said Flora. 'What do you hope to do with the money? Or shouldn't I ask?'

'It's a bit of a secret,' said Geoffrey. 'I'll tell you if I get what I need.'

'It won't be me—'

'It's not for a cruise,' broke in Edie, but Flora couldn't tell if this was a bit of a disappointment for her.

'You'd have to tell me if you were going away,' said Flora, 'so I could keep – what have you decided to call them?'

'Flora and Fauna, after you, and, well – Fauna sort of goes, doesn't it?'

Suddenly overcome with emotion, Flora hid behind another forkful of pie. 'That's so sweet!' she squeaked, as soon as she decently could.

'We really should be getting on,' said Geoffrey. 'We haven't got all night.'

'Flora is staying over,' Edie reminded him. 'Although I think she should have an early night. She looks all in. Have some more veg?'

Flora nodded. As long as she was eating, Geoffrey couldn't teach her to count in twos, fives and tens. Or threes and eights, or any other complicated way there might be that she had never heard of.

'And you've got homes for all of the kittens?' Edie spooned carrots and peas on to Flora's plate.

'Well, Charles was going to have one, to live in the office, but I don't know . . .'

'That Annabelle! She always was selfish,' said Edie.

'But if he loves her . . .' said Flora.

'Well, I hope he does, but they never seem very lovey-dovey, do they?' She turned to her husband.

'No one knows what goes on in anyone else's marriage, Edie.'

'But they're not married yet, are they? More pie?'

'No, thank you. I can hardly move as it is. It was so delicious.'

'You could do with feeding up a bit. Nothing but skin and bone, you are.'

'Stop fussing, Edie. Flora and I have got work to do.'

'There's apple and rhubarb crumble for pudding.'

Even her desire to put off Geoffrey's crash course in auctioneering didn't make it possible for Flora to accept this offer. 'I'd love some later, but I need to have a bit of time to digest this.'

'And we must get on!' insisted Geoffrey.

'I'll just make a cup of tea for you both, and then leave you in peace.'

'The thing you have to remember is that you only deal with two bidders at a time. There may be other people waving their numbers in the air who think you haven't seen them, but until one of the other two drop out, you just ignore them.'

'Right,' said Flora, writing this down.

'And you know about the book?'

Of course Flora knew about the book, but Geoffrey obviously felt it was his duty to explain everything. 'The place where the bids that people have placed are written down?' she said, to indulge him.

'Yes. And you have to make sure that the person in the room is not at the same place in the bidding as the amount on the book.'

Flora thought she understood this, but did feel a bit blank. 'Don't you just pretend that they're a person and that they drop out when their bid's been overtaken?'

Geoffrey had to think about this. 'I think so. Anyway, Louisa will keep you straight on that. She's very good.'

'I don't know why Louisa couldn't do the selling.'

'She could if your voice gives out completely, but this is your opportunity to take your proper place in Stanza and Stanza. It's all very well you having all these good ideas, but until you've been on that podium you won't be seen by the world as a proper partner in the business. You'll just be the pretty blonde.'

Flora had spent quite a lot of her life being seen as the pretty blonde, and while it did have a lot going for it, it wasn't her preferred sobriquet. 'OK, I'll do it, but only if Charles doesn't get back from the dentist.'

'Of course. Now,' said Geoffrey, 'you know about the counting? When you get someone to open, you go up in fives. If that won't wash you do threes, but then jump to the ten.'

Flora realised she had a long evening in front of her.

'Tell you what,' said Geoffrey. 'Me and Edie will pretend to be punters. You run the auction. I'll help you.'

Eventually Edie sent Flora to bed, having run her a bath and put Lily of the Valley perfumed bubbles in it. She was very glad to go. Her brain had turned to soup and she felt more confused about the whole process than she had done before Geoffrey started. She climbed into the little narrow bed in Edie's spare bedroom and fell asleep almost instantly, knowing her hair would be a sight in the morning and that she'd left her hair straighteners in the cottage.

'Annabelle phoned,' said Louisa, as soon as Flora and Geoffrey arrived. 'Charles's appointment is at twelve. He wanted to come in this morning, but I told him not to. We don't need him and he's in a lot of pain.'

'Poor Charles,' said Flora, weakly. 'Louisa, what time do you think Bob will finish? I mean, um – how likely is it that I'll actually have to do some selling?'

'Flora! Why don't you want to do it? You'll be great! And it's such good experience for you. After all, you are the senior partner.'

'No I'm not! Not really, the thing with the will was just a sort of fluke.' She frowned. 'Anyway, I didn't think anyone knew about that.'

'Oh, nothing's a secret in this place.'

'So tell me what time we'll get to the books that Geoffrey can't do?'

'Well, Bob's very fast, so we'll get through his really quickly. Then Geoffrey. He hasn't done it for a while so he'll probably be a bit slower.'

'And if he's truly my friend, he'll spin it out until Charles gets here,' put in Flora.

'Which means we should get to the books at about two.'

'Plenty of time for Charles to get back from an appointment at twelve!' said Flora, relief flooding over her.

'I suppose so,' said Louisa.

'I do wonder why he didn't make the appointment for earlier, though,' said Flora.

Louisa shook her head. 'Have you any idea how diffi-cult it is to get a dentist appointment in this town? They always keep one at about midday for real emergencies, otherwise you have to wait weeks.'

'Oh.' Chastened, Flora went to check what else needed doing, grateful that she would be too busy to worry too much about having to conduct an auction. For once the words 'cheer up, it may never happen' seemed appro-priate.

She was doing a stint in the little café area, selling rolls and cups of tea in between washing up. She liked it in there. You got to see all the punters, you could over-hear their opinions of the sale, but the work wasn't too stressful and was almost completely free of any deci-sion-making. She'd just coped with a little flurry of customers when she checked her watch. It was half past one! Where was Charles?

The almost-octogenarian Bob was getting through the remaining furniture in record time. He'd once sold cattle at auction and hadn't lost the rapid delivery required, in spite of his bad heart.

'Slow down!' Flora urged him from the back of the room when she'd abandoned the café, leaving any other customers to make their own tea. She'd sold all the rolls already.

Virginia loomed up beside her. 'Geoffrey's on next, then you.'

'But where the hell is Charles?' Flora whispered. 'His appointment was at twelve, and it's half past one. He should be back by now!'

'Stop fussing about where Charles is and just focus on what you've got to do. I'm willing to bet that when you come down from the podium you'll be aching to go back up there again.'

Geoffrey apparently had only a few lots to sell, either that or the time it took him to sell them whistled past so quickly that Flora blinked and missed it. Virginia took her elbow and marched Flora to the front of the building, just as he was finishing.

'You're going to be fine,' said Louisa, as Flora, her legs shaking, climbed up beside her at the desk.

Geoffrey winked. 'You'll need this,' he said, and put a gavel into her hand. 'It's Charles's. He told me to make sure you had it.'

Flora clutched it tightly, willing the years of experience it had gained with Charles to flash into her like a bolt of electricity. At the same moment she realised that Charles had never intended to be there, either because of the dentist, or because he thought it was good experience for her. She loved him and hated him in the same heartbeat.

She thought about the time at school when she'd been the compère for the end-of-term show, how she'd held the audience's attention, in spite of being terrified. She thought of her drama classes, how she'd been taught to think herself into the role. She thought of Charles, how she wanted to do well for his sake, and for Geoffrey and Edie and everyone else who'd been so kind and welcoming to her. She glanced down at the ledger in front of her, checked to see where the porter was standing, holding the book up, and took a deep breath. She looked at everyone and waited until they were all looking at her. Then she smiled – as brave a smile as she could manage – and began.

'A fine example of *The Caine Mutiny* by Herman Wouk, nice edition, good condition, who'll start me off? A hundred pounds? No? Fifty then, yes! Fifty pounds I'm bid. Fifty-five? Yes? You, madam . . .'

She soon got into the swing of things. She found she had taken in Geoffrey's coaching with regard to counting in threes, fives and tens, and with Louisa at her side keeping her on track with the book, and both phones in use, she found she was exhilarated. It was like spinning plates, trying to keep all the balls in the air at the same time. She was surprised how quickly she learned to identify the bidders, to keep their attention. Virginia was manning one of the phones and having her calm presence was an added support.

Halfway through she noticed Charles, standing at the back. But she hadn't got time to decide how she felt about this, she was too preoccupied with what was going on.

Sips of water kept her throat lubricated when she thought her voice would fail and eventually, when Geoffrey came to relieve her, she realised she was exhausted.

'I thought you couldn't do it because it wasn't ethical,' she said to him as he waited for her to give up her seat.

'My books are all sold. Do you know you raised over twenty thousand pounds for me?'

'Did I? I realised we were getting some good prices, way above the estimates, but I didn't know which, or how many of the books were yours, of course.'

'Go and get a cup of tea. You deserve one.'

Flora's knees nearly gave way as she climbed down and the audience, most of whom had learnt that it was her first time, gave her a round of applause.

Virginia was there and hugged her tightly. 'Well done, Flora! You were fantastic! You did so well. We all knew you would.'

Suddenly, everyone was congratulating her on her success.

'That's thousands of pounds' worth you've sold – and for far more than it's worth, going by the guide prices,' said Louisa.

'But you know the guide prices are always fairly low to encourage people to come,' said Flora, embarrassed.

'Those last two bidders just competed with each other for your attention! They must have known they were paying over the odds.'

'Well, as long as everyone is happy. I think I did make a couple of mistakes with the book.'

'Yes, but you put it right by inventing an imaginary bidder,' said Louisa. 'Did Geoffrey tell you to do that?'

'He certainly did. He was coaching me for hours last night.'

'Well worth it! You've made him thousands!'

'I'm glad about that, but we can't stand around here feeling smug, we've got loads to do before we can go home.'

Then she was caught from behind and turned round. Almost before she registered who it was, Charles had his arms round her and was crushing her half to death. 'Well done, Flora,' he breathed into her ear. 'I knew you could do it.'

Then he kissed her, full on the lips.

For a moment, it was just a kiss between friends, a congratulatory kiss, that she might have exchanged with anyone, but then, for the briefest moment, it took on a quality of passion that made her catch her breath.

They broke apart, both astounded and horrified. They stared at each other, neither knowing what to say. A lifetime passed before Flora licked her lips. 'Um . . .'

'So,' said Annabelle in a flat voice. '*Flora Pulls It Off!* Or something. How does it feel to be the title of a girls' school adventure novel?'

Flora tried to laugh. 'Er – fine.' She looked at Charles's white face and knew it was a reflection of her own. 'I, er . . . excuse me. I think I'll just pop to the Ladies'.'

She was washing her hands when Annabelle came into the room and stood with her back to the door, so they couldn't be interrupted. Flora felt shaky, a mixture of shock, guilt and a nervous reaction to her performance as an auctioneer.

'What the hell do you think you're doing?' Annabelle looked hot and bothered, but her gaze as she stared at Flora was icy.

'I . . . I don't know what you mean,' Flora stammered. How much had Annabelle seen?

'Don't give me that. I saw you. You and Charles.'

'Oh,' said Flora weakly. 'You mean when he kissed me just now? It was just over-excitement, Annabelle, really, don't read anything into it. He was just—'

'I'm not talking about the kiss, Flora,' Annabelle said furiously. 'That was a bit of meaningless sentimentality. I mean the look.'

'Look?' echoed Flora weakly. 'What look?'

'Oh, grow up, Flora,' snapped Annabelle. 'You're in love with him, aren't you?'

'No—' said Flora hotly.

'Don't try to deny it! It was plain as a pikestaff.'

Flora shook her head. Everything suddenly seemed to be happening so fast that she didn't know what to think. Charles's kiss had been unnerving enough, but Annabelle was right. It was the way he had suddenly pulled back, the way they had looked at each other, that gave everything away.

She felt an inappropriate little rush of pleasure. Charles didn't just think of her as his little cousin, he thought of her as a woman. And clearly found her attractive. But what about Annabelle?

'Look, I'm sorry, Annabelle, really, I—'

'Honestly, Flora, I don't want to hear it. I can't imagine there's anything you could say that I'd want to hear. But there's one thing you should know. Even if Charles did think you were more than just a minor irritation in his life, he'd never leave me for you.'

'Why not?' Flora was surprised to find she'd spoken out loud.

'Because without me, he'd lose everything.'

'Everything? What do you mean, everything?'

'I mean he'd lose the company. He'd lose Stanza and Stanza.'

'That can't be true.' Flora didn't understand. 'I'd know about it, if that was the case.'

'Not necessarily. He doesn't tell you everything, you know,' Annabelle said nastily. 'In fact, he doesn't tell you much at all.'

'So *you* tell me then. How would he lose the company if he left you?'

'The office building needed completely rewiring. My

father paid for it, with Charles's half of the business as collateral.'

'You mean, your father lent Charles the money?'

'Sort of, but the arrangement is that the debt will be written off when we get married. So however much he loved you – even if he does, which I sincerely doubt – he'd still never leave me. His precious company will always be more important to him than any woman.'

'I see. Well, thank you for making things clear to me. And I hope you'll be happy knowing that Charles is only marrying you for your father's money!'

'Not "only", darling, but he has got an awful lot of it.' She looked pityingly at Flora. 'I did try to tell you. I thought I'd made it quite clear how things are. Charles and I are going to get married, we've always been going to get married, and that's that.'

Flora's mouth filled with salt water and she knew that, unless she was very lucky, she was about to be very sick. She also knew she couldn't retreat to a cubicle and throw up where Annabelle could hear her. With a huge effort of will, she swallowed hard and pushed past Annabelle.

'Excuse me. I've got to go.'

She stood in the corridor for a few moments, feeling sweat prickle along her hairline, wishing she could just die of humiliation and not have to endure the process of going back into the saleroom, where everybody would want to talk to her. She opened the door to a storeroom, obviously used by the playgroup, and full of tricycles and scooters, space hoppers and lorries. There was hardly space for her, too, but she squeezed in and stayed there until she heard Annabelle leave the Ladies'; then, when her nausea had passed, she emerged, feeling her life was as much of a road smash as the pile-up of plastic vehicles behind her.

She had to go to the little room they used as an office to get her bag. She didn't know if it was good or bad that only Charles was in there.

'Flora! Are you all right? Where have you been? You look awful!'

'I just feel a bit shell-shocked,' she said, trying to brush it off. 'The excitement, I suppose. How's your tooth?'

'Oh fine, now. Shall I drive you home?' He stared at her with what was unmistakably an echo of the look in his eyes after they kissed. 'We need to talk, Flora. I want to—'

'No.' She stopped him before he could get any further. She had to sort things out in her mind before everything got any more confused, and the last person she could talk it all over with now was Charles. 'No, Charles, sorry.' Good, she was sounding more composed. 'I would like to go home, but I don't want you to drive me. Really. I'll be fine. Could you just pass my bag? It's in the bottom drawer of that filing cabinet.'

He looked hurt and confused. 'But, Flora, I don't want you going home on your own when you look so ill. And we have to—'

'I really will be fine on my own.'

Looking into her eyes, he could see her determination and backed off gracefully. 'You were a star today, Flora. I saw it all. And we can talk tomorrow, can't we?'

Flora regarded him, feeling she didn't know whom she was looking at. 'I'm glad I didn't let you down, Charles.'

And then she left, too miserable to weep.

Chapter Twenty-Four

Flora felt overcome with loneliness and despair once she got back to the cottage. She put the kettle on and then realised she didn't want tea, so she opened a bottle of wine, poured a glass, and didn't want that either. She knew that a really good cry would release some of her tension and be healthy, but tears wouldn't come. She collapsed on to the sofa and let Imelda and the kittens comfort her. The kittens weren't interested in her for long, but Imelda was satisfyingly soothing. She sat on Flora's lap and purred loudly, dribbling as she kneaded Flora's knee with her paws. Flora sat there with her eyes closed, stroking Imelda on automatic pilot.

'This is ridiculous!' she said aloud. 'You came to the country to learn about your family business and you've done it! You've learnt about it and improved it and today you made thousands of pounds for Geoffrey. You should feel ecstatic! The whole thing with Charles is neither here nor there, really. He was engaged to Annabelle, and he's still engaged to Annabelle. Nothing's changed.'

But something had changed. That kiss, that look, and Annabelle witnessing both. Even if she'd wanted to, she felt she couldn't pretend nothing had happened – Annabelle wouldn't let her. And Annabelle held the whip hand – over her, over Charles and, currently, over Stanza and Stanza. A lot of things now made sense.

She went into the garden to ring her mother. She wasn't ready to talk about Charles yet. When she'd got her thoughts together, she would, but not now. But her mother knew she might have had to do some selling today and would be longing to hear how it went.

At first the call went to plan. Her mother was even more excited that Flora expected.

'Oh, darling, I knew you'd find out what you were really good at eventually!'

'What do you mean?' Flora was indignant. 'I'm good at lots of things. People always want to give me jobs and hate it when I leave.'

'I know, I know, but an awful lot of that's because you're blonde and pretty. And they were just jobs. This is a career, and you're good at it in spite of being blonde and pretty.'

Flora didn't want to pass on what Louisa had said about the last lot, when she thought the two bidders just kept bidding so they could watch Flora. 'I've never thought that not being a dog to look at was a disadvantage. People have been very kind to me. Do you think that's why? That's a dreadful thought.'

'Well, maybe, initially, but if you're just a pretty face they won't go on indulging you. That's what I mean, really. This is a job where looks don't count. I'm so proud of you, darling.'

'Thanks, Mum.'

'Your dad's here. Do you want a word?'

Flora really wanted a hug, but a word would have to do. After a long chat with her father, who wanted to know exactly how it all worked, Hermione came back on.

'So, what about you and Charles?'

'We're not – a "we", I mean. He's with Annabelle and will be for ever.' She sniffed. The tears she had tried to force away earlier threatened now.

'Are you sure?'

'Yes! He kissed me after I got down off the podium and Annabelle saw.'

'But everyone would have kissed you, surely?'

'Not like that. And we looked at each other. That was the worst, the most revealing part. Then she followed me to the Ladies' and told me that if Charles . . .' She gulped back a sob. 'That even if Charles wanted to leave her for me he couldn't because . . .' Another hiccup. '. . . he owes her father loads of money and he put up his half of the business as security.'

'Why does he owe Annabelle's father money? Was it gambling debts or something?'

'No! He had to have the office building rewired.'

'Oh, good. I mean, I'm glad it wasn't anything dreadful.'

'Quite dreadful enough. Mum, I've got to leave. I can't stay around and watch him marry Annabelle. And I couldn't ask him to do anything that would risk him the business.' This realisation had been filtering through to her slowly, but now it had arrived it was perfectly clear.

'But are you sure it's true? This story? Before you do anything irrevocable, check that Annabelle's telling the truth. She might easily have made it up. Phone Geoffrey. He'll know.'

'There's still the kiss thing. She knows I'm in love with Charles—'

'And is he in love with you?'

Flora was silent for a long moment. 'I think so. I mean, that's what it felt like. When he kissed me, and then when he looked at me afterwards. But—'

'Don't turn your back on the business you love and have put so much into without making sure there's absolutely no choice. Ring Geoffrey. And then ring me back.'

Geoffrey answered the phone, sounding very cheerful. 'Hello, dear! How nice to hear you. I didn't see you to say goodbye, are you all right?'

'I'm fine, Geoffrey,' she said, realising she sounded anything but. 'Tired, of course, but otherwise fine. I was just wondering if you could tell me something. I was thinking about the wiring in the office building.' She hoped Geoffrey didn't think it a strange thought, but she had to know if Annabelle was telling the truth.

Fortunately, Geoffrey didn't seem to think her thoughts were all that strange. Or if he did, he didn't mention it. 'What about the wiring?'

'Does it need redoing?'

'Oh, I shouldn't think so. They had it all redone about a year ago. Annabelle's father paid for it all.'

'How on earth do you know that?'

'I had to check the bills. He wouldn't write any cheques until I'd reported that the work was done. Annabelle was very cross that her father had asked me to do it. You know she never had any time for me.'

Good manners forced Flora to continue the conversation for a bit longer, then she rang her mother and reported the news.

'Oh, love! My heart bleeds for you! My friend said that the hardest part of motherhood was watching them break their hearts and being able to do nothing about it. Now I know what she means.'

'I'll be fine, Mum. I'm strong. I've just got to decide what I'm going to do now.'

There was another long pause.

'Well, darling' – Hermione stepped into the silence – 'you know we're always thrilled to have you. If you'd like to come and stay—'

'No, Mum,' Flora said tiredly. 'It's a lovely thought, but I need to be practical, and you're not exactly round the corner, are you? I think I do have to leave though – I can't face Charles.' A memory of his face looking worriedly at her after her confrontation with Annabelle came back to her. He'd been very keen to talk – presumably about their kiss – but whatever it was he wanted to say, she couldn't bear to hear it. If he wanted to tell her it was a mistake, and he was in love with Annabelle and Annabelle alone, it would break her heart. But if he told her he was in love with her but tied to Annabelle by Stanza and Stanza, that wasn't any better. She couldn't ask him to give up the business he cared so passionately about – and to be honest she didn't really want to know what choice he would make were he forced to make that decision. No, there was nothing for it. She couldn't stay in Bishopsbridge.

'I might go and see Emma for a bit,' she said slowly, thinking it out. 'But you must promise not to tell Charles where I've gone. He might want to follow me to make sure I'm all right, but I don't want him to. Do you understand? Leaving is going to be quite hard enough, but it'll be even worse if I have to talk it all through with him. I couldn't bear that.'

Reluctantly, her mother agreed.

When she disconnected she burst into tears and drank the glass of wine.

After that, and some bread and Marmite, she felt robust enough to ring Emma. She might not be in, but Flora thought she could leave a message, warning her that she might be getting a visit very soon. But, luckily, Emma was there.

'Sweetie!' she shrieked. 'How are you?'

Flora felt utterly exhausted, suddenly. 'Well. I've just conducted my first auction. It was brilliant. Very exhilarating.'

'So are you celebrating with a glass of wine?'

'Mm.'

'So why don't you sound happy?'

Flora bit her lip. Crying was healthy, but it did interrupt conversation rather. 'Because the rest of my life has gone pear-shaped.'

'Is it Henry?'

'Henry? No! Charles! I'm in love with him, Ems, and he'll never leave Annabelle.'

'The one that William wanted to paint? She did have a sort of heavy, pre-Raphaelite sort of beauty. Well, just get him away from her. Should be easy, pretty girl like you,' Emma said briskly.

'It's not that simple. Even if I could, if they don't get married he'll lose his half of the business. Oh, my God. Can you imagine sharing a business with Annabelle's dad! How scary!'

'But it would be OK, because you'd have Charles.

413

Then you could do anything.' Emma paused. 'Is he still as stuffy as ever?'

'Pretty much. I'm just so in love with him I don't mind any more.'

'He is extremely attractive, in that Mr-Darcy-in-need-of-an-enema kind of way.'

'Emma! That's very unkind. You should see how kind he can be—'

'He's not being very kind if he's breaking your heart,' she retorted acidly.

'He's not doing it on purpose!'

'I know, I know, I'm sorry. I'm just a bit off men at the moment.'

'Oh, Emma, I'm so sorry! I've been so wrapped up in my own problems – are you and Dave OK?'

'Yes, because he doesn't live here any more.'

'What?'

'Life is so much easier without him. Man-free and proud, that's me. Jeremy rings me from time to time but we haven't met up yet.'

'Does that mean . . .'

'What?'

'That I could come and stay for a bit? I've got to get away from here.' Then she told Emma everything. When she'd finished, Emma said, 'Get in the car as soon as that glass of wine has gone away, and get your arse up here!'

Flora rang Geoffrey, although it was quite late, and arranged to leave Imelda and the kittens with him, early in the morning. Then she cleaned. She knew she wouldn't sleep and so didn't even attempt to go to bed until the cottage was as gleaming as it could be. Every plate, cup and knife was washed and stacked in a freshly wiped cupboard. The future Mrs Stanza would not be able to criticise her housekeeping.

When the physical exercise of sweeping and wiping and dusting had finally exhausted her, she had a bath in what was left of the hot water and fell into bed, Imelda on top of her.

She awoke at dawn and packed her clothes. Downstairs she saw the teapot on the mantelpiece. Should she leave it? Or take it as a souvenir? Or would her heart break all over again whenever she saw it? Without consciously making a decision, she wrapped it in the cashmere sweater of her father's that she had once lent to Charles and put it in her little flowery shopper, along with her make-up.

Loading Imelda and the kittens into the Land-Rover, which she was now going to steal, made her cry again. The little cottage had been the kittens' only home. They'd been so happy here. Flora had been so happy here, in a way. She sniffed hard and wiped her nose on a tissue she found in her jacket pocket. It was one her mother had given her, and it had shoes printed on it. The sight of it made her cry even more.

Flora had forgotten how awful London traffic could be, even on a Saturday, and realised that while the Land-Rover was perfect for country roads, it was a bit hefty for the back streets of Clapham. But someone was on her side because she found a parking spot right outside Emma's house.

Emma must have been looking out for her, because as soon as Flora opened the car door she came running

415

down the steps. She hugged Flora for some minutes. Then she said, 'That's an awfully big car.'

'I know. And it's not even mine. Mine's still parked in the yard behind the office.'

Although she'd been away for less than a day, and wouldn't normally have gone into work on a Saturday, she felt a terrible pang of homesickness. 'It's great to be here. I've missed London.'

Emma frowned. 'Let me help you in with your stuff.' Then she looked at Flora's bags. 'Is that all you've got?'

'I didn't take all my clothes down with me. I'll have to get them out of the loft in the flat.' Usually the thought of delightful, but forgotten, little outfits to rediscover would have given Flora quite a thrill. Now they just seemed like clothes that belonged to a former life.

'Well, come in, do. I've put a bottle in the fridge, or is it too early?'

As Flora gathered up carrier bags and cases she decided that getting drunk was the only option. 'I don't think it's too early at all. It's nearly lunchtime.'

The wine set Flora properly weeping. She curled up with her feet on the sofa and alternately sobbed and drank and told Emma her woes, until Emma got up and made cheese on toast.

'Sorry, Ems, I am being the most complete pain, I know. Do you want to talk about Dave?'

'No. Not being in love with Dave any more, if I ever was, I don't want to talk about him.'

'Fair enough. Is there a corner shop that might be open?'

'Just off the main drag. Why, what do you want?'

'More wine and chocolate. At times like these a girl

needs her props and so does her friend. We need a few good DVDs, too.'

They spent the rest of the afternoon and evening eating chocolate and watching their favourite films. When Bridget Jones said, 'I choose vodka,' they both cheered.

Eventually it was bedtime, and Flora staggered into the spare bed feeling drunk and slightly sick. 'I'll feel fine tomorrow,' she said. 'I'll be strong again tomorrow. I just needed today off.'

But she didn't feel fine the next day. She pulled on the cashmere sweater over her pyjamas, having put the teapot on the windowsill in her room. It was stupid, she knew, but she felt the sweater was her last link with Charles, the nearest thing she would ever have to having his arms round her. She didn't tell Emma this. She knew how tiresome broken-hearted girlfriends could be but she couldn't snap out of it, no matter how sternly she ordered herself to.

When Emma came home from spending the day with friends Flora was still in her pyjamas. She had made a cursory attempt to clear up the dirty tissues and chocolate wrappers from the day before, but she hadn't washed her hair or put on make-up. Even brushing her teeth seemed like a waste of time, though she did at least force herself to do that.

Emma didn't comment, and cooked them both some pasta. She was being such a good friend, Flora realised. I must pull myself together soon or she'll go off me, and then where will I be?

The next day, Flora was immersed in a programme about couples buying property abroad when her mother rang.

'Darling,' she said carefully, 'I don't want to make you feel even worse, but there's something I think you should know.'

'What? Nothing's wrong with Dad, is it?'

'No, no. Nothing like that. It's just that we've had a wedding invitation. From Annabelle's parents. To Charles and Annabelle's wedding,' she went on as Flora still hadn't reacted.

'Oh.' They'd obviously been sent out a couple of days before Flora had left. Annabelle wouldn't call it off now, and Flora's last faint hope evaporated. 'That's it, then.'

'It does rather look like it.'

'Well, it's only what I knew already.'

'I know. But I'm really, really sorry, darling.'

Flora ate a packet of custard creams even though she didn't like custard creams, possibly hoping that the nausea would be a distraction from her utter misery.

When she heard Emma's key in the lock, she flew to the kitchen and began to peel some onions to chop. She had to have some excuse for her newly red eyes and nose.

'Oh, Flo, what now?' Emma demanded, not convinced that pulling the brown skin off an onion could have had that effect so quickly.

'Mum rang. She's had a wedding invitation. They're definitely going to get married. My life is over.'

'No it's not! You knew they were going to get married. You're no worse off than you were before.' Emma was obviously trying to ward off another Niagara-sized weeping session.

'I know, but I suppose that deep down I'd been hoping that they'd had a huge row after I left. I suppose I hoped that kissing me might have made Charles think twice, that he might have decided to cancel – or at least postpone – the wedding, but I shouldn't have let myself hope really.'

'Well, you're not to let it make you slump into despair. I know it's hard but lounging around all day in a sweater that's far too big for you isn't helping.'

'It's a lovely sweater,' said Flora, clutching its softness.

'It is, but it's making you soft. You'll have to get out – do something about getting a job. You can stay as long as you want, but I can't manage the rent here on my own. If you don't pay me rent, I'll have to find someone else.'

'Emma!'

'Tough love, sweetie. And you'd be so much happier if you were doing something.'

'I'll need a job before I can pay you.'

'Haven't you got savings? Didn't they pay you at the auction house?'

'Not really, not in a way that would count as being paid in London. I didn't have to pay rent, you see.'

'Well, I'm sure you'll pick something up, if you're not too fussy. I'm not sure if Sotheby's will take you on just like that, though.'

Flora smiled obligingly. 'No, but when I've sorted myself out a bit, I will think about working for an auction house. It's so exciting.'

Emma wasn't very enthusiastic. 'But I've a feeling if you want to work for one of those places and live in London, it helps if you've got a private income.'

'You're probably right. Maybe I should find a country

auction house who wants to take on an apprentice. I can always do bar work in the evenings.'

'Or you could get better-paid work. You've had loads of quite high-earning jobs in the past.'

'They were just jobs, not careers,' said Flora. 'I don't know if I'd be satisfied with that now.'

'Well, don't be too fussy. And why don't you go and have a shower and wash your hair? I fancy going out tonight. Some people from work are meeting up at a new wine bar. You can come and meet them.'

'Oh, Emma, do I have to?'

'Yes! I don't want to leave you here on your own, and besides, I said I'd be bringing my pretty friend.'

'I'm not pretty now,' said Flora glumly.

'But you would be if you did something about yourself! Get in that shower!'

An hour and a half later Flora was in the sort of bar that had been her natural habitat before she went to the country and ruined herself for civilised life. She tried really hard to be bright and amusing and live up to the reputation Emma had created for her. If her heart had not been broken, it would have been as easy as breathing. As it was, every smile, every flickered eyelash, every little hand gesture felt forced. Fortunately, it seemed to have the right effect.

'So, Flora, what do you do?' came the inevitable question from Emma's boss, who was called Tim.

'I'm between jobs at the moment, but I've just finished helping run an auction house.' She smiled and sipped her spritzer, wishing she could go home and put her sweater back on. 'What about you?'

Flora ran the conversation on auto-pilot until Tim said,

'We're sponsoring an art exhibition. I know nothing about art, don't even know what I like, but apparently it's a good marketing tool.'

Flora began paying attention, wondering what William would have to say about the word 'art' being included in the same sentence as 'marketing tool'. 'You don't need any extra help, do you? That's just the sort of thing I'm good at.' It would be easy, and it would get her out of Emma's hair.

'What? What are you good at?'

She shrugged, smiling, trying to blag herself a job. 'Talking to people, handing out leaflets, showing people artworks. I can do it all.'

Tim frowned. 'Well, I suppose we could do with some extra help. Do you know anything about merchant banking?'

'No, but I'm very good at learning things by heart, and acting, and believe me, I can sell ice to Eskimos.' She delivered him a full-on smile that didn't often fail her. Charles was the only man who had seemed immune to its wattage.

Tim smiled. 'I think you've talked yourself into a job, Flora.'

'You see! I'm just the girl you need.'

'I'll need you to wear business clothes.'

'I know just what you mean! Darling little suits, crisp shirts and heels.' Or perhaps no shirt, just a hint of cleavage. She would have to raid Emma's wardrobe. Her own darling little suits were currently suffocating in black plastic bags in the Lancaster Gate flat. She didn't have a key and wouldn't be able to arrange to retrieve them in time.

421

'You seem very keen.'

'I am! It's just the sort of job I love. You can leave me in total charge, and I'll cope. I'm good at responsibility.'

Tim's scepticism was gradually worn away until he was convinced that Flora was just what he needed. The pay was quite good, too.

In the taxi home, Emma was just as enthusiastic. 'I knew it wouldn't take you long to get a job. I said you always fall on your feet. And while it might not be the most demanding job in the world, it'll get you out there. You'll have loads of fun.'

Flora sighed. 'I know you're right about me needing to get out into the world, but I think "loads of fun" is a bit beyond me at the moment.'

Flora, wearing one of Emma's suits, the button of which came a little far down even for Flora's liberal attitudes, was sipping water from a bottle. The gallery was full of people screaming at each other. No one seemed to be looking at the art, but a lot of people had come up to chat to her about merchant banking. To a man – and they were all men – they knew more about it than she did but they all stayed to hear her patter and offer to get her another drink. Several had slipped their business cards into her pocket. It was quite good for the ego, she decided, and promising when it came to looking for more permanent work. One of those City types would have a vacancy for her, doing something. She had many more skills now than she had when she'd lived in London before.

There was a small lull in proceedings and Flora was resting her voice, rehydrating, waiting for the next man bored with art to come up and be told things he knew by a girl who didn't know them, when she saw what seemed to be a familiar head bobbing through the crowd. She dismissed it as her crazed mind seeing Charles where Charles could not possibly be, and then he appeared.

Her mouth went numb and she broke out into a sweat. She tried hard to form her mouth into a semblance of a smile but it wasn't a very convincing attempt. Speaking was beyond her.

'God, it's taken me a long time to track you down!' he said crossly. 'Why the hell didn't you leave a forwarding address?'

Flora tried to work some saliva into her mouth so she could speak. 'Hello.' Her voice was husky and she cleared her throat. 'What are you doing here?'

'I've been looking for you!' Charles seemed irritated, as if they'd had an assignation and she'd failed to turn up.

'Why?'

'Oh, for God's sake, Flora! Have you got a coat? No? Good, then come on.'

'Just a minute!' Flora's backbone re-formed itself. 'Who are you to tell me to "come on"?'

Charles frowned down at her, confused. 'Flora, I've come to take you home. Now come on.'

'I can't leave here, I happen to be working, in case you didn't notice!'

'Standing round handing out leaflets is not what I call work!'

'Well, sorry about that! It's the best I could do in the time! I've only been in London a short while—'

'And it's time you came home again.'

423

'No it's not! I'm working. Now please go away and let me do my job.' She smiled over his shoulder, to make out there was someone waiting for her attention.

Charles clicked his teeth and took her bottle of water out of her hand. He looked for somewhere to put it and, failing to find anywhere, dropped it on the floor. 'No one's that bloody indispensable,' he misquoted back at her, as she had when he hadn't wanted to take time off for the dentist. 'Come on.'

Chapter Twenty-Five

Flora found herself being grabbed by the wrist and pulled. As digging her high heels into the parquet floor would have been both difficult and embarrassing, she allowed her body to follow her wrist. 'I can't go anywhere with you, Charles,' she said when they got outside. 'And if I leave early, I won't get paid and I need the money.'

'What do you need money for?'

'To pay my rent. And I've got a flat to look at when I've finished here.' That wasn't true, but it sounded good.

'Look, Flora, it took me a long time to track you down—'

'How *did* you track me down? Don't tell me my mother told you where I was?'

Charles pushed his hair out of his eyes. 'Can we have this discussion somewhere other than in Cork Street?'

'Where do you suggest? Shall we ring up Rent-a-Boardroom and hope they've got one available?'

Charles smiled. 'A restaurant would be good. I'm starving.'

Excitement, adrenaline, and sheer pleasure at being with Charles again, even if they were fighting, made Flora's heart give a little skip. 'OK.' She struggled to sound non-committal. She didn't want to give Charles the impression she would just go meekly home with him.

'There must be one somewhere round here.' Still holding on to her, they walked past several places that were closed.

'A lot of restaurants are closed on Monday nights,' explained Flora. 'It's something to do with the fish. Or that may just be chip shops.'

Charles scowled down at her, as if despairing of ever understanding her.

They turned into a little side street down which could be seen an awning and fairy lights. Sounds of a busy restaurant emerged. They got to the door; the maître d' regarded them sadly and shook his head, 'I'm sorry—'

'Listen,' said Charles, polite but very firm, 'we're hungry, we need a small table for two. We don't mind if we have to sit by the kitchen, we don't mind if there's a bit of a draught, we just want somewhere we can eat.'

'Certainly, m'sieur. If you would just wait here, I'll see what I can do.'

While they were waiting, Flora looked around her. It seemed as if there wasn't a spare square inch to sit down in the entire place. However, not many minutes after their arrival, the maître d' came back to them.

'We have found a little corner for you.'

They squeezed past other diners and Swiss cheese plants until they came to the corner described. Even with the table pulled out, Flora could hardly get behind it. She collapsed on her seat with a giggle, which she partly put down to nerves. Charles took the menu from the waiter, who had followed their progress with difficulty.

'Steak frites, salad, and – can I see the wine list? That all right for you, Flora?'

'Are you ordering my food for me, Charles?'

'Yes. Have you got a problem with that?'

Flora sighed. 'Not on this occasion.'

Charles scanned the list that was on the other side of the menu. 'We'll have the Barolo, please, and some water. Sparkling or still, Flora?'

'Sparkling,' she said meekly.

She didn't approve of men ordering food for their companions as a rule, but in this instance it was quite nice. After all, if he'd ordered something she hated, or just didn't fancy, she'd have said something. And she was too intrigued by Charles's presence to fuss about it.

The wine came with satisfying alacrity. 'I don't need to taste it,' said Charles. 'I'm sure it's not corked.'

The waiter tried not to show he was offended and poured them each a glass of wine and then retreated. He was obviously experienced enough to know when customers wanted to have a good row in peace.

'Now, Flora. Oh, bread. Thank you.'

Flora took a bit of bread and nibbled it. She realised she was hungry, too. She hadn't eaten anything except nibbles since breakfast.

'As I was saying. Why did you run away? You must come home!'

'I didn't run away! I went away for the weekend and decided to stay on for a few days. It's not at all the same.' She didn't want to explain why she'd gone, it was too humiliating, too painful.

'You may have told Geoffrey that, but it didn't fool

427

me. And if you only went for the weekend why did you get a job? And you said you were looking at a flat!'

Flora checked her watch. 'Thank you for reminding me. I'm due there at nine. It was the only time they could see me. I mustn't miss the appointment.' Her pride made her keep up this pretence. It made her feel more in control, somehow.

'You're not going to look at any flat! What is going on with you? You come down to Bishopsbridge, cause havoc at every turn—'

'I did not cause havoc! I caused . . . prosperity, publicity, a lot of good things. And we made loads for Geoffrey's books.'

'I know. I was there. We must let you have another go sometime, when you're more experienced.'

Flora was on her feet before he'd finished speaking. He grabbed her wrist. 'Only joking, honestly. You were a star, and everyone has gone on and on about it ever since.'

Flora regarded him suspiciously. 'Tell me, Charles, honestly, did you deliberately stay away so I'd have to do the sale?'

Charles raised a comical eyebrow. 'If I tell you, will you promise not to throw anything?'

'No. I won't promise,' she snarled, 'and you've betrayed yourself by asking that question.'

'Think how disappointed you'd have been – Geoffrey would have been – if you'd done all that coaching and studying and then didn't get to go on stage. It would have been like the star turning up at the theatre at the last moment when the understudy has been told she's going to go on.'

Flora allowed herself to subside. 'I suppose so. Did you see it all?'

'Yes, I did and I was genuinely impressed. Geoffrey did a really good job of coaching you.'

'Don't I get any credit?'

'You know perfectly well you're a natural. And people love you.'

Flora felt a smug little smile start at the corner of her mouth and bit it back, glad she didn't have to go rushing off into the night in a huff without having had her steak frites. 'I'm not a natural at all. Geoffrey spent hours coaching me.'

'Well, it was worth it. I didn't dream we'd get anything like that for them.' He frowned. 'Geoffrey was of the opinion that people kept bidding just so they could get your attention.'

'It's not true. People aren't idiots. It was the website that did it. People heard the books were on sale and turned up to buy them. Nothing more than that.'

'I'm not jealous of the punters.'

'Good.'

'So why did you go?'

Flora exhaled, fiddled with her napkin and ate some more bread. It was lovely that Charles had come after her, but it didn't actually change anything. He'd still lose the business if he chose Flora over Annabelle – assuming he wanted to, that is. He wasn't behaving terribly like a heartbroken lover right now; instead he'd reverted to his bossy older cousin persona. Nothing had really changed, and so Flora didn't feel she could be honest with him about what had happened. She decided instead to be a bit economical with the truth.

She fixed her gaze on a flaw in the tablecloth. 'Annabelle saw us kiss. She got the wrong end of the stick and' – she forced herself into an attempt of careless laughter – 'thought there was something going on between us.' Charles's expression changed, but she found she was unable to read it. She carried on regardless. 'So she told me that if you and she didn't get married, you'd lose your half of the company.'

Charles shook his head. 'But why did that make you leave?'

'What do you mean? I couldn't ask you to—' She checked herself. She couldn't say she couldn't ask him to choose as that rather presupposed that he wanted her, and she wasn't sure if he did or not. 'I couldn't ask you to jeopardise the company. It's your life.'

'I thought it was your life too, Flora.'

'It was – is' – God, this was difficult – 'but it has been yours for longer.'

'I see.'

'So what are you doing here?' she asked. 'You and Annabelle are going to get married. Don't try to deny it! My mother got the invitation.'

'Oh God, I'm sorry. I expect Annabelle's mother sent them out before she knew we'd broken up—'

'Broken up?' Flora couldn't believe what she was hearing. 'You mean you and Annabelle have broken up?'

'Yes, Flora. I rang you on Sunday, and got no answer. I asked Annabelle if she knew where you might be and she told me that she'd sent you packing.'

Flora's head was spinning. 'But if you don't marry Annabelle, how will you pay back her father for the rewiring?'

'I haven't a clue about that, either. I expect I'll think of something.'

'Charles, this is so unlike you!'

'I know. I think I got bored with being like me. I'd rather be more like you. I'm living in the office flat. I'm going to pick up my kitten as soon as we get back.'

'Is that the royal "we"?' she asked cautiously, not wanting to misinterpret.

'No! It means both of us. You've learnt a lot, you've become really useful.'

'You said I caused havoc.'

'It means the same.'

Flora backtracked. There was too much to take in all at once. 'You still haven't told me why you came to find me. Or how, for that matter.'

'I'll take the fifth on that last bit.'

As Flora had a strong suspicion her mother was involved, she let that pass. 'What about the first part of the question?'

'We need you, Flora! And you can't expect Geoffrey to look after your cats for ever.'

'There's only Imelda, and two of the kittens are his anyway.' She frowned. 'Do you want to go on living in the flat? Because if we sold it, we could raise enough to buy Bob and possibly George out. Perhaps there'd be enough to pay off Annabelle's father, too. If not, there's still my half of the company. We could raise a loan on that. The wiring couldn't have cost that much.'

'You'd be prepared to do that?'

'Uh-huh.' Flora was suddenly aware how much she had exposed her feelings.

'For me, or the company?'

She swallowed. 'The company, of course.' This was a lie, but she felt too vulnerable to tell him the truth.

'So you do care about Stanza and Stanza?' he asked softly.

'Of course I care!' said Flora and, a second later, she realised she'd been tricked in a way she'd tricked Charles in the past.

'So why did you run away?'

'I told you. I thought you'd lose the company if I stayed. Why did you come after me?'

'Do you really need to ask me that?'

Flora's vehement affirmative was interrupted by the appearance of their food. She was grateful. It gave her time to think. What reason could she possibly give for running away that didn't involve her feelings for Charles? And Annabelle. She cut herself quite a large bit of steak so she couldn't possibly be expected to answer difficult questions for some time.

'It was quite hard to track you down,' said Charles who, having taken a smaller mouthful, was able to speak quite soon.

Flora nodded, chewing.

'I had to get in touch with Henry in the end.'

Flora frowned. 'How did he know where I was?'

'It was he who suggested we got in touch with Emma.' He frowned. 'And strangely, although they were supposed to be friends, William didn't have Emma's number.'

'Oh?'

'No. Fortunately your mother had it. She told me where you were working.'

Flora made a note to either kill or hug Emma and her

mother later, depending on how things worked out.

'So were Emma and William old friends?'

Flora shrugged. 'Maybe not.'

'Still, he paints a very good portrait.'

'Oh, did Annabelle get it done? What's it like?' She picked up her glass.

'It's very fetching. She's naked.'

Flora sprayed red wine all over her plate, the surrounding table and even, a bit, on Charles. The waiter rushed up, to see if she needed patting on the back. He was sent away by Charles's frown.

'Didn't you know?' asked Charles. 'I thought you were in her confidence.'

Flora shook her head and sipped some water. 'She never told me she was going to have herself painted naked! It seems so unlike her!'

'I don't know about that. Since you did your Trinny and Susannah act on her, she's been a changed woman.'

Flora suddenly became very hot. If she hadn't meddled with Annabelle's wardrobe, thrown out the pie-crust collars, got her to stop doing her shirts up to the neck, she and Annabelle might not have been any happier, but at least Charles might have been. He must have liked the pie-crust collars.

'I'm so sorry,' she whispered as guilt flooded over her.

'I don't think you're aware of your powers, Flora,' he answered, looking maddeningly inscrutable.

Flora got hold of herself. 'Oh, come on, you can't blame it all on me! She's a strong-minded woman, Annabelle.'

Braced by his unreasonableness, she attacked another section of steak. She didn't bother with the chips, delicious though they were, she needed iron, a few red corpuscles, to keep her emotional flag flying.

'So you don't take responsibility for Annabelle behaving out of character?'

'No!' She concentrated on deepening her voice so she didn't sound too mouse-like. 'No. You can't take responsibility for the actions of adults in their right minds. It's just neurotic, blaming yourself for everything.'

'A moment ago you were blaming yourself for Annabelle's improved dress sense making her skittish, now you won't accept any culpability for her having her portrait painted naked.'

Flora suddenly wondered if that was all that was going on between Annabelle and William. Despite her threats to Flora, it seemed Annabelle had ended up relinquishing Charles quite quickly – maybe William had been a factor. After all, taking your clothes off in front of a man was a very intimate thing to do, even if only in the capacity of artist's model. She didn't mention this rogue thought.

'Only you would use a word like "culpability" in conversation, Charles.' She took another sip of wine. She had been about to say that it was one of the things she loved about him. Not because it was in any way lovable, but because it was so characteristic of him.

'Are you going to eat your chips?'

'No. Do have them.' She watched as he piled his plate with frites. 'Honestly, how you can eat so much . . .'

'What?' Charles chewed stolidly.

'At a time like this,' she managed, deliberately being unspecific.

He put down his knife and fork and glanced at his watch. 'Half past eight?'

434

Flora folded her lip behind her teeth to stop herself smiling. 'I said a time like this, not this specific time.' Then she remembered her fake appointment to visit a flat. She thought it was about time she referred to it again. 'And if it's half past eight, I must go. I've got to get to Islington, and I have no idea how long that'll take me.'

'Too long. And why go to Islington anyway?'

'I told you, to look at a flat.'

'But I told you I've come to take you home.'

'Well, I can't possibly go. For one thing, the Land-Rover's in a residential parking space outside Emma's house.'

'I must remember to report the fact that you stole it to the police.'

'It's half mine, anyway. And apart from Imelda, who I am sure is perfectly happy being fed sardines by Edie, give me one good reason why I should go back to Stanza and Stanza?' She took a breath and carried on, in case he didn't give her the answer he wanted. 'The business is picking up no end, you can buy out Bob and George and get all their business, the website works brilliantly. You can really become profitable.'

'Did Geoffrey tell you he wants to buy into the business?'

'No, really? How fantastic!' That must be the plan for the money the books had raised that Geoffrey was being so mysterious about. 'He knows so much about everything and the extra cash would come in very useful.' In fact, Flora realised, it would be more than useful – it would enable Charles to repay Annabelle's father's loan. And Annabelle's hold over Charles would disappear.

'Extra cash is always useful.' Charles smiled ruefully. 'But it would go to you, not to the business.'

'What?'

'You'd get the cash, not the business, because it would be your shares he'd be buying, wouldn't it?'

Flora shook her head. 'Not necessarily, they could be some of yours. But if he wants to buy some of mine, that's fine by me. In fact, if he wanted to buy me out entirely, that would be great.'

Charles frowned, rattled for the first time. 'But, Flora, I thought you loved the auctioneering business.'

'I do,' she agreed in a small voice. 'But it doesn't have to be Stanza and Stanza, does it?'

'No other business has your name on the letterhead, Flora. Doesn't that mean anything to you?'

'Yes, it does, but . . .' Tears clogged the back of her throat. She felt very tired, and very despondent. Charles had travelled all the way up to London to ask her to come back, but it now seemed very clear it was only for business reasons.

'But what?'

'It might be better if I became an auctioneer with another auction house, somewhere else.'

'Why?'

'Because . . .' What could she possibly say that would make any sense?

'There's no reason at all, is there?'

She gave a little shrug and looked into the middle distance which happened to be the specials board. There was a reason, a very good reason, but not one she could possibly give Charles.

'Would you like pudding?'

'No, thank you.' She regarded him. 'But don't let me stop you. Why not have the profiteroles?'

'There's something I want more than chocolate-covered pastries.'

'What?' Flora scanned the blackboard again. 'Tarte au citron? Tarte tatin?'

'No, you silly creature, I want you. Come on.'

He tossed a large sheaf of ten-pound notes on to the table and got to his feet.

Rather than face the embarrassment of his high-handed behaviour with the matter of the bill, Flora allowed him to take her arm and rush her out of the restaurant and on to the pavement, which had suddenly become quite busy.

'Now where?' demanded Flora, trying to remember she was a twenty-first-century woman and therefore not to be hauled about willy-nilly.

'A hotel, I think. Taxi!'

A taxi pulled up and Flora got into it. Charles collapsed on to the seat next to her.

'Where to?' asked the taxi driver over his shoulder.

'A decent hotel,' said Charles. 'Can you recommend anywhere?'

Flora hid her face in her hands, trying not to die from mortification. 'What will he think?'

Charles looked down at her and chuckled. 'Frankly, my dear, I don't give a damn.'

Behind her hands, Flora laughed.

Chapter Twenty-Six

❧❧❧

Flora was still hiding behind her hands when the taxi drew up, several minutes later. It wasn't surprising, really: they were in the centre of London; it was stuffed to the gills with hotels.

'This should do you. Small and discreet, just what you need, sir,' said the taxi driver.

Flora clambered out of the taxi and stood next to Charles, blushing, while he paid. She followed at a safe distance as he strode up the steps to the hotel. What could he possibly say at the desk that wouldn't make the whole situation look incredibly sordid? She hung around in the foyer, studying the modern art which surrounded her, indifferent to her state of acute nervousness. It wasn't that she didn't want to rush up to a bedroom with Charles, it was just that the process of getting there was toe-curling, to say the least.

'Come here and sign this,' said Charles. His words were commanding, but his tone was gentle. Flora signed obediently, hardly glancing at the nice-looking young woman behind the desk.

'As you see, we haven't got any luggage so could you kindly send up toothbrushes, toothpaste and – do you need anything, darling?'

The 'darling' made them seem married but as it was

the first time he'd used that endearment it made her blush even more.

'Some sort of moisturiser would be good,' she mumbled, still not looking up.

A horrid thought occurred to her. What about contraception? But if she reminded him about it now, he'd ask this nice woman for some condoms to be sent up with the toothbrushes and then she really would die of mortification. Such a death might be a medical first, but she was quite sure it was possible.

It wasn't the sort of hotel that told you which floor your room was on and expected you to find it. Although there was a conspicuous lack of bags to carry, a young man – gorgeous, Flora noted, and therefore even more embarrassing – took them along carpeted corridors and down a little flight of stairs to their room.

Once inside the room, after showing them the wardrobe, the mini-bar and how to work the television, he left them to it.

Flora went straight to the bathroom to inspect the shampoos and shower gels and found them to be Molton Brown – very satisfactory. When she went back, she found that Charles was inspecting the mini-bar.

It wasn't so much a bar as a cupboard with a fridge in it. Inside the fridge was gin, vodka, champagne, white wine, and the usual jelly beans and mixers. Outside was whisky, red wine, a disposable camera, snacks and something called a Comfort Pack.

Flora seized it and pulled off the top. 'Oh look! It's full of useful things! Sticking plaster, painkillers, a sewing kit and—' A packet of three condoms fell out on to the bed.

'Only three,' said Charles after a moment. 'That's a bit of a disappointment. But I expect they'll send up more if we ask.'

Flora allowed her gaze to meet Charles's head on for the first time since they left the restaurant. 'I can't believe we're doing this when we haven't even kissed properly.'

He smiled at her and opened his arms. 'Then let's kiss – properly.'

His arms folded round her and his mouth locked on to hers as if drawn by a magnet. He tasted minty, and she realised that he must have eaten a breath-cleansing sweet at some point. She wished she'd done the same – there was something in her bag – but she hadn't thought of it. Then she stopped worrying, stopped thinking, even, and just gave herself up to the sensation.

At first it was clumsy, too passionate for technique, and it took a few seconds before his lips took control and Flora felt her body melt into his. Her knees gave way and they subsided on to the bed, first sitting, and then lying on all the bits and pieces from the Comfort Pack. Then he really applied himself to what he was doing and Flora began to catch fire.

He was just battling with the safety pin that was holding Emma's jacket together at the top of her breasts, when there was a knock on the door, so discreet that Flora was sure the knocker knew what was going on inside the room.

Charles got up to open it, and Flora fled to the bathroom so her flushed cheeks, rumpled hair and general dishevelment weren't exposed to whoever it was came with the toothbrushes. Where did Charles learn to kiss like that? she wondered. Surely not from Annabelle!

440

Banishing Annabelle firmly from her mind, she undid the safety pin while she was waiting for Charles to deal with room service. It seemed to take a long time to deliver a couple of toothbrushes and some moisturiser.

When she came out Charles was opening a bottle of champagne.

'That didn't come out of the mini-bar. It wouldn't fit,' she said.

'It's complimentary. For honeymoon couples.'

Flora opened her eyes wide. 'But we're not on our honeymoon! And it can't possibly look as if we are.'

He shrugged. 'Maybe they mean honeymoon in a more metaphorical sense.'

Flora bit her lip and blushed.

'I must have a shower before – we get too carried away,' he said. 'I've been on the road all day and must stink.'

Flora hadn't thought he stank. He had a pleasant, metallic, masculine odour, of course, but she'd liked the way he smelt. Now he'd mentioned it, she began to feel self-conscious about how long it had been since she had had a shower herself.

'I might have a bath. I must stink, too.'

'I'll go first, then I'll bring you a glass of champagne while you're in there.'

At least the first time he saw her naked she'd be covered in bubbles – Molton Brown bubbles. Flora found the thought surprisingly erotic. But she realised any thought connected with Charles was surprisingly erotic. She picked up the small pot of moisturiser that had come with the champagne. It smelt divine. This was a very expensive hotel. The taxi driver must have thought

Charles looked affluent and she supposed he did. His suit was well cut, his shoulders were broad and his shoes were shiny. Very Alpha Male. She giggled.

The Alpha Male marched back into the bedroom wearing only a towel round his waist. Flora had never seen his naked back before, or indeed his naked anything. His muscles were surprisingly impressive for someone who, as far as she knew, didn't work out. She looked away. The sight of him made her catch her breath. She shot him a quick, provocative glance as she moved behind him to get to the bathroom.

Hotel baths fill very quickly and it was only moments before Flora was in hers, the bubbles forming a protective layer. She wasn't usually self-conscious about her body, but it had never mattered as much before. She'd yearned to be with Charles for so long and had never thought it would happen. Now it was happening, she wanted it to be as good as possible. She realised she hadn't had a hot bath since she'd left the cottage and the feeling of the water around her was both shocking and relaxing. She closed her eyes, thinking of what lay ahead.

She heard him come into the room and opened her eyes as he sat on the edge of the bath and handed her a glass. Putting out her hand to take it revealed, she knew, her naked breast, partially concealed by foam. She saw his eyes go to it, and bit her lip. Her initial shyness and embarrassment were rapidly turning to lust. It must be the combination of hot water and cold champagne.

'You're very beautiful, you know, Flora.'

'I'm not beautiful. Quite pretty when I'm done up, but not beautiful.'

'To me you're beautiful, and have been from almost the moment I first saw you.'

Flora sipped her champagne and tried to think what she'd been wearing. Not quite enough, she remembered, and very unbusinesslike shoes. 'I thought you were terribly stuffy.'

'I was. Still am in some ways, but better than before, I hope.'

'You're OK,' she said into her glass. 'I quite like you.'

'I do a great deal more than like you, Flora. I love you, very much indeed.'

'That's all right then.' This time she looked at him over the glass.

'Are you ever going to get out of there? Or do I have to come in and get you?'

'I don't usually get out until I've turned into a prune. A pink prune.'

'I can't wait that long.' He took her glass and set it down.

'Pass me a towel, then.'

'No. You can share mine.' He pulled her up out of the bath and into his arms. For a moment she just stood against him, the tips of her breasts just below his pectorals, but not touching. He looked down at her speculatively, then, without touching any other part of her, he ran one finger lightly down her spine. She caught her breath and he drew her towards him, and his hands slid all over her body. Then he put his hands on the back of her waist and held her close. They kissed for a long, dizzying time before he pulled away and she heard him swallow. 'Come on.'

Still welded together they got from the bathroom to

the bed, where they collapsed, kissing, only moving when Flora realised she was lying on top of a packet of safety pins.

Charles stripped the covers off the bed, scattering the Comfort Pack. He had lost his towel by now and as he scooped her up and tossed her on to the bed, Flora giggled breathlessly until his mouth came down on hers.

'You can't ring for more condoms,' said Flora. 'I won't let you.'

'Well, what do you suggest we do, then?'

Flora thought about it and then glanced at the clock radio. 'It's five to midnight. There's probably something open still. You could ask at the desk.'

'Then I might as well save myself the bother of going out. They'll know what I'm going for. Besides, I'm hungry again.'

'Order some sandwiches, then – or something.'

Somehow she wasn't surprised when, emerging from the bathroom a little later, she found not only club sandwiches, chips and two huge portions of profiteroles, covered with chocolate sauce and cream, but two packets of condoms.

'Charles, you didn't ask for them? From room service? How could you? And I thought you were respectable!'

'I was until I met you, then I realised that it wasn't a lot of fun. Have some chips. I suddenly wanted to eat all the things we didn't eat at the restaurant. And there are a lot of good things you can do with a profiterole.'

Flora looked at her lover with admiration. Not so stuffy, after all.

Previously unaware how hungry she was, she picked

up a sandwich and wondered how to get it into her mouth. Then she pulled out the cocktail stick that was holding it together and, somehow, took a bite. After a couple of mouthfuls she suddenly had a thought.

'I must ring Emma,' she said, horrified that it hadn't occurred to her before. 'She'll be worried if I don't come home!'

'Surely not. You're a grown-up, after all.'

'I can be home late, but I can't not come home at all without telling her. Where's my phone?'

'Use the hotel phone.'

She shook her head. 'Can't remember her number. Pass me my bag, could you?'

She watched as he reached over for it and saw the muscles in his back ripple. If they moved to a really warm country, she decided, they need never put clothes on again. But perhaps having all that male beauty covered most of the time was in a way actually more exciting.

She took the phone and got back on to the bed before pressing the relevant buttons. She pulled the sheet up a little to partially cover herself. It would be more enticing if he couldn't look at her completely naked. After all, if he'd gone to the trouble and embarrassment of ordering the condoms, it would be an awful waste not to use them.

Emma had begun to worry. 'Did you meet someone nice at the gallery and go out for drinks?' The optimism in her voice was almost painful.

'No. I'm in a hotel.'

'Darling! Why? Check out immediately and come home.'

'I haven't got any clothes on.'

'What! Then get dressed! Have you just had a bath? I expect they'll make you pay if you've messed things up.'

'I have messed things up.' Flora looked at the chaos about her. Clothes, bedcovers, and now plates of food, all over the place. The box of safety pins had come open and was now scattered on the carpet. 'And I've no intention of getting dressed.' She shot Charles a look which caused him to come and sit on the bed. He took her breast in his hand and caressed her nipple with a knowing finger. 'Don't do that! Emma? Sorry. You may have gathered I'm not alone.' She giggled, in spite of trying not to.

There was an audible silence from the other end of the phone. 'Darling, I know you're hurting just now, but do you think a one-night stand is going to make you feel any better? How will you look yourself in the mirror in the morning?'

Flora felt it was time to put her friend out of her misery. 'It's all right, I'm with Charles.' Then she held the phone away from her ear while Emma screeched.

'Oh my God! That's so romantic!'

'It is, rather. But, obviously, I can't talk much now . . .'

'I want all the details, just as soon as you can tell me. Oh, that's so sweet! I'll let you go now.' She was still cooing as she disconnected.

Charles held a hot thick-cut chip out towards her. Flora opened her mouth and closed her eyes. It was delicious. He went on feeding her chips until she opened her eyes again. 'Can I have pudding now?'

* * *

Flora had made an effort with her appearance. She had washed all her underwear the night before and used her emergency make-up kit to good effect. She hadn't bothered with the safety pin to keep her décolletage to a discreet minimum and her hair was a little wild. It had been washed (by mistake, while they were in the shower) and conditioned, courtesy of the hotel, but she hadn't had her frizz-controller and mousse and the other things she used to tame it with. But she felt her attempts at respectability weren't too despicable.

Charles, wearing yesterday's shirt and a very satisfied expression, stood at the desk with complete lack of embarrassment.

'There you are, Mr Stanza,' said the girl on reception, handing him the bill. 'We do hope you enjoyed your stay.'

'Oh, we did, very much,' said Charles. He signed the credit-card slip and then opened his wallet. 'Do you have a staff box?'

The girl indicated a discreet brass-bound opening in the wooden desk. Charles posted a couple of notes in it. 'The room service was really excellent,' he said.

'Good. That's very kind.' The girl caught Flora's eye and smiled. 'I do hope you enjoy the rest of your honeymoon, Mrs Stanza.'

Flora opened her mouth and shut it again as she realised what had happened. Because they had the same surname, the hotel had assumed they were married. There were advantages to keeping things in the family.

When they reached the pavement she allowed her giggle to emerge. 'They really did think we were on our honeymoon, because of our names being the same!'

447

Charles frowned. 'Yes.'

'I expect you've got used to being engaged now. You were for such a long time.'

'I'm thoroughly fed up with it, actually. I think I'd definitely prefer to be married. What do you think?'

'I might quite like to get married, one day, when I've had plenty of time to decide what my dress should be like, but I'm not taking your slot at Bishopsbridge Abbey,' she said firmly.

'So you probably don't want me hanging the picture of Annabelle naked above our bed?'

'No,' she said patiently, 'I wouldn't like that. Although I must say I am quite curious to see it.'

He kissed her nose. 'I might ask William to do one of you.'

She squeaked and hit him.

Their journey back to Bishopsbridge took longer than their separate journeys to London had taken. This was because Charles flatly refused to allow them to drive their own cars home. He insisted on Flora parking the Land-Rover at the house of a friend of his who lived in Richmond.

'If I got home without you, I'd be lynched by practically the whole town,' he explained as he handed her into his car. 'Now I've got you, I'm hanging on to you.'

As they fought their way through the traffic and on to the motorway, Flora was contemplative. She was ecstatically happy but she wanted to make sure that Charles was, too. 'Were you upset when you and Annabelle broke up? You'd been together for ages. Your heart's not broken?'

'What do you think?' He looked at her so lustfully his feelings on the matter were fairly clear.

'It's your heart I'm talking about, not – you know.'

'Annabelle and I were just a habit, really. We'd both become so accustomed to the idea that we were together that we'd stopped thinking about it. And once we thought about it, I think we both realised that we'd changed and moved on since we got engaged. I was – am – very fond of her in a way. You never saw her at her best, but—'

'I made her "her best"!' Flora was indignant. 'Without me she'd still be wearing pussy-cat bows and skirts just the wrong length.'

'Well, anyway, she's out of our way now.'

'Charles, you don't just want to marry me for the sake of the business, do you?'

Risking both their lives, he leant over and kissed her nose. 'When I knew how much in love I was with you, all my feelings for the company felt pretty pathetic in comparison. If you wanted us to sell up, I'd do it in a heartbeat, for you.'

'Oh,' said Flora in a very small voice, trying not to cry.

There was a garland of flowers round the architrave of the house. Everyone, all the porters, were gathered in the doorway. Geoffrey had a tray of champagne. As they got out of the car, Flora said, 'How did they know when we were coming?'

'I rang from the last service station, when we got petrol.'

'But you're not supposed to have your phone on in service stations!'

449

'I know, I'm such a rebel,' he said dryly, and then laughed.

They walked up the steps arm in arm. 'It's like getting married,' murmured Flora before she found herself being embraced by Virginia.

'Welcome back! We've missed you!'

'I was only away for – oh!'

Geoffrey gave a note and acted as conductor and then what there was of the choir, mostly sopranos, but with Geoffrey, Fred from the ironmonger's across the road, and a couple of other men and some altos obviously roped in for the occasion, broke into 'Brightly Dawns Our Wedding Day'.

Flora laughed and cried at the same time. 'That's so lovely!'

'Here,' said Edie, at her elbow. 'This person might cheer you up.' She put Imelda into her arms, who instantly started purring and putting cat hairs on Emma's black suit.

'Imelda, how lovely to see you!'

When Flora looked up again, she saw that Edie had the kittens with her as well. She was led into what was once the boardroom but was now set for a party. Louisa, grinning like mad, was protecting the plates of food.

Having put Imelda down, Flora hugged everybody, even people she realised she'd never met before, and Geoffrey opened more champagne. Everyone congratulated Charles, who was holding his kitten. They were kissing him, patting him on the back, and generally behaving in a way that they never would have done before.

'We're not actually married, you know,' said Flora, taking a glass of champagne from Geoffrey.

'Just as well. The whole choir is looking forward to singing at your wedding. By the way, can you ring your mother? She's a bit worried.'

Flora stifled a scream, found her phone and the cupboard under the stairs, and rang her. 'It's all fine! I'm so happy. Charles came and found me in London and took me to a hotel and – well, you can guess the rest.'

'And are you engaged?'

'Not officially, but we have discussed it.'

'For one dreadful moment I thought you were going to say you were married.'

'No, no. The choir want to sing at the wedding.'

When her mother had enough details to be going on with, Flora reappeared from the cupboard to find everyone assembled for toasts.

'To Flora,' said Charles, 'who's not only put the sunshine in my life but has had some jolly good ideas for the business as well.'

Everyone laughed.

'To Stanza and Stanza,' said Geoffrey, 'which I suppose could either mean Charles and Flora, or the auction house. But whatever, may it go from strength to strength.'

'I'll drink to that,' said Charles.

'Oh no, Imelda's stolen a sandwich,' said Flora.

'No, she didn't,' said Edie. 'I gave it to her. No reason why she shouldn't join in the celebrations, is there?'

'By the way, Virginia,' said Flora later, 'do we know what happened to Annabelle?'

'Well, about half an hour after Charles left, Annabelle stormed about, clearing her desk, slamming cupboards and generally being very upset. But then, a couple of days later I saw her in the ironmongers, looking so different I almost didn't recognise her.'

'I did give her a make-over,' murmured Flora.

'But it was her whole body language that was different. She seemed all dreamy and disorganised and was carrying a wicker basket.'

'Oh my God,' muttered Charles.

'Well,' broke in Louisa, thrilled to be the bearer of good gossip. 'I've got more recent news!'

'What?' chorused everyone.

'My mother met hers at a fête. She was furious! Annabelle's mother, I mean. Apparently Annabelle's run off with an artist and is living in a gipsy caravan in the woods!'

'William!' said Flora, looking aghast at Charles who had started to laugh.

'Good for Annabelle,' said Charles. 'Who said she was inflexible?'

'Not me, darling,' said Flora, trying to scoop up the black kitten and failing.

Charles picked it up without difficulty and presented it to Flora. It sat on her chest, between them, looking bemused.

'Will you, Flora, take this black kitten as a symbol of my undying love?'

'No!' said Flora, trying not to become sentimental, 'I gave you the kitten.'

'Have this instead then.' He rummaged in his pocket and produced a twist of tissue paper.

Inside was a tiny diamond and jet brooch in the form of a cat. It had emerald eyes and a distinct look of Imelda.

Flora looked at the brooch and then up at Charles.

She nodded. She couldn't speak. He kissed her nose.

'You think he'd have got her a proper ring,' someone murmured in the background.

'They'll need to choose that together,' said Geoffrey and then, a moment later, 'If this kissing's going to go on much longer, I think I'll get back to work.'

If you enjoyed Flora's Lot, *why not
try Katie Fforde's irresistible new novel . . .*

Practically Perfect

Anna, a newly qualified interior designer, has decided
it's time to put her money and her expertise where her
mouth is. She's risked everything on buying a tiny but
adorable cottage so she can renovate it, sell it on, and
prove to her family that she can earn her own living.

Outside, the chocolate-box cottage is perfect, but inside
all is chaos: with a ladder for a staircase, no downstairs
flooring, candles the only form of lighting and a sleeping
bag and camping mat for a bed, Anna's soon wondering
whether she's bitten off more than she can chew.

Her neighbour Chloe comes to the rescue, providing tea,
wine and sympathy – and a recently rescued greyhound,
Caroline. But just as Anna's starting to believe she's
found the perfect idyll, the good-looking yet impossible
Rob Hunter arrives on the scene, putting up more
obstacles than the Grand National. Can Anna get over
all of life's hurdles?

Read on for an extract . . .

CENTURY

Chapter One

The candle at her side flickered, and Anna shifted her position on the pair of steps where she was perched. She was beginning to regret having the telephone connected so promptly. There was very little mobile reception and without a conventional phone she'd have been almost unreachable. As it was, her ear was getting hot and her hand was getting cold, but her sister was still interrogating her. Anna didn't bother to cut her short – it would only involve another telephone call later – she tucked her free hand into her sleeve and listened politely. The bib-and-braces dungarees she was wearing were fairly warm when she was moving around, but now she was getting chilly.

'So why was it you moved there again?' asked Laura for what felt like the hundredth time. 'You know, property's much cheaper up here in Yorkshire. We could have done the project together. Much more fun.'

Anna embarked on her explanation again – rather patiently, she thought. 'I didn't want to be so far from London, and Amberford is a much more desirable area. Commutable from London, just. We've been through this.'

Laura sighed. 'I just don't like you doing it all on your own, so far from us. And I really wish you hadn't rushed into buying it, without me having a chance to see it first.'

In fact Anna did feel a bit guilty about this. 'I'm sorry, but I had to decide very quickly. There were lots of other people after it. It was such a bargain.'

'You were a cash buyer,' Laura pointed out rather snappily.

Anna sighed. 'I know, and that's partly thanks to you. But so was the other guy. It would have gone to him if I hadn't been a position to write a cheque for a deposit on the spot.' She paused. 'I'm eternally grateful, Lo. Without that loan I couldn't have done it.'

'You know I was happy to lend you the money, and you're paying me more interest than I'd have got from anywhere else, I just don't trust you to buy—'

'I know you don't,' said Anna, quite gently considering her frustration. 'But it's time you did. I know you're my older sister, but I am an adult, you know.'

'Twenty-seven is not—'

'Yes it is.'

'I don't mean that, of course you're an adult, but this is all your capital and a bit of mine. It's your inheritance.'

'I know the money didn't come from the tooth fairy.'

Anna wished she'd supplied herself with pencil and paper and a space to sketch – she could have got on with some drawings while all this was going on, not that it would have been possible in this light. She just hated wasting time.

'What I'm saying is,' Laura continued, 'you won't get that money from Granny again. And you could lose everything, you know.'

Anna shifted uncomfortably on the step. 'I watch all the same television programmes you do. I'm just as aware that the property market goes down as well as up, all that stuff. I haven't lived the last five years with my head in a sack.'

Laura sighed again. 'I expect I'm just jealous. It was such fun doing up the flat in Spitalfields together.'

'It *was* fun,' Anna agreed, 'but I'm a big girl now. I'm a qualified interior designer. It's time for me to go it alone.'

There was a silence. Laura was obviously still not convinced. 'So how much money have you got left to live on?' she asked, setting off on a new tack. 'You won't be able to do everything yourself, however handy you are with your Black and Decker and your Workmate – and I admit you are quite handy. And you still need to pay the mortgage.'

'I took out a slightly larger mortgage so I can use some of it to pay it—'

'That doesn't sound sensible—'

'But I thought I might get a part-time job anyway,' Anna said soothingly before Laura could get any further, 'just to get to know people.'

'Ah! So you're already worried about being lonely and you haven't even spent a night in the house! Sell it quickly, and do the same thing up here, where I can keep an eye on you. You might still make a bit of a profit. You could get in touch with the other man who was interested—'

'No, Laura! I love this house! I'm not going to sell it.'

Laura pounced like a cat on a daydreaming mouse.

'Ah! I knew it! You've fallen in love with an investment project. Fatal mistake.'

Anna cursed herself for letting slip this sign of weakness. 'I didn't say "in love",' she said, knowing she sounded pathetic. '"In love" is quite different from loving it.' She bit her lip while she waited to see if her sister bought this rather specious argument.

'OK.' Laura seemed resigned at last. 'Just promise me you'll sell it when it's done. Falling in love is always a mistake.'

'I know.'

'With men or with property,' she continued menacingly.

'Come on, Laura! You and Will are ecstatically happy. You and the boys could rent yourself to cornflakes ads as the perfect family!'

Laura laughed, trapped by her own argument. 'I know, but—'

'You've all got good teeth and shiny hair. You eat the right food—'

'This conversation is not about Will and the boys,' said Laura firmly.

'I know,' Anna admitted, 'but I was hoping I could steer it in that direction. How is Edward's spelling coming on?'

'Anna!'

'OK, but I really want to know if Jacob has got off that vile reading book.'

'Oh yes.' Her sister was momentarily diverted from sorting out Anna. 'At last. But getting back to you, and falling in love—'

Anna accepted the inevitable. 'You don't trust me to

fall in love as sensibly as you did?' Will was the perfect husband – not only loving, good-looking and a good provider, he also did DIY.

Laura was silent for a moment, possibly realising that falling in love with the right person was about luck as much as anything else. Anna enjoyed the respite.

'You make me sound terribly bossy.'

At the other end of the phone, Anna nodded agreement.

'But I'm just looking out for you,' persisted Laura. 'Mum's a bit taken up with Peter these days and doesn't pay attention to what you're getting up to.'

'Mum's entitled to be obsessed with her new husband. I am an adult.' Although Anna was beginning to wonder if this was true, her sister seemed so unable to accept it.

'And of course you're just as capable of falling in love with the right man as I am. As long as I've checked him over first.' But at least there was a smile in her voice now.

'Fine. I promise I won't marry anyone without consulting you. Oh, I can hear the boys. You're needed, Laura.' Never had her nephews' shrieks sounded so endearing.

'Oh yes, better go. Speak soon!'

'Right.' Anna uncrossed her fingers, and then replaced the receiver on the handset and tucked it back into the little niche in the wall. It was only a white lie, she told herself as she stepped down to the floor. And you have to fall in love with a project a little bit, to really throw your heart into it. As for falling in love with the right man, that ship had sailed, too. She'd fallen in love with the wrong one years ago, and even knowing he was the wrong one didn't affect her feelings. One of the reasons

461

she had come to look at the house in the first place was because she remembered Max saying that his mother lived near here. It had seemed like a good omen.

Anna blew out the candle and then reversed carefully down the ladder that was currently her staircase. Sometimes she let herself fantasise about meeting his mother, or running into Max while he was visiting her. She always chuckled at this dream in spite of herself. If he did run into her, she'd more than likely be wearing dungarees and builder's boots, and while she had always been a jeans and sweater girl, her clothes were even more utilitarian now than they had been when she was a student.

Still, she'd carried the torch for a very long time and it still burned as brightly as when Max had been the guest lecturer at college.

He'd been the hot young architect, coming in to talk to them, and she'd just been one of the students, taking notes. She was willing to bet she wasn't the only one who'd fallen in love with him, either. He'd been so dynamic and vital. Not really handsome, but with such a massive personality that his looks didn't matter. But she'd never talked about him to anyone else and, thank God, this included her sister. She hadn't wanted to find out that he'd slept his way through half the class but passed over her. Then, at their Graduation Ball, he had picked her out and danced with her. It was right at the end, and Anna had had to leave because there was a whole group of them sharing a minicab home. There'd just been time for Max to write his number on a menu. 'Call me,' he'd said, his voice a husky whisper.

Anna had fully intended to call him, even though the

thought was more scary than finals had been, but some hideous bug had laid her low for days. The first day she felt well enough to go out she had been on her way to the chemist when she saw him – with a woman. She had rushed home and torn up the menu and then burnt the pieces. It was only a couple of days later, when the last remnants of the bug had left her and she felt less wobbly, that she realised she'd been incredibly stupid. The woman could have been anyone: his sister, a colleague, anyone. She'd regretted her folly ever since.

Anna went to the place where the electric kettle and the toaster were plugged into the only part of the house where they could be. There was also a small wash-hand basin there, so it counted as a kitchen. To satisfy the demands of the building-society-turned-bank, she had left the slightly rusty cooker and cracked sink in place until after she'd been given a mortgage. Luckily for her, the address, and the relatively small amount she needed to borrow, meant the valuer didn't actually need to go into the property. She had secured her money on a 'walk by' – which normally would have been a drive by – and so the cottage was hers.

Of course the mortgage didn't seem small to her, it seemed enormous, but from the building society's point of view, it was fairly insignificant.

While she made herself a cup of tea, using the last of the milk, she forced herself to stop thinking about the man she hadn't seen for three years and calculated how long it would be before Laura could stay away no longer and would descend, handyman husband in tow, to 'sort her out'.

Anna loved her sister dearly, and when they'd lived

together they'd got on fine. But since Laura was no longer able to supervise her dates, steer her wardrobe in the right direction, and generally mother her, the word 'bossy' was becoming more and more appropriate. If she'd known where Anna intended to spend her first night in her very own home – investment project, she corrected herself hurriedly – she'd have had a blue fit. She would not consider a sleeping bag and a camping mat a suitable resting place, even if Anna did have a couple of blankets she could pull over herself. But without Laura adding her capital to hers, her mortgage would have been much larger.

And surely Laura wouldn't blame Anna for falling in love with the cottage, at least a little bit. It was heavenly! Or it would be when it had floors, a staircase, a proper kitchen and a bathroom. The previous owners had ripped all these things out and then either run out of money or interest. The estate agent was rather cagey about it.

Anna had tossed and turned her way through a week of sleepless nights while she waited for the surveyor's report. She was certain he'd discover some major problem: the reason why the previous owners had abandoned something with 'such terrific letting potential' as the estate agent put it. When no such reasons were revealed, Anna felt it was probably because there was so little left in which to discover death-watch beetle, dry rot or perished timbers. The ground floor had been stripped of almost everything, including most of the floorboards. There was no staircase, so the only way to the first floor was via a ladder. Here there was at least a floor to walk about on, but there was no bathroom.

And the very top floor, the attic, which in Anna's mind's eye was already the most wonderful bedroom-bathroom-dressing-room suite, was very much as it had been hundreds of years ago. Anna planned to sleep up there when things were straighter downstairs, but at the moment she felt she needed to be nearer things. Up in the attic, the rest of the house could burst into flames and she would be unaware of it until it was too late. She'd bought and installed a smoke alarm, even without her sister's prompting.

Its lack of amenities had made the house very cheap, considering its position, both in the country as a whole and in Amberford in particular.

It was part of a row of cottages which stood behind long gardens and overlooked the village. Laura would say that having the garden open plan would detract from the value. But there was a smaller, enclosed garden at the back, and if your children needed lots of playing space (and Laura's two boys definitely did) there was an attractive bit of common land not far away. A church, a school and a pub, and an easy journey to a mainline station, made it a very desirable spot. There was even a shop and a post office and, not too far away, a Chinese takeaway.

Of course it only had two bedrooms, and Laura would say that cut Anna's target market down considerably. Anna had already prepared her speech saying it made it an ideal second home, although she didn't like the idea of second homes making once-thriving villages barren and empty during the week.

She had yet to meet her neighbours, and because it was beginning to get dark and people would be putting their lights on, a walk along the row would tell her which cottages were occupied permanently, and which were not. She needed a few things from the shop anyway; now would be a good a time to investigate discreetly.

It seemed strange walking so close to people's windows and although she couldn't quite resist looking inside, she made her glances oblique and fleeting. She was grateful that she was the end cottage (she would tell her sister that 'end of terrace' was better than 'mid') so no one could look in at the building site she currently called home.

Her immediate neighbour was definitely a permanent resident. Anna could hear children and there were lights on everywhere. A sideways glance through the kitchen window as she passed showed a reassuring amount of mess. Anna's sister was terribly organised and it was what they argued about more than anything else. Anna didn't want to find herself living next door to another neatnik.

The next house was either a holiday home or belonged to someone not yet home from work: a commuter, possibly. The curtains were open but no light showed. Anna could see hints of a very stylish, modern kitchen, full of expensive appliances.

The house next to that was clearly occupied by an elderly lady. Her windowsill was covered with china ornaments, visible in front of the curtain that was already drawn. A cat sat on the porch, evidently dismissing Anna as a blow-in, and refusing her offers of friendship.

The first cottage in the row, and the last one Anna

passed before she reached the main road, was definitely a holiday cottage. The Christmas decorations were still up, even though it was mid-March. Going by the quality of the decorations, which were of the tasteful corn-dolly and red-ribbon type, she judged the house was not owned by disorganised people who just didn't get round to taking them down. More likely they were spending the winter somewhere warm.

Out of the five cottages, three – possibly four – including her own, seemed occupied which, considering how small they were, was not a bad ratio.

The shop bell jangled in a friendly way. It was a small supermarket, with a couple of short rows of goods and a counter for bacon and cheese. The man who stood at the counter, doing the crossword, looked up when she entered and smiled. 'Evening.'

'Evening.'

'Can I help you?'

'I think I can probably manage,' said Anna, feeling a little shy. She was used to the anonymity of London shops, where only the proprietors of shops you used very frequently ever spoke to you.

'Well, let me know if there's anything you can't find. Just moved in, have you?' he added later, when Anna had put a few things into her basket.

'That's it. I just need some basic provisions.'

'So you've moved into Brick Row?'

'Yes. How did you know?' This omniscience took some getting used to.

The shopkeeper smiled. 'It didn't take much detective work. We knew the house had been bought by a young woman; you're obviously dressed for work; and

467

who else would come in here just before closing, at this time of year, whom I don't know?'

Anna smiled. 'I suppose it does make sense.'

'Don't worry, we're not all nosy round here, and those of us that are are well meaning on the whole.'

Anna placed her basket of goods on to the counter so he could ring them up. 'I'm sure you are.'

She walked home feeling very satisfied. The shop didn't sell fresh meat or fish but otherwise it seemed to have everything else Anna might need and the town was only a short bike ride away. Amberford was perfect, well worthy of being fallen in love with, and if being there without a car caused a few problems, well, she'd deal with them as they came up.

As Anna walked back along the lane she saw a young woman standing by the front door next to hers, looking anxious. Anna was pleased to see her as she'd been intrigued by the row of three small pairs of Wellington boots, arranged in size order, on the windowsill of the cottage. She overcame her shyness and smiled. The young woman smiled back, still preoccupied.

'Hello,' she said. 'You've moved into number five? You're very brave! It hasn't even got floors, has it? I was going to invite you round for a bath, but just now we can't even have one ourselves. I'm waiting for a plumber. He promised he'd be here before two, but I don't suppose he'll come now.'

'Oh dear, what's the problem with it?' Anna asked.

Presumably hearing her voice, three small boys abandoned their toys of mass destruction and clustered round their mother, eager to see whom she was talking to.

'Blocked drain,' the woman said with a grimace. 'I've

pulled out the plug and nothing happens. It's full of cold soapy water. If these three don't have a bath at night, they take ages to settle. And it's beginning to smell.'

'Well, I might be able to help,' said Anna.

The woman's face lit up. 'Really? How?'

'I have a few building skills, which is just as well given the state of my house, but, more to the point, I have a tool that unblocks drains. I'll just pop home and get it,' Anna offered, 'if you'd like me to.'

'I'd love you to! I'll put the kettle on. Or open some wine?'

Anna grinned back at her. 'I'll be back in a minute.'

It took Anna a little longer than that to find the tool that she and her sister had had cause to use so often in the Spitalfields flat. When she knocked on the door of her neighbour's house and was let in, she found an agreeable amount of chaos.

'I'm Chloe,' said the woman.

'Anna.'

'And these are Bruno, Tom and Harry. Two, four and six, only in reverse order.'

'Hello,' said Anna, suddenly shy in front of three pairs of inquisitive eyes. 'I've got my gadget, if you'd like to show me upstairs.'

They all went up the steep and very winding staircase to the second floor, where the bathroom and the boys' bedroom were. The boys grabbed hold of her and towed her towards it.

'We haven't had a bath for two days!' said the eldest, who was probably Bruno, but might have been Harry.

'My husband's away,' said his mother. 'He would be, just when there's an emergency.'

Anna didn't think a blocked bath plug quite quali-fied as an emergency, but accepted that some people might well do, and Chloe obviously did. She rolled up her sleeve as far as it would go, which was not far enough.

'I don't suppose you'd all like to go downstairs while I do this?' she suggested. 'I want to take my jumpers off.'

'We want to watch,' announced one of the boys.

'Yes, we do,' said another.

Anna sighed. 'OK.' She undid her bib and peeled off the two jumpers that covered a long-sleeved T-shirt. Fortunately that sleeve rolled up obligingly high, and she plunged her arm into the cold, scummy water. 'Right, pass me my plunger, would you?'

'This is so cool,' murmured Bruno.

'You're right there,' said Anna, shivering. 'Very cool indeed.'